JUSTICE

FOR NONE

Also by Gene Hackman and Daniel Lenihan

Wake of the Perdido Star

Also by Daniel Lenihan

Submerged

JUSTICE
FOR NONE

Gene Hackman
and
Daniel Lenihan

ST. MARTIN'S PRESS NEW YORK

www.stmartins.com

Library of Congress Cataloging-in-Publication Data

Hackman, Gene.
    Justice for none / Gene Hackman and Daniel Lenihan.—1st U.S. ed.
      p.   cm.
    ISBN 0-312-32425-1
    EAN 978-0312-32425-4
    1. World War, 1914–1918—Veterans—Fiction. 2. Fugitives from justice—Fiction. 3. African American men—Fiction. 4. Women journalists—Fiction. 5. False testimony—Fiction. 6. Male friendship—Fiction. 7. Race relations—Fiction. 8. Illinois—Fiction. I. Lenihan, Daniel. II. Title.

PS3558.A3114V47   2004
813'.54—dc22

                                       2004040549

First Edition: June 2004

10 9 8 7 6 5 4 3 2 1

This book is dedicated to:

The sound of corn growing
from rich, dark Illinois soil
on a still summer night.

———

Just hold your breath and listen.
Listen hard, now. You can hear it.

JUSTICE
FOR NONE

It was hot. Southeast Illinois hot. The Heitzberg grain elevators loomed over their eastern neighbors on Main Street. Lou's Better Lounge, closed since the start of Prohibition, was completely cast in the elevators' limp shadow, but even shade provided little relief.

"Hot enough to fry eggs on the sidewalk," someone muttered as he shuffled by the motorman. Boyd Calvin thought about that. He fantasized passersby dissolving in sunny-side-up confusion in the concrete skillets that paralleled the trolley tracks.

Though it scarcely helped with the heat, Boyd let the streetcar sit in the shade for several minutes until he could see his westbound counterpart swing around the wayby at Bells Park. The single-track line a block ahead was in direct sunlight. Most of his regular passengers at this time of day understood this. Some didn't.

A middle-aged man in a worn coat approached Boyd. "Excuse me, young man. What seems to be the problem?"

"You'll have to stay behind the yellow line, sir." Boyd's left hand rested on the accelerator; his right firmly clenched the brake handle. He chose not to explain that they were waiting for the westbound trolley in the shade instead of the sun.

Sparks flew as the westbound car self-switched into the wayby, its spring-loaded contact pole rolling along the charged overhead line as the two cars passed. Boyd noticed much bigger flashes far overhead, reflecting brilliantly off the ominous clouds building in the east. He eased forward and nodded to the other motorman, an old-timer with a fixed smile whose uniform cap sat squarely on a head that bobbed as if unattached. Boyd dreaded this run. The route took him several miles east, past the

Soldiers' Home, or "Old Soldiers' Home," as most people called it. He never could figure out if the name meant it was a place for old soldiers or that the home itself was old. He certainly hadn't been old when he was there. Even now, at twenty-eight years, he should have been in his prime. The "Home" always triggered unwanted memories; it really wasn't a home at all. The various places Boyd had lived were just places to stay. His only real home had been made by his wife, Laurel, and he had managed to wreck that relationship, but now there were thoughts forming in his head. He would try again with her. Boyd knew she'd give him another chance. He'd needed room to breathe, some air. Maybe they'd have a child. There had been several attempts at children, but it seemed Laurel had problems. We'll see, he thought, we'll wait and see.

The sweltering day turned to muggy night as Boyd's third round-trip brought him to the western turnaround. He swung out of his seat and walked outside to the rear of the car. Grabbing the rope that held the contact pole and pulling it down, he cut off the electricity. He then secured the long pole into the hook above the car. Tonight it was hard to spin the heavy trolley on the turntable, its ancient mechanisms resisting his efforts. Finally, using the heavy switch bar, he was able to urge the metal monster around, turning her within her own forty-foot length. A sense of fulfillment overrode his fear that he wouldn't be able to manage it someday. Sometimes, the elation he felt over such small victories confused him.

When Boyd returned to his operator's chair, his soaked shirt was clinging to his back, his uniform pants sticking to his legs. He removed his matching jacket and folded it at his feet next to his lunch pail. He checked his pocket watch, the worn engraving depicting remnants of a stag leaping in the woods. Five minutes before starting his last run, he switched off the lights and sat in the empty car, staring at the long track stretching for what felt like miles in front of him.

Lightning lit up the eastern sky. Boyd counted six seconds before the sound rumbled past his deserted car. Even though he had expected it, he was startled by the thunderclap. Sweating even more, anticipating the next far-off boom, he must have missed the flash; the sound crashed around him without warning. He gripped the brake handle with both hands.

Not now.

Boyd bent over, trembling. The summer storm moved closer, hot winds pushing the troubled skies directly down the iron path toward the trolley. He watched as lightning danced along the overhead wires, sending sparks cascading to earth. He lowered his head. A bolt hit a tree down the street and everything went white; even with eyes shut he could see the powerful light. He looked up to see a tree ablaze.

He was back in France, in the Argonne Forest.

"Corporal Calvin, put out that fire." The lieutenant, lying on his left side, was trying to unleash his pistol.

"Yes, sir," Boyd answered. Crawling to the officer's side, he could see that his leg was turned at a peculiar angle, his stomach exposed and ripped, the blood going dark as it poured rapidly onto already wet earth.

Lieutenant Eddie's hand found the flap of his holster.

Boyd slid the heavy Colt out of his reach, its sticky presence cold.

"You've been hit, sir. I'll send someone back for help," Boyd shouted. He looked over his shoulder.

What was left of the squad was scattered along a ravine, huddled under an embankment. Their faces were white, lit from the burning tree.

"One of you men crawl back down that ravine. See if you can get help."

No one moved.

"You hear me, damn it?"

Boyd could see the men were frozen. They had been under bombardment for two hours, and each time they tried to move, raking machine-gun fire pinned them in this ravine. A copse of trees along the edge had provided some protection, but with the tree on fire they were exposed.

"Sir, it's Boyd." Shouting above the mortar fire, he turned to the fallen lieutenant. "We're in a bad way here, sir. What do you want I should do?"

The officer tried to fix on Boyd. "Prepare the men to counterattack.

We'll flank them and kill all the bastards. Roll me off my side, Corporal. I've pinched my leg."

Boyd eased the lieutenant onto his back. The man's left leg was gone, an impossibly large area of wet mud marking where it had been. Responding to some nameless reflex, the lieutenant suddenly bucked up from the earth as if shot. "Oh blessed Jesus, please."

The officer's eyes opened wide, startled with pain. He bit down hard on his lips, the blood frothing from his mouth onto his muddied face. "Take it away, take it away!" he screamed. His arms were beating the earth until Boyd pinned him with his body. Boyd could feel the Lieutenant's warm blood soaking his own woolen pants. He glanced to the top of the embankment to see the other men. No one blinked. They watched as Boyd brought the officer's pistol up to the mortally wounded man's head. Blood from the Lieutenant's wounds sprayed in rhythmic spurts onto Boyd's face as he looked for approval from the man. He would have sworn the lieutenant nodded, said yes with his eyes.

A round from either the Germans or the Allies washed the trees and trenches in white phosphorescence. The tree shadows wavered as the burning white globe drifted slowly to earth. Boyd could see the squad. They were still fixed in place. He wasn't sure if they disapproved of what he had done. Whistles in the distance and hard crisp voices in German shouted orders.

"I'm crawling the hell downstream. If you want to follow, help yourselves," Boyd yelled to the squad. He shoved his Enfield rifle, pocked with mud, in front of him as he squirmed down the damp ravine. After thirty yards he looked over his shoulder and could see that some of the men had followed. But most had taken off in the opposite direction. Still breathing hard from the effort, he heard machine-gun fire ripping up the ravine. Several rifle shots answered, then all was quiet. One of the three soldiers who had been following him rose, dropped his rifle, and ran past him, following the stream and disappearing around a bend in the ravine. Boyd told the men behind him to stay down. He could hear them talking, and in spite of his command, they got up and sprinted just as a star shell exploded overhead. They ran in the direction of their pal, leaving Boyd alone.

Boyd knelt and buried his head in his crossed arms. But he wasn't kneeling in the mud of the French forest. His knees were encased in dark blue cloth, his feet clad in heavy brogans. An embossed metal plate, a rounded worn foot bell, came into focus . . . and voices. He wasn't alone.

Two passengers, washed by the summer storm, boarded the dark trolley. They glanced at him expectantly. Boyd raised his head and nodded as he worried his knuckles into the scar tissue of the old wound at his hip. He turned on the lights, released the brake, and rattled off the turnaround. The storm vanished as quickly as it had appeared, but Boyd's hands still shook as he signaled with his bell to waiting passengers standing under awnings along Main Street.

The storm left him angry. He didn't like losing control. He knew that once they started they would have to play themselves out—the "brain-crashes" and "go-backs." "War strain," people said, as if that explained everything. Nightmares from the war. But his nightmares didn't come at night, and they were real. The heat in his chest, the smells, the bright colors. They were real. The closer he got to Laurel's neighborhood, the more upset he became. He was short with people when they didn't have correct change and rude when they were slow. "Come on, come on. Got things to do." *Got people to run over.* Twice he started when people were only half up the step, throwing them just enough off balance to irritate them. By the time he reached Laurel's house, he was livid. It was her fault. She had left him.

Laurel Wheaton had been barely seventeen when she married Boyd, just before he went off to be a part of the war that would end all wars.

"Dang you, Boyd," she'd said, "you don't have to do this." She'd looked into his eyes. "Yes, I suppose you do, don't you?"

Boyd had nodded, grinning stupidly, his face alight.

Laurel had seemed saddened that he exhibited such joy at the prospect. She needn't have worried. It wasn't a joyful Boyd Calvin that came home to Vermilion.

He was with the American Expeditionary Force for a year but gone from home for two and a half. When he returned, her visits to him in the hospital were chaotic, filled with accusations from Boyd. He remembered Laurel skipping easily across the ward-room floor.

"What's up?" Boyd asked.

"What d'ya mean, hon?"

"You come in here all giddy and girlish. Seems to me like something's happening on the outside."

"Oh, sweetie, please, I just want to love you. Nothing's going on."

Boyd covered the back of her neck. "I know, Laur—it's something always eating at me. I'm sorry."

The memories of their relationship, marred with separations, drunken bouts, and several miscarriages, made Boyd's grip tighten on the wheel.

He didn't expect to see her on this trip, but maybe later she would answer his two-one-two bell signal as his trolley rattled past her bedroom window. Boyd changed his foot bell as he passed. An answering flick of her bedroom lights calmed him abruptly. It was like that when she answered. He was suddenly able to catch his breath, and felt the flush leaving his face.

Boyd was back to some semblance of normal by the time he finished his run. He could hardly remember the last half hour, but he was breathing again, and it was air, not something evil from that forest, not something that sets lungs on fire.

*S*omeone *was* calling for help. As hard as he tried, he couldn't get to him. He struggled to rid himself of the tangled ropes holding his arms and legs. Boyd pushed against the soft restraints as he heard more loud voices. Finally, he awoke, the sweaty sheet wrapped tight around his damp arms.

Voices rose from the stairwell of the cheap hotel. Boyd gasped for air as he tried to decipher the loud sounds. Sitting up in the narrow cot, he squinted bleary-eyed around the tiny room. Nothing had changed. The faded wallpaper was still bubbled and peeling. The trim paint on the door and windows was cracked in a thousand different patterns. The drip from the small sink continued. Home.

It seemed only minutes since he had put his head down on the damp pillow, but the noise was incessant. He began dressing, thinking only of what he would say to the offenders. From the top of the lobby stairs, he could see the room clerk, several women, and an unshaven drunk all yelling simultaneously. It was the monthly upheaval over late rent, and suitcases were spread out over the lobby floor. Boyd slouched to the worn marble steps. His friend Claudia needed a little help again this month. He tried to catch the attention of the beleaguered room clerk, who finally glanced his way. Boyd pointed to himself and pantomimed paying the older lady's rent. The clerk nodded and went back to quieting the residents. Boyd's legs burned as he trudged up to his third-floor room. He would try once more to rest.

Three dollars a day bought him a window, bed, sink, and mirror at the Grant Hotel in Vermilion, Illinois. June 5 was much like June 4, still too hot for Boyd. His head had barely hit the pillow when the stark images

7

returned. He didn't want to think of these things, but he was their prisoner. He knew what would happen when he lay down, but he needed
more sleep, brain-crashes or no. Boyd stood by the chipped enamel sink
in his room, staring at the hollow-eyed image in the mirror. He hadn't
rested well. Trying to sleep during the day was hard for him. Each door
slam became an event, each truck backfire a calamity. The walls of the
cheap hotel reverberated with the din. He would wake with a start, as-
tonished that there wasn't someone standing over his bed waving a gun.
No matter, he needed more sack time. He edged to the bed and flopped
back down. He was a workingman, for God's sake. Nobody respected that
anymore.

After only seconds of lying down, they came.

A mortar exploded in the field above him. Rifle and machine-gun fire
from both ends of the wet ditch. Boyd tried to stay dry but the cold night
soaked through him. The shallow water smelled of musty hay. He worried that phosgene had settled in the creek.

He pulled himself up the edge of the slimy bank to see movement
somewhere down the stream. Soldiers were pushing aside broken
branches and speaking softly. He couldn't tell what they were saying.
Then he heard a whisper.

"Was ist das, Leutnant?" They had found something.

An American voice shouted nervously, "Surrender. I surrender.
Sprechen Sie Englisch? Ich will mich ergeben. Verstehen Sie mich?"

Private Veeder. Don't do it, Veeder, they'll kill you.

Boyd crawled farther out of the water. Lieutenant Eddie's body lay in
front of him. As Boyd moved next to him, a single shot rang down the
ravine. He could hear laughter imitating Veeder's pleas.

"Sprechen Sie Deutsch, Ami?"

Boyd had seen a log over a shell hole on the embankment. Taking a
deep breath, he hooked the lieutenant's right arm with his and quietly
dragged him to the fallen tree. He crawled into the hole and pulled the
lieutenant's broken body in on himself. Single pistol reports echoed along
the ravine as the Germans shot the wounded and dead where they had
fallen. He knew they would be able to see him but prayed that when his

time came, their coup de grace would not penetrate the lieutenant's body. It did. A German officer fired twice into Lieutenant Eddie's corpse. The Germans' laughter masked the grunt Boyd expelled as the second bullet entered just above his right hip. He clenched his jaw and squeezed his eyes as the German soldiers continued down the ravine.

Midafternoon. The water Boyd splashed on his face gradually awakened him. His tap produced neither hot nor cold water, just some tepid mixture that never satisfied. He splashed the lukewarm fluid under his arms and between his legs, and patted himself dry with a soiled shirt that hung from a nail by the mirror.

Still ragged from his lousy sleep, Boyd stepped through the now deserted lobby on his way to his boss's office. He reached up and slapped the tattered awning. The G in Grant had been torn. Someone had taped it over so it spelled "rant," which appealed to Boyd's sense of disorder.

Walking the two blocks to work got his blood pumping somewhat. Boyd felt he had to be sharp to face his boss; he was always getting after him about something.

Chuck Decker's office was wedged between a dismantled trolley and a locked cage for lost and found. Decker's shirt, dark rings under the armpits, clung to him; his hair was brilliantined to a helmetlike sheen. Jim, a mixed hound, lay across the threshold.

"Corporal Calvin reporting as ordered, General Decker, sir." Boyd stood at exaggerated attention just outside the open door, an innocent look on his face.

"Knock off the horseplay." Decker's voice boomed in the cavernous shop.

Jim slunk away, ears down, tail dragging. Boyd could see several of the mechanics in the back of the shop nod to one another knowingly, then renew their work with vigor.

"Boyd, goddamn it. I've got a letter here telling me how you passed up these people late at night, they having to walk home and all."

"Where exactly was that, sir?"

"What the hell difference does it make where it were? You left these people stranded." Decker looked briefly at the letter. "Corner of Dayton and Main, as if it matters."

"Well, there you are. When it's wet or snowy there's a grade there that I got to get a run at, especially if I'm driving number sixty-five. She's a bitch 'cause I don't think the electrodes are making good contact with the dyno and I just don't have the power to make that little hill there. I'm all intent and everything and I probably didn't notice them a-waiting and—"

"It's June, for Christ's sake. There ain't no snow. They happened to be niggas. Explain that to me if you please."

"Can't explain it. I didn't see them 'cause it was dark, I suppose."

"Have a seat." Decker shuffled some papers on his desk, apparently trying to make a decision. "I know you've had your problems, son, and I'm trying to be fair with you. But you do not have the right to ignore people just because you don't like their color or the way they part their hair or the smell of their aftershave. Your job is to transport people from point A to point B and that's it. Do you understand me?"

Boyd nodded.

"As you know, we're probably all going to be out of a job in a few years. The trolley is dead. But some of us good little boys might just be considered for the buses when they come along. Do you get my drift?"

Boyd wasn't listening. He had read the bulletins and heard the other motormen talking. The mayor had explained on the radio how the new bond issue would cover the cost of transformation from electric trolley cars to gasoline buses. He could not link the things together for himself. It didn't concern him much if he drove a streetcar, sold shoes, or pumped gas. He hadn't purposely ignored the colored folks. He hadn't known many coloreds, but they treated him all right and he went his own way.

"You're on number sixty-one tonight." Decker heaved his way up from his workplace, his belly scraping the desk drawer, a button flying to the floor. "Watch the slipper brake, it needs work. Lincoln Square to the east end."

"I thought I was driving from point A to point B, sir." Boyd remained straight-faced.

Decker reddened. "Get the hell out of here, smart aleck."

"Just one thing, sir. Would you authorize an advance? A friend needs some extra change, and—"

"Yeah, see the accountant."

*B*oyd *felt* the joints in the track rumble under the iron wheels. There it was, the place where part of him still lived. *Come on, be there.*

He had screwed up, nothing new there, but he still loved her. She had looked beautiful the day Boyd left for duty overseas. On his ten-day leave after basic training at Camp Lewis in Rockford, they walked from her house toward the station, stopping to watch a mourning dove peck hopefully at the frozen ground of a fallow garden. The bird flew off, her woeful cooing lost in the distance.

At the station, they huddled under the covered platform of the depot. The army had trained him well and he was ready to take on the world. He felt needed. Boyd swung up on the steps of the train and reached down to clasp Laurel's warm hands.

"Please be careful, will you?" Her face was sad.

"Of course. This thing'll be over quicker than you can say 'Jack Robinson.'"

The conductor called all aboard and Boyd waved with his service cap when the train began moving. Laurel dug in her handbag as if she had forgotten something. She produced a small American flag from her purse and struggled to unwrap it from the tiny sticklike pole. She finally dropped it to her side and watched as the train pulled out of the station.

Laurel had forbidden him to come to the house for months, but most of the time she answered his signals, and it always calmed him. She at least still acknowledged his existence.

But nothing. No response to his signal. He tried it again and still nothing. Continuing to the end of the line and turning the trolley around on

Georgia, he started back. Slowing the car as it passed in front of the white frame house, Boyd saw the bedroom light on, the shade drawn. A figure stood in silhouette against the beige background.

He stomped on the foot bell. No movement. But something moving in the crab apple orchard behind the house caused the moonlight to cast another person's shadow against the clapboard wall. Boyd could feel the heat rising in his neck and swelling to his cheeks and forehead. Entertaining at eleven-thirty. He'd just have to see about that.

*B*oyd paused. He had just ridden up on Decker's bicycle and leaned it against the chicken-wire fence by the back garden. Boyd had borrowed his superintendent's bicycle; he didn't think the old guy would mind. Fact is, he would probably never know. He heard two men talking nearby, and several people pointed toward the back of Laurel's house, as if they had heard something. They gave no indication of having seen Boyd, and he wondered what had happened.

The window shade to the kitchen had been pulled down but there was a small slot at the bottom through which Boyd managed to look. A man he had never seen was sitting at Laurel's table, leaning over, holding one hand to his forehead as if in deep thought and writing with the other. He was talking to himself.

Anger went to Boyd's chest. He clenched his hands and forced himself to relax. He took in a deep breath.

Moving quietly to the back porch, he tried to decide whether to knock. Then the man inside cleared his throat and spoke.

"Come in. I'm almost done here. Come in."

Boyd turned the glass knob and pulled the screen door open. The man sitting at the table leaned back in his chair as Boyd entered the kitchen.

"I'm Ralph Sheridan and I'm just about finished up here." The man pushed forward and smoothed his hand over the book in front of him.

"That's my Bible you got there, mister." Boyd's voice shook as he spoke but he didn't understand why. "I gave that to Laurel."

He looked past the man to the tiny bedroom doorway, with its flowered drape covering, expecting Laurel to burst through at any moment, pointing fingers and hurling epithets.

14

The man gestured toward the bedroom with a pencil. "She's not in there." Then he nodded his head in a direction where Boyd's view was blocked because of the half-open door. He closed it behind him and glanced where the man had indicated.

A bundle of clothes and a pair of legs stuck out from under the kitchen table. Deep red blood spread along the linoleum floor. Laurel.

Boyd steadied himself against the table. Slipping to his knees, he reached for Laurel's hand. It was wet.

Boyd looked over the tabletop at Sheridan, who had turned back to the Bible and now seemed to be underlining some passage. And then for the first time Boyd saw the pistol lying next to the book. The next moments were a blur. Boyd heard himself screaming Laurel's name over and over. Then the deafening sound of a pistol shot as it ricocheted off the walls of the tiny kitchen. Sheridan's head snapped back, his mouth fell open, his empty eyes stared at Boyd.

Boyd heard a shout in the distance to call the police. Another voice yelled for a shotgun because "there's someone standing in the kitchen." The small .32 caliber pistol's nickel-plated finish reflected lamplight off its surface. The bone handle lay shattered on the bloody linoleum. Boyd lifted the weapon and turned it over in his hands, the barrel still hot. He backed toward the kitchen door, never taking his eyes off the terrible scene. The door jammed as Boyd tried to wrench it open. He turned and pulled with full strength—he had to get out.

Once on the porch, he could see people in the yard, unsure of themselves. Someone yelled that a man had a gun. One barefoot fellow in bib overalls shouted to Boyd, wanting to know what was going on.

Boyd's ears rang as he shouted, "Don't know. They're dead, all dead." He jumped from the porch and stumbled, then began to run.

The man with the shotgun yelled out, "Come on back here and tell your story, mister." But by that time, Boyd was in the alley, dodging garbage cans and running for his life.

*T*he *alley* wound snakelike behind the dark houses. A tough old mongrel followed Boyd and nipped at his pant leg. The mutt had started tagging along soon after he left Laurel's house. Each time Boyd took his eye from him, the dog would growl and gnaw away at his already tattered trousers. Hands on knees, Boyd contemplated the animal, who had finally stopped barking and just stood waiting. "Go home," Boyd gasped. The mongrel tilted its head inquiringly. Still fighting for air, Boyd moved backward from the dog, hoping that if he got far enough away, the animal would get discouraged. A woman some fifty yards back slammed her outhouse door and stepped into the alley. Boyd moved slowly into the shadow of the high wood fence. He slipped to one knee and pretended to tie his shoe.

The woman's heavy form was wrapped in a flowered housecoat, the chenille fullness doing nothing for her allure at this hour. She called her dog back home to mama, and the old dog's ears drooped as he reluctantly turned.

Boyd turned back to the alley and started to run again, this time not as desperately. His left ankle stung from the bites, his sock damp from a trickle of blood.

The full moon lit his way. He shoved aside the long-stemmed flowers, their prickly stalks stabbing at his neck and face. He couldn't get enough of the thick warm night air into his lungs. Oh Jesus. She looked so pitiful lying there. What had happened after that man spoke to him? He'd had a Bible in his hands. Was he writing in it? Who was he?

Running almost two miles before slowing to a walk, Boyd made his way over a backyard fence and slipped softly into a garden. The tomato plants beat against his torn ankles and he swore. Someone coughed from a nearby bedroom window as he caught his breath.

The streetlight behind the oaks cast long, crooked shadows of arms and legs against the buildings. Tree limbs hung languidly in these witching hours before dawn. Boyd stopped on the sidewalk and listened as a siren moaned in the distance. He barely felt the pain in his leg. His right ankle had been somewhat protected from the dog by the clip that kept his pant leg from getting caught in the sprocket of the bicycle. The bicycle. God. He'd left it at Laurel's. He looked back in the direction of her apartment. He had to keep moving. He had to get to his room.

Boyd started toward his hotel, walking through the Heights, Irishtown, Elmwood. He hid behind a large oak as a police car flew by. A rat scurried across the alley behind the Grant. Boyd quietly scraped his shoe on the graveled alley and whispered for it to scoot. The rat ignored him. Boyd watched from the alley as someone moved in the third-story hall window of the hotel.

He had to get to his room. He watched carefully as the figure in the third-floor window stopped and rubbed a clear spot in the dirty glass. A cop stared out at the dark building lining the alley.

The police were waiting for him. Boyd eased back into the overhang of Rick's Alley Garage and Auto Parts. The two-story dry goods store shared a common wall with the hotel. If he could get to the roof of Miller's Notions, he could reach the fire escape and make his way up to the roof of the Grant.

Boyd stood on a rotting wood fence and grabbed the tiled parapet of the roof. He pulled himself over the ledge and crouched as he ran toward the side of the hotel. The ladder of the fire escape was just out of reach. He got purchase with his large work shoe and jumped for the bottom rung.

He missed on the first try and lay in a panting heap, listening for voices. None came, so he tried again. This time he clawed his way to the first rung and swung himself up to the platform of the second floor. On all fours he crept past the window where the cop had stood and made his way to the hotel's roof. The door was unlocked. Thank God for the hotel owner's rotten kids, always playing on the roof.

Waiting at the fourth-floor landing, Boyd heard the cop, pacing below, start up the stairwell. Boyd played with his room key, his fingers tracing its familiar ridges and bumps. He tossed it lightly in the air, his palm sweating, and eased it back into his pocket. He would need to distract the cop. He went back to the top of the building. There were several broken tiles lying on the tar paper next to the door; he grabbed them and walked to the edge. Measuring the length of the throw to the landing of the cop's window and taking a deep breath, Boyd lofted the tiles into the air. Their lazy arc carried them perfectly onto the steel fire escape, where they exploded into small, hard ceramic pieces, shattering the window. Shrapnel rained down on top of Miller's. By this time Boyd was back at the roof door, making his way down the hotel stairs. He ran as quietly as he could, praying the cop would still be at the window trying to figure what the hell had happened. He flattened himself against the wall and peeked around the corner of the third-floor corridor in time to see a uniformed policeman's torso stuck completely out of the jagged window. Boyd darted across the hall and slipped his key into the lock on his door and in one swift movement swung into his room, wincing as the latch clicked. He stood in the darkness, his back pressed hard against the thin wooden wall. A door slammed and someone raced down the hall, loud footsteps pounding toward the roof. It wouldn't be long before the cop figured out what was what.

He held his hands over his mouth, trying to subdue the painful gasping of his breath. What did he need? Money, clothes, food. He had no food. What else? Boyd grabbed a small leatherette valise and threw a few of his things into the bag: his life savings of thirty-eight dollars stashed in a pair of socks, razor, toothbrush. More voices in the hall. Raising the window he tossed his case down onto the awning at the front of the hotel. It bounced once and flew into the street.

Straddling the sill and feeling for the brick cornice with his toe, Boyd lowered himself to the top of the second-story window, the plastered arch slippery in the night air. Squatting on the thin ledge, he realized he was committed. With not enough strength to go back up, going down seemed almost impossible. Finally, he lowered a foot along the window below him, feeling for a hold. He was startled when he felt two hands, one on the back of his ankle, the other on the toe of his shoe. Boyd pressed his face against the rough surface of the building.

"All right, you got me, Officer."

The hands pulled Boyd's leg farther down the wooden edge of the window until it was resting on the sill.

"I gotcha, but that don't mean I want you." His friend Claudia sat back onto her perch in the window, smoking.

Boyd brought his other leg down and rested, his limbs dangling.

"It's an interesting way you've chosen to leave the building."

Out of breath, Boyd lowered himself slowly to the top of the awning's metal brace. Before his head disappeared over the edge of the window, he struggled one finger to his lips and shushed Claudia. He crouched on the metal bracket, figuring his next move. There was plenty of noise in the hotel. Half the lights were on and people were scurrying about.

Boyd reached for the long metal pole used to crank the awning up and down. With one hand holding the bracket, he slid the other down the pole and hugged the slender pipe, trying to slide slowly. His toe got caught in the crack of the rough bricks halfway down. He struggled for a few minutes, then stopped to catch his breath. His legs were cramping when he heard her chuckle. Claudia had scampered down the interior stairs and was gaping up at him. "Not a pretty sight, Boyd. Not a pretty sight." His weight and exhaustion caught up with him and he plunged the last ten feet, the crank handle catching him right between the legs. He grunted and lay curled on the hard pavement.

"Didn't your mama ever teach you that it is impolite to touch yourself like that in public?" Claudia stood back and puffed on her ciggie. "Course, you never knew your mama, did you, baby." She tugged at Boyd's arm, helping him to his feet, then went into the street and picked up Boyd's bag. She held it behind her back like a schoolgirl.

As he half crouched, the pain swelled in his groin.

"If you're leaving the hotel, perhaps I might suggest the Salvation Arms," Claudia continued. "It's quite a lovely establishment. Matter of fact, it was just recommended to me yesterday."

He extended his hand for the bag.

"Not till you say those three magic words."

"And what's that?" Boyd felt exasperated.

"Claudia, you're beautiful."

Boyd sucked at his lips. "I ain't got time for this crap. Now give me the bag."

Claudia stood muttering, shaking her head, smiling. "Uh-uh. Nope."

"All right, you're beautiful. Now I got to go. Give me the case." Boyd studied Claudia, her worn nightgown hanging limply from a shrunken frame, her mussed hair on end. The older woman had befriended Boyd, and they had helped each other out of various scrapes. She was like a kindly aunt to him, or sometimes like a wicked stepmother, but he cared deeply for her, and smiled inwardly at her pitiful image.

"Are you in trouble, Calvin?" Claudia used Boyd's last name when she was caring for him.

"Yeah, I reckon I am." They stood for a moment under the awning.

Claudia passed the battered valise to Boyd and touched his scraped arm. "Get that looked after, kiddo," she said, her hand wandering up to his face.

Nodding, Boyd took the bag. He began limping down the sidewalk toward the bus station.

"Thanks for the help with the rent, Buster Brown. I'll remember you in my will." She let out a loud cackle, then tried to stifle it with a weathered hand.

Boyd looked back to see her standing forlornly under the tattered awning, the "rant" hanging over her head. He turned, not wanting to see her tears.

*M*aj. *Dale* Hennessy carefully studied the wall above his dresser. From flat on his back in his mother's old bed, his pictures and plaques were the first things his bleary eyes focused on each morning. Unlike the ones in his office, which officially confirmed *what* he was, these were a testament to *who* he was—among other things, a hero. It said so, right there on the certificates of valor accompanying his Distinguished Service Cross. An ivory-framed sepia displayed a younger, jauntier Hennessy astride a motorcycle, wearing shiny black boots that reached to his knees. A side arm hung on his waistband, and a county sheriff's patch adorned his sleeve. There were more pictures in little frames on the dresser. Hennessy with a handsome woman as tall as his own five feet ten inches. She wore flats instead of heels so as not to appear taller.

Hennessy kicked the sheet off with his good left leg. If a person was tired enough, it was a simple matter of physiology: he should be able to sleep. It hadn't worked that way for him, not for a long time. His mother would tell him he was snoring, but he had no memory of sleeping; what the hell did it matter if you slept if you never experienced waking up? How could he explain how painful and frightening it was not to sleep?

The stiffness of his right leg and pains in his hip were nothing compared to that fear. He counted sheep, goats, goats wearing hats—nothing helped. He got up and walked, drank warm milk, sometimes even did the deed with his hand under the sheets, feeling ridiculous. He drank wine and that only made it worse; he'd doze off for an hour and wake up with the whirlybeds. He often felt there was some sort of conspiracy against him, between his ears, in the gray matter.

21

Gray matter? It wasn't gray. Hell, he'd seen it in trenches, it was brownish white and had the consistency of cooked cauliflower. It's funny the things that he shared with some of the patients under his care, a knowledge of things so bizarre when compared to normal, everyday life. They might not be well-read or sophisticated, but they all shared knowledge of exposed brains in the fresh morning air. They knew what it felt like—and smelled like—to wander into an exploded cow at night. When he finally did sleep he thought of those cows more than anything. Not bombs bursting in air but cows bursting at night. They'd bloat in the hot sun all day and just when you'd think they'd be cooled down, they'd contract around a jagged rib and boom! Nothing in God's brown-and-red-stained earth smelled as awful as internal cow.

He felt himself sweating profusely. He got up to check the block of ice in the pan. Plenty. He glanced at the clock: two-thirty. The wail of a siren filled the darkness with a grim notice that others were having problems at least as great as his own. Not much later he realized his alarm clock was asserting that it was five-thirty. Thank God, he must have slept.

When he arrived at the home, it wasn't yet 7:00 A.M. and he already had a crisis on his hands—hooligans caught on the grounds by security. His secretary had assumed the role of angel of mercy and the temperature was already rising enough to ensure another miserably hot day.

"Let them go. Give them a talking-to and let them go."

"Betty, please. Something's got to be done about this sort of behavior. These hoodlums need to be taught a lesson."

"Perhaps, but they're just kids, what harm did they really do?"

"Harm? Why, trespassing, showing no respect for property, indecent exposure, and basic hooliganism."

"Well, I expect they'll mend their ways. Having had a taste of Clancy will probably make them straight shooters for a month of Sundays." Betty was an excellent secretary and a proper lady, but she was also a mother. Hennessy believed motherhood was a condition that forever clouded a woman's judgment. It made them worthless on juries and an impediment to sensible discipline.

From the door to his office, Dale Hennessy could see through a glass partition into the holding room where Chet Clancy, his chief of security, was glowering down at three teenage heads bent in contrition. "I'm going to call the police."

"Why don't we just have Clancy take them home, Mr. H? After their parents get through with them, Clancy won't seem so bad."

"If they're old enough to be malicious and destructive, then they're old enough to go in front of a magistrate, especially that Bertrick boy. He's the ringleader, you know."

"Yes, sir, but the only damage was a few bent strands of barbed wire and"—she raised her eyebrows in an attempt at conspiratorial humor— "most of the real damage was to that Bertrick boy's rear end trying to climb back over the fence."

Hennessy would have none of it—it just wasn't right. Damn kids hadn't only trespassed, they had run around naked, screaming at the Soldiers' Home residents—"the loonies," they called them. Loonies indeed. A hell of a way to treat veterans—heroes one day, the next day kids are crawling over fences to mock you. And something else troubled him: the mention of barbed wire tweaked something deep inside him, something that left a cold, heavy weight in his stomach. He began drumming his fingers absently on his desk, only half listening to the case being made for leniency.

"He may be from bad seed, that kid, but we can't be treating him like Capone quite yet."

"Capone's a businessman at least, not a randomly destructive lout."

His comment didn't even break Betty's stride. "I know you don't like it when the old soldiers are made fun of, but teenagers will do just about anything to get a rise out of anyone."

"Let me talk to Clancy."

As Betty stalked resignedly to the holding room, Hennessy glanced around him at the residue of his life. It was all there in soft sepia photographs, hard-edged plaques, and official certificates adorned with self-confident signatures. He lived less than a mile from where he had grown up, in a place to which he had once vowed never to return. At forty-five years old he was commanding officer of a home for broken men. And not all genuine invalids. People were right about some of them being just slackers.

"Come on in, Chet," Hennessy said loudly in the direction of the hall.

Hennessy heard the big Pole with the Irish last name make his way toward his office. For about the length of a tennis court, you could hear the man breathing through his mouth. It was difficult to understand how he ever sneaked up on anybody. The man was a self-important bully, but that was fine; he didn't need to hear from any more apologists this early in the morning. He'd get a no-nonsense appraisal from his security chief. There was no room for misdemeanors in Clancy's world. There were only felonies and atrocities, the latter term usually reserved for matters concerning Bolsheviks, Germans, or Jews.

Hennessy eased back into his cushioned throne; he grabbed up his cane to use as a pointer and a sort of scepter, his staff of office.

"Good morning. Hear you apprehended some petty criminals. Good work."

"Yes, sir, Major, I put the fear of God in them."

Hennessy said nothing. By way of encouragement he pushed a brass ashtray across the desk with his cane and jutted his chin toward a leather chair. Clancy pulled a deck of Lucky Strikes from his neatly pressed and double-starched shirt pocket and politely offered the pack to his boss—who gave in return the perfunctory head shake of a man who neither smokes nor condemns those who do. It did bother Hennessy that the man smoked Luckies. They seemed too small for his hands. He always held his right hand in front of him chest level, fingers extended like he was saying the Pledge of Allegiance, with a tiny white fag barely extending between the meat of his third and fourth fingers. Perhaps he would buy him a box of cigars for his birthday.

Clancy made the usual flourish of submissive gestures, indicating he was horrified to see the pristine inner sanctum of the Soldiers' Home violated by barbarians whom he neither feared nor tolerated and would crush like bugs at the merest whim of his master. For some reason, today Hennessy found the loyal pit bull demeanor somewhat comforting.

"When I catch dem they say, 'We not doing nothing.'" Clancy's large hands gestured in front of him, giving form and substance to the words of his captives. Smoke from the Lucky emanated from somewhere deep in his cavernous lungs, pulsing out in cadence with his own words.

"What exactly *were* they doing?"

"At exactly 1:32 A.M. they enter grounds, Major. I know this because I always look at my watch when I respond to violation-of-perimeter calls."

Violation of perimeter? Jesus, sounds like a prisoner-of-war camp.

"They come in under the fence except for the big one; he come over the fence and cut his flesh on the concertina strands."

"Uh-huh, what happened then?"

"I was hiding in bush with two guards and the boys are falling and laughing about the big one's wounds. And the big one says they should dance like devils under the moon."

"Dance like devils under the moon?"

"Yes, sir. So they take off their clothes and start running toward section C, yelling like wild Indians."

"And at this point you apprehended them?"

"Yes, Major."

Hennessy felt his concentration wander. His mind was made up; the details were of no interest. He saw his own reflection in the mirror behind Clancy and checked that he appeared appropriately attentive before tuning the man out of his consciousness.

His reflection had shown the face of a terminally bored man, one dissatisfied with more than the day's events. Even the way he sat in his chair bespoke a stiffness to one side of his body, nothing dramatic, just enough to make him appear . . . imperfect? The mirror also revealed the back of the big Pole in front of him—you usually didn't see that much of anybody at one time. There he was, an immigrant, one of the huddled masses yearning to breathe free, dutifully reporting to his lord and master his latest accomplishment in oppressing anyone out of lockstep with authority.

But look at the character he was reporting to—a gaunt figure, a man with a lean and hungry look, prematurely balding, thin-lipped, slightly pale except where the summer sun in Hell's Half Acre, Illinois, had left shiny pink splotches on his nose and forehead. Now there was a study in third-generation virile American manhood, a warrior's warrior. Having faced the Hun, he would hardly flinch at defending the heartland of America from incursions of junior high school marauders.

After dismissing Clancy, he sat back for a moment, listening to the big man's footsteps receding on the tile floor. They seemed tentative, as if reflecting his disappointment at not being called on to administer justice to the young hoodlums. Hennessy shivered; there was something disquieting about Clancy's demeanor of spurned executioner. Then he gathered himself for his confrontation. He never seemed to do this sort of thing right.

As he entered the holding room—the tank, as they sometimes called it—Hennessy found himself in an unexpectedly aggressive, outspoken mood. The boys were about fifteen years of age, features drawn from being up all night and in obvious awe of his uniform and what he hoped was a no-nonsense bearing. They were side by side on a bench behind a long, weathered cedar table.

He pushed the door closed slowly and deliberately behind him and stared from one boy to the other. The only one that returned his stare was Jimmy Bertrick, no surprise there.

Finally, Harold Shaw ventured, "Sir, I might say, sir, we really didn't mean to—that is, our families work—and, well, we were just doing something crazy, having fun, and—"

All three of them almost evaporated in their chairs at the resounding crack of the cane on the tabletop.

The room was completely silent when Major Hennessy said in a very low voice, almost a whisper, "Dance with the devil, is it?"

Silence.

"You want to dance with the devil under the moon?" The boys' jaws seemed to hang to the soiled necklines of their undershirts.

He walked behind them, brushing between their backs and the glass partition. There was the smell of dirt and stale clothes and nervous fear. He'd smelled that before in much finer bouquets mixed with French and Belgian mud, much darker than Illinois mud. And bloodstains, he'd tell them about bloodstains. He raised the cane over his head. He didn't intend to strike anybody, he just did it on impulse. Two of the boys flinched, raising their arms to protect their heads. Ah, so they could see his reflection in the glass on the other side. Again, the Bertrick boy was the exception. He just bowed his head as if to let it happen. What a strange reaction.

Hennessy walked back around to the front and proceeded to stare at each one again. The Bertrick boy wouldn't look up. Then Hennessy boiled over, surprising even himself.

"Listen, you little shits, I've been to hell, and it might be the only place I'm comfortable. For one thing, it's not as hot as this goddamn town. Look at me!" All eyes but Bertrick's were frozen on the Major. "Do any of you really want to dance with me?"

No answer.

"What do you tough guys think you're going to do when Betty out there calls your parents to tell them you're at the youth cell at the county jail? Think you'll want to strip and laugh about that?" Silence. "Maybe I should turn you over to the soldiers. You think these men who've seen blood and brains splattered on their shirts while defending their country are going to care a damn about doing you in?" He was over the edge now. This was not like him—he had to get a grip. He heard his secretary walk up to the outside of the room, seemingly uncertain whether to come in or to leave. But he couldn't back off. That little Bertrick bastard's shoulders were bobbing while he stared at something interesting on his feet. The little shit was laughing at him.

"Okay, we'll just find out how tough you are. Betty, ring up this big shot's father."

"Sir." Freddy Fallon, the least of the three in size or mettle, spoke softly. "Major, he ain't got a phone, none of us do, and also . . ."

"Also what?"

" 'Also what?' " Jimmy Bertrick was suddenly staring up at him, eyes blazing through something shiny that covered them. "I'll tell you 'also what,' you stuffed-up gimp, 'also what' I ain't got a father." Hennessy suddenly knew the boy's shoulders hadn't been shaking from laughing. "I ain't got a father 'cause the pig got so bored beating up me and Mom that he shot hisself right in his goddamn mouth." Hennessy suddenly felt like he needed to sit down. Bertrick didn't—he stood, eyes wide and red, full of tears, nose running and mouth spewing something dark from his soul. "Also what—his brains and blood was on my sister's shirt just like you said. He was in the war, too—took his gun home, he did. So fuck them old soldiers and fuck him and fuck you."

Hennessy heard the last words in Bertrick's list trail off behind him, because he was headed back to the sanctuary of his office and his chair. He heard the yelling dampen further as his secretary slammed the door of the tank. She appeared in front of his desk a minute later, one hand kneading the other, wordlessly awaiting orders.

"Betty." His voice was strangely calm. "Tell Mr. Bertrick in there and those other boys to go home and not come back here anymore."

"Yes, sir."

"And please, no visitors whatsoever until I tell you . . . I . . . I don't want to be disturbed for the rest of the day. I have some work I need to do." As his secretary closed the door quietly behind her, Hennessy began studying an oddly shaped stain on the wall. It was just above the dormant radiator. For some reason, he found that he was becoming an expert on wall and door stains. They were a sort of art form, he had decided—water, varnish, blood—the art of the unintentional. There were important messages that time had etched in wood and plaster if you made the effort to look for them. And they never let you down or expected more from you than you could give.

Walking the deserted streets of Vermilion, Boyd headed toward the bus station but kept changing direction every several blocks, hoping for inspiration. He stood in a used-car lot, leaning against a Model T Ford with its shiny black finish reflecting colored lights that proclaimed "Great Deals, Best Prices."

He slipped down to the running board and looked across the street at the bus station's faded gray siding. A lone bulb over the entry cast a weak light onto the painted running dog on the wall. Someone inside was moving around, turning on lights. The door opened and a man with an industrial-sized broom swept a pile of dust and bits of paper out onto the large parking lot. The man strolled out to the curb and looked both ways, checking his watch. He danced a few steps with his broom and drifted back to the building. Boyd could see him making coffee and donning a green eyeshade, preparing for his day.

Deciding not to ask about a bus until the last minute seemed wise. He would wait until he saw one drive up and then just buy a ticket and board. The destination didn't matter. He would get far enough away and then decide what to do once he got there.

The night sky started to fade, turning blue-gray. Moisture rose from the earth, getting suddenly colder. Boyd slipped his hands under his armpits and shivered. His head drooped and he fell asleep, dreaming of giant spiderwebs clinging to his arms and legs. A multilegged insect stared at him, its green eyes darting and its mouth making strange honking sounds.

Boyd awoke to car noises. His cheek stung where he had laid his head against the sleeve of his coat. A police car sat not thirty feet from him. A cop leaned out the window and motioned for the bus dispatcher to come to the curb. He honked again and the man turned his head and ambled out to the squad car. The two conversed briefly, the dispatcher making motions to the north and looking at his watch again. Whatever was said seemed to satisfy the cop and he drove away, calling out, "See you later."

Boyd slipped out of the car lot, eyeing the dispatcher, certain the cop had told the clerk to be on the watch.

Walking for a couple of hours to the edge of town, he was thankful for the beginning of day; it seemed easier not to be seen with people going to work and children off to school. When he reached Adams Elementary he cut across a cornfield, the wet stalks soaking his pants, the damp earth sticking stubbornly to his large brogans. A sound like a pistol rang out across the fields.

Boyd ducked and turned to see a woman snapping a wet pillowcase before pinning it to her clothesline. He could see her watching him over the top of her bedding, her fingers smoothing the wrinkles from the wet sheets and towels. Boyd knew this woman. She was Bea Collier. Her son David, a classmate of Boyd's, had drowned while ice-skating at the lake when he was a junior in high school. Boyd would never forget her at the funeral; prostrating herself on the casket, screaming and pounding her fists on the closed bier, the husband trying to calm her. She wouldn't know who Boyd was, but he would never forget her. The woman turned and called to someone in the house as Boyd vaulted the fence and disappeared across the road into a large wooded tract.

A large turkey vulture lit on a tree and spread its wings to dry in the sunlight. The creature gazed at Boyd as he sat on a rotting log. He put his hand against a smooth rock and watched the farmhouse. A man hiking up his suspenders had come from the small cottage and stood talking to Mrs. Collier. He watched as they gestured to where Boyd had disappeared into the woods. He watched them for several minutes, but didn't believe they would call the police. They certainly hadn't heard about the murders, and they wouldn't be that upset about his trespassing on the cornfield. But just to be sure, he made tracks.

The sun was full up by the time he reached the Wabash River. He left the woods on the east side and walked the dirt roads, carefully ignoring two offers of rides. Shaded by elms and oaks that soared upward as they gained strength from the muddy waters, Boyd walked the rich bottom-land bordering the Wabash.

He stopped under a covered bridge. The day had turned humid. Sinking to his knees and rinsing his neck and face, he was startled to see dried blood on the sleeve of his dress shirt. Boyd scrubbed frantically at the stubborn stain with sand and muddy water. After several soakings, the stain disappeared, and he sat breathless on the dirt bank. A car rattled over wooden planks above him and he dropped his head, then immediately realized the occupants could not see him. His uniform jacket lay next to him. He hadn't changed clothes at the hotel. The sleeves were badly wrinkled where he had tied them around his waist. He looked inside his scratched, dirty valise, then closed it.

He hadn't eaten since the day before at the Lucky Diner, and then it was just a chocolate doughnut. What a mess. Why did he have to run? He should have stopped and thought it out. Ralph Sheridan. He couldn't remember where he knew him from. He had definitely shot her. "We're almost done here," he'd said. Almost done?

He felt weak, needing food and something to drink. The river water was dangerous but he had to take a chance. A man in a wooden rowboat came in sight and Boyd lay back slowly in the shadows of the bridge. The man, wearing a red long-sleeved underwear top, stood in the boat, balancing himself gracefully as he cast a line toward the shore, gently reeling it in, then casting again, each time seemingly with great satisfaction. Boyd envied the fisherman, whose life seemed uncomplicated. He stopped casting as his boat drifted gently under the bridge. He placed his pole at his feet and looked Boyd squarely in the eye, as if he had been aware of him lying there all along.

"It's one day at a time, brother, take it as it comes." He smiled. "You look troubled. Get yourself a pole and reap the benefits of this great Indiana river." The tall stranger expertly flicked his wrist and the line leaped out toward the reeds on the far shore. "What'cha go by, Bud?"

Raising his hand to his face as if to shade his eyes, Boyd answered, "Some people call me Tom."

The man nodded. He looked at Boyd as his boat, now some distance away, caught a sunken branch and spun toward the far bank. Reeling his line in, he settled his straw hat on his head. He sang off key, the words almost lost in the moving river.

Boyd sat up; his hands shook as he hugged his knees.

*T*here *came* a measured and formal knock on Dale Hennessy's door.

"Betty?"

"Major, there's someone here to see you, sir."

Major? No Mr. H. Must be someone from the outside—serious visitor.

"Come on in."

Hennessy offered his greetings to two men with the unmistakable bearing of plainclothes police. "Sorry, this has been a busy morning. Gentlemen, how can I help you?"

"Major," interjected Betty. "These men are officers from the Vermilion Police Department. This is Detective Sergeant Petrel and Detective Manion."

"Major." A narrow-faced but thoughtful-looking sergeant of detectives held out a wiry hand. Hennessy took it and in turn shook the hand of his heavyset, moonfaced partner.

"Vermilion? City police? This isn't about the boys, is it?"

"Boys, sir?" The detectives looked at each other.

"Nothing, sorry. I guess there's a problem with one of our people on the outside?"

"Possibly, sir. Do you recall a patient by the name of Boyd Calvin?"

Now it all made sense, the divine order of the day, where that downward spiral to the depths was taking him. Boyd Calvin—sweet Christ on a crutch!

The story the policemen told him was bizarre, but if anybody could get into such a pickle, who other than Boyd hard-luck-professional-loser Calvin? He agreed to help the police—what else could he do? Within minutes they established that he knew Boyd as well as anyone and subtly implied that he was the one responsible for his being free to commit crimes.

When they departed, he briefly renewed his careful study of his favorite stain. It was droopy, and star-shaped, and made no sense at all. What could explain such a stain? What could explain the behavior of Boyd Calvin? Why couldn't Boyd just fade into anonymity like the hundreds of other patients that he had released from his care? Boyd was the classic bad penny; no sooner had you got rid of him than somebody slipped him back again. Or maybe Boyd was like a stain—simply there, obtrusive, drawing attention just by nature of what it was: anomalous—something that didn't fit in the order of things. And now, the police? Killed somebody? Not something Hennessy would ever have predicted, but with a guy like Boyd . . . who was to say?

For thirty minutes he pondered those questions, until he could stall no longer. He would have to join the policemen.

With less grace than usual, Hennessy went through the hated ritual of getting into his new 1928 Ford coupe. He stepped up on the running board with both feet like a child, then held on to the roof and did a contortionist's twist of his lower body to accommodate his stiff right leg. As his hands went through the everyday motions—making sure the shift knob was in neutral, pulling the choke, pushing the starter button—his mind was somewhere else. When the car rumbled to life, a tabby cat jumped from the canvas roof onto the engine hood, doing a curious mincing dance on the hot metal before it leaped into the azaleas.

He had been asked by the good detectives to join them at places where people had reported seeing Boyd. Sergeant Petrel seemed to think Hennessy would have some insights into Boyd's behavior, but when he arrived at the Grant they had little to ask him, and he had even less to offer in reply. He was not as surprised as the detectives that Boyd had returned to his room at the hotel. They thought it more daring and premeditated than they would have expected of the man, but Hennessy knew Boyd ran deeper than people would expect. He was a loser but a complicated loser.

The whole business made him uncomfortable. True, he had been a policeman for a time before the war, and an officer in the military police, but that was enforcement, not sleuthing. Driving a motorcycle along Illinois roads was not the same as conducting a murder investigation. Indeed, when he had been wounded in France, it was while riding a motorcycle—but in a sidecar, as befitted an officer.

He couldn't quite put his finger on what troubled him so much about this Boyd business. But it was more than that; it was Boyd himself. Something in the nature of the man just rubbed him the wrong way. Boyd was insolent, but that wasn't unique. There were a lot of hard cases who went through a stay at the home with a chip on their shoulder, but Boyd was worse somehow. He had never accorded him the respect due his rank— even the most insolent usually called him "Major." The wound to his leg took him out of the field in law enforcement and a meaningful career in the military, but that was old news. If things had gone right for him he might be leading an investigation like the one he was being asked to visit as a consultant.

Now there was talk that someone had seen Boyd near the rail yard. There was already interest from newspaper and radio types. Detective Manion met Hennessy at the gate to the Chicago and Eastern Illinois yard and told him there was "a news lady who came all the way from Chicago" assigned to the case. She must have started down at dawn to be here already. Unlike the aloof Petrel, Manion was having trouble hiding his excitement over the presence of big-city press. She was parked at the other end of the yard and had specifically asked to speak to the Major. Manion jumped into Hennessy's coupe and pointed the way. "I'll introduce you to the lady, Major."

When they rounded a warehouse near the main junction, there was no trouble finding the scene of the last Boyd sighting. Three patrol cars clustered around two lonely freight cars. Uniformed officers talked to a group of hobos who were gesturing in the manner of men anxious to please their interrogators. Someone that fit Boyd's description had apparently walked by their jungle camp in the wee hours and asked about southbound freights. Hennessy saw lots of nodding and hand talk to unresponsive cops listening with arms folded, some rocking back and forth on their heels.

"Gentlemen?"

They turned at the sound of the high-pitched voice.

A lady sat on the running board of a lone deuce coupe. It had a convertible top, like Hennessy's car, but sat only two in front. It was angled to provide shade from the late-afternoon sun. Her heels were planted carelessly in the muck, and a long white cigarette holder dangled from her lips, holding the unlit stub of a cigarette.

Fanning herself with a folded map, she jumped up from her perch without losing her step and walked toward him with a pad and a crumpled newspaper in hand. She had what Hennessy's mother would have called a "flapper sort of look; definitely not marryin' material."

"Delighted to meet you, Major." She extended her hand, turning a set of baby blues on him. She radiated a skin-deep respectfulness that Hennessy had often seen in people who wanted something from him. He had to admit she was not unattractive. Taking her hand warily, he wondered how she already knew his rank. She smiled and said, "You can call me Myrna Logan."

Major Hennessy said nothing; he could feel Detective Manion's jealousy beside him.

"So, what can you tell me about Boyd Calvin, Major?" She addressed him by rank as one would address a Boy Scout leader "Master," as if humoring his little boy's world of status about which he didn't give a hoot.

He had to get on top of the situation. "Well, I'm not sure what you want to know, Miss Logan."

"Myrna."

He gave a weak smile at the correction. "I know some things about him because he was a resident at the home."

"The asylum?"

"Asylum? It's not an asylum, Miss . . . Myrna, and I think you should be clear about that in anything you write."

Her half smile told him she had been playing him, and he was irritated that he'd fallen for it.

"Now, there are some things I can share with you, but others are privileged. . . . Boyd . . . Mr. Calvin was under our care from 1920 to 1925, and then for a short time again in 1928. He was, for the most part, a model patient."

She's not writing.

"He suffered shell shock at Argonne Forest and, well, he had some other problems and—"

"So he's a nut?"

"Now look, Miss Logan, I don't think that's appropriate and I don't think you should be referring to war veterans as—"

"Excuse me, Major, you're right." She placed her hand on his arm and confided softly, "I'm sorry, it's so hot out here, Major, I forget my manners."

He hated himself for being disappointed when she removed her hand.

"We're getting off on the wrong foot. Now we do know that Calvin committed these murders, don't we?"

"Oh, he done it all right, Miss Logan." Manion apparently couldn't help himself. "Nope, there ain't much doubt about that."

But Myrna never took her eyes off Hennessy even as the detective assured her their quarry was an honest-to-goodness double murderer. "Do you have any doubt about that, Major?"

"I guess I had the mistaken notion that we had juries and courts to decide guilt and innocence."

Manion rolled his eyes and opted for silence.

"True, true. I would almost think you had some real doubts, though."

"I don't have anything, including any more time, Miss Logan."

"Just one thing, Major. Who would technically be responsible for releasing a patient before he was ready?"

"That would be a panel with my concurrence, Miss Logan. We have a rating system of red, green, and yellow for persons who have had emotional problems. Some of these men have been at the home since serving their country in the war with Spain, a war in which the color yellow as applied to journalism had some significance, if you recall?"

Hennessy turned and made his way stiffly but with restored authority and dignity back toward his car. Manion seemed confused but blessedly held his tongue.

There was a slight grinding sound as Hennessy slipped the gearshift into reverse. He was still feeling righteous when he had to slam on his brakes because Miss Logan, Myrna, whoever the hell she was, stepped in front of his car as he was about to accelerate out of the rail yard. Her cigarette was now lit and she had adopted a hands-on-hip pose. Her stance was accentuated by, he had to admit, a fine figure. He recalled Boyd often using the term "put together," and this woman was definitely that. Except for the weather making her look a bit like she had been rode hard and put up wet, she reminded him of some motion picture star.

"Look, Dale, no reason to be testy," she whispered into the car. "We need to talk in private, away from Sherlock Holmes here."

"I believe the police are the proper people to answer your questions."

"On some things, but not Boyd Calvin, the person. Please meet me this evening at that diner, you know the one north of town on the Dixie Highway?"

It was incredible. After what he had said to her, she was unfazed; all business and all . . . legs and a sort of mocking smile.

"Pearl's? You mean Pearl's?"

She must have seen the place on her drive to Vermilion. "Yeah, that's the one. Plenty of ice, a little breeze from the river. I saw it on my way down."

The hand was back on his sleeve. He found himself against his better judgment nodding and mumbling an okay.

A light rain made the humidity worse near the river. The breeze had fled the muggy night. Mosquitoes seemed to be the only truly content life forms in the area—even the damned lightning bugs seemed sluggish and depressed.

When Hennessy arrived, his freshly changed shirt already soaked with perspiration, Myrna was perched on a bench outside the diner, scribbling madly in her notepad.

"Do you really have that much to write about already?"

"Oh, it's you, hi. Sure, I have plenty to write. Atmosphere . . . atmosphere and detail. Take this pencil—it's an Eagle number two High-Writer, not just a pencil. I'm sure because I just checked and wrote it down along with some evocative comments about these unpaved county roads, the deafening hum of night insects, and the funny way they get loud and shut down like a whirring motor heeding some divine command—pretty nifty, huh?"

Again, in spite of himself, Hennessy found he was intrigued.

"Have you said anything about the heat?"

"Yep, and the mosquitoes." As if to illustrate, she suddenly slapped one senseless on her lower leg, daintily picked it off with her fingertips, and discarded it.

"How about the fragrance of wet corn in Illinois soil, from that field over there. Can you smell it? I collect smells of wet earth, remember them from all over."

Perhaps the first genuine smile he had seen from Miss Logan creased the edges of her mouth. "Why, Dale, how observant. Don't mind if I use that, do you?"

"Feel free."

As they made their way into the bar she small-talked and he came to accept that he enjoyed her company. She was a study all right, Chicago hard and brusque on the outside with maybe a hint of some kind of caramel filling. Hennessy had heard of front-page girls before. Women who did honest-to-goodness hard news reporting just like men. But he had never met one. The society page and gossip columns seemed to be written by women, but Myrna was the real McCoy. Hennessy nodded to various men who recognized him, and found himself basking in the attention he was receiving from being in the company of a classy woman. "Quite a dish you got there, Major," said Max the barkeep when she was out of earshot. He ignored the comment but couldn't say it displeased him.

He quickly learned more than he would have expected from his news lady. She was thirty-five years old, never married, one of only three lady field reporters on the whole *Trib*. She had been assigned recently to Radio/Write, a division that shared its story text with a local affiliate of CBS Radio in Chicago. She liked gin, white roses, red wine, and the Paul Whiteman Orchestra, not necessarily in that order. And, her girdle was pinching.

Suddenly it occurred to Hennessy that he didn't have much excuse left for not leveling with Miss Logan, since she had just shared everything with him but her cup size, and that was probably available for the asking.

"Now the bulls, Dale, they're convinced Boyd did this. You have been glaringly noncommittal."

"I thought we were going to talk about Boyd, the person."

"See what I mean?"

He smiled. "In short, I don't really have a strong opinion, but I would say I find it more than a little surprising that Boyd would do something like this. No real reason, it just doesn't seem to be the Boyd I knew."

"But you have to admit it's a tight case." She started counting off the reasons, extending one dainty finger at a time. "Hell, he was seen fleeing the scene, he's known to be a bit wacky, he supposedly walked in on some guy nudging his ex-wife"—her ring finger went up, indicating point four was coming—"he finds 'em doing the horizontal refreshment, and"—all five delicate fingers extended—"pow, pow . . . what could be more natural?" Hennessy was happy for the fast-increasing darkness as he felt his face redden, he imagined to the color of summer beets.

"Well, there is the issue that they haven't been living together for years."

"Come on, Major. What would you do? You wouldn't be a little hot if Mrs. Hennessy was— is there a Mrs. Hennessy?"

"No."

She studied him for a second, drink raised halfway to her lips. "I didn't think so."

Beating the back of his trousers with angry hands, Boyd picked up his disheveled coat from the ground, snapped it several times, and patted his right hip pocket, where he concealed the pistol he'd taken from Laurel's kitchen. Another car rattled overhead, the noise drowned by laughter and what sounded like Russ Columbo singing one of his love songs.

Boyd waited several seconds by the bridge, looked both ways, then sprinted across the wooden structure. He was heading east, deeper into Indiana.

On the other side of the bridge, the land seemed to change as the fields became lined with tall oak and maple trees, the ditches on either side of the road thick with chickweed. Boyd thought a small shed with weathered sides and a broken roofline looked abandoned. He pulled a couple ears of immature corn from the waist-high stalks as he made his way to the shack. The interior was strewn with rusty farm implements. Sitting on the dirt floor and leaning against the rickety door, he peeled the green husks from the hard seed corn. After fighting to stay awake while eating, he rolled his coat into a ball, making a pillow, and fell into a deep sleep. He woke several times in the night, listened to the owls and crickets, and fell back again.

In the morning his hip ached from the dirt floor chafing his old wound. Shaking himself off, he started walking the fence farthest from the road, dodging in and out of the tree line. He found this to be hard work, so he made his way back to the road.

After an hour walking, Boyd finally heard a tractor coming up behind him. The model D John Deere's metal treads bit into the hard-packed dirt, exhaust banging out of the tractor's vertical muffler. A boy no older than thirteen motioned for Boyd to jump aboard. Boyd stood on the drag bar, clutching his small bag with one hand and gripping the back of the seat with the other.

"How far you going?" The boy pushed the hand throttle.

"All the way into town." Boyd didn't know exactly where he was, so he didn't specify which town.

"Yeah, town's far. I don't go all the way but I'll take you to our drive. It's 'bout three miles. This's all our land." The boy indicated both sides of the road, his hands leaving the solid spoke steering wheel.

"What's going on with school? You out?"

"Nope, don't go, much. Excep' when Ma insists. Says it's good for a person."

The boy stood with the wheel held lightly at his waist, his legs strad-dling the giant transmission. Boyd rested his forehead on the seat back and watched the metal lugs on the tractor wheels toss fist-sized chunks of earth into the air.

The white farmhouse sat back from the road. A tired-looking woman in a worn cotton dress stood by the mailbox watching the tractor ap-proach, the thinness of her face accentuated by her hair pulled back in a severe bun. She clasped her hands firmly at her waist, holding the mail. The boy turned into the farm's drive, stamping the clutch and pulling back the throttle.

"This here man needed a ride, Ma."

"You live around here, do you, sir?"

"No, ma'am, I'm over by Springfield way, just heading to Indianapolis to see some folks." Boyd dropped his eyes at the lie, then tried to recover. "Sure appreciate the lift from your son, ma'am." Boyd stepped off the drag bar, dropping his valise to massage his legs.

"You look tuckered. You can come up to the house and rest." The woman started toward the house.

"Oh, I think I better keep moving, ma'am. Thanks just the same."

She turned to Boyd. "We're Christian people, young man. My husband and I never met a stranger. Now stop your palaver and come meet my husband, the Reverend Merle."

Boyd felt trapped but needed water; he followed the woman to the modest frame house. A windmill just behind the dwelling creaked a steady strain. A man six foot five or better stood by the pump. His overalls were undone at his waist, revealing his undershirt dark with sweat. He splashed water from a bucket onto his face and hair.

"Reverend Merle, we got company."

The reverend appeared to be a good twenty years older than the woman. His features grew dark as he appraised the stranger. He didn't speak but went back to his washing, eyeing Boyd while he rinsed his arms.

"Little Merle picked up this gentleman by the west forty. I told him we would be obliged to have him for lunch and prayer." The woman stepped back, then waited, as if expecting either to be scolded or praised.

"Do you love God, son? Do you embrace His holiness and accept His spirit?"

The reverend stood braced, a strange challenge on his sunburned face.

Boyd felt caught between the couple. He glanced back at the woman and started to speak. "Well, sir, I—"

"Speak up, son." The man chuckled. "You needn't try to tell any tales, I've heard all the sinners' lies and their backpedaling. Their hopeless, pathetic stories. Now just tell the Gospel truth, do you accept the Lord Jesus and all His teachings?"

"I can't very well say that I do, sir, when I don't know all His teachings. I was what you might call a reluctant student at Sunday school. But I sure—"

"Wash up for lunch," the reverend interrupted Boyd. "What's your name?"

"I go by Tom, sir."

"Well, Tom, we don't stand on formality here. Wash up and come in the house. It's time to break bread."

Boyd knelt by the pump, priming it by taking the remaining water from the bucket and pouring it down the housing that encased the well shaft. He moved the pump handle and let the water trail over his neck and hair. He drank the cold water and wondered if he should just walk away from this free meal. The question was answered when Merle called to him from the screened back porch.

Religious images dominated the walls of the neat farmhouse. The woman and boy were seated at the table, heads down, mouthing some prayers. The reverend sat and began grace.

"O heavenly Father. Thou hast blessed—" Merle looked up at Boyd. "I told you we don't stand on formality. Damn it, sit."

Boyd didn't like being talked to like this, but he was hungry and didn't want to make a fuss. So he sat. Boyd could see the woman's hands shaking slightly and that the boy had his eyes open under his partially bowed head, watching his father, expecting . . . he didn't know what.

"Merle junior, turn the radio off till after lunch."

The boy nodded. "Don't forget your farm report from WGN at one o'clock, Pa."

"Do you know Chicago, Tom?"

"No, sir, can't say that I do."

"Evil city, Tom, evil." The reverend looked at Boyd as if expecting a reply. "Why don't you lead us in saying grace?"

"Well, sir, I'll try, but truth be told, I'm not right up to speed."

"Just start," the reverend insisted.

Boyd stammered, his mind a blank. "O Jesus. Thank us—I mean, thank you—for all your generous harvest and the bountiful portions on this wonderful day. We thank you in God's name, amen."

The reverend brought a large forkful of mashed potatoes to his mouth and began chewing. "I think what you meant to say was 'thank you for the bountiful harvest and generous portions,' right, Tom?"

Boyd played with his food. A couple more words from this bumpkin and he was storming out of there.

"Oh, never mind me, Tom. I get on people's nerves sometimes. The deacons at McFarley Methodist couldn't take a joke, either. They saw fit to dismiss me after twelve years of dedication and hard work."

The woman looked up from her food. "Merle, our guest probably don't want to hear all that. Please, dear."

Soaking a hard biscuit into his pork gravy, Boyd thought he'd better get what he could before another fracas.

The reverend began a speech to his wife about the iniquities of the so-called Christian brothers who had unceremoniously expelled him from the church and how he would rise up against them and bring the full power of the Lord to smite them mightily. Merle junior stopped eating and toyed with his spoon.

A pocketful of biscuits and a fistful of pork chops later, Boyd was out the door and heading for the road.

Reverend Merle called to him as he passed the mailbox.

"Where the hell is your manners, boy? Most folks would offer to do some chores or such. We feed you, treat you to a decent Christian meal, and the first crack outta the box you're hip swinging down the path. Well, sir, I . . ."

He trailed on in that manner as Boyd ate his chops. At one point he turned and heaved a pork bone back toward the quaint farmhouse with a "God bless you all."

Farther down the road, Boyd could see a small rural community rising from the distant cornfields. Must be Franklin. Boyd started to feel better. The food helped, and the prospect of getting off this road and soaking his feet in a creek bed felt good.

The noise behind him startled Boyd. It was a tractor moving at full speed. He had been daydreaming and hadn't heard the John Deere until it was almost on top of him. Boyd could hear the throttle retarding, and the tractor slowed beside him.

"Tom, isn't it? My, my, the people you meet when you ain't got a gun." The reverend then pushed the throttle all the way forward, heading for town as if in an awful hurry.

Boyd stopped. What had he meant by that? Maybe he'd listened to the farm report. Boyd could see the dust from the tractor a half mile ahead; a hay barn and silo were tucked a quarter mile off the road. Dropping down into a stream bed, Boyd began to run; he knew he didn't have much time.

He fell several times in the rocky stream bed, the cool water a shock. The pistol slipped from his pocket into the water and he thought about leaving it, but wiped it off and jammed it into his pants. Looking toward town, where the tractor had disappeared, Boyd left the stream bed and ran the last hundred yards down a wagon lane with high weeds down the center that seemed to be veering in the direction of the barn.

The building was locked. An old padlock under a leather flap kept all who would steal from this barn at bay. Boyd quickly circled the structure and found a smaller entry to the silo. He wriggled through the slats that kept the silage intact. The smell overpowered him and he gasped at the ripening damp mixture. He climbed the ladder to the second floor and found the entrance to the loft blocked by hay. He pulled several bales out past him and let them drop, splitting open as they hit the rotting silage. Finally, he had enough room to crawl into the vast loft. Daylight shone through several small openings, the dust from the hay turning the air to tiny particles.

He tried to catch his breath, wondering how much time he had. The sound of an approaching wagon sent him to the south wall. He watched through a crack as two men rode toward the barn. They didn't look like the police, and besides, there hadn't been enough time. The two farmers unlocked the large barn door and propped it open. The older man urged the two horses pulling the flatbed trailer into the barn, and began loading hay.

Boyd crawled to the edge of the loft and watched as the men stacked the hay from the first floor. He watched them carefully, expecting at any moment for them to come up the steep wooden steps. They had almost finished their work when the younger of the two stopped and put his hand to the back of his neck, looking to the loft. Boyd pulled back and buried his head in the dry hay.

"You say something, Pa?" the young man asked.

"What? What's that you say?"

The younger man cupped his hands to his mouth and spoke louder. "I said, did you say something?"

The other man looked at him. "Whenever you want to stop for lunch, it's fine with me, yeah."

The younger man went back to work just as a bell rang out toward town. "You hear that?"

"Did you hear that, Phil?" The older man walked out of the barn and looked around.

"Sounds to be Willard, trying out his new police car."

"What?"

"Never mind, Pa. I said it's the police. They're coming this way." He raised his voice and the older man nodded.

Boyd swore to himself as he lay flat on the loft floor. These two rubes were going to get him in a whole lot of trouble. They seemed like decent enough people, but he was worried. He watched as the police car came careening down the dirt road, the dust cloud behind rising fifty feet. The father and son farmers stood watching as their police chief raced past the access road.

"Old Willard seems in a right hurry, Pa."

"Seems in a hurry, don't he?"

"I said that, Pa."

"What'd you say?" The old farmer turned and gave his son a dirty look. "If you'd speak up, damn it, I'd hear ya. Always mumbling, 'nough to drive a body crazy."

The son motioned toward the road. "Willard's backing up, look."

The police car backed down the town road and turned into the small access to the barn. The elderly farmer watched the police car come at him. "Drivin' awful fast, hope the old fool can stop."

Chief Willard of Franklin, Indiana, slid his new roadster with the brass bell on the hood to a stop just short of the barn door. The two farmers stepped aside.

"Walter, Phil." The police chief made his acknowledgments as he opened the door, wrenching his girth from under the wheel. "Putting up hay?"

"No, taking it down, Willard."

"Ah yes, I see that."

Boyd fought to keep from sneezing. Dust from the hay floated in the hot air and swirled around him.

Chief Willard pulled a red-and-black handkerchief from his back pocket and wiped his bald head and brow. "Reverend Merle says he saw a young fellow walkin' toward town like a half'n hour ago or so. Seen the likes of him?"

Phil stepped toward the chief. "Haven't seen no one about at all."

"Haven't seen no one about, Willard," Walter repeated.

Boyd continued to watch and listen as the group below talked about him. He took short shallow breaths and tried not to be heard.

"What's this fellow done, Will?"

"Desperate fugilist from the law, as I hear it. Merle says he heard on the news that they was looking for a fellow what killed two folks over by Vermilion. Killed them. He lit out, armed he is, and considered dangerous. Merle gave him lunch and was a bit suspicious of him. Then he drove in and told me, being his phone's down. I ain't heard nothing 'bout it, but old Merle is usually pretty reliable. So if you was to see anyone about, let me know, would you?"

"Sure will, Chief."

Willard pushed his way back into the cramped squad car, tipping his hat to Walter and Phil. He spun the car and sped back down the narrow road, sliding sideways as he headed away from town, bell clanging.

Boyd pushed back from the wall, his hands shaking. He waited for the two men to finish their work. They wrestled the last bale onto the wagon, and Phil closed the barn doors and snapped the lock in place.

"I locked the barn, Pa."

"Did you lock up, son?"

"Yeah, Pa. I locked up." Sitting down on the back of the wagon, Phil rubbed the back of his neck again and looked up at the loft. Boyd breathed deeply as he watched the two of them disappear down the country lane.

He rolled onto his back and slept deeply, the relief spreading through his body.

The day started early for Hennessy. He was called by Sergeant
Petrel at 6:00 A.M. and told of a Boyd Calvin sighting at a
farm outside town. A woman doing her laundry had seen Boyd and recognized him immediately. When Boyd approached her she called her
husband. Knowing better than to tangle with the man of the household,
he had run off "like the murderin' coward he is."

Myrna was already at the scene when Hennessy arrived. Her car wasn't
around, so he figured she must have ridden with one of the detectives.
She seemed rather subdued, just nodding in his direction when he caught
her eye.

Mrs. Collier was happy to repeat her story, adding a part she had previously forgotten—how she'd had to hold back her husband from taking
after Boyd. "Jake was a mind to give that Calvin fella a talkin'-to, but I
tole him let the police handle it."

Jake looked to Hennessy as if he would probably be partial to letting
the police handle most things. The man stood with his head lowered,
nodding assent to his wife's account, hands in his overall pockets except
when one leathery paw moved furtively to his nose.

"Well, he was here," offered Manion, "no doubt about it. They identified him down to his shirt color."

Hennessy was looking at his shoes, intent on banging dirt clods off with
his cane. The sun had climbed to its 9:00 A.M. reserved spot in the sky, and
the heat had already driven Myrna under the shade of a nearby elm.

"Look, Major." Petrel spoke to him intently. "I'd like you to meet
Lieutenant Stanton, with the Illinois State Police. He's letting us keep the

lead on this, as is the county sheriff. But Indiana is something else. We want to keep this local, don't need G-men here."

Hennessy listened politely but wasn't sure what this had to do with him. From what he could remember from seeing different layers of police operate in the past, this case would have gone to the state folks or at least the sheriff as soon as Boyd was on the lam. But once he crossed the state line, the feds could take over. There was law enforcement politics at play here, and he had no investment in the outcome.

Petrel continued. "This Calvin is probably armed and dangerous, and he's headin' for the Indiana border if I don't miss my guess. What can you tell us about him—what can we expect when we find him, a shoot-out?"

Hennessy shrugged. "Sounds like he's pretty shook up. If the Collier fellow could run him off without a gun, I suppose he's not inclined to shoot people."

"Yeah, but he wasn't cornered. How's the rat gonna act when we get him in a trap?"

Petrel appeared to be demonstrating to the state police lieutenant that he had the situation well in hand, up to and including special consultants from the military in the form of Hennessy. Myrna perked up at the question and moved a little closer to hear the answer.

"I don't have any reason to believe that Boyd Calvin is homicidal."

"You mean a reason in addition to two dead bodies?" asked Manion with a sneer. A look from Petrel shut him up.

"Well, I don't know as people who commit crimes of passion are dangerous to anyone else. If, in fact, he committed any crime. You asked me and I'm telling you: Boyd gave no hint of murderous proclivities while at the home." He was aware that he might sound as if he were covering his rear.

"Gentlemen." Myrna reentered the fray. "What do we tell the citizens of Illinois and Indiana is being done about this? An armed man, a possible double murderer, is wandering through the countryside with two notches on his gun handle. Do the police have any idea where he's heading?"

The lieutenant immediately dummied up and let Petrel speak for all of them. He's been around, Hennessy figured. No news is good news until they find the suspect.

"Don't worry, we're gonna nail this crumb." Petrel's voice had a real edge to it.

Myrna glanced at Hennessy, as if to see how this was all registering, but said nothing. When the detective stalked off toward his car she turned to him, a slight frown on her face. "Kind of a scary guy."

"Who?"

"Wedge-head," she said, nodding toward Petrel. "You could split a log by laying him facedown on it and hitting him with a mallet."

Hennessy tried to remain expressionless, but he felt his mouth twist into the beginnings of a smile.

"He seems to really have an attitude about Boyd. I mean Fatso and the minions just figure he's guilty and that's it . . . but Petrel really doesn't like him."

"Indeed."

Myrna duly noted that Manion often had an entourage of admirers—uniformed cops that lurked in his vicinity hoping to learn from his erudite assessments about a world composed of felons and women's body parts. She had dubbed his coterie "Manion's minions." Like many things about Myrna, Hennessy found this habit both intriguing and irritating. He accepted her way of naming things but refused to do it himself. "Look, Dale, I got a ride out here with the bulls. Mind taking me back to Vermilion? I enjoyed our talk last night."

"Suit yourself." He took note of the fact that he was no longer "Major," but Dale. On some level, he found that it pleased him.

As they motored toward town, two police cars passed them, claxons sounding, headed in the other direction.

"Okay, so Boyd first entered the home in 1920?"

"Yeah, it was—" They could see in the distance a third car, state police, and decided together that they should find out what was happening. They both stepped out of Hennessy's coupe and flagged the fast-approaching roadster. It began to slow, whether for Hennessy's brass-covered army uniform or Myrna's legs, he wasn't sure.

The exchange was brief but courteous. There was another Boyd sighting miles farther into Indiana. The station house couldn't reach the detectives or the lieutenant with their radio transmitters—the officers would have called back to acknowledge on the nearest farm phone if they had. "They must be in a dip or something," the young officer opined knowingly to Hennessy, though his eyes were glued on Myrna, who was standing a few feet behind. He was heading for the farm road to inform his superiors. "The others are meetin' an Indiana State Police escort at the state line."

Gravel sprayed from the police car's wheels as it took off again, rumbling over the "Hoosier Highway" into Indiana.

"Jesus."

At Myrna's request they stopped at a package store and Hennessy came back a few minutes later with a bottle of Old Kaintuck bourbon. It still had a label just as if it were perfectly legal, although there was no telling what was really in it. The fellow minding the store had given them two glasses "since there's a lady in the car" and asked only that they return them on the way back.

But now there was steam coming from under the engine hood. Hennessy decided they had to wait awhile before continuing, because the coupe was overheating—something it tended to do when he let the engine idle too long.

Myrna apparently saw this as an ideal opportunity to prompt Hennessy to pick up where he had left off. She listened attentively to his brief medical history of Boyd Calvin—counseling for nervous disability due to shell shock, along with treatment for chronic pulmonary edema caused by the ravages of phosgene inhalation. There were many incidents involving Boyd, but they didn't seem to add up to a person capable of cold-blooded murder. He had been released from the home in 1925 and had kept himself employed more or less since that time.

"So later, he came back briefly. Why was that?"

"A complaint . . . by his wife."

"She claimed he beat her up, right? That's what Fatso said."

"Right. She also claimed he smashed the expensive picture frames her new rich boyfriend gave her."

"Swell. Mean-spirited besides being jealous."

"Yeah, except she later admitted she might have dropped the box of frames herself."

"Really?" Myrna seemed to be mulling the implications of this possible new window into Laurel's soul. "Well, at least that must have made Boyd happy."

"What?"

"Vindication. You know, having his side of the story confirmed."

"That's the funny thing. He never had a side to the story. He never challenged hers."

Myrna's raised brow invited more commentary, but he had little to add. She grabbed the bourbon off the seat and took an unladylike slug straight from the bottle. "So how'd he get released again?"

"It's not like that. It's an administrative action. He wasn't really confined for any specific sentence, just to the limits of my discretion, I guess."

Myrna walked around to the front of the car, stepped on the bumper, and lifted her behind up on the fender near the driver's door. It was a fairly athletic act, to Hennessy's way of reckoning. He realized also that he was not totally unaffected by the distilled essence of cornfield he had been sipping. He watched with more than purely objective interest as Myrna drew her legs up, planted her elbow on her knee, and assumed a chin-in-hand position that reminded him of something: maybe a Norman Rockwell print or maybe news photos he had seen of those Chicago gun molls.

"What made you decide to let him go?"

"I think the fire had a lot to do with it."

"The fire, tell me about the . . . eh, fire."

He glanced up at the sound of a particularly loud hiccup to see an unrepentant Myrna looking him dead in the eye, chin resting on her folded hands. *Good grief, she's getting snockered.*

Suddenly they were interrupted again by a rumbling cloud of dust that indicated a gaggle of police cars coming toward them, also heading for Indiana.

"Let's go," she said. They got back in the car and took off.

Myrna remained silent for a long time, taking a few disinterested pulls at the bottle, having ignored the glasses. But when she did speak, her tone was cold sober. "Look, Dale. This guy did it. It makes for an interesting story to play all these angles, but let's cut the malarkey. Where are the other suspects? You and me—we know he did it, right?"

"Maybe. But I don't like the way people treat the patients—I mean veterans—with problems, and they make an awful easy target for the red-necks. I think we ought to make a point of sincerely representing a man like Boyd in the court system."

The sun was just touching the treetops in the west when Boyd awoke. He lay staring at the rafters of the old barn, trying to figure out where he was. The light had changed to long shadows sweeping across the baled hay. The buildup of heat in the loft from the day was stifling. Then he heard it. The damnable bell again. Boyd rolled onto his stomach and watched as Willard's police car turned into the small lane. This time he wasn't alone.

Two black four-door Fords, each with shiny spotlights on the driver's side, followed the police chief's now slow-moving vehicle. They took their time driving the quarter mile to the barn. Staying back a reasonable distance, the men got out, six of them, and they were clearly being cautious. Phil stood in a circle with them behind one of the black Fords.

Boyd watched as the young farmer started toward the barn, keys in hand. One of the men dressed in a suit and tie stopped him. They conferred for a moment and Phil handed the keys to the suited man. Then all the men seemed to act at once, spreading around the barn like locusts. The one who seemed to be in charge and had taken Phil's keys reached into the backseat of one of the black cars. As he came out his gray fedora tipped down near his eyes. He glanced around and settled his hat, then raised a megaphone to his mouth. "We are agents of the Bureau of Investigation. Boyd Calvin, we know you're in there. Come out peaceably. Now!"

Boyd lay still. The BI. What were they doing there? He heard a shot and tried to bury himself deeper in the prickly hay. He could see the perfect hole just three feet above his head.

"You idiot. Why'd the hell you do that?" the special agent in charge shouted at the police chief.

Willard stood alone behind his squad car. He leveled his Smith & Wesson on the vehicle's rooftop. Smoke seeped from the long barrel. "I hear he's armed and I sure's hell don't wanna take no chances."

"Well, just back off, will you, Sheriff?"

Willard dropped his oversized weapon to his side, looking disappointed. "It's Chief to you, G-man."

"Boyd Calvin! Come out." The megaphone made the words sound mechanical and menacing.

Boyd considered what to do. He watched as several men gathered again around the trunk of the first black car. Suddenly they turned as if one to look back up the weeded lane at Reverend Merle and his family hustling toward them on their tractor, Merle junior and the missus standing on the drag bar, grinning. Boyd could see the agents stop the reverend and speak for a few moments. Then the reverend sat, seeming to wait for the show.

One of the BI agents looped a canvas bag over his shoulder and knelt down, speaking to the agent in charge, who was busy loading a machine gun on the running board of the Ford. The older man handed him the keys to the barn, then pointed and patted the younger agent on the back. The man sprinted toward the barn. Boyd lost sight of him as he stood next to the doors. He could hear the heavy lock being unfastened.

The doors opened but the agent didn't step inside; instead he took a can from his pouch, pulled a pin from a handle apparatus on the top, and tossed it into the barn. Thick smoke erupted from the can with a loud *pop*. Boyd watched as the smoke rose to the loft. Gas. They were going to gas him.

The mixture enveloped Boyd as he crawled toward the silo door. His throat burning and eyes tearing, he made his way through the small opening and started climbing down the metal rungs. The gas hadn't reached the silo yet as he dropped down to the broken hay bales. He quickly covered himself in the scattered hay and buried his head alongside the wall, searching for an air pocket in the damp silage.

A muffled voice nearby called to him. "Boyd Calvin, I'm going to drop a canister right down your trousers if you don't come outta that silo right now."

Boyd dug his way out of the clumped hay and looked up. A man wearing a gas mask and holding a machine gun peered down at Boyd from the small silo opening. Coughing, Boyd rose with his hands over his head. A flashlight shone into his eyes from below the slotted door.

"Keep your hands high, young man. You armed?" The agent trained an automatic pistol at Boyd.

"Yes, sir, I think I am, sir."

"What do you mean, you think you are?"

"Well, sir, I don't know if this piece works, sir, it appears to be broke."

The agent crawled through the slats, the flashlight never leaving Boyd's face. "Put out your hands."

Boyd complied. The handcuffs pressed hard against his damp wrists.

"Boyd Calvin, I place you under arrest for interstate flight to avoid prosecution for the murders of Ralph P. Sheridan and Laurel Sue Calvin."

N*ot much* piss and wind left in him now, is there?" Detective Manion leaned against the cage, keys clinking steadily against the hard metal. "Is there, Big Bad Boyd?"

When Boyd didn't respond, Manion's blustery features gained intensity. "Hey, killer," he hissed, "you listening to me?"

Hennessy and Myrna stepped back against the flaking wall of the small lockup.

The jailer at the end of the hall stood up, his chair scraping the floor.

"Detective, the state's attorney says you're not to question the prisoner until after the grand jury convenes later this month, you hear?"

"Yeah, I hear." Manion glanced at Hennessy and Myrna.

Boyd sat on his bunk, face buried in his hands. His cell was at the far end of the L-shaped corridor and the first to be visible head-on to anyone entering the block.

"Thanks, Detective, I'll take it from here." Petrel sounded slightly annoyed in his abrupt dismissal of Manion. The latter tipped his hat to Myrna as he departed. As there were only four holding cells in the entire lockup, it was painfully obvious that the man was strutting a trophy capture. Petrel hung back several steps as Hennessy approached Boyd's cell. Only one other cell was occupied, by a black man who returned the newcomer's gaze with an unblinking stare.

"The nigga here is accused of raping a white woman in Mackerel Town." Petrel spoke as if the man was behind glass and out of hearing, not two steps away. "You go on and talk to Boyd if you want but I gotta stay here." Petrel looked in at Boyd. "Oh yeah, the tough guy here decided he didn't want to go to jail after all, damnedest fight I ever seen.

57

Took four of us to get him down the hall and through the door, screaming his lungs out. Yellin', kickin', and spoutin' all kinda crap about how
he can't be locked up, he couldn't be confined, poor baby. You popped
me in the mouth, jackass. I won't be forgetting that anytime soon." Petrel
draped his arms through the bars, daring the prisoner to come close.

Boyd remained still.

"Thank you, Sergeant Petrel. May we spend a few moments alone
with him, please?"

Petrel shrugged and walked back to join the jailer at the end of the
hall. He sat on the man's desk as if he owned it.

Hennessy leaned on his cane in front of the painted gray bars. He
couldn't help but remember the many times he'd locked up drunken soldiers, almost always repentant, usually vomit-sodden and polite to a fault.
The man sitting with head in hands seemed different. Cold and distant.

"Boyd, how're you doing? Been treated all right? It's Major Hennessy,
from the home."

They waited for an answer. Silence.

"Is there anything I can do for you?" Hennessy looked back at Myrna.
"You want to speak to him?"

Myrna nodded but stayed against the wall. "Mr. Calvin, my name is
Myrna Logan. I work for the *Chicago Tribune*."

Boyd kept his head in his hands and turned away in a manner that
strongly suggested the interview was over.

"I'd like to express my condolences for the death of your wife, sir."

A small gasp came from Boyd at the mention of Laurel, but nothing
else.

Hennessy could see that Myrna's little flanking maneuver on Boyd
hadn't worked. He tapped the bars gently with his cane, thinking.

"I'd like to hear what you have to say about all this. If there were extenuating circumstances or possibly you were provoked in some way?
That will be a matter for the courts. I'll certainly be called as a character
witness. I can quite quickly show almost any jury that you've had problems and that this may not be the cold-blooded act that it appears to be."

Hennessy immediately felt rotten. He'd done exactly what he had disapproved of in others, accusing Boyd without the benefit of trial. "Listen to me. I don't mean to imply that you're guilty, but things don't look good. I'd like to help you if I can." He wanted to reach in and shake Boyd out of his stubborn trance.

"Mr. Calvin, you know that under our judicial system you are entitled to an attorney." Myrna's voice was soft and insistent. "If you're indigent, I'm sure a public defender would be assigned to you." She paused. "If you'd like to speak to me and my readers, it might be possible for my editor to give you assistance in some manner."

Hennessy shot Myrna a murderous look. "Miss Logan, you might want to save all that for another time."

Without moving, Boyd whispered, "Take your dogfight outta here, will you?"

"I didn't hear you, son."

"You heard me. I said get out!" Boyd shouted down into the concrete floor.

"What's going on?" Petrel called out.

Hennessy raised a hand to assure the officers that all was well.

"Boyd, listen to me a moment. You were seen going into your wife's residence. People heard shots. You were seen leaving the house threatening onlookers with what looked for all intents and purposes like the murder weapon. The murder weapon was found on you. For God's sake, man, what else is there?"

No response.

"Boyd, are you all right? Do you realize what's going on, how much trouble you're in? Remember how the Germans had that mine you could step on and nothing would happen? Then you'd lift your foot and the damn thing would go off and blow your butt into the middle of next week? You're standing on that mine right now, Boyd. Be careful of your next step."

Silence.

"Okay, we're going to leave, Boyd. But I'm coming back, and the two of us are going to talk."

Hennessy felt Myrna move next to him.

"Maybe we should let Mr. Calvin rest, Major," she said, her warm presence burning the Major's elbow. "Boyd, if I may call you that, please feel free to contact me."

She seemed sincere enough to Hennessy, if a tad self-serving. They made their way down the hall. Petrel started closing the door behind him, but they could clearly hear his last comment. "Calvin, you're sure to be dimming the lights at Joliet after not too long, and it'll be good riddance in my book." Petrel turned his attention back to his guests.

"Didn't get much, did ya?" He smirked. "I'll bet you dollars to a doughnut that ol' boy will crack before the night's out."

They started through the sally-port door when they heard a weak voice call out from the cellblock.

"You're wrong, Major. I didn't do it."

They stopped.

"I didn't, goddamn it, I didn't."

Hennessy sighed and turned to Myrna, who remained strangely quiet.

Petrel, standing several feet ahead of them now, motioned for them to follow him out. Hennessy thanked the detective and made his way back toward his car, the mute Miss Logan following a few steps behind.

He jammed his good foot down on the starter and they drove away in silence.

*T*here's a Mrs. Falk to see you, Calvin."

"Don't know any Falks."

"Well, she knows you." The jailer swung an old captain's chair as he walked toward Boyd, Claudia trailing behind him. He dropped the chair in front of Boyd's cell. "She can stay as long as she likes, but no touching."

"Goodness gracious, Boyd, did he have to say that?" Claudia glanced at him, tucking her skirt primly under her knees as she sat on the worn chair. "Hope you don't mind visiting for a spell. I had some time to kill and I thought I'd drop by."

She patted the arms of the chair nervously.

Boyd sat on the iron cot. A heavy smell of Evening in Paris laced the air. Perfume did not mix well with the odors of urine and dampness in the ancient basement. The jailer at the end of the hall rattled a set of keys as he hung them on a peg.

Claudia smiled and looked at Boyd, hoping for some recognition. They sat for several seconds, not speaking. Boyd looked at the wall's faded green paint as Claudia hummed softly.

"I made this dress myself, what do you think?"

Boyd glanced at the worn cotton garment.

Claudia chewed her bottom lip. "Well, I mean, not recently. Oh . . . it's been several years ago, I guess. Got the pattern out of the catalog. Sears, you know, just snipped it together, easy as pie." Her voice got high at the end and she gave him a big smile. "Use to sew all the time when I was on the road. Had to make all our own costumes. So it comes quite naturally to me." She stopped for a moment and took a small compact from her beaded bag. "The light is very poor in here." She moved her

61

head from side to side as she examined her powdered face, the stained puff racing over her wrinkles. She licked her lips and ran her tongue over her teeth. "My sister and I were on the Chautauqua Circuit for years. Bet ya didn't know that, didya?" She clicked the compact shut and dropped it ceremoniously in her bag. "We were the Flying Falks, tumbling and songs. My, my, what a time we had. Verna was actually the acrobat. Oh, I could do a couple of tricks, handsprings and somersaults and the like, but Verna was the one they came to see. She could do, sometimes, a dozen back flips while the audience clapped and counted 'One, flip. Two, flip. Three' . . . Meanwhile I'd be singing 'I'm Falling for You.' Did you ever hear it? It goes,

'I'm falling for you, my dear, I'll never be blue, my dear.
There are birds in the sky and I'll never know why.
But I'm falling for you, my dear."

Claudia's beautiful clear voice seemed to be trying to make contact with Boyd. "After each phrase, you see, she'd do a back flip and the audience would shout out the number. Sometimes it went on so long that I had to start the whole song over. Verna didn't seem to care. She loved the audience. She'd always finish with a leg split and a big grin on her face. The pit band loved our act. Probably 'cause they had such a good view up Verna's knickers." Claudia laughed and slapped her hands together, burying her face in embarrassment. "Verna always managed to snare one of the band members, usually the drummer. She died young, Verna did. TB it was. I don't know . . . she came to me one day and said, 'Kid, I'm real sick.' Wasn't long before she was in a sanitarium, and then after that, nothing."

Claudia seemed to be remembering her sister and the good times. "I don't mean to rattle on such. Boyd, it's just that I don't know what to say, sweetie. I feel bad 'bout what happened with you and whoever that girl and fellow was. I just want you to know that you're all right by me and if there's anything I can do, please tell me." Claudia moved her chair closer to the cell and had both hands on the bars, peering in. "Won't you talk to me, Boyd?"

Boyd glanced at Claudia and shook his head. The old gal let her hands slide down the bars in defeat. "Do you recognize my belt? I swiped it off the drapes in the lobby of the Grant." She got up and made several circles, letting the velvet rope swing out from her body. The jailer at his desk swiveled his chair around as if he did not want to be seen laughing. Claudia's dress lifted to her knobby knees and one rolled stocking came down to her thin calf, her buckled shoes scuffing the cement floor as she danced in the jail. She paused to tug at the wayward garter. "Boyd, if you talk to me, I'll tell you a secret. Okay?"

"Uh-huh."

"Your mother and I were the best of friends."

He looked up quickly.

"Oh, that got his attention, folks." Claudia did a little la-da-de-da and sat crossing her legs, plopping her hands in her lap. She cocked her head expectantly. "Well?"

Boyd opened his mouth but nothing came out. "I—I—what are you saying?" he blurted finally.

"I knew your mother, Bettina. We were chums in Chicago after I quit the circuit. We worked in the five-and-dime on Halstead and she was the finest human being I've ever known. Period." Claudia sat back in her chair and sighed.

Boyd listened.

"She was pregnant with you when I met her. Course she didn't know that at the time, but we were the best of friends. My God, but that woman could laugh. We would howl at work, always finding something funny. Old Mr. Busybody Franklin always looking over his shoulder from across that store, doing his cluck-clucking and shaking his finger at us. But your mom would just look at him and he would practically pee his britches. Oh boy, we got away with murder." Claudia gasped, realizing what she had said. "Oh, excuse me. That was just an expression, dear." She got up and stretched. "Worked late last night. Oh, darn. I forgot to tell you, I got a job."

No reaction from Boyd.

"Yeah, got a job down at the Lucky. Not exactly a waitress, just cleaning up and such. Pays the rent, get a meal . . ." Claudia sauntered down the short hall to the first cell. "Hello, young man. What's your name?"

"Me? Well, my name be George, ma'am."

"Well, George Maam. How are you keepin'?"

"I'm just fine, ma'am." George smiled, pointing a gentle finger at her. "You're one of those people that always makes a body laugh. Ain't you, ma'am?"

Claudia looked all around as if to make sure no one was listening. "Let me tell you a little secret. Life is just what you make it." Arms out wide, she danced quietly in the narrow hallway. "You make of it only what you can." She went into a soft-shoe shuffle, keeping perfect time while making popping sounds with her mouth and slapping her hands softly on her thighs. The black man grinned.

George called out, "What's your name, miss?"

"Claudia, George. And what, may I ask, brings you to these humble surroundings?" Claudia stood, head high, panting, in the dingy hallway as if she were attending the annual cotillion ball and she was Queen of the May.

"Well, ma'am, they say I done some bad things to this girl downtown."

"Hey, miss," the jailer called out. "If you want to be Florence Nightingale, do it somewhere else. The colored man don't need any of your help, he's going to Joliet with your friend, where he'll have plenty of his kind to tell his backwoods stories to."

Claudia breezed down to the jailer. "Oh, Morris, don't be such a stick-in-the-mud. I was just being sociable, and besides, if anybody around here is backwoods, it's you."

Morris sat straight up in his chair and dropped his paper. "Listen here, miss. I'll kick your skinny behind outta here quicker than Dixie if you don't watch your mouth. Now go on back and talk to your killer friend and leave blackie here alone."

"Morris T. Adams. Underachiever. Does well at recess and playtime. Doesn't relate well to his classmates or teachers. Has difficulty reading and comprehending at his grade level. Recommendation: after-school study, but the student refused with the following note from his parents:

'Morris is needed at home for the evenin' chores. Thank you.' Do I recall correctly, Mo?"

"Well, I'll be damned. Miss Falk. I thought there was something familiar 'bout you when you came in. Haven't seen you in a coon's age. How've you been?"

"Fine, Mo, just fine, and you?"

"Oh, can't complain." Morris stood and grasped his right thumb with his left hand like a schoolboy.

"Sit down, for heaven's sake."

The jailer seemed to be waiting for further instruction.

"Nice chatting with you, Morris. And please, as a favor to your old third-grade teacher, take good care of Mr. Calvin, would you, please, and also my new friend, George?" Claudia sashayed back to her chair at the end of the hall with a "Toodle-oo" to Morris and a wave to George. "Well, Mr. Calvin, what's to become of you? Are we gonna hafta spank your butt or what?"

Boyd looked to Claudia.

"Can't see me as a schoolteacher? How'd she ever manage that? Why, I always thought she was just some kinda white trash that hung out in hotel hallways at night, servicing the boys that sneak around. My, my. Schoolteacher, friend of my ma's, failed opera singer, what else? Well, Mr. Smarty, there's plenty else. But we don't have time for all that now. What I want to know is what's to become of you? Do you have a lawyer?"

Boyd shrugged. "Huh-uh."

"Well, 'huh-uh' isn't good enough, Boyd Calvin. I'm gonna see what I can do 'bout rustling you up a lawyer." Claudia sat for several long moments, her face softening. "Keep your chin up, sweetie. Old Claudia loves ya. And if you've done a bad deed, I'll still be here for you. Do you hear me?"

Boyd nodded.

"I'm gonna go now, kid. I'll come back and visit with you tomorrow if that's all right. Your arraignment hearing is not for another week, so just hold on, okay?"

She looked like she wanted to reach in and touch Boyd. Instead, she gripped at her wrinkled housedress and slowly smoothed the pleats that had gathered at her lap. She straightened her knockabout hat; her gray fringes peeked out from under the rose-colored brim. She turned slowly. "Bye, love."

She was halfway down the hall when Boyd called out, "Was she really a good person, Claudia?" He was now standing right up against the bars.

Not turning, she called back, "The best, the very best."

The tiny opening high on the back wall of Boyd's cell looked out on Main. He moved the small footstool under the window and, after several attempts, managed to grasp the two steel bars. He pulled himself up to the edge of the window at sidewalk level. People were scurrying about, shopping, loafing; there was Claudia, getting ready to cross the street, her arms waving, her mouth moving a mile a minute, speaking to two strangers. Lord knew about what. She waved to a black man driving a horse–drawn ice wagon. She did a funny little hop while trying to pull up her rolled stocking and crossed the street.

*B*oyd *paced* the eight-by-six-foot cell. A glossy film crept slowly down the walls of the jail, the cell stifling in the June heat.

"Least you got a window." The voice came from George, the man three cells away.

Since they were the only prisoners in the tiny jail and he had the only window, Boyd assumed George was talking to him. "I got one but I can't do much about it, now can I, boy?"

"I am not your boy." George chuckled. "Always the white man's way—reply to a friendly word with some smart remark."

At the end of the hall, Morris glanced up from his paper and then went back to his reading.

"Mind your own, fella, and I'll mind mine," Boyd said. He fell onto the cot, inadvertently banging his head sharply on the welded frame. He swore loudly and held his head, stomping on the damp cement.

"Don't hurt yourself, Massa Boyd, sir. The authorities will be a might ruffled if they can't hang your lily-white ass." George stood next to his cell door, long, lean arms dangling relaxed through the vertical bars. "After you been here awhile, you'll feel right at home. You'll find no need to be hurtin' yourself that way. Eventually a body finds a way to excuse one's sins and each day you'll look more and more innocent till finally you'll be seeing yourself as Jesus the Lord Almighty himself, I swear."

"Oh dry up, will ya? I don't need your bullshit." Boyd had moved to his cell door, where he ran his right hand high onto one of the bars while rubbing his head with his left.

"Are you a southpaw, my man?"

"What do you mean?" Boyd said.

"Are you a lefty?"

"How'd you know?"

"Oh, just figured, you know. The way you were rubbing your head. It just took what my pa used to call an educated guess."

Boyd paused. "Was he?"

"Was he what?"

"Educated."

"No, he wasn't, but he read a considerable amount, and my ma had graduated business college and insisted we, my sister and I, finish at least high school."

They stood for several moments in silence.

"What are you really in here for?" Boyd asked.

"I didn't do what they say, if that's what you mean. But yeah, I did it." George smiled. "I'd been doing it off and on for over a year. But this par-ti-cu-lar time"—George raised his eyebrows and looked down his nose— "we got caught and missy decides to scream bloody rape." George spat on the jail floor.

"You fellas shut your traps back there, there's no conversing 'tween prisoners." The jailer went back to his reading.

"I didn't think we were conversing, Morris. I thought we were just talking."

Morris threw his paper down and swiveled his chair to get a better look at Boyd. "I'll come down there and converse on your hard head in a minute, mister."

"Oh, he didn't mean anything, boss." George winked back at Boyd. "He was just having some sport with you."

Morris moved quickly toward the sally-port door.

"Hey, Morris, could you bring back a couple sody pops and a few candy bars?" Boyd thought it fun to get old Morris's goat.

"Yeah, boss, and while you're at it, some chitterlings and black-eyed peas for me, the colored man, Mr. George M."

Boyd and George hooted at Morris down the hall. Morris reached the sally-port gate with a wicked smile on his face.

"I hate a man who has no sense of humor, don't you, George?"

"Sure do. Like my daddy always said, 'A man without a smile is a man what lacks education.'"

The door burst open and Morris came raging back to the cells. He had picked up a nightstick and was now accompanied by Ross, a beefy policeman with a no-nonsense look. Morris poked his stick into the cell to keep George back while Ross unlocked the cage.

"Well, Mr. Big Mouth, it's time I had a little sport, don't ya think? And speaking of black eyes, peas or otherwise, you gonna be quite a spell before you can eat anything, let alone chitterlings."

Ross rushed George and tried to pin him against the back wall. Boyd couldn't see what was happening but could hear the awful thump of the nightstick as it struck the defenseless prisoner.

"Hey, stop that! Stop it, do you hear?" Boyd screamed. "You bastards!"

When they stopped he could hear loud panting and a moan. Morris and Ross spoke in low voices. Boyd strained to hear and then said, "I'm going to report both of you guys, do you hear me? Goddamn it. Do you hear? Who in the hell do you think you are? You lousy bastards." Boyd was blue with rage as he shook the heavy steel cage door. "What in the hell did he do to deserve that? You sons a bitches."

Morris stepped out of the cell and pointed his club at Boyd. "You're next, killer, your turn's comin'. You shut that flap of yours and just sit tight. We're just takin' a breather in here."

Boyd again shook his cell door but stopped when he heard George call out.

"Don't worry 'bout these crackers, white boy, they hit like a couple Girl Scouts. My mama's whacked me harder than these—"

The beating started again. Enraged, Boyd grabbed his stool and began pounding it against the bars. In desperation, he leaped off his cot and grabbed the bars that shielded the high window on the back wall. He took the broken stool leg and jammed it through the thick glass.

"Hey, hey, anybody. There's a guy getting murdered in here!" Several people on the sidewalk turned but kept walking. "Hey, damn it, we need help down here!"

A woman pushing a baby carriage paused. "What's wrong, young man?"

"They're killing a guy in here, get some help, quick."

"Is this some kind of joke?" The woman moved closer. "Because if it is, I'm—" But she stopped to listen as the screams and shouts from George's cell got louder. "Oh my God . . ." She pushed her carriage to the police-station door.

Boyd could just barely see as she took her baby from the carriage and hurried to the front door of the station. Boyd hung from the bars at the window until his fingers turned white. He yelled several times more and then slid down the wall, finally dropping to the damp floor. The noise from the far cell had ended. He could still hear the heavy breaths being taken by the two policemen and an occasional painful gasp.

"That's the most cowardly damn piece of business I ever heard. Both of you so-called policemen ought to be ashamed of yourselves!" Boyd shouted at George's cell door. The sally-port entrance rattled as someone let himself in. "Morris? Where'n hell are you?"

A policeman with gold pins on his lapels and stripes on his sleeves moved stiffly from the gate and proceeded down the short hall. "Calvin's got visitors." He looked into George's cell. "What you doing in there?" The police sergeant stopped at the cell door. "What happened here?"

"They beat the shit outta him for no good reason. That's what happened, the bastards." Boyd clenched his teeth.

Claudia and a tall, thin older man stood uncomfortably in the dimly lit hall.

"Are you fellows all right?" The sergeant was halfway into George's crib. Boyd couldn't make out the muffled reply of Morris and his big friend.

"Yeah. But why beat him?" the sergeant asked.

Again an inaudible reply.

The sergeant stood for a moment, then turned to the visitors. "You folks step back into the room beyond the sally port and I'll call you."

Morris and Ross stepped out of the cell and into the hall. "The big buck tried some funny stuff. I'm telling you, the nigger don't know his place, and when I went to talk to him he took a poke at me through the bars." A deep laugh and something garbled that Boyd couldn't understand came from inside the cell. The sally-port door slammed open and an excited officer leaned in. "Say, there's a woman out here with a baby says she heard screaming down here. Is everything all right?"

"Yeah, Bill, tell her thanks for being a good citizen and all. Everything is fine, just some prisoners having a good time." The sergeant whirled on Morris.

"You're in some deep trouble this time, Morris. You, too, Ross." He grabbed Ross by the arm and headed him out the hall, getting nose to nose with him. "Tell those people—Miss Falk and that lawyer—to come on in. Do you think you can manage that?" Ross lumbered away, head down.

The sergeant turned to Morris. "You sit at your desk and try to think how in the hell you're gonna justify beating the crap out of a prisoner under your care. Even if he is colored."

Boyd sat down hard on his cot.

"Boyd, this is Mr. Freeman. Mr. Freeman is a retired lawyer who worked around the county for some fifty years. He's a friend of Mr. Weiss's, the owner of the Grant, and has kindly agreed to talk to you," Claudia said as she and the man she had brought with her were shown into the cell area. "He has worked on lots of famous cases around the county."

"Now, Miss Falk, let's not overstate the facts. I have been a practicing attorney for a number of years here, and—"

"Well, darn. Can't you tell him about the Malby murder case? You know, getting those rednecks off—"

Boyd listened as his two visitors spoke as if he weren't present.

"Oh, Miss Falk, that's ancient history. I'm sure your friend here doesn't want to hear all that nonsense."

George was being led out holding his left side with both hands; his chin was still up, but he was limping. Boyd called out, "I'm your witness, George. Remember that. Damn it, remember."

George turned halfway around. "Much obliged. I'll try and bring you back some sody." He laughed even with a welt forming on the side of his face, blood on the back of his head. "And some candy bars and chitlins."

Boyd raked his fists lightly against the bars, then looked at the old gentleman standing outside his cell. His high, stiff collar was slightly soiled;
his suit hung limply on thin shoulders. A perfectly bald head with bifocals perched on a large hooked nose gave him the appearance of a
turkey sticking his head out of a fallen log.

A giant smile showed large, yellow teeth. "So pleased to meet you, Mr.
Calvin. You're in good hands." He made an "okay" sign. "Claudia has
told me all about you."

Boyd was sure Claudia had gone to considerable trouble to acquire
some help, but this guy didn't look like he'd make it through the day, let
alone a trial. Boyd looked up as he heard voices again in the sally port.

Morris pouted at his desk. "Ya can't go in till the others leave."

"Why?"

" 'Cause I say so, that's why."

Hennessy and Myrna stood by Morris's desk. Another well-dressed
man with a black briefcase waited in the background.

Boyd had trouble focusing on what Claudia and her lawyer friend
were saying. He was still in turmoil from the beating incident; things
seemed to be happening faster than he could keep up with.

Claudia motioned for Mr. Freeman to hold on for a second and put
her hand on Boyd's shoulder.

"Damn bastards. Goddamn bastards beatin' on that colored fella like
that."

"What'd he do?" Claudia asked.

"Nothing I didn't do."

"Okay, now settle down, sweetie, and listen to old Claudia."

"Yeah, why? Just what in hell are you doing, Claudia? Ain't I in enough
trouble without getting help from you?"

"I'm tellin' you, Boyd. This here is Mr. Freeman, he's a genuine lawyer
recognized by the Illinois bar."

"Bar and grill, maybe."

Freeman stepped backward, as if struck.

"Now you stop that, Boyd. I spent most of the morning talking to Mr.
Freeman, and he's willing to help us, if you let him. Not many lawyers are

going to help you unless they're appointed by the court, and everybody knows they're mainly window dressing."

"Well, at least they're walking upright. Freeman here looks like he's fixing to fall over."

"I'm fixing to give you one upside your head, young fella." Freeman's voice didn't have that carnival barker's tone it'd had minutes before. The old bastard looked like he actually might be thinking of taking a poke at him.

This mollified Boyd. "Okay, Jack Dempsey. Calm down. Now just what is it you can do for me?"

"Not a goddamn thing if it wasn't for Mrs. Falk here. She's a real old friend, and for some reason I can't understand, she gives a hoot what happens to you."

"Yeah, so why would you be more than window dressing like the lawyer the court will give me?"

"Because I care." He quickly followed with, "Not about you, that is, but about Mrs. Falk." It was hard for Boyd to fathom why this geezer would care about Claudia, but then, he had learned a lot of things he couldn't fathom about Claudia in the last two days. "Also, I'm getting paid better than some wet-behind-the-ears pipsqueak in a three-piece."

Boyd's eyebrows raised. "Paid?"

"That's none of your nevermind, Boyd," Claudia said, and seemed to really mean it. "If you're gonna look a gift horse in the mouth all day, Mr. Freeman and me'll just be on our way."

"Okay, okay," Boyd grunted with a shrug. He took a drag on a Chesterfield and leaned toward his makeshift ashtray, a Coke bottle half full of some nameless brown sludge of cigarettes and a liquid, presumably Coke. He tapped the cigarette on the rim and the ash fell neatly down the neck. Freeman took the one available chair and pulled it up in front of Boyd while Claudia stood to the side and started humming to herself.

"So, will you tell me what happened, Boyd? The judge is going to have an arraignment tomorrow. There's no doubt he'll convene a grand jury, and there's no doubt, either, that they'll hand down an indictment. So, what's it gonna be?"

"Seems everybody's got it all figured out anyway. Don't know what good it would do me saying I didn't kill anybody."

"Actually, sometimes saying you didn't do it helps, guilty or not. In this case it's probably too damn obvious that you did do it and you can only make it worse denying it. Might want to throw yourself on the mercy of the court."

"I thought you was supposed to be my lawyer—you sound more like that damn state's attorney."

"State's attorney? You spoke to the state's attorney?"

"Mr. Fancy Britches was here all right. Came in with Morris and Petrel and had me give a statement."

"You have a lawyer there at the time . . . a court-appointed attorney?"

"Hell no. They just asked me a bunch of questions and called me a liar, kinda like you're doing."

Freeman gave a thousand-yard stare toward the corner of the cell and was quiet for a moment. Claudia continued her humming; Boyd recognized the plaintive strains of "Amazing Grace."

Freeman's bifocals kept fogging for some reason and the man kept peering over and under them, anywhere but through the glass panels. He had a comedic-tragic demeanor about him that was starting to intrigue Boyd. Suddenly he straightened and pointed a finger in Boyd's face. "Boy, don't you be bullshitting me anymore, tell me straight so's I can get my bearings on all this. You're saying people are calling you a liar and not listening to you. I'm asking you once and for all, in front of God: You saying you didn't kill them people?"

In answer, Boyd shoved the butt of his Chesterfield down the spout of the Coke bottle while exhaling a deep lungful of white smoke. He grabbed up the bottle and held his hand over the rim to smother the cigarette. It couldn't reach the liquid through the ugly raft of soggy tobacco. It occurred to him that his mouth tasted very much like he imagined the contents of the bottle must taste. It almost made him sick to think about it.

Claudia's melodious refrain contributed to the background noise in the cell. "To save a wretch like me . . ."

Freeman started drumming his fingers on the hat he held in his hand. He sighed and made to leave, then turned back one more time to Boyd. "You kill those people?"

"Nope."

Claudia turned to the two of them and sang, ". . . but now I'm found." She said it with an upward flourish of her hands, freezing her recitation of the lyrics of the old hymn with that optimistic refrain. Freeman removed his spectacles and started rubbing a hopelessly soiled piece of cloth on the lenses. Now Boyd knew why the damn things were always fogged.

The old lawyer asked simply, "So you want me to represent you or no, Boyd?"

"Reckon . . . probably."

"Well, okay then. Don't say anything more to anyone. I'll come back and talk to you later. If you decide you want me, I'll be seeing you alone from now on."

Claudia strutted over and gave Boyd a peck on the cheek and, like a grand lady of the ball, put her hand out to the old lawyer. "It's time to let Boyd be for a spell."

"Can I bring you back anything when I come see you tonight? Can we do anything for you?" said Freeman in parting.

"Nah—well, wait a minute, yeah, you can do something. Bring me back some chitlins, I'm really hankering for some chitlins, okay?"

"Chitlins? Okay, Boyd. Whatever suits you." Freeman tossed the words over his shoulder as he headed down the hall.

Boyd listened to a slight commotion at the end of the hall, and Morris walked toward him.

"You got more people coming to see you than flies swarming on a turd."

"Go to hell, coward."

"Pipe down, Boyd." Morris was having trouble maintaining an authoritative demeanor after all that had transpired. "Settle down, hear? And I'll lead these people back here."

Boyd felt like everything was spinning. "Wait. Morris, you tell 'em to wait . . . and let me use the head."

Each cell had a slop pot, but with visitors coming down the hall soon, the jailers often let the inmates use the two-holer head, which was the pride of the Vermilion jail. It had a brand-new chain-pull flush toilet. For some reason the city fathers had neglected to put in a meeting room for counsels, but had included a state-of-the-art shitter.

Morris was obviously unsure how to deal with this new development, but Boyd figured he was even more concerned about the trouble he was already in for beating on George. "Okay, Boyd, but no trouble or you're in for it."

Boyd walked quietly down the hall and broke to the right in front of his new visitors while Morris explained that the prisoner was "just taking a nature call and will be back in a minute." Boyd didn't have to go to the bathroom but needed simply to be alone for a few minutes. That reporter lady and Hennessy and some stuffed shirt he had never seen were all standing there solemnly as he walked by, but he didn't acknowledge their existence.

His breathing got back to normal and his nerves settled down. He had no idea if Freeman was a total joke or not, but at least the old lawyer had some sort of plan. He started to leave and noticed blood on the lavatory sink. That was George's for sure. That goddamn Morris reminded him of those Germans . . . over there. Something about that mindless cruelty. It made some kind of sense in war, but when he saw it for no reason in everyday life it twisted him inside.

As Boyd trudged back to his cell, Morris told the assembled guests they could follow him down to the cell but they had to talk through the bars, no going in. The reason the last folks had been allowed was that they'd had Boyd's lawyer with them.

Boyd saw an annoyed grimace pass over the face of the starched shirt. Miss Logan seemed truly agitated when their little procession reached Boyd's cell.

"Boyd, now look, it's me, Myrna, we met yesterday."

"How could I forget?"

"I told you then that we'd found you a first-rate lawyer—all you'd have to do is talk to us a little bit and tell us what happened."

Before Boyd could respond, the attorney took over for Myrna. He had a deep, resonant voice, clearly trained to comfort and convince. Boyd thought he sounded like a radio preacher.

"Mr. Calvin, I'm Donald Devlin, and I represent a firm that has had great success with this kind of case."

"This kind of case?"

"Yes, our criminal division specializes in capital murder and other violent crimes. Our civil side handles the full range of torts."

Boyd wasn't at all sure what a tort was, but he did have a question. "So what can you do for me that would be different than what Mr. Freeman can do?"

"Mr. Calvin, we would have the full resources of a well-respected firm able to concentrate on your unfortunate situation. In short, you'd have the same consideration a rich man does when he goes before twelve of his peers."

Boyd thought Devlin sounded as if he were speaking in parables, and Boyd never did much understand them.

"But I already have a lawyer."

"All you have to do is sign a writ, which I could draft up in fifteen minutes, after access to a typewriter. It would explain how you are relieving him of his duties—why, we'd even pay him for the time he spent coming in to consult with you. Don't worry, he won't object."

Boyd considered the offer. Devlin's manner was so reassuring and confident that everyone seemed to think Boyd would see the obvious advantage of using him over Freeman.

"How would you get me off?"

"I would make sure the jurors appreciate the strain you were under when you encountered the scene that so upset you at your wife's home."

"What do you mean?"

"After all you'd been through for your country and then to go home and find a man romantically involved with your wife . . . it must surely have put you over the edge. . . . No jury would send you to the death chamber once they understood that."

"Romantically involved? That's what you call it?" Boyd was becoming increasingly agitated. "I told them both"—he nodded his head toward Hennessy and Myrna—"that I didn't do it."

"Admitting to yielding to a moment of understandable confusion and outrage, a crime of passion with extenuating circumstances—it's something any jury could be made to understand. Even her lover knew they were sinning, underlining that passage about adultery and all. Believe me, throwing yourself on the mercy of the court is not such an unreasonable choice, once the court has been suitably informed."

Boyd sighed and walked to the window through which he had summoned the woman during George's beating. "You don't believe me—you're trying to just keep them from executing me?"

"It's not a matter of what I believe but rather what a jury can be made to believe. However, we can talk about strategy later."

"No we can't. Like I said, I already have a lawyer."

*M*orris, *when* did I come in here?" The days had melded together. Boyd couldn't remember if he had been in jail a week or a month.

"Calvin, suit up. You and this black yea-hoo you call your friend are going over to the magistrate's to confess your sins. You been here nine days, if it matters." Morris had taken Boyd's tin plate with the remains of his oatmeal. He ignored George as he passed his cell door.

"You not going to speak to me, boss man? Damn, I don't think I'll be able to sleep tonight." George leaned against the bars and winked at Boyd.

Boyd pulled on his motorman's uniform coat, brushing the sleeves and stretching the material in a vain attempt to get the hard wrinkles to fall.

"You boys are breathing a wart on your nose." Morris spun the cell keys around on a brass ring. "I wish I could go with you lads to see how old man Wilson is gonna settle your hash."

Boyd exchanged looks with George and shrugged.

Morris shackled them along with another new prisoner. The heavy cuffs were hooked into a steel chain wrapped around the three prisoners' waists and linked together. The men were forced to walk front to back as they made their way through the county jail.

Morris turned his charges over to an Officer Blake, and they started their walk across the town square. The midday sun seemed much more vivid to Boyd. He welcomed the noise from the cars and trucks and it felt good to be alive, but Boyd wondered if people thought of him as a murderer or someone who had been wrongly accused.

As they waited on the corner to let the eastbound trolley car pass, several passengers craned their necks to look at the strange entourage. The motorman stomped his foot bell several times and waved. Boyd nodded and dropped his head. He wondered if he'd still have a job after this.

The two-tiered old county courthouse stood like a cheap wedding cake. Its stone cornices had softened, and the once proud gargoyles that supported its roof were blurred and pitted.

Lawyers and friends of defendants crowded the stifling courtroom. Boyd sat in the first row with George and the new prisoner. They were in the company of several prisoners from the county jail in various stages of either sobering up or nursing wounds from fights—in some cases, both.

"All rise," called the bailiff. "Court is now in session. The honorable Carl Wilson, chief magistrate, presiding. Be seated."

The judge charged into the courtroom. His light blue sweater peeked out beneath his black robe. An unlit homemade cigarette protruded from narrow, mean lips. "Call the first case, Bailiff." The judge settled back into his chair.

"The people of the state of Illinois versus Earl Fount, Your Honor."

Without moving, Judge Wilson asked the clerk, "The usual charges?"

"Yes, Your Honor."

"Stand up, Earl." The defendant next to Boyd shot to his feet. "Mr. Fount, how many times have you been before me in the past twelve months?"

"I don't recall, Your Honor."

"Would you like me to refresh your memory?" the judge asked calmly. "Are you represented by counsel, Mr. Fount?"

"No, Your Honor. I didn't think that would be necessary." He flashed a toothless smile.

"Well, Earl, you're probably right. How do you plead?"

"Guilty, Your Honor, with an explanation."

"Go on, Mr. Fount."

"Well, Your Honor, it was payday and a few of us fellows got together and one thing led to another and—"

"You got drunk as usual, stripped yourself naked, and urinated on the Abe Lincoln statue in Collins Park across from the hospital, am I right?"

"Yes, Your Honor."

"Now how would I know all that, Earl?"

"Because I've done it before, Your Honor, but—"

"You've done it before, exactly." Judge Wilson grabbed the defendant's file from his desk and scribbled quickly across the bottom. "Thirty days in the county jail, suspended. Now get out of here."

Earl made smacking sounds with his lips while Blake released his handcuffs.

"See you soon, Earl," Officer Blake said.

"Good luck, guys." Earl nodded to George and Boyd. "Wilson is not too ornery today." The old drunk made his way past the bar separating the court from the gallery.

"The court calls George Matthews."

A slim, eager young man stepped forward and motioned for George to stand next to him. He turned to George and quietly explained, "I'm Phil Green, your attorney, Mr. Matthews."

George looked at him and grunted.

"How do you wish to plead, George?" the attorney asked.

"Shouldn't we talk some about this before I plead?"

"Well, it's a fairly cut-and-dried case, George. . . ."

The judge startled the courtroom by cracking his gavel down sharply. "Damn it, Green. Now is not the time to be palavering with your client. The felonious crime with which you are charged, Mr. Matthews, is rape with bodily harm inflicted on one Millie Mae Moss, perpetrated on the third day of June 1929. Do you understand the charge against you?"

"I suppose I do, yes, sir."

"How do you wish to plead, Mr. Matthews?"

"Not guilty, Your Honor."

"Not guilty?"

"Yes, sir, Your Honor."

"A not guilty plea requires a trial by jury," stated the judge. "You understand that, don't you, Mr. Matthews? Have you discussed this with Mr. Green, your attorney?"

"I just met this fellow right now, Judge." George took a deep breath. "This is sumthin' I didn't do, so I don't see as how there's much to discuss."

"The court doesn't take kindly to the wasting of its time, Mr. Matthews, but if you're sure that's what you want, then that's your right." The judge glanced at his calendar. "Trial set for September twenty-third. Next case." The judge seemed genuinely agitated as he only half listened to the next few cases that were called. He either dismissed them because they seemed annoying to him or exacted what looked to Boyd like extremely harsh punishment.

"The court calls Boyd Calvin in the matter of the people of the state of Illinois versus Calvin, the charge being two counts of murder."

"And how does your client wish to plead?"

"We wish to plead not guilty, Your Honor."

"You realize, of course, that this matter will have to be held over for the grand jury."

"We are aware of that, Your Honor."

"Have the young man rise."

Freeman signaled for Boyd to get up.

"Young man, before I ask you how you plead, let me just say this: I intend to do all that is humanly possible to keep Vermilion and its environs as clean and free of human filth as I possibly can. Now having said that, how do you wish to plead?"

Freeman turned quickly and whispered into Boyd's ear.

"I plead not guilty, Your Honor." Boyd's voice cracked.

Judge Wilson gathered his papers and exited. Overhead fans beat the humid air. Boyd's trial hadn't even started and already he was in deep trouble.

Boyd and George were reshackled along with two other black prisoners who had been through arraignment as well. They were led from the county jail to the street.

Blake clasped the two sets of prisoners on either side of himself and started moving across the wide public square. The afternoon heat had settled into the concrete and wound its way up Boyd's pant legs. Sounds came from the direction of the jail, a high-pitched chant booming up the narrow street. When they were halfway across the square, Boyd could see several hundred people gathered in front of the jail, some carrying placards. A few people stood on the running boards of their cars; others were crowded onto horse-drawn wagons, yelling and waving fists in the air. Officer Blake stopped. "This don't look too good, boys," he said.

George pulled Boyd toward him with the chain. "They're coming for me."

"What're you saying?"

"The crowd, they want me."

Boyd stared at the ragtag assembly. They indeed wanted something or someone. He looked down at his handcuffs.

Blake had stopped his charges on the sidewalk near a drugstore. He turned to his other two black prisoners and looked them hard in the face. "I'm going to let go of you for a moment. Don't make me chase you now, you hear?"

The two men nodded.

Blake turned back to George and Boyd. "Going to unshackle ya. But don't think I'm being easy. You follow me into the jail and there won't be any trouble. You try and run for it, I'll shoot your butts, hear?" He moved the men up against the wall. They were a block from the jail and the noise had intensified. Blake's hands trembled as he tried to unlock the restraints and pull the chain from around their waists. "I'm doing this to give you all a chance in case that mob goes loony on us. Now behave, hear?"

A shotgun blast rocked the city streets. Someone on the jail steps shouted for the crowd to disperse. Several more shots were heard as policemen fired in the air.

"Give us the nigga! Give us the nigga! George Matthews dies! George Matthews dies!" Blake shook so hard he finally had to give the keys to George, who unlocked both his and Boyd's shackles. He calmly passed the key back to Blake.

George's hands were steady as he wound the long chain around his fist, letting the end dangle below his knees. Boyd could see uniformed policemen on the jail steps trying to reason with the crowd. Blake had moved all four men up against the wall of the drugstore. People inside were peering out the window, trying to see the show. Blake could not seem to unlock the two black men's cuffs.

George and Boyd squeezed against the wall, trying to shrink into its rough brick surface. Something whistled past Boyd and splattered against the wall. An egg burst just inches from his head and both he and George ducked, squatting on the hot pavement. Blake whirled and drew his pistol. Boyd saw two young men across the street hide behind an ice wagon.

"Down here!" they shouted. One of the young fellows broke out from behind the wagon and ran shouting toward the crowd. "Down here, damn it! Down here! He's down in front the drugstore!"

Several of the rabble turned and listened, and in a few moments the entire group had the information. With renewed enthusiasm, the mob started to move down the street. The police on the jail steps still occasionally fired in the air, but no one paid attention.

Blake turned to George and Boyd. "You're on your own," he said as he tossed his keys to the other prisoners. Blake walked toward the crowd.

George moved along the wall, never taking his eyes off the crowd. "Let's make tracks, Mr. Boyd."

Their waists still bound together with heavy chain, the two other black prisoners moved to the center of the sidewalk, one of them holding the keys to freedom unused in his hand.

Blake fumbled with his pistol as the crowd ran toward the group. Rocks and sticks flew as a stone hit Blake in the forehead, knocking his hat to the ground. He staggered for a moment and fell to his knees, blood streaming down his face. A round from his pistol ricocheted off the sidewalk. Someone in the crowd went down and screamed.

The two black men bolted back across the street toward the courthouse. One fell, dragging down the other, but they quickly rose and sprinted down the alley behind the old stone building.

George and Boyd, hidden by spectators leaving the drugstore, continued moving down the wall. A small girl cried and fell as she was hit by a rock. The crowd seemed to hesitate for a moment as Boyd moved around the corner of the building and began to run.

Trees from Collins Park drifted past Boyd as his arms pumped out of rhythm with his leaden feet. Someone was coming. He dug harder and dared not look back. *Gonna be killed. Not fair. Gonna be hanged. Oh Jesus.*

The pounding behind Boyd became louder. He finally glanced over his shoulder, fearing what he might see.

But it was George, teeth showing, eyes sparkling.

Boyd laughed in spite of himself.

"Where you think we oughta go, boss man?"

"Don't know . . . just keep running?"

George struggled with his breathing, fighting for air.

"Seeing as how . . ." There was a long pause as he drank in the humid afternoon. "Yes, seeing as how they want to"—thirty steps, then—"hang my sorry butt."

The two ran some distance in silence, then collapsed onto the soft grass near a playground.

"I don't see anyone"—Boyd stopped to look around—"following us."

"Let's get behind something," George said. They made their way through the park into a wooded area that bordered Mill Creek.

"I don't know exactly what you did, George. But you sure upset a lot of people."

George grabbed a broken stick and limped through the heavy thicket.

"No—there's just a lot of people what got led into thinking they were more upset than they really were."

Boyd listened as a roar went up along Mill Creek valley. It sounded as if Red Grange had scored a touchdown. A siren wailed to underscore the mob's delirium. Dogs could be heard shrieking as if on the scent of a wounded animal.

George mumbled something to himself, making marks in the dry earth with his newly found walking stick. He started along the path, brushing away branches and swinging his stick as if batting away some invisible demon. Boyd watched him carefully.

"You ever see a lynching, Boyd?"

The two men stopped and turned toward the distant sounds.

Boyd didn't answer.

George made his way carefully down the wooded path, thick with early-summer hawthorn and dogwood. He squatted often to pull off the cockleburs stuck to his socks and to gather wild tiny raspberries, which he alternately ate quickly and stuffed into his pockets. Boyd rested on a large stone and gazed back through a crowded brush of ironweed. George turned to the north, then east, listening, apparently trying to determine if the sound was changing. Boyd followed, glancing back along the path every few seconds.

"When we lived in Tuscaloosa . . . bunch of us were fishing . . . me and a few of my school buddies skipped school and just went fishing."

George leaned down to put his hands on his knees, breathing deeply for several moments. Filling his lungs one last time, he resumed walking.

"Well, we were sitting by the creek, trying not to catch anything, when we heard a noise. Something like what we're hearing now." George looked up as if hearing the crowd for the first time. "Only not so loud. It was a bunch of crackers coming down the path hollerin' and laughin'. Cuttin' up, so we scooted into the brush on a little hill overlooking the fishing spot."

George paused, rubbing his eyes and running his shirtsleeve across his nose.

"They was all liquored up, those old boys, and right in the middle of the mob was my uncle Leonard. He was bleeding pretty bad, cuts on his head and arms. They'd tied his hands and was leading him down the path like a goat."

Boyd tried to walk away but George followed, still telling his story. Boyd sped up, hoping George would tire of the pace and stop talking.

"When they arrived at the clearing below our little hill, they gave Uncle Leonard a yank and he went flying on his face. 'Get up, nigga, we hate to see you a-crawlin.' They laughed and booted Uncle a couple times, and he got to his feet. Never forget the look on his face. He was trying not to show fear and at the same time have some kind of dignity, the blood and dirt makin' a pitiful mask of his face. 'I sur, sur-lay . . . did, di . . . no . . . not . . . me . . . mean, ni-ni-no harm.' 'Spit it out, nigga, what's ya trying to say.' They taunted him, all the time Uncle Leonard kept trying to stutter his way through some kind of explanation, all the time grinnin' a shit-eatin' grin."

Boyd looked back at George. "Why you telling me all this, for Christ's sake?"

" 'Cause I'll be leaving you soon to parts unknown and I want you to remember me from this little tale. Got it, boss man? It just so happened that the little ol' fishing spot had a big tree at the edge and there was a wonderful knotted rope swing that some white kids had rigged up so that they could shoot themselves out over the water, then drop. Well, I guess you can imagine what happened next. They hoisted my uncle Leonard on their shoulders, looped the rope around his neck, and pushed him out over the pond. But those crackers weren't so expert at killin' folks. The rope was too long and uncle just flopped halfway down the water. The rope pulled tight and the water was around his waist.

"By this time all my fishing pals had slipped away through the thick undergrowth. I stayed, watching. Hoping, wishing I could do something. Uncle was gagging and fighting with his bound hands trying to relieve the pressure from the rope. The redneck bastards waded in and pulled him back on the shore, looped the rope once more around his head to shorten it, and pushed him out again.

"Uncle was really screaming now, pulling, trying to climb the rope, his legs kicking the water into a foam. They went out and got him again, tugging him back to the bank. 'I'm goin' for a nigga ride, fellas. Give me a push.' One of the men in bib overalls and a blue straw hat jumped on Uncle's back as his shit-head pals pushed. I looked away but I could still hear a terrible cracking sound along with a rebel yell.

"Strange what you remember: All that was going on, and I can still smell that bitter goldenrod, my face buried in those thick stems. I stayed head-down in the bush. They seemed to sober up quickly then. As they left, the man in the overalls walked quite close to where I was hiding. I got a good look at his face as someone called to him, 'Bobby Tom, you looked right smart whoopin' and hollerin', waving that hat out over the water. Where'd you learn that? 'Oh, I went to Negro ridin' school, graduated with honors.' They laughed in a way I never forgot."

George and Boyd walked along the creek side for several miles, not speaking. The sun was just starting to disappear in the west when they stopped to rest on a broken tree trunk that formed a bridge across the small strip of water.

"I wanted you to hear all that, not 'cause I wanted to shock you, but 'cause I like you, and you seem a decent sort . . . for a cracker."

Boyd tried to be angry at George, but the black man's grin melted his resolve.

"Damn, boy, don't you have a sense of humor? Nah, come on, I'm just funnin' with ya, but listen, I want you to know if they catch us together, you run, hear? They'll probably let you go, but just be on the safe side and hightail it."

Boyd sat nodding. He was struggling with the realization that he liked this fellow—maybe more than any other man he had ever met. George was irritating, obnoxious at times, but he always seemed honest and able to say just the right thing to Boyd to engage him, always with a bit of ginger.

"How old were you when all that happened?"

"I say 'bout thirteen, I reckon. Old enough to know that I had seen something that would change my life. I cried for what seemed hours afore I could go to Uncle. I lay there trying to decide whether to fetch my daddy or to try and do for Uncle. His neck was all funny lookin'. Stretched and swollen. His eyes were open and his tongue was way out his mouth. He had messed hisself. His arms had locked up around his chin, like he was praying. I tried to pull him out the water but I was just a little kid. I finally climbed up the tree and with my puny pocketknife cut the rope. I remember thinking the white kids will probably lynch me if they find out who cut their rope swing. Uncle had slipped completely under by the time I got down but I managed to pull his head and shoulders up out of the water.

"I undid the rope, thinking how many times did I watch Uncle get ready to go out, funnin' on a Saturday night with a joke for me and a laugh. Doing his tie so carefully, always with a fresh shirt, and here he is now, his neck all swollen, him all beaten, his clothes sodden and spoiled. I sat in the water with his head in my lap, making some promises to Uncle, promises I kept three or four years later.

"But finally I started to get cold and I let Uncle slip back in the water. I tied the rope around the base of the tree and started toward home to tell Daddy.

" 'What you doin', boy? You got yourself all wet and ruined your school clothes. I told you afore, change them clothes before you—' He stopped, as he could see I was crying. I couldn't catch my breath. 'It's Uncle Leonard. They kilt him by the tree. By the fishing hole, they kilt him. I saw it. Daddy, I couldn't do nothing. I shoulda but I couldn't. . . . '

"Daddy was never the same after that. He ran hard to the spot and was there long before I was. He had dragged his brother onto the bank and was on top a him, hugging him, tryin' to squeeze life back into his bruised body."

George got up and walked away, beating the blackberry bushes with his walking stick. He would stop every few strokes and sob, great gushes of air pouring out of him.

They continued to walk, the night sky glowing at their backs. Reflections of the town lights bounced off the clouds. North of town, a bonfire glimmered.

George and Boyd reached a small creek bed that reflected the moon. Boyd slipped to his knees and bathed his face in the tepid stream. He hunched over and breathed deeply, let the warm water drip softly back into the shallow creek. He could hear George's bones protest as he slumped across from him next to the small waterway.

"Gonna rest a spell, massa."

Boyd listened as George's breathing slowed and changed into a soft snore. He sat back and ran his hands over the dried grass. An owl hooted as it swept across the sky. Moments later, he could hear a small animal's high-pitched scream as the bird of prey pounced. A cloud passed in front of the moon. Boyd couldn't get George's story out of his head, and somehow the picture the words created in his mind started getting all confused with the recent hell in his own life.

The creek blackened to dark blood as the water reflected off the red clay banks of the stream. Laurel's blood on the linoleum kitchen floor of their modest apartment swam before Boyd's eyes. Who was that man at Laurel's? Boyd had never seen him before. He seemed older and tired. Why would Laurel take up with such a person? The image of the man's macabre grin . . .

He had loved her, had tried to remake his marriage, but it hadn't worked. He realized maybe part of it was his fault. Well, maybe more than part. The more he thought about it, the more pain he felt. He lowered his head onto the warm earth.

Boyd clasped his hands over his mouth to keep George from hearing his stifled sobs. He could almost feel the crushing weight of her body on his. He breathed deeply the smell of fresh-cut hay. His hands clenched the tufts of weeds on the bank. Was he in a cave? Far-off thunder shook the earth.

He raised his head cautiously above the shell hole. The Germans had disappeared. Boyd tried to push Lieutenant Eddie away from him. Each time he moved, the body seemed to settle more permanently onto his. *Fill your lungs and relax. You got the lieutenant in here, you can get him out.*

Boyd's adrenaline had been replaced by bone-deep weariness. He looked up through the skeletal branches of an oak tree at the deep blue sky. He pushed again. Lieutenant Eddie had become stiff. His head was frozen in place, tilted to one side and staring down at Boyd. The branches above created a wicker cage. Boyd jammed his heels into the soft earth and shoved again, his arms aching as he rolled the dead weight off of him. A burning cough erupted from his chest. Once free, he lay panting, frantically clawing Lieutenant Eddie's blood from his face. The lieutenant lay next to him, stiffened arms reaching for the sky.

Boyd squeezed his right hip, examining the wound. The bullet from the German's Luger had missed the bones and passed through, leaving a ragged hole out of his waist as it exited. The pain wrapped his body so completely he couldn't tell if it was inside or outside. With his bayonet, Boyd cut a large chunk of the officer's woolen blouse away and wrapped the heavy material around his own bare waist. The Sam Browne belt worn by the lieutenant secured the bandages. The shoulder strap swung freely to Boyd's knees. The first few steps Boyd took were agony, but when machine-gun fire cut through the high tree branches, the pain was forgotten. Boyd followed the Germans' direction of retreat for thirty or forty yards until he came upon the balance of his squad. They were spread around in a wide part of the ravine in the position of a clock.

Veeder had been shot in the face as he tried to surrender, Bailey in the back of the head. He had been on his knees, praying. It looked as though Walsh and the rest of them had tried to run but were cut down. Boyd picked up a discarded canteen. He shook it and looped the strap over his shoulder. These were good guys. Someone had to pay for this.

Boyd retraced his steps and tried to think. The lieutenant had brought them down the ravine for a half mile; Germans seemed to be on all sides; they were cut off from the 308th. . . .

He slipped quietly into the stream bed, placing each foot carefully, making his way west. The moon came up and cast long, eerie shadows across his path. The sound of the water against his boots was much too loud, the noise bouncing off the close ravine walls.

"Was ist das, Willi?"

"Nichts. Das ist nichts, du Esel."

German voices. Boyd dropped onto the cold earth and crawled quietly to the embankment, pulling his Enfield rifle up level with his shoulders. He pulled the bolt back halfway to check that he had a round in the chamber and eased the rifle shut. Safety off. He slid forward, his right arm extended, his hand clasping the carrying strap of the long rifle.

Germans at the top of the ridge. They were ten feet above him and probably looking down the ravine in the direction he had come. He couldn't continue down this creek bed. He had to go back a ways, out-flank them.

Boyd slowly pushed back, keeping the Germans in sight and never turning his back until he reached the turn of the ravine. He crawled up the embankment and made his way into the dense woods. Dried sticks sounded like pistol shots as Boyd attempted to circle. He kept the moon off his left shoulder, trying to give the lookouts a wide berth. German voices came from his right. Boyd dropped to the ground. It sounded like fifteen or twenty of them had gathered, singing. "Deutschland, Deutschland über alles, über alles in der Welt."

Jesus, what the hell to do? Germans on both sides. Boyd lay for several minutes facedown, trying to decide whether or not to surrender. He couldn't stop shaking; his hands danced like crazy.

Boyd stood and damp leaves clung to his uniform. He unslung the Enfield from his shoulders and pulled back the bolt all the way to unload the rifle. He felt it was safer to show them he was harmless. He raised the weapon with both arms above his head and started to call out but heard slurred speech. *Drunk Germans. Veeder said . . . what . . . as he tried to surrender? Will they listen? . . . Will they just make fun of me and then kill me?* He slowly brought the rifle back down to his waist, gently pushed the bolt forward, and seated it. He retraced his steps, trying not to make noise. After several hundred yards, he came back to the ravine. He was farther upstream.

"Halt."

Boyd froze. They had moved.

The voice was no more than twenty feet away.

"Was gibts?" A pause. "Heinz?" A longer pause, then a different voice.

"Heinz, bitte reiche mir das Getränk."

They want Heinz to give them something. Boyd dropped to one knee. He fired two quick rounds in the direction of the voices. A scream.

"Mutter, Mutter, bitte hilf mir, hilf mir. . . ." The voice trailed off.

Another man shouted, "Ich werd das Arschloch erwischen," then fired a burst of machine-gun fire. But his direction was off. Boyd picked up the German's muzzle blast. He reseated the cartridge in his rifle and sighted the Enfield carefully, took a deep breath, and slowly squeezed the trigger.

Boyd sprinted across the second German's field of fire and leaped headlong into the ravine, landing on his hands and knees. Voices from the drunken German party could be heard. They were running toward their comrade's trench. Boyd scrabbled to his feet, moving quickly through the rocky creek bed. He finally fell at the base of a shattered tree. Fighting for air, he looked up to see three sets of eyes staring at him in shock; the troopers from his squad who had earlier fled.

The moon was full up as George and Boyd skirted the west rim of Mill Creek valley. They quickly made their way around the few houses along the ridge.

The bonfire on the distant ridge gave off a strange dim light. The black man had kept a steady pace, limping slightly but soldiering on. "Where we headed?"

"Just a closer walk with thee," George replied. He grinned. "Something my mama used to sing."

Boyd watched the last fading glow. "Looks like it's overlooking the old shale pit, that fire." A vague silhouette waved a hat at the moon, and antlike figures walked toward cars and wagons. "How far do you reckon they are from us?"

"Not far enough, brother. If'n they spot us, they could relight that fire in a jiff and start another wiener roast without blinking an eye."

George walked the hard dirt path as if born to it. Occasionally they would come upon a fence that would stop abruptly at the cliff edge. George would swing around on the last post, his body momentarily thirty feet in the air, while Boyd lumbered over the top of the barbed-wire strands, snagging his shirt and pants.

"Have you always lived in the North, George? I mean since you came up, have you lived only in Vermilion?"

"We'll try and make our way over to the Bottoms. I got kin there what will put us up for a night or two. Then I'll be headin' out. . . . No, I've lived all 'round the Midwest, lit here 'cause of family, cousins, aunts, and such. Good folk, poor as church mice but decent and God-fearin'."

Boyd said nothing for several seconds.

"Don't worry, Calvin. You'll be all right. They might stare at ya a bit, but in the end they'll feed ya and bed ya down. Oh, you might have to sleep with a couple of the kids, but they don't wet the bed much anymore. At least not so you would notice it." George smiled. "Besides, as tired as we are, it won't matter much."

It was three in the morning when George and Boyd stood by the chicken coop of George's cousin. George tossed pebbles at the second-story window and glanced at Boyd, who stood nearby.

"Fred, it's me, George, hey." George tried to whisper as loud as he could. "Fred, wake up, damn it."

The dormer window slid up, and through the screen Boyd could see a candle held next to a sleepy black face.

"Who is it?"

"It's me, Cousin George. Let us in."

Boyd could see the face turn briefly back into the room.

"Are you in trouble?"

George laughed. "What you think, Cousin?"

"Yeah, you're in trouble."

Boyd could hear the resignation in his voice, some swearing, and a woman arguing. A baby started to cry, and a soft voice hissed, "Ought to make your damned cousin put that child back to sleep, Frederick. I swear."

George looked at Boyd. "What'd I tell you, Calvin. Welcome with open arms."

George motioned to Boyd to follow him. They walked back through the modest house and out to the screened porch. Cousin Fred gave them a couple blankets to lie on and went back to bed.

"It'll be cooler here, help yourself." George pointed to some tattered pillows lying on an old wicker settee. Boyd spread his blanket on the floor and stuffed a pillow under his head. He could hear George in the corner, his breathing already steady.

Crickets chirped in the tiny garden. Somewhere, a cat screamed in pleasure or pain. Boyd took several deep breaths; his body pulsed, the muscles waiting for the signal from his brain to relax.

Boyd's hip dug deep into the cupped planks of the porch floor, the blanket too thin to soften this strange bed. Hands behind his head, he stared through the leaves of a giant elm, its dark branches pointing toward the twinkling night sky.

Laurel swam above him, her diaphanous nightgown brushing softly over his body, her right arm patting his shoulder. And then her kisses, at first gentle on his forehead and cheeks. Her hot breath racing across an ear. Then he reached for her and she was gone.

What happened to her? Was she really dead? He didn't kill her, he knew that. She was already dead when he came into the forest. No, she wasn't killed in the forest, but in the . . . He couldn't remember.

A beautiful view from the clouds. He could see the town square and the hotel. The car barn lit up as if for a celebration. Boyd swooped down. Old man Decker and the gang stood next to number 68 with long-stemmed glasses in their hands, looking under the trolley car. The lead mechanic tipped his glass in the air. "It was the slipper brake, what got him." The rest of the shop gang and the other motormen all saluted. "Here, here." Old man Decker raised his glass especially high. "If I told him once, I told him a thousand times, you got to stop for everybody, don't matter what color—now this." Decker drank deeply. "Martin, fix that slipper brake, damn it." They acted like children, laughing as if it were the funniest thing they had ever heard.

A pat-pat on Boyd's shoulder and Laurel was back, her warm tongue traveling across his face. Once again he could hear the gang from the car barn giggling. "Boyd. Boyd!" Someone was calling. It didn't sound like Laurel, but he could feel her presence. Her body floating just above his, her warm breath insistent.

"I think Sparks likes ya, Boyd."

Boyd's fingers came up to his face, catching Laurel's furry paw in his hand. "What?"

"Sparks don't cater to just anyone, and he's been working on you for a couple minutes. I think you made a friend."

A large shepherd mix stood next to Boyd's temporary bed. George held a steaming cup of coffee in his hand. Two children stood in the kitchen doorway, bubbling with laughter.

"How ya like your coffee, black?"

Boyd rolled away from the dog and rubbed his wet face. "I'll have whatever Sparks is having."

"Black it is, then. Bacon and eggs in five minutes."

WEDNESDAY, JUNE 19

*D*ale Hennessy wiped the sweat from his brow with an already soggy handkerchief. The last two days were a blur. Boyd and some crazed black rapist had escaped from custody, and Vermilion was in the biggest uproar he had ever seen. Some kids said they saw the Negro and someone who they thought looked like Boyd run down into the old quarry and try to swim to the other side.

"They seemed to all of a sudden lose their heads and up and drowned . . . from panic, I reckon." Hennessy listened to the boy recount the story to Myrna and a pair of nodding police officers. The latter, arms folded, gave the impression that the whole episode made perfect sense in the grand scheme of things criminal. They'd seen it all a hundred times.

Claudia and Freeman were also present for awhile, but Claudia, looking haggard, left rather than enter the cordoned-off area where the search was about to begin in earnest.

Afraid their cars would overheat on the steep gravel road, Hennessy and Myrna left them at the lip of the quarry and walked down to the site, where a crowd of curious onlookers had gathered. Many of them seemed in a festive mood. As they passed through the rope barrier that isolated the work scene from the gawkers, Hennessy could hear crude commentary from tobacco-chewing philosophers and redneck jesters.

"The nigga's probably standing on the white guy's shoulders."

The gallows humor had apparently been flowing thick and heavy. "Bait the hooks with watermelon and find the nigga. Boyd'll float for sure once we yank the coon off his shoulders." Several blacks formed their own knot nearby, and Hennessy noted that while some of the older

96

ones tended to sheepishly smile along with the gibes, a few of the younger men cast cold stares at the loudmouths.

Hennessy couldn't believe how quickly the police, with help from the *Tribune,* had been able to secure the services of a drag team. A group of locals were solemnly tugging a set of hemp lines across the quarry bottom with some sort of weighted apparatus at the end, supervised by two confident-looking gents wearing straw hats. If they caught up on something, they stopped and looked around expectantly until one of the straw hats came over and expertly checked the feel of the line. The expert would shake his head, and the process would continue.

The quarry had a benefit Hennessy would never have expected. It was cooler down at the water's edge. This was surprising because it seemed the hottest place in all Vermilion was at the tree-bare rim of the quarry, with exposed stone soaking up all the sun's rays. At water level things dramatically changed. The north face of the sheer rock hole was almost perpetually in shadow and on the lake surface the deep water below acted like the source for a great swamp cooler.

The men helping with the drag operation were trying to maintain an air of detached importance, but they couldn't seem to prevent themselves from casting looks at Myrna. She looked like she had stepped from a sauna, her skirt and blouse molded to her full features as though painted on. She seemed to be wearing nothing but a brassiere on top, the moisture having rendered the blouse almost transparent. She has to know, Hennessy thought, but if she did, she didn't let on.

"Can it get any hotter?" She directed the question to Hennessy, but said it loud enough for the whole group to hear. Then, with purpose, she stalked off when she saw that the photographer she had requested from the *Trib* had in fact arrived on the scene and was starting to take pictures.

"I can see two good reasons for liking that woman," Sid offered. He was one of the uniformed minions of whom Myrna seemed so contemptuous.

"They *do* satisfy." Manion's imitation of the new Camel cigarette advertisement was met with appreciative chuckles. He glanced over when it occurred to him Hennessy could be listening, frowned uncomfortably, and turned away.

Hennessy ignored them and walked in closer to the action. He found himself strangely fascinated with the operation. Some of the draggers were now in a wooden rowboat about twenty yards away. One man was plying the oars while one of the straw-hatted men tossed a hemp fishing line with something dark on the end into the dark green water and methodically retrieved it, hand over hand, each time he threw it out.

Then Hennessy noticed one of the lines heaped on a wooden pallet just to his left. It was balled up as if it had snagged on something and been temporarily tossed aside, hopelessly tangled. He studied the grim tool that lay still dripping at the end of the line. It was a smooth, torpedo-shaped lead weight that Hennessy recognized as the type suspended inside the frames of most windows.

The weight was neatly spliced to the line, and down the sides of the smooth lead surface were fixed a series of treble hooks, the type he'd sometimes used to fish for largemouth bass. The thought that the nasty-looking hooks were meant to sink into clothes and flesh gave to the affair a reality that made him grimace. He thought about the onlookers. What made people find something like this amusing? The thought that his fellow citizens could stand there and joke about dragging men from the depths with things like that, hooked in them God knows where, was disturbing.

Manion suddenly appeared by his side, seeming intent on being helpful. Hennessy thought perhaps it had to do with the detective's being afraid he had heard the lewd comments about Myrna.

"Major, let me introduce you to the guys." Then he quickly turned to Myrna. "Miss Logan, your people at the *Trib* sure helped out in getting these men here so fast."

The detective wasn't waiting for replies. He yelled over Hennessy's awkward attempt to stop him from bothering the workers. "Hey, Toole, we talk to you a sec?" The man signaled with a nod that it would be fine to approach through the busy hive of helpers.

Manion, already stepping over a pile of wet lines and weights, spoke toward the ground in a loud voice. "This here's Major Hennessy from the army, the Soldiers' Home we got here in Vermilion." And stepping directly on the raft, he gestured with his thumb. "That there's Miss Myrna Logan from the *Chicago Tribune*."

Hennessy, irritated that Manion had pushed them into the operation, responded apologetically. "I don't mean to get in the way, just wondered how it was going?"

Before the dragger could respond, Myrna piped up. "Bet it's hotter'n hell hauling those lines."

Hennessy cleared his throat in advance of asking a question. He felt compelled to say something because Myrna had surprised him with her sudden animation. She had been quiet, almost morose, for a couple of days after Boyd turned down her lawyer. Hennessy had had strong words with her in the Lucky Diner because he felt she had gotten out of line with Devlin after leaving the jail. She had told the attorney, "Donald, get over it. Mudville's full of surprises."

Devlin had responded in his obnoxious manner about the paper "sending a woman to do a man's work," and it had gone downhill from there, with Myrna offering the gentleman the opportunity to kiss her posterior, in a tone and volume that could be heard in the diner's parking lot. In the middle of Hennessy's explaining why behavior like that from a woman was unacceptable in Vermilion, she had muttered, "Bye," then disappeared for two days. Now she was acting as if nothing had happened.

"Mr. . . ."

"Toole. Kendall Toole, Major."

"Okay, Mr. Toole. How successful are these hooks when hunting for a body in a place like this?"

"Barring bad entanglements and considerin' the fact this here lake is only about two or three acres' surface area, it should be real successful."

"I must say it seems kind of crude. . . . I mean, you could hook them anywhere, the nose, the eye."

"Yeah, well it don't seem to bother the victims none—at least we ain't never heard one complain." That elicited a round of conspiratorial chuckles from the newly formed drag fraternity.

"Heard some people around here talking about using dynamite," added Hennessy.

"Actually, sometimes that works okay, but only after they've had a chance to get ripe and bloated and are on the verge of floating anyway. . . . Also gotta make sure you don't toss the sticks too close to the bodies. Mess their innards up and they'll never float."

With that, Toole's men, or "Toole's ghouls," as Myrna quickly dubbed them, paddled their master to the point the pair had allegedly last been seen.

Myrna and Hennessy found a shady spot and sat down. Her blouse was wrinkled but she didn't show through anymore.

There were a few false alarms from the draggers. After an hour had passed, suddenly one of the linemen called, "Got something here for sure." He passed the line to Toole, who deftly hoisted the line toward the surface. It was obvious he thought they had something, too.

The onlookers hushed as a form became visible under the raft. Toole's assistant reached down and grabbed hold of a black arm. "That's the darky!" someone yelled.

But a helper yelled back, "Hell, he's got two of 'em."

Another figure clothed in prison garb was barely visible, bobbing next to the first victim. "And there's Boyd. . . . Didn't I tole you we'd find 'em like this."

"Hey," said the line helper. "This fella Boyd, he's a white guy, right?"

"Whaddya mean?" shouted Manion.

The response from Toole was to lift two arms manacled together from the water. Two heads drooped below, face-to-face, mouths open, a thick slime pouring from one of them. The crowd went quiet. Then there came a low, intense murmur. The two victims were very real, very dead, and very black.

The days crept by. Boyd wandered around the house counting the fish on the living room wallpaper. Fourteen varieties before the pattern repeated itself. He figured about ten repeats, so that made 140 fish on one wall, times four, minus the door and window openings made. He sat reading the encyclopedia. The books looked new, or at least never used. The crisp pages stuck at their fake gold edges.

"The man said I owed it to my family to expose them to the wonders of the universe."

Juanita, Frederick's wife, busied herself around the sitting room. She picked up a lace doily from a small end table and put it on the arm of the couch. She stood back, looked at it, and moved it back to the table. "The white devil sat right there and said that. The cheater. Said I could pay easy payments, two dollars a month for a time, then a balloon at the end. Well hell's to Betsy, I didn't know what was a balloon." She dug viciously with her broom at some imagined piece of dirt in a corner of the room. "Well, I paid and I paid and then finally I got tired of it and stopped and then the rotten heathens wouldn't let me be, they kept writin' these here threatenin' letters." Juanita changed her voice to what seemed to be her idea of a snotty person. 'Dear Mother, we realize you are up to your lovely ears with your children and all, and your monthly obligations are the last of your concerns. But if you could please remit your last three payments on your books of knowledge, it would be appreciated.' " Juanita snorted as she drew out "appreciated." "I'd like to appreciate that boy's white ass with this broom handle."

She looked at Boyd as if realizing for the first time he was white. "Listen, mister, I . . ." the apology stuck in her throat.

Boyd sat quietly, the open book in his lap.

Juanita drifted into the kitchen. "They finally came to the door, the white devil what sold me the set and some other ghost turd that said he was a marshal or some such crap." Her voice rose from the kitchen so Boyd could hear. " 'Are you Juanita Matthews?' I said, 'Whass it look like?' Then, looking down official-like at his paper, he said, 'We have a failure-to-comply here that says you owe Lawrence and Lawrence Educational Books a balance of twenty-eight dollars,' or some such, and I says, 'Take the damn books. Go on, take them and your shittin' balloon at the end, go on, take it all.' Well, they started whistling a different kinda tune, then. I'll tell you." Juanita stalked the kitchen.

"Well, they obviously didn't take them, Miz Matthews, so I guess you won after all." Boyd chose his words carefully.

"I don't know that I won anything. Yeah, I still got the books, but so what?" She stood defiantly, hands on hips, staring at Boyd.

"Those are nice books, missus."

"Well, I knew you'd say something like that, being you're . . ." She stopped. Her shoulders were bunched and her hands clenched the broom handle. She took several deep breaths and started sweeping the kitchen noisily.

Boyd remained still, the book heavy in his lap.

Later at supper, he was quiet. The family passed their food back and forth, offering him equal shares and making comments about other relatives, friends, and current local news, and occasionally reprimanding the children. George's aunt, Jolene, walked over from Rabbit Town with a covered dish to join them for supper.

"Y'all hear 'bout James Collett; he left his wife and ran to Chicago with his young cousin. I guess the family is fit to be tied." Frederick reached for the mashed potatoes and gave himself a hardy dollop of gravy.

"Well, I would imagine they would be. That boy always had a roving eye, I swear."

"He's got a big mouth, too, always going on about how he does this and that and t'other. I swear, I think Gladys is well shut from that boy."

"Oh, I don't know, I 'spect she'll have a tough time roundin' up some-one to take his place."

"What you mean?"

"Well, she ain't the slickest thing to come along the pike."

"Don't you talk 'bout Glad like that." Juanita dug her fork into a chop.

"Well, you'll have to admit she's got a big ol' butt on her."

"I don't have to 'mit nothing of the kind. She's what you might call a full-size lady. But I think she has a very sweet personality."

Juanita tried to defend her position amid laughter at the table. "She was smart in school and everybody always said she would mount to somethin'. . . . Don't you snicker at me, Frederick Matthews. I'll box your ears." Juanita grinned. "Well, anyway, I feel sorry for her. That boy had no right to just up and leave her like that." The table fell silent for several moments. "But you get any ideas like that, Mr. Matthews, and I'll come to bed with your razor in my hand."

Even Aunt Jolene, a staunch Baptist, got a rise. She spat out her mashed potatoes on her plate, the children thinking it the funniest thing they had ever seen.

A knock at the front door prompted Juanita to ask George to get the door. Still, Boyd cautioned him with a look as he stood.

George spoke before he opened the door. "Yeah, what is it?"

A uniformed policeman stood on the porch. "Is this the Matthews residence?"

George recognized the cop. "Yes, it is, Officer. What can I do for you?" George leaned back, hiding his face with his hand.

"May I come inside, please?"

"Yeah, sure."

Boyd turned at the sound of the white voice. Everyone at the table looked to Boyd and then slowly up at the policeman standing in the liv-ing room.

"Is there a Jolene Matthews here?"

"Yes, I'm Jolene." George's aunt slowly folded her napkin and laid it carefully next to her plate.

"Well, ma'am, I'm sorry to have to tell you that your nephew George Matthews has . . . well, he's passed. I guess you could say, rather, that he, well, we found him."

Jolene looked all around the table.

The policeman stammered, staring down at his shoes.

Jolene looked at the cop. "You found him? I don't understand."

George had moved back behind the policeman and to one side. Boyd sat rigid in his chair. His mouth was full but he was afraid to chew. He felt as if someone were drilling a hole in the back of his head.

Jolene moved toward the cop but stopped at the end of the table with her back almost against Boyd's; she was hiding him. Everyone at the table remained still. There wasn't much reaction to the bad news, and Boyd thought the cop sounded puzzled.

"Yes, ma'am. We found him in the old shale pit."

"Yes?" Jolene gave the cop a hard look.

"He was dead. I mean to say that he was drowned along with another fellow. . . . I'm real sorry, ma'am."

"What you sorry for? That he's dead or that you was the one to have to tell me?"

"Well, ma'am, it's just that you're having a nice supper and I hate to spoil it. I mean to say I went over to Rabbit Town to tell you at your house and you wasn't home."

"No, I wasn't, was I. I was here."

"Yes, well, I can see that. I asked your neighbor where . . . and it's just that, it's just that I would have rather given you the bad news at your home where you might have been more comfortable."

Boyd detected choked sounds disguised as grief.

George buried his head in his hands and drifted toward the side bedroom. "Oh Jesus, oh Jesus, not Cousin George. He was the best, the bravest, handsomest, sweetest human being. Oh no."

"Papa, did the man say Uncle George drowned? But he couldn't—"

Frederick gave his young son a wicked look and clamped his hand over the youngster's mouth. Jolene's eyes never left the cop's.

"Well, I guess I will be goin' now, ma'am. So sorry for the loss of your son."

Jolene walked the officer to the door. "He weren't my son, Officer, but my nephew, what lives—lived with me."

"Oh yes, of course, miss, I knew that. Sorry, and sorry once again for havin' to tell you under these circumstances. Remember, miss, that these things have a way of healin', I mean to say that in time the pain tends to get better. No, not better, but I mean it gets less worse or to put it another way, it goes away. The pain does—grow less deep." It seemed the officer ceased attempting to be sympathetic and moved to leave, since he wasn't getting any help from Jolene.

Boyd wanted to turn and watch the scene at the door.

"You take care yourself, mister. And remember, the Lord loves all us lonely fools."

"Yes, miss, thank you and good day to you." The cop walked up the darkening street.

The house fell quiet after the policeman left. Frederick walked to the downstairs bedroom door. "You can come out the bedroom now, Mr. Sweetest, Handsomest."

George was smoking a home-rolled cigarette. "Damn, that were a close one, damn." He sat back down at the table. The food had grown cold. Only the children were still picking at their meal. "That cracker stared me plumb in the face. Damn, I don't get it."

"What don't you get? You mean you never realized the whites think we all look alike?" Jolene glanced at Boyd but kept on as if he weren't there. "Well shoot, didn't surprise me a'tall that he looked right through you."

George shook his head. The rest of the family slowly put their knives and forks on their plates but made no attempt to get up.

"Mama, can I be 'scused from the table?"

"Yes, sweetheart. Go out in the back and play with your sister."

The family watched silently while the children ran outside. Not taking her eyes from the youngsters, Jolene slowly wiped her mouth with her paper napkin. "You gonna get caught, George, I tell ya."

"Auntie Jol, I'm fixin' to light outta here late tonight. Probably goin' to Chi-town, visit Marvin and the kids."

"Why you think that old boy didn't recognize you, George?" Frederick asked.

"Don't know, Freddie, but sure as hell he's goin' be back, soon as they figger out they heard the story wrong and it ain't me and Boyd here what they pulled out the shale pit." George looked at Jolene and Juanita. "Would you all look after Boyd here for a while?"

"Where we gonna hide him? In a shoe box?" Juanita laughed as she said it, and the table seemed to loosen up a bit.

"Yeah, I'll wrap him in tissue paper and hide him in my closet." Jolene reached over and patted Boyd's hand. "Speakin' of tissue paper, you 'member that fat cracker what use to run Thomson's down in Appaloosa?" she asked Juanita.

Boyd watched this family, and he knew they loved one another in such a trusting way.

"Thomson's. You mean the shoe store? That devil always had a grin on his face and a big hello at the door and then he'd still do his tissue-paper trick." Juanita had gotten up to tend to making coffee.

Boyd's curiosity got the best of him and he nodded toward George. "What was the tissue-paper trick?"

George looked around the table. "Juanita, you want to tell our massa Boyd what the tissue-paper trick was?"

"Go on and tell him, he's your friend."

George moved his chair back and rocked it on its hind legs. "When you went into the shoe store at Thomson's and finally found the pair you wanted and asked to try them on, old fat-ass Akins—"

"Thass right, Akins, thass his name," Juanita called out from the kitchen.

"Well, Akins would say, 'Here, son, lemme just wrap your foot with this tissue from the box so you don't get any shoe stain on those nice clean socks.' So he'd very careful-like wrap your foot and slide it into the 'offending' shoe. . . . Do you 'member what he'd always say? . . . 'By golly-gee, those shoes were made special for you, boy.' George was up on his feet at this point, his stomach extended, imitating Akins with a phony grin on his face.

Frederick jumped in. "I asked him once why his white customers didn't get this special treatment, and he just winked and whispered in my ear, 'Sanitation.' I looked at him and his little pig eyes got hard. 'A word to the wise.' "

After several moments the family started to clear the table. The men took their plates to the kitchen as the women wiped away the crumbs and folded the worn tablecloth. Boyd started to take his plate to the kitchen, but Juanita abruptly snatched it from his hands.

George watched for a moment, then called to her as she cleared the plates into the garbage pail. "Juanita, have you met my *friend,* Boyd Calvin?"

Juanita turned and nodded to George. "Yes, I know. . . . I'm sorry, Mr. Calvin. It's just the thought of that Akins cracker just got me riled. Sorry."

"That's all right, Miz Matthews. I guess I'd be riled, too, if I was treated that way."

The thing of it was he had never been treated that way. He had suffered a lot of indignities, some justified, others not. But to say that he knew how a black person felt being treated as less than human was beyond Boyd's experience.

The evening wore on. Boyd sat in the dining room, watching the family. Sometimes they were argumentative, but with an affection for one another that seemed so outright as to be almost embarrassing. They cared for one another in a way that felt utterly foreign to Boyd.

George had assembled a few things: a hairbrush with a broken handle, a toothbrush, and an almost empty tube of toothpaste. His cousin gave him a couple of old shirts, and George put the lot into a heavy two-handled paper bag. He hugged Jolene for a long moment, embraced Juanita and Frederick, and then picked up the two children. Juanita had fixed sandwiches and hard-boiled eggs and put a bottle of milk in his bag.

The family gathered at the back door, whispering with George for several minutes. The lights were out so as not to draw attention to George's leaving. All their good-byes said, George turned to Boyd.

"I've asked my family to look after you for a while." George could see that Boyd was uncomfortable. "What you think you're gonna do?"

Boyd shook his head.

"You could come to Chi-town with me, but I don't think you'd like it much."

Boyd nodded.

George's baby-girl cousin snuggled further into his arms. "I could go to Chicago, Unca George."

"You gotta stay here, sweetie, and help your mama." George passed the children to Frederick. "Take care, Freddie, Nita, kids, love ya, Joly." George slipped quietly through the screen door and was gone.

The family moved about the house not saying much. Frederick turned on the radio; Juanita and Jolene continued to clean the kitchen.

Boyd felt he couldn't stay. The family had agreed to keep him but he knew it would be uncomfortable. His hands gripped the back of the kitchen chair. "I reckon I'll be leaving, too, folks."

No one spoke.

"I wish to thank you for feeding me and giving me a place to put down my head."

Frederick handed Boyd a jacket that had been hanging from a hook in the hallway.

"We enjoyed your company, Mr. Boyd, and like George said, we'd be happy to put you up for a while. But if'n you feel the need to move on, we understand."

Jolene stuck out her hand to Boyd. "Good luck, may God's wishes be with you, and praise Him."

"Thank you, miss."

Juanita put some leftover bread and a small jar of preserves into a sack. "Sorry it's so little, but things are kinda short right now."

Boyd thanked her and stepped out into the backyard.

His eyes were trying to adjust to the dark. The path through the vegetable garden was moist; Frederick must have watered it with his leaky hose. He picked his way through the rows of greens and, at the gate, looked back. He could see the family standing in the kitchen, talking, looking occasionally out into the darkness.

He waited for a moment, trying to decide which way to go. A soft wet tongue licked Boyd's hand. Sparks waited to be petted. Boyd crouched down and smoothed his hand quietly over the dog's shiny coat.

"Where should I go, boy? Huh? Tell me." The dog cocked his head to one side and whined. "I know, Sparks, I feel the same way."

Boyd thought he could walk half an hour to the north and perhaps make it out of town. Maybe catch a freight. Or go south to the town center. And do what? He turned south. He didn't really know why. It just seemed right.

In the blackness, a naked lightbulb swung slowly on the back porch of a clapboard house. The moon had not risen yet. Another home was alive with music; a blues guitar led the way for a family of singers, their silhouettes lit by what looked to Boyd like a kerosene lamp. The warm glow from the houses was in sharp contrast to the way Boyd felt, for he knew he had very few people he could turn to. Major Hennessy might try to help him, but he didn't think he could ask him to hide a fugitive from the law. The woman with the Major seemed interested, but maybe only because it was her job. Old man Decker from work would probably turn him in to the police. Freeman would probably feel obliged to do the same. Under normal circumstances he could have gone to Laurel's house. So his tired feet brought him inevitably to the Grant Hotel and his only real friend, Claudia.

The hotel's dim canopy lights cast soft brown shapes against the cracked gray sidewalk. Boyd stood across the street and gazed at the forlorn structure. He missed it. Its smells, the way the walls seemed to lean, the peeling paint. It was familiar.

He watched the lobby for movement. Climbing up the back way was not something he wanted to do. Boyd waited for the night clerk to move, but he seemed to be asleep in his chair behind the desk.

Boyd was soft-footing halfway up the lobby stairs and watching the clerk intently when the man awoke. Looking at him, he said, "Boyd," and slumped back in his chair, instantly asleep.

"Claudie," Boyd knocked softly. He hoped she hadn't changed rooms. "Claudie."

"Who is it?"

"It's me. Boyd."

The thin wooden door swung open and he stepped into the dark room, stumbling against a stuffed chair. "Thanks, Claudie." He could hear rustling behind him and then Claudia's cotton robe brushed against him as she passed by to get back to her bed.

"We best leave the lights off." Claudia pulled the sheet over her.

"Ol' Pete woke up when I was coming up the stairs but he went right back to sleep. I don't think he'll be makin' any rounds soon."

"Well, in terms of the lights being on, I was thinking more of your well-being, as to having to look at me in my present state, being awakened in the middle of the night. If you get my drift, bronco."

"Oh, I'm sure you look fine." Within moments, Boyd's head dropped back on the overstuffed seat back, and his hands lay limp on the rounded arms of the chair. His breathing became deep. The warm wind from the open window dried his perspiring face.

"Oh, by the way, Mr. Boyd, was there something you dropped by to talk about or did you just want to rest for a moment in my chair?"

Boyd sat up. "I guess you heard what happened the other day on the square?" he asked.

"Heard? Oh, you mean the little riot, the drowning of a couple people in the shale pit, the stomping and serious injury of a police officer, the wounding of a little girl, the escape of two yahoos to Lord knows where without letting certain people know where they were? Yes, I believe I did hear something along those lines."

Boyd could hear Claudia breathing.

"Boyd Calvin, you got yourself in a whole pack of trouble. That stupid cop fired his revolver into the crowd and then gets in the middle of them, getting himself injured. The little girl is gonna live but just barely." She paused for a moment.

Boyd could hear sniffling.

"Goddamn you, Boyd. Now they also want to accuse you as an accessory. I think what happened was he fell and got himself run over by a wagon, car, or horse, but regardless, they still want to lay the blame on you and George." Claudia pulled her knees to her chest and wrapped her arms around her thin legs. "I talked to lawyer Freeman. He says if I hear from you, let him know. . . . Am I hearing from you? Well, come on, shug, people have gone to considerable trouble for you. Old man Weiss, he of the bratty kids and owner of a certain Grant Hotel, has extended a helping hand with the lawyer. Freeman himself has cut his fee because he believes in you. I want to help, but Boyd baby, you have got to show some initiative or people will lose interest."

He closed his eyes. "I don't know. I can't think straight. What should I do?" Boyd could hear Claudia move from the bed. What seemed like an apparition passed him and moved to the closet behind.

"I was walking home from the Lucky tonight and I said to myself, 'Claudia,' I said, 'you know, you really don't have to have an opinion about everything.' " A thin flannel blanket came drifting over his legs. He could feel his shoes being untied and pulled off. The last thing he remembered was a motherly kiss on the top of his head.

The kiss came back harder than he expected. Hennessy had surprised himself with his own impetuousness, but Myrna's response was startling. Smiling at him over a tinkling glass of whiskey sour, she seemed to be inviting his ardor. But he was still afraid he might be rebuffed. He needn't have worried. Myrna's hands had somehow found their way inside his shirt, and when she pulled away he was aware of a slight stinging from a gentle bite on his lower lip. The effect on him was electric—he felt the hair stand up on his neck and his heart begin racing.

He cast a guilty glance toward the window—no one there, door locked, but had the innkeeper's daughter seen them? Old man Jericho's teenage girl was usually at the desk this time of night. Myrna's cabin was pretty far from the reception area, but this . . . this was crazy.

How had it all started? Things were definitely out of control. All he had done was invite her in for a drink. They were passing his place on the way back to the home after another fruitless day of Boyd-searching. Okay, so he had been fixating on her all day, but Christ, when a woman dressed like that . . .

And then what? She had flounced onto his ottoman and looked at him in that curious, inviting, almost laughing way of hers. "Dale," she had said, "what are we gonna do?"

"Do?"

"You know what I mean. Look at us. We're both tired and lonely and hot—and honey, face it, we're randy—randy as alley cats."

He had almost passed out. All he could say after a moment in the glare of her mocking smile was, "Not here . . . not in my mother's place, not here." So he drove them to the Cabins by the Dixie Highway Inn and Auto Court in silence. Now they were there, and Hennessy was losing his last shred of sanity.

His mouth was dry but he could feel himself perspiring through his shirt, and the heat in his cheeks told him his face must be flushed. Everything below his waist was in a state of confusion. Growing in step with his heat was a decided sense of panic. Memories of the hayloft at his father's farm and a migrant worker named May kept popping back in his head.

"Dale, you rascal you." She had pressed him up against the door in a standing clinch and was now fumbling with his tie while she kept her lower half pressed against him and the stirring chaos under his belt. "I thought I felt your eyes playing with my bra strap all afternoon, and from all the hopping around I'm feeling in your pants, Mr. Hennessy, I suspect you kinda like ol' Myrna."

She kept talking, but it wasn't registering—something about "showing this city girl a good time." Damn it, he would show her all right. There had been a time when some of the finest flowers in Vermilion had been plucked by Dale Hennessy, and he felt a surge of power building between his thighs. Part of him was enthralled, but part of him resented being talked down to like a country hick. "Big boy," "rascal," eh? We'll just see about that. See if we can't get a few squeaks out of you, lady.

Then, somehow, they were doing it. It was dreamlike. He was on top of her on the creaky bed—both of them half dressed. He felt like he had just sunk into a world of woman and flesh that he hadn't known since . . . since, maybe never. Her fingers dug into his buttocks. Christ, she was wanton. The smell and feel of her was overpowering, and suddenly he was spent. It was obvious from her pulling at him and urging him on that she didn't know he had finished. He tried some vain efforts to keep moving to satisfy her, but it didn't work and he felt a confusion—a familiar shame—wash over him.

He rested his face in the crease of her neck. She stopped moving beneath him and tried to push his head back to look in his eyes. "You okay, tiger?"

"Fine. I—guess you weren't finished—"

"Hey, hey, it's okay, big fella. Don't worry, you felt great."

He hoped whatever he had given Myrna was better than nothing. She snuggled reassuringly and resisted his efforts to pull away. Somehow, Myrna's consoling him made it worse.

Christ, why had he done it? He knew Myrna had just begun her journey to fulfillment and that he had lived up to his own lowest expectations. All of a sudden he was sobbing, and he felt her fingers running through his hair. Then for a long while they lay there, quiet.

Hennessy felt himself slowly sink somewhere deep inside himself. He started taking stock of the world outside of Myrna's warmth and her fingers playing over his scalp. Must make a ridiculous picture, he thought. Tangled in the bedspread, Myrna's blouse open, her brassiere someplace, skirt up over her belly. And underpants? Probably the same place as her bra. He could tell by the movement of air on the hairs on the back of his good leg that it was bare. His gimp side still had trousers wrapped on it.

He was conscious of that intimate stickiness shared only by lovers. It left patches of moisture that seemed to cool quicker than the skin around them. Soon he was aware of her rhythmic breathing and that her fingers had stopped moving. Asleep. Hennessy slowly disentangled himself and lay back, using her outstretched arm as a pillow. There was something about it all that reminded him of those paintings he'd seen in Chicago, the ones people were calling surreal. Drained is how he felt, like the water had all run out of the tub.

Hennessy began searching the ceiling for stains. Not one to be found, so he checked the varnished wood door. Sure enough, there were monsters apparent in the mahogany swirls for anyone who looked. But there, in the corner, not far from the brass doorknob, was the most vivid image of all—the shape of a woman with thick Matisse-like legs wrapped tightly around her lover. The man was diminutive and seemed to be missing a head, but that didn't seem to bother the woman. The strain lines in her legs indicated she was enjoying the moment.

Myrna moved her arm from under his head and pulled the edge of the spread up from the floor and over her feet. It was still too hot to cover anywhere else. "Sleepy, tiger? Mmm, I am."

"I guess so. Maybe."

"Dale?"

"Uh-huh?"

"Nice of you to be considerate of your mom's feelings. Is she home most of the time?"

"No, it's not like that. . . . She isn't around anymore. I mean, she passed away a few years back."

"Oh."

After a few moments of silence, Myrna rolled over and presented her backside to him. Then she reached around and tugged him toward her. She obviously liked to be snuggled when she slept. He glanced one more time at the Matisse lady on the door and complied.

The clock on the small table by Claudia's bed was unreadable from Boyd's position in the chair. He kicked off the thin blanket, and his bare feet made sucking sounds against the rough wood floor as he crossed the tiny room. Boyd picked up the clock and turned it toward a pale blue light coming through the window. Two-thirty.

His talk with Claudia had distressed him. Her tiny body lay as if floating on the hard bed. He should leave, just slip out into the night without recriminations and good-byes. He pulled on his shoes and socks and wrapped an extra shirt around his waist. The box with his pitiful belongings that Claudia had taken from his room was only half full. A lifetime in a cardboard box, and not even full. He put on a striped engineer's hat and backed toward the door.

"Not gonna say good-bye, kiddo?"

Boyd turned toward the door. "I didn't want to wake you."

"Uh-huh."

Boyd could hear her as she sat up in bed. He waited what seemed several minutes but nothing was said. Finally, Boyd whispered, "I've gotta go, Claudie. I know I won't get a fair shake in Vermilion."

Claudia said or grunted something.

"What?"

"I said, 'Bullshit.'"

"What do you mean?"

She started crying. "Oh, Calvin, baby, you can't keep running. They're gonna catch you and hurt you bad, don't you see?"

Boyd continued to stare at the crumbling paint on the thin hotel-room

115

door. A sign at eye level declared 'No Visitors after 9:00 P.M.' There he was, breaking the law again.

"Come over here and sit on the end of the bed."

Boyd couldn't see Claudia. The streetlight cast a strong light around the cracks in the torn green blind that covered the single window. The end of the wood bedstead looked like a gravestone. Boyd stared into the void where Claudia's raspy voice began telling him a story.

"Your mother and I worked in the five-and-dime till she was really showing and they kicked her out; old man Franklin said something about it being unseemly for a woman to be in the marketplace all big like that when she should be home doing whatever pregnant women are supposed to be doing. I asked him, 'And just exactly what is that?' 'Is what?' he says, and I say, 'You know something, Mr. Franklin? Your problem is your belly; it's so big you haven't seen your wienie in years and you probably wonder if you still have one.' Old Franklin screamed, 'You—you little tart. You follow right along with your impregnated friend!'

"Your mom and I strolled out into the bright Chicago sunshine carrying on something fierce." Claudia smiled.

Boyd strained to see the older woman's face. "Was my mom really a good person, Claudie?"

"As I told you in jail that day, she was the best. I'll never forget what she said to me on Halstead as we walked back to the apartment we shared. 'Claudia, I'm scared, baby, I'm really scared. I don't feel well.' I told her, 'Bettina, it's just that ol' Franklin got under your skin, sweetie.' 'No, I haven't felt well for weeks and it's not just morning sickness, I have a deep pain in my stomach, real deep.' Well, we walked on home in silence, but it wasn't long after that you decided you would relieve your mom of some of her burden and just popped out one night kinda unexpectedly. I did what I could. Finally a midwife came and tried to stop the hemorrhaging, but it was too late. I held her hand till the end. Her face was gaunt and white. Lips dry and pulled back from the pain. The pillow soaked with her sweat. The police came, and finally, an hour after she passed away, a doctor came. He said something about your being cyanotic and 'blue baby' and some other sort of medical folderol and they whisked you away also. I'll never forget the date. September fifteenth, 1900. I sat in that room for hours, staring at her bed, not believing what the long night had brought." Claudia was crying hard.

Boyd's eye caught the light from the street. "What happened then?"

"I lost you, baby. I just plain lost you." By now she had stopped trying to recover and wept into her pillow.

"I went to Evert Hospital in Chicago over the next few days. No one knew anything about the baby. You know, you. Your mom's body had been cremated and taken to a potter's field in south Chicago there. Wasn't any record of a child. The morgue said that a man they thought was a Dr. Miller came in, signed some papers, and left. There was no record of a Miller. Then after several years of searching records and such, I finally found you."

"Where was I?" His breathing grew irregular.

"You were in a home, a foster home. I tried to get you out but nothing seemed to work. The woman who had you had maybe six or seven other kids, and she was a real bitch, let me tell you. I begged her to let me take you. But of course she couldn't do that 'cause you were a ward of the state. I don't know how much she was gettin' to take care of you. But according to her, it wasn't enough. Anyway, I would come to visit you every week or so and then suddenly one week I arrived and the house was empty, just completely empty. Mail was in the box and a note on the front door to the water company instructed about how they should shut off her service, please, and mail the bills to this such-and-such address in California. Well, I wrote that woman maybe a hundred letters and they all came back undelivered, address unknown, no such person and so forth. That was the last I seen of you till you moved into the Grant here a couple years ago. Course, I didn't recognize you till I heard your name. Oh, your name—always got bastardized. . . . Oh, sorry, 'cuse me, sweetie, didn't mean anything by that."

"It's okay, Claudie. Lord knows, I was called that enough times. One of my first memories is of Uncle Donald, who always called me 'little bastard.' 'Hey, you little bastard, pick up those socks,' and like that. Course he called all the other kids names, too, so I guess I shouldn't feel bad. If there ever was a bastard, it was that guy. He beat me silly if I needed to be punished. The kids all called his missus Aunt Lumpy—course not to her face. Anyway, she would send me into the basement. 'Uncle Donald will be home from work soon and when he gets here, I'm gonna tell him what you said, how you sassed me, and I'll let him settle your hash, young man.' Damn, I'd wait in that dank basement till that mean son of a bitch came home. It was always the same. He would come down those basement stairs and on each step he would pronounce, as if surprised, 'Did' step 'you' step 'talk' step 'back'. . . . By the time he got to the bottom he had his belt off and was swinging. I would bounce around trying to dodge him. Course that just pissed him off even more. But I would get behind the furnace or scrabble up the coal pile until he turned the belt around buckle first. Then I would bend over and take my medicine. In some way the waiting in that dark basement was worse than the beatings. It seemed like hours sitting on the steps or under the stairs on a pile of old newspapers, trying to figure out what it was I had done and how I could get away from this mean bastard."

"I'm so sorry, Boyd, I am, sweetie." Claudia caught her breath.

"Ah, it's all right, I finally left one night with a couple other guys and we made it 'bout a hundred miles 'fore they got caught. I don't know why I wasn't nabbed. Guess I was just naturally slippery."

"What did you do then?"

"Oh, I just bummed around a couple years workin' on the section gang for the C & EI, picked strawberries for Vermilion Farms, jerked corn for DeKalb. Finally, when I was old enough, I got married, joined the army in '17, spent a year in France and Germany, then some tough time in Leavenworth."

"What's a Leavenworth?"

"Oh, it's a little establishment the army has for its bad boys." He dropped his head. "Let me tell you, there were quite a few Uncle Donalds at Leaven."

Boyd got up, raised the blind, and watched a policeman across the street step into a storefront and check the door. His eyes followed the portly cop as he methodically made his rounds doing what he could to protect the good folk of Vermilion. He wondered what the cop would do if he stuck his head out the window and shouted, "Hey, Officer, it's me, Boyd Calvin. Desperate killer. Mad–dog fugitive. Striker of army officers, assassin of a certain Lieutenant Charles Eddie. Killer of citizens of the German Empire, widower of Laurel Calvin, and . . ."

He watched the cop for several more moments before slowly pulling down the tattered blind.

"I'm going to Chicago, Claudie. I'll try to find work. I've got a friend there, if I can find him." Boyd walked to the door. He waited for her to say something. The room was not only dark, it seemed empty.

She didn't speak.

He wanted her to shout at him, "Be safe, take care of yourself, and think of poor old Claudie once in a while and eat well."

She said nothing. It was as if she had vanished, as though he were in the room by himself. Boyd started to speak but instead quietly turned the worn brass doorknob, taking the first step of the hundred miles to Chicago.

G oddamn it. Don't you white folk tell time?"

A disheveled Juanita leaned out the second-story bed-room window. "I mean, for Lord's sake, it's four in the morning. I'm gonna buy your sorry behind a clock so's I can get some sleep."

Boyd stood below the window trying to look contrite.

"Sorry, Juanita. I was hopin' Frederick would be awake. You know, gettin' ready for work." He stood for a moment while Juanita turned to speak to someone.

"Mrs. Matthews, I'm just trying to find George, and, oh yeah, I don't remember if I thanked you for the bread and preserves."

"Freddie says George is probably at a friend's house on the South Side of Chicago. There's a bar there, name of Pat's. Corner of Prairie and Thirty-fifth Street. Ask there."

"Oh, thanks. Prairie's, corner of Thirty-fifth and what?"

"No. Damn it. Pat's, Pat's. Thirty-fifth and Prairie."

"Okay, right. Thanks again, Juanita."

"Don't you 'Juanita' me, and don't you come cattin' around in the middle of the night no more. I got to get my sleep."

Boyd thought she must be aware of the way she looked. Their eyes met.

"Take care yourself, Boyd, and be real careful in Chi-town. They got some mean sum-a-bitches up there. All kinda Polacks, Krauts, and such, not to mention some big ornery niggas what would think nothin' about walkin' right through your skinny butt." Juanita gathered her thin night-gown around her ample breasts and went back to her bed.

Boyd grinned at the reference to Krauts and Polacks. Juanita was not that different from him. Suspicious and ill-tempered to one and all.

120

Boyd made it to the double tracks of the New York Central several hours later. He waited under a bridge while several trains sped by. Tall trees opposite the bridge housed a family of flying squirrels. Boyd watched as they soared from the high branches to earth; landing at a dead run, they searched for nuts, then scampered back to their lofty perches.

The sun was finally driving shards of piercing light through the trees and into the gloomy space under the concrete structure. A face slowly materialized across from Boyd, a grizzled man, fifty-odd years old, with filthy clothes, sitting against the opposite wall.

"What's up?" Boyd asked.

"Nothin', just a-waitin' for number 12, be by in about an hour, stops just south of here to take on water, then if a body wants to ride, ya just step out and swing aboard 'fore it picks up speed—that is, unless Tusco happens to be on board."

Boyd nodded. The hobo focused so hard on Boyd across the ten-foot gap that he felt as if the man were trying to read something on the wall behind him. Finally Boyd got up as if to stretch his legs and walked out into the beginning day. He glanced back, and to his relief, the man was still staring at the wall.

Boyd skipped a rock across a small pond that had formed on the west side of the trestle. The hard-packed earth around the pond held rocks in several places, piled in circles to contain a fire. Morning dew made the rocks a glistening necklace around the black ashes in the pit.

Boyd walked into the paths of a wooded area adjacent to the railroad tracks. Several bedraggled men, shaking out thin blankets, slowly made their way toward the trestle. Boyd walked back to the embankment that supported the tracks. He didn't want to get into any kind of extended conversations about who he was and where he came from. He tightrope-walked the steel rail for a quarter mile north, then skipped over to the other side and walked back.

The sun was full up by now. He could feel the beginning tingle of a vibration in his shoes, then a solid rumble in his legs as the freight train announced her presence a mile down the tracks with a wail and a tiny puff of smoke. He could see the hoboes taking cover behind trees and bushes. He dropped down to the gravel embankment, scaled a low barbed-wire fence, and sat on a pile of forgotten splintered, creosoted railroad ties.

The train came to a halt several hundred yards down the track. The engine of the freight sat huffing at the water tower. Boyd could see the hoboes restlessly peering from their hiding places. He got the distinct feeling it was more of a game they played, this hopping of trains, rather than any pressing need to travel to distant cities and towns.

A brakeman could be seen at the end of the twenty-car string. He waved his arms to the engineer, who ducked back inside. The locomotive belched white steam from her boiler as the train wheels slipped and then caught; the crashing of the couplings taking up slack alerted all the 'boes strung along the right-of-way. Boyd immediately realized he had made a mistake. He had tried to distance himself from the group, but now he was last in line, and it was working against him. He had given the train a long way to build up speed. As the locomotive passed he began running, looking over his shoulder at the hoboes who had already swung aboard. He didn't know if he was going to make it. He was running about as fast as he could. Boyd noticed the leering faces already aboard the empty cattle car. He missed the large open side door and grabbed for the steps of the ladder at the end of the car, his foot sliding along the slippery metal rung. He pulled as the momentum of the train flung his body between the couplings. His arm stretched around the edge of the cattle car, and he was afraid he might slip off until he found a projection to lever his feet against. After considerable effort, he found himself lying on his side on the deck of the rumbling freight.

Boyd tried to smooth his breathing. He slowly recovered and slid his feet carefully along the slatted boards of the open car. He saw once again the blank faces of the men inside looking back at him. Boyd remained quiet. Four hoboes sat at one end of the empty car and two lay out at the far wall.

"You ride the rails a lot, do ya, bo?"

Boyd could feel a man's gaze on him. "Yeah, some."

The man's bib overalls stretched tight over an extended stomach. His dirty white dress shirt with sleeves rolled halfway up his swollen arms didn't look as if it belonged to him. Gaudy lipstick stained the collar, and the name Philip was embossed over the breast pocket. His lank hair hung down across his eyes, long sideburns melting into a pockmarked face. His hands and arms were streaked with dirt and some reddish mix. Boyd could feel that he was trouble. His stomach roiled as he took deep breaths and tried to stay in control.

"Some? Uh, I don't think so, bones."

Boyd shrugged and turned away. He could swear that the other men in the car were salivating over the possibility of a scrap. The freight beat steadily as it struck the joints in the rail every forty feet. Wind from the open door stirred dust from the floor.

"Did ya pay your dues, bo?"

Boyd shook his head. There didn't seem to be any way around this guy. "I don't know what you mean, pay my dues."

"You can't just jump on a train and 'spect to ride for free, do you?" Several of the other men grunted as if agreeing. A grin appeared on the rotund man's face. "I mean, fair's fair, my friend." He seemed to gain strength from his comrades' approval. "How much you carrying, bones?"

"What?"

"How much you carrying? Why don't you let me hold a five. That should do it." Someone in the back said, "Yeah, five, that's the going rate." Boyd looked straight into the fellow's eyes.

"Look, Philip, I ain't got no five to give you, and even if I did, I wouldn't give it to you. Now let's all be friends here and let it go."

"Who you calling Philip? We're talking 'bout dues here, you little shit. And by the by, name's Ron or Ronnie, or some call me Ronald, but not Philip. If'n you're looking at this shirt, that's from a fellow what I woke up in the middle of the night with a razor to his throat when I couldn't find any *dues* in his house. I put on one of his shirts and then his wife paid till eventually I was all duesed out."

Several of the men laughed nervously. Boyd thought they enjoyed his boldness, and after all, weren't they all brothers in some way? He started thinking it would be easier to pay the guy. But he thought better of it.

There would be no stopping this group once he showed his small stash. The freight-car door was just about eight feet from where Boyd was sitting, but he would have to pass Big Guy to get to the door—and the train was moving over thirty miles an hour.

Big Ron cracked his knuckles when he spoke. "We watch, you know. You can never tell when a railroad dick might swing aboard with a group like us." The man's piggish eyes narrowed. "When you swung aboard at Vermilion, you grabbed the handles at the end of the car. Real 'boes don't do that 'cause you could swing into the coupling between the cars. See, bones, I'm helping you out, that should be worth some dues. You grab at the front of the car so's you just swing into the side of the freight, thass how I knowed you owed dues, bones. You a rookie."

Boyd patted his pockets. He got up and slid his hands down his pants front, then stopped and reached into his back pocket. The big guy smirked and looked at his fellow travelers. As he turned away, Boyd drove his booted foot into the guy's chest, then kicked his knee and bounded toward the door. A deep-sloped embankment came up after a small stand of trees, and he waited before he jumped. Big Ron had rolled over on his stomach and was getting to his feet when Boyd felt he could wait no longer.

He jumped, catching a ten-foot sapling a glancing blow. He hit the gravel and landed hard, tucking and rolling, his head pointed down, away from the steep embankment. Although almost upside down, he could see several heads sticking out of the door of the freight as it sped away. Ron was shaking his fist and bellowing unidentifiable words.

Boyd's left arm was scraped and his right shin bone stung from the gravel. His head whirled from the fall. The train's rumbling sound diminished in the distance. Ron was gonna be in his thoughts and prayers for a while, that fucker.

The sun was almost overhead and the heat began to build. Boyd made his way to a road parallel to the tracks and was, as far as he could figure, heading north across flat terrain. Corn on both sides of the road stretched to a grain elevator in the distance, the only building within miles. Boyd figured it must be about eleven o'clock. He reached for his cap and realized he had lost it. It struck Boyd as strange that the other hoboes gravitated to the lummox on the train. He felt confident that if he hadn't leaped, they would have taken his money and maybe more. There was something evil about people who took sides against a weaker opponent.

Boyd realized his situation was of his own doing: If he had not run from Laurel's that night, maybe he could have explained things. But that always seemed to be the case. When in trouble, run. It had certainly been true in the army, and, Boyd thought, maybe even before that. He had run from his foster home, where there had been trouble. A lot of it, and very little else.

The dusty road finally curved gently toward the west. He could see several houses on each side of the road, their neat yards, white fences. It had the makings of a small town. Boyd came upon "Crete, Population 28." A horse trough and hand pump sat in front of a general store, and what looked like a church tucked behind a cemetery. A handwritten sign hung in the store's window: "For funeral today and tomorrow, I'm closed. Open the day after."

Boyd could hear someone chopping wood in the distance. There didn't seem to be anyone in sight. He primed the pump and bathed his face and arms, the water stinging the scrapes on his arm. He was reminded of the last time he had pumped water, at the Reverend Merle's. The wood chopper stopped his work and began to whistle, but Boyd still could not see him.

Farther down was a crossroad.

Boyd walked to the corner, trying to see in all four directions. At this point he felt tempted to take a ride south, but on reflection, realized it wouldn't do him any good except for the company. There didn't seem to be a pressing need for him to stand in the middle of the road in the midday sun. He climbed a small fence that enclosed the cemetery and sat under a crab apple tree. Boyd picked an apple off the ground and looked at it. He thought if the roots went down far enough, they would penetrate something that he didn't want to think about. He wasn't sure he wanted to be sucking on an apple that got its nourishment from Lord knows where. But in the end, he stuffed several of the tart fruits into his pants pockets.

Down the westerly road, Boyd could see a truck coming. He stationed himself on the northeast corner, but the man driving the open-bed truck never looked at Boyd. Instead, he drove on to the store and sat in the vehicle while he read the sign. Boyd could hear him swearing softly. He backed the truck around in the road and turned north at the crossway.

"Jump in, son." The gangly man wearing bib overalls and a straw hat spoke loudly over the noise of the truck. "Where you heading?" he asked.

"Going to Chicago, sir, if'n I can make it."

"Oh, you'll make it, it's just fifteen miles or so. I'm just headin' up to Steger to get some hardware. Forgot 'bout old Bob's aunt passing away. Other day, guess the funeral was yesterday or maybe it's today or, well, can't rightly say. Not that it matters much, it's just that I came all the way in from Monee to get a dang tool. . . . By the way, you know how to fix a chimpanzee?" He waited with a deadpan look on his face. Boyd remained silent, not knowing if the man was offering a job, and finally shook his head.

On the punch line, the old farmer pounded the wheel of the truck and burst into laughter. Boyd couldn't understand him and it wasn't until much later that he managed to piece it together. But he didn't think it was such a bad joke. Matter of fact, he would have to remember to tell George when he saw him. After the man dropped him off in Steger, Boyd got successive rides to Chicago Heights—first in a Hupmobile driven by a female preacher pulling a small trailer with a tent in it. Then Boyd got on the back of an Indian Chief motorcycle driven by a fellow who said he was a salesman; they sped into the suburb of Chicago called Harvey after having fallen only twice on the hard-packed dirt road.

Boyd sat on a trolley-stop bench, nursing his wounds. He was almost reluctant to ask directions to Thirty-fifth and Prairie, since he'd already had a pretty full day.

He stood across the street from Pat's Place for a while and hadn't seen a white person pass through the doors. Thirty-fifth and Prairie was deep into Chicago's South Side. Black ghetto. Boyd got a number of strange looks while standing on the corner trying to decide whether or not to go in. Finally realizing he had no choice, he pushed the swinging doors gently and slipped inside.

The noise of people enjoying themselves hung in the smoke over the bar, which was lined with black women and men, all of them with a foaming glass of near beer and a second glass of clear liquid next to it. The liquid most likely was liquor of some kind, moonshine or some illegal drink the proprietor had obtained from who knew where. Boyd was surprised they drank so openly and without fear. Maybe, he thought, the authorities are afraid to come in here. He was having second thoughts about it himself.

A slim old black man, his deeply lined face the color of coffee, sat on a high stool near the back wall of the bar. He wore a slouch hat and a faded denim shirt. The worn guitar that rested in his lap had a large metal plate on the front. He sang in a deep voice that resonated.

Boyd eased up to the end of the bar, next to the service area.

A waitress serving beer on a tray glanced his way. "You all come in here to bust us, handsome?"

Boyd nervously placed a fifty-cent piece on the counter.

"No, ma'am, I just . . . I mean, I'm looking for someone, a friend, is all."

The waitress moved closer to Boyd. Her white apron stretched tight over her chest. She balanced her drink tray in her right hand and mock-whispered in his ear. "You can look for a friend all you want, but you ain't gonna find nobody more friendly than me." She sashayed over to a table heaped high with empty glasses and food remains. The four occupants of the table all turned to Boyd. He could hear them chattering.

"Who's your boyfriend, Shirleen? He look a might pale, sugar." Boyd heard them enjoy a laugh while three wooden overhead fans tried to keep time to the bluesman's tune. The *slap, creak, slap* was just slightly off beat. Boyd turned and was greeted by a six-foot-seven, three-hundred-pound bartender in an undershirt that barely covered his chest. He leaned his arms against the bar. "Whatcha want, Jack?"

Boyd stumbled, trying to sound in control. "Looking for a beer. I mean looking for a friend. I'll have a beer, though."

The man stepped back and took a hard look at Boyd. "We only got near beer. Famo or Vivo is what we sell. If'n you want something more potent, we don't got it, brother." The bartender waited. The large mirror extended the length of the bar. Boyd could see almost everyone turning toward him. Several of the patrons along the bar stopped what they were doing and looked at Boyd.

"Near beer is fine. Just fine. Oh yeah, and a couple those hard-boiled eggs, if you could."

The bartender slowly walked to the dispenser and poured a beer, the golden liquid spilling over the top of the tall glass. He reached into a large crock and produced two pickled eggs, gave them a sharp rap on the counter, and plopped them on a saucer with salt and pepper shakers and a paper napkin. "That be thirty cents, my man."

Boyd shoved his fifty-cent piece closer toward the bartender. "Keep it." He exhaled and watched the man.

"She-it, for me?" He raised his voice a notch so the other patrons could hear him. "Damn, brother, I don't rightly know what to say."

Boyd realized he had made a mistake trying to buy the man for twenty cents. "Sorry, I'm new to Chicago. It's just that I was looking for a friend who supposedly hangs out in here from time to time."

"Well if'n your friend be in here he won't be hard to spot, will he? He'll right likely stick out like a sore thumb, won't he?"

"He's a colored fella himself, sir." Boyd smiled self-consciously.

"Oh, is he now. And what would this colored fella be named, my good man?"

"His name be, I mean, his name is George Matthews. 'Bout six one, thin, muscular guy."

The bartender leaned against the back bar. Boyd nodded and drank his beer. The eggs tasted good, with a slight tang of vinegar to them. After wolfing down his meal he started out. Shirleen winked at him. The bartender kept working, but Boyd could see he never took his eyes off him.

"I know you know him, Tiny. I can see it in your eyes. Tell him I'll be back tomorrow night about the same time. Thanks."

The sound of the bluesman drifted into the street with him. The night air felt good. It was hotter outside than in the bar, but it still felt good.

Early morning, and Boyd had been walking for thirty minutes. For the last ten, he had become aware of a sickening smell. He knew he was heading in the right direction. The owner-clerk of the fleabag hotel where Boyd had stayed had given him directions for "Work you will find good, plenty." He could barely understand the man but his wild gesturing convinced Boyd there was work to be had. "Follow these mens now."

Seven or eight bleary-eyed guys with lunch sacks and battered tin pails trudged slowly down the middle of the dark street. Boyd followed them dutifully from the hotel lobby, and they were joined from time to time by other men stumbling down the steep steps of the row houses. From the cross streets they drifted like ghosts into the predawn haze to join this procession. Boyd could smell the rich odor of the stockyards, of nearly fifty thousand animals slaughtered each day.

As the streets lit up, the smokestacks towering over the packing plants loomed through the gray light. Thick, oily smoke drifted to earth in the heavy dawn air.

A large group of men milled around in front of the Dunfield plant. Boyd stopped and inquired of one, "Waitin' for a job, are you?"

He looked at Boyd and shrugged, mumbling something to him. Boyd moved on and started to speak to another sleepy-eyed worker. The group ran toward a gate where a fellow holding a clipboard shouted, "Day laborers, need ten!" He repeated himself and then gazed out onto the thirty or forty heads. All eager. Some of the men old and sickly looking. Others just weary.

"You, Petra . . . Janus, come on." The men he picked out grinned immediately and stepped quickly through the wooden gate, the foreman jotting their names down and again peering out toward the crowd. "I need strong men not 'fraid to work. Who'll it be? What's your name, fella?" He pointed at a heavyset blond man.

"Name, Helmut, work damn hard, you betcha."

"Come on then." The foreman picked several more until he had his ten able-bodied men. He turned his back and huddled his group behind the fence. Boyd moved closer, trying to figure how in the devil he could get a job. The group had started to move away from the gate when Boyd called out to the foreman.

"How in the hell does a fellow get work round here? Do you have to be a foreigner?" Boyd had caught the man's attention. "Ain't there no jobs for 'mericans, damn it?"

The foreman spoke quickly to one of the men in the group and they started walking briskly toward the plant. He turned to Boyd.

"I want men I know, men what can do the job, men what ain't scared of work." He studied Boyd. "You don't seem to fall into none of those boxes."

"The hell I don't. I fall into the box what ain't afraid to work. . . . Try me."

Once again the man sized up Boyd. "Shovel guts?"

"Wha—what?"

The foreman got a half grin on his face. "Ever shovel da guts? You know, cow's insides. Offal?"

Awful? Boyd hesitated for a moment, waited just a beat too long. "Yeah, sure, over at Armour's. I cleaned up, doing whatever."

The man rocked back and forth on his heels, trying to decide. "Tell you what. I got a guy what's been workin' wit' me only couple weeks. He don't look like he can do the job. Work alongside this guy the rest of the week, I'll decide on Friday what to do 'tween two a ya."

"Okay. Show me where."

The inside of the packinghouse smelled like nothing that Boyd had ever known. The dead animals in France, the horses and cattle, didn't compare to the overpowering stench that greeted Boyd at the large double doors. But the smell meant work.

The foreman walked Boyd down a wide concrete aisle. Shouting and yelling in a half dozen languages, men attacked large slabs of beef; cleavers and flensers flashed with speed and skill. A ripping noise permeated the building as others stripped the hides from the dangling carcasses. Boyd could hear the bellowing of thousands of animals pushing against wooden pens, crashing violently into one another, all of them agitated and restless.

The two men walked through a courtyard, heading for another structure. "These buildings are where we do all the dressing of the cattle. Your job's to keep the floor clean so's these guys don't fall and bust their butts. Got it, comprende?"

Boyd nodded. "Yeah, got it."

"Like I said, you gotta work with this Elrod. He's a nice guy. He'll break you in."

It turned out that Elrod was crippled. He was a man of about fifty, small-boned but muscular, with quick darting eyes. Shoulders slumped, he walked with a heavy limp. He took a step, then kind of threw his right leg out in front of him as if he didn't have much control of it.

"Say, your name is . . . what?" Elrod turned slightly to Boyd as the two of them headed toward a tool bin.

"Didn't say, but it's Calvin . . . Calvin Boyd." It was just the second time Boyd had called himself Calvin, the first being a minute before with the foreman, who had looked up suspiciously when Boyd stumbled on his own name. He knew people were looking for him but it was the only name that Boyd could think of.

Elrod limped steadily forward. "Been trying to convince ol' high-pockets all along that we need more help on the floor." The man rattled on about the foreman, who Boyd eventually found out was named Luis Pantalon, Spanish or Italian or something.

Boyd followed Elrod to a line of men driving large cleavers into suspended sides of beef hanging from an overhead trolley arrangement. They split open the sides and a small quick man with a hooked knife expertly trimmed out the stomach and intestines. The bloody package plopped on the wet floor and was kicked aside by the knife-wielding man, who never even looked down. Elrod poked Boyd excitedly.

"There, you see it? Jump in there."

The quivering mess got scooped up with his long-handled shovel. "Where I put this, Elrod?"

"There in the corner. That hole, quick."

Why quick? Trying to keep away from the stench coming up from below, Boyd rapped his shovel over the edge, where there was a three-foot hole in the concrete.

"What happens to it now?"

"It gets processed down below for a lotta stuff. Some of which you don't want to know 'bout. Especially if you eat sausage."

Boyd gagged and turned so the older man couldn't see his face. *Oh shit.*

"Don't fret 'bout it, young'un. We all done it. If you upchuck, make sure you do it where the inspector can't see it." Elrod nodded toward a man in a dress shirt sitting on a stool halfway down the long line. With a clipboard and other paraphernalia in his lap, he looked as if he was fighting to stay awake.

"He'll shut down the whole line and make ya clean up both sides for fifty feet real good. High-pockets don't like to shut the line down, hurts production, ya know." Elrod seemed to love his job. He would stalk along the line like a hungry dog, his eyes eager, hands gripping the long-handled shovel. Prowling, waiting, he'd pounce on the offending entrails and scoop them into the dreaded hole. Stepping back, using his shovel as a crutch, he would momentarily stare at the hole as if it were the gateway to hell and he had once again escaped its clutches.

Boyd worked up and down the line, his pants tucked into his socks, his heavy rubber boots covered in blood and other unidentifiable bits and pieces of white mucuslike material. The thought of food hit him hard in the stomach. Boyd dropped his shovel and ran to an open door. The air outside was not much better than in, but he took in great gulps and once again defeated the pressing need to vomit.

By the end of the day, Boyd was exhausted. Not from the physical work but from the stress of trying to keep from being ill. The walk back to the hotel was a welcome relief as the odors receded.

It was getting dark as Boyd rounded the last corner with the hotel in sight. Pat's Place was just across the street, and although weary, Boyd pushed through the swinging doors and walked quickly to the bar. Unlike the previous night, the place was only a third full. *Guess it's early.*

"Tiny, were you able to run—"

"Name's not Tiny, fella, and don't call me that, ya hear?"

"Yeah, okay. I was just wondering if you—"

The bartender walked away before Boyd had finished his request. Boyd stepped back from the bar and called out to the man.

"Hey, Midge. If'n you see my friend George Matthews, would ya tell him his friend, Boyd, is stayin' at the Western just down couple blocks on the right?" Boyd looked around to make sure everyone in the bar had heard him.

The bartender shouted back, "Don't be comin' in here, Whitey, all full of yourself, shoutin' out orders to me. And don't be callin' me Midge or Tiny."

But by that time, Boyd was well on his way.

By the end of the third day in the stockyards, Boyd was beyond exhausted. The cheap rubber boots that helped keep the refuse off his pants and socks were already saturated and cracked, and he was looking forward to Friday's payday. His nightly visits to Pat's had become almost a joke. He would pop his head into the tavern, and Tiny, if he saw him, would show his teeth and, with the index finger of his right hand, describe a circle indicating to Boyd that he was to turn right around and continue back the way he had come. This forced Boyd to have several abbreviated conversations with the bartender over the top of the swinging doors.

"But would you at least tell him I been around, would ya do that, please?"

The bartender shrugged as if he didn't know what he was talking about. "Who?"

"George Matthews."

It was the same routine on the third night, when Boyd noticed a man interrupting their conversation. "I know that fella. Was in here awhile ago talkin' to you, Pat." The bartender put his finger to his lips to quiet the man as Boyd spoke.

"Ah, Pat, Pat, I thought we was friends." Boyd tried to get a tear in his voice, hoping the bartender would help him out.

"Why you bother 'bout some nigger name of George Matthews, anyhow?"

" 'Cause, Pat, George and I are friends."

"But I don't know that, just 'cause you say it's so."

"I know you know who I'm talkin' about."

"I ain't mittin' nothin' of the sort, but if—"

Someone brushed past Boyd at the swinging door and disappeared into the crowd. Boyd could see the bartender's eyes follow the man intently. Boyd tried to pick the man out but could not in the gloom of the tavern.

"Pat, that's your name, right?" Boyd slowly tried to ease his way into the bar. "All I'm asking is, if you see . . ." Boyd's voice trailed off as George Matthews emerged from the crowd and walked toward him.

"Damn cracker, I didn't 'spect to see you up here. What ya doin' draped 'cross that door like that. You look a fool, Boyd. Hell, I just walked pass you like you was a piece a dog doo, then I hear that familiar cracker voice and there ya be. What you gettin' on Pat about?"

"I was just trying to leave a message for you that I was here and stayin' at the Western."

George signaled for Boyd to come through the doors. "Come on, I'll buy you a drink."

Boyd looked to the bartender and saw that he gave George permission. Boyd wondered what George would have said if he was refused a drink.

"What's with you and Pat?"

"Oh, I guess I got the needle in him the first time I came in here. I called him Tiny and then Midge for midget, and, I don't know, I guess he just don't cater to white folks, eh?"

George nodded his head. "You musta been actin' the fool to get Pat riled up. What you drinkin'?"

"Oh, just those beers."

George went to the bar and spoke to Pat for a minute. When he came back, he had two beers and the obligatory glass of clear liquid. "Pat was trying to look out for me, not wanting to speak out too much with a stranger and all. What you been up to?"

"Oh, hell, don't know. Left Vermilion couple days ago, thought we might hook up and go to work somewhere. Find a job, save some money, hitch to California, pan for gold."

"Pan for gold?" George asked. "You nuts or something? Brother, I got plans and purposes. Fact is, I got something maybe you and I could kick around a bit."

He took a long pull at his drink, never taking his eyes off Boyd. Tinny blues cut through the babble of the smoky tavern. The slouch-hatted black man's frame was bent over the patched guitar, his arthritic hands moving slowly over the strings.

"Hear that?"

"What, the guitar?"

"Yeah. First time I heard that kinda music, I musta been seven, eight years old. It was my uncle Leonard, played guitar and sang. He lived with papa and me. You know him, you 'member I told you about how he died?"

The two men sipped their drinks and tried to recapture their last moments together and the camaraderie they had felt. "That cracker cop was a case, wasn't he?"

Boyd turned. "You mean at the house?"

"He looked straight at me." George washed the harsh whiskey down with a swig of beer. "Damn, I 'bout shit."

Boyd didn't answer. It was one of the most intense couple of minutes he had ever spent.

George leaned over the bar. "They all look at us like we're apes or something." He crooked his head at Boyd. "You know I don't mean you, don't ya?"

Boyd nodded. "Yeah, sure. It's just 'them,' right?"

"Yeah, right." Boyd and George laughed quietly.

"Ready for a joke?" asked Boyd.

"Sure—hey, Pat, give us another round." Boyd told George how he had hitchhiked to Chicago and about the old farmer who had picked him up. Pat set their drinks down as Boyd said, "Do you know how to fix a chimpanzee?"

George thought a bit. "No."

Boyd exploded with laughter. "With a monkey wrench."

George burst out, too, as Pat stood behind the counter with a blank expression. "I don't get it."

George winked at Boyd. "You know . . . fix a chimp with a monkey wrench."

Pat scowled. "Is this some kinda black-and-white thing? You know, racy or something?"

Boyd could tell George was trying to smooth Pat's feelings. "No, Pat. Just playing with words. A chimp and a monkey wrench, that sorta thing."

Pat collected the change for the drinks and mumbled away.

George said, "You may be right when you call him Midge . . . for the size of his brain."

The two men tried to stifle themselves as Pat glanced at them over his shoulder.

George moved closer to Boyd and said quietly, "Got a job for us this weekend. Doing some loading and unloading. Friend of mine just got outta Joliet trying to find his way and all. Got this sweet deal Saturday night over by Gary, Indiana, suppose to meet him in Calumet City. He'll drive us over to Gary and we help out on some trucks. Anyway, we get thirty dollars apiece, and if all goes well, a bonus. Don't know what it's all about, but sounds legit. What you say?"

"Yeah, right, sounds okay. I didn't tell you but I got some work in the packing plant in the stockyards. Just started, suppose to get paid tomorrow, so the weekend's fine. It'd be nice to pick up a few extra greenbacks."

They scratched around for a few more minutes, made plans where to meet on Saturday afternoon, and parted.

Boyd stood in the middle of the street watching George kick at some refuse. Spirits high, George seemed to float as if suspended by his dreams.

*H*ennessy *was* still unsettled from his evening with Myrna, but she wasn't showing anything. She had dropped by unexpectedly after he returned home from work and immediately started grilling him about background material for her story. He poured her a drink and readied himself for the assault.

"I've been clacking away on my typewriter and something keeps bothering me."

"What's that?" He had a feeling he knew.

"It's the way you keep making excuses for Boyd. Either there's something you haven't told me, Dale, or you're even a stranger bird than I would have guessed."

"I'm not making excuses. I just don't know as I see Boyd killing people like that . . . but it's complicated."

"What happened in that fire, Dale?" Myrna swished her drink around absently in her glass, her gaze half distracted, half sultry. Hennessy was beginning to recognize that as a warning that her wheels were turning.

"Well, it's not just the fire, it's the whole story of his residence."

"What do you mean? I thought he was being treated for gas inhalation and shell shock."

"Well, he was not voluntary for the first two years, he was under directed observation."

"What? Are you telling me he was committed?"

"It's not like that . . . not with soldiers. It's not really committed, it's more like involuntary residence."

"Invol—Christ, Dale, he was committed."

"Have it your own way."

"But why?" Myrna was now standing, one hand on her hip, the knuckles of the other showing white on the glass, and her eyebrows raised in a prosecutorial "Oh really?" expression. Hennessy felt his composure slipping away.

"Why was good ol' Boyd an involuntary resident?"

Hennessy began choosing his words carefully, like a man who knows he has to come clean sooner or later, and it may as well be now. "There was some controversy about his mercy killing of an officer . . . some lieutenant."

Myrna placed her drink back on the table and flounced back in the chair. Hennessy couldn't remember a more deafening silence. Finally, her fingers tapping on the table broke the spell, but she still had nothing to say.

"Now, that's what I mean. I knew you'd make a big deal out of it." Hennessy hated the sound of his own voice when it carried no conviction. "It's really not like it sounds." He tried to articulate more resonantly, more confidently, in control.

"Sure, and just how does it sound to you, lover boy?" Her voice was cold and matter-of-fact.

"What?"

"You know what I mean. Us riding in cars, being pals, sharing our thoughts. You doing me like I was barmaid making an extra buck. But when it comes to confiding in me, you're all mum and manly."

"Hey, now wait—"

But Myrna would have none of it.

"Nah, that didn't mean we were close at all, did it sweetie?" This really surprised Hennessy. The last thing he'd ever expected from this tough front-page girl was that she would have her feelings hurt. Somehow, in a woman's unfathomable way of seeing the world, he had stolen her virtue and hurt her feelings. But this was no act, she meant it, confirming for him that women were absolutely, totally incomprehensible.

"Look, Dale. You lied to me. How come there was nothing about that in the arraignment? You were questioned, weren't you?"

"Yes, but this was not the official reason for his being at the home.

That's all they asked me, the official reasons. Hell, he was just a kid, seventeen, eighteen, when it all happened."

"So he was young. What is with you? You don't think it's relevant that—" She stopped suddenly as another question occurred to her. "By the way, sweets, just how did baby Boyd help this officer into heaven? It didn't happen to be through a gunshot, did it?"

He knew his silence answered her question. "And what kind of gun . . . his rifle?"

Hennessy stood up abruptly, at least as abruptly as he could with a game leg. "I think we've taken this just about far enough." Then, still wilting under her glare, he sat back down. "It was with the officer's sidearm, his pistol. . . . Boyd shot him in the head."

Myrna exhaled slowly, rose, grabbed her bag, and stalked out of the room, slamming the door behind her. Incomprehensible. Hennessy had just given her everything he knew and she still acted like he was an absolute cad.

A minute later the bell rang. It was her. She walked in with a casual air, raised the shade, pulled over a different chair than the one she had occupied moments before, and stuck her purse in an empty flowerpot. "Okay, Major, let's start over."

Hennessy felt strangely relieved. He knew she must be sensing the relief in his voice.

"Sure, let me explain. I really think you're taking it the wrong way. I didn't mean to mislead you."

"Sure you did, sweetie, but what's a girl to do?" Her manner now was flippant yet strangely businesslike.

"So, Boyd's a swell guy but he just happened to pop his officer, the good lieutenant, the same way he did two other—oh, wait, pardon me, the same way *someone* did the late Mrs. Calvin and her beau. Correct?"

It was a rhetorical question. Hennessy frowned and let her continue. "But my bedtime buddy Dale doesn't think this is important enough to tell me." Before he could protest she began again. "Dale, what in God's name happened in that fire? You never did tell me that story, and now, dumplin', I'd really like to know."

"What's the fire got to do—"

"Don't know, but something. Tell me what happened in that fire and I won't be bothering you with more questions—or anything else for that matter—for quite a while."

Hennessy didn't want to think about what "anything else" meant, so he ignored the implication and tried to match the cool, detached manner that was Myrna's choice of the moment.

"It's like I said, he really helped out."

No reaction from Myrna.

"He was in the far-gone wing but we also have, or had, the catatonics there. Lots of the men are, uh, confused in that ward."

"So?"

"Well, we couldn't get them to come out of there and so I went and grabbed a big fellow and tried to push him toward the door and some of the orderlies were helping me, but it got very . . . confused, you know, and, well, then Boyd sort of took over."

"Took over?"

"Yeah, he ordered the men to get on the floor and move toward the door, and they did it."

"So?"

"So, that's it. But with men like that, they had to, you know, trust somebody."

"But you were the one who actually got them out of there, right? I've seen your valor award for doing it."

"That was really nothing, I was just doing my duty."

"Aw shucks, ma'am, 'tweren't nothin'."

Hennessy wouldn't rise to it. She was mocking him but damned if he would rise to it. "Make fun all you want, but that's what happened."

"So, since Boyd helped get the nuts out, you figure he couldn't be a murderer?"

"You had to be there."

"Guess so."

Myrna got up, grabbed her purse, and exited again. This time she didn't come back.

Hennessy sat back in his chair and made himself ignore the stains. He sat there peering deep inside his own mind. A scene kept playing through his head like a needle stuck on the phonograph. He was scuffling along a smoke-filled hall, terrified, trying to get the men to follow him. He was trying everything he could but no one was listening to him. Then he froze; he suddenly knew what it was to panic. All he could think of was getting himself out, but he didn't know how. Then a voice, the voice of a young man—young but authoritative—said, "This way, you dumb shits, keep down, damn it." Then a hand grabbing him roughly by the collar and dragging him. "C'mon goddamn it, this way, c'mon."

Finally, Hennessy pushed the memories away. He relocated the varnished door. There was a giant, one monster gargoyle of a stain, he had never seen before. He set to studying it.

Elrod was hard at work long before the 7:00 A.M. whistle blew. Boyd watched as the man limped willingly toward a pile of bones that he had been shoveling into a tallow-laden wheelbarrow. It seemed to Boyd that some men relished work, always piling in when there was something to do.

Elrod glanced at Boyd and spoke without hesitation. "This'll be your last day, young'un."

"How do you figure that?" Boyd wondered what he meant.

The crippled man stretched his back, his quick eyes taking in the floor, ceiling, dead animals. "I told you the other day when ya started that we needed help on the floor, but ya see ol' Luis is a tricky bastard, and, well, you'll see. . . ."

Boyd was puzzled but went about his work.

After lunch, Luis spoke to him. "You doing good, man. Keep up the work. I like you, you good worker, keep it up."

Boyd drove his shovel into a pile of entrails. The bloody mess oozed over the sides of his shovel as he guided the whole mess to the hole in the concrete. He could see Luis and Elrod arguing at the other end of the line. The afternoon dragged on, the heat building and mixing with the noxious fumes of the dead animals.

Boyd swept close to the door and Elrod came by with a wheelbarrow loaded with horns and bones.

Elrod called out, "Got to get these horns to the button maker's, otherwise we can't button our pants. And oh yeah, we can't comb our hair 'cause there wouldn't be any combs and my wife couldn't pin her hair back without da bone hairpins." The little man pushed the barrow with his funny little hop and hunch. "Not to mention, I brush my teeth once a week whether they need it or not, and that be with a bone-handled toothbrush. If'n I smoked a pipe." Elrod gave a nod. "Thass right, a bone pipe stem." After he dumped the wheelbarrow, Elrod shouted to Boyd as he went back for another load, "They make shoe black, fertilizer, gelatin. Phew. All kind of shit. I tell you, my man, there's no end to what you can make from a damn cow." Elrod dropped the wheelbarrow and pinched his nose. "Did I mention fertilizer, oh yeah."

At five o'clock, Luis approached Boyd. "Calvin, I got bad news for you, man. Big boss says I got to cut back. So you're fired, hombre. Pick up your check at the oficina. Bye for you."

Boyd leaned against his shovel. He wasn't really disappointed. It just didn't seem right the way it was done.

"He's a snake, I tell you. That man's got no honor." Elrod eased up to Boyd. "Ya see what he does, is, every two weeks or so he'll hire a guy part-time, usually for a couple days. Helps with the floor. But really what the prick be doing is trying to get me to work harder." He never looked at Boyd. "If it means anything, you lasted longer than most."

Boyd thanked him, and the two men shook hands. He walked over to the glory hole and dropped his shovel into the black abyss.

Boyd was halfway to the door when he heard Elrod's voice.

"Can I have your boots?"

"What?"

"Your boots, can I have them?" An unabashed smile from the crippled man.

Boyd stood on one leg as he pried his boot over his leather shoes. The second boot stuck hard, and Elrod scuttled quickly across the floor and pulled along with Boyd.

"I wouldn't have asked if'n I thought you were going to need them, but if I had to guess, you got bigger fish to fry, right?"

Boyd wiped the boot debris off his hands. "Yeah, right." He pointed his finger at the new owner of his boots and smiled. "See ya, El."

The walk back to the hotel seemed longer tonight. Men dropped off on either side of him, some with a wave of the hand, others just drifting in an exhausted haze. Others seemed energized and anxious to get to the bars or back to their wives and children. As for Boyd, he had nowhere to go other than his tiny room at the Western. There wasn't much to look forward to except the temporary job that George had set up for tomorrow night. If he had bigger fish to fry, they were a long way out in the lake.

For several days, he had been thinking about going back to Vermilion. He asked himself what the worst thing was that could happen. Imprisonment? He knew he couldn't handle any serious jail time. But he also knew this darkness about Laurel's murder had to be cleared from his mind.

M*yrna sat* back and exhaled a long drag from her Marlboro from the side of her mouth. The cloud engulfed Hennessy's head for a moment before being carried toward the open window by a stray breeze. She never took her eyes from Freeman, who was in animated discussion with Hiram Vedeler, but Hennessy knew she had done it to him on purpose. Marlboros were supposed to be a lady's cigarette that kept them healthy and happy and slim, but he didn't believe it. Myrna would no more be able to stop eating sweets because she smoked than he would be able to hold off the cough that tobacco smoke always caused. He glimpsed a flash of satisfaction in her expression when he started hacking, although she quickly offered an "Oh my, sorry, Dale." She made a big flourish of putting her cigarette out and turned back to listen to Vedeler.

Hiram Vedeler was Vermilion's only real stockbroker with access to the ticker tape, and he seemed to Hennessy to be dominating the conversation at their end of the living room. The gathering at Dr. Bingham's house was a staid one, but the guests were beginning to liven up after a few drinks. It helped that the house was a three-story colonial that allowed the oppressive heat to escape upstairs, leaving the living area at street level comparatively comfortable. The Binghams' party extended through the whole downstairs, including the large kitchen, where most of the women were gathered.

There was new money in Vermilion, and Vedeler was the golden boy of the nouveau upper middle class. He had been holding forth to Freeman and several other doubting Thomases on the merits, indeed the magnificence, of the American free market system. James Lavoy, who owned

Vermilion Savings and Loan, and Todd Brenner, head of the chamber of commerce, were both nodding supportively. But Dr. Bingham just puffed his pipe impassively.

"You can't lose. Hell, you can't afford not to be in the market anymore."

Freeman's frown and slow head-shaking indicated to all he didn't agree with Vedeler, but he kept quiet. Hennessy glanced over at Myrna, whose eyes seemed to glaze over any time the subject of stocks and investing surfaced at the table. She had already whispered to him an unflattering assessment of "Vedeler the Peddler," as she dubbed him, and he sensed her patience might be wearing thin—a dangerous state of affairs. Hennessy knew that the distance thoughts traveled between Myrna's heart and her mouth was obstructed by little in the way of judgment.

"There's money to be made, I'm telling you—all it takes is a little self-confidence and moxie."

"Keep mine in the bank, myself. Thank you, Mr. Vedeler, but I'm a saving man, not a betting one." Dan Murphy summed up what he and a fellow farmer from west of town felt about the trustworthiness of the entire financial world. Hennessy hardly listened; he had heard it all before.

"But that's just it, there's risk in betting—where's the risk in the market over the long haul? A couple little bumps last year, but it's hard to pick a stock that won't do better than the bank."

Freeman finally gave voice to his misgivings. "Yeah, well, I had some money in the market until that scary business in March."

"That's right, my friend, exactly!" Vedeler had a checkmate tone to his voice. "When those with no stomach for a little risk bail out, that's when fellows who believe in the American way make money." Looking around at his audience as if explaining the end of a fairy tale to children, he added, "I made a small fortune for my investors when the fainthearted sold in March. Why? It let me buy low, so we could"—he solicited several in the group to chime in with—"sell high."

"Aha, he's got you there." Jim Lavoy good-naturedly slapped Freeman on the back and led a chorus of appreciative laughter to Vedeler's trump line.

Hennessy hoped he was the only one who could hear Myrna's murmured remark that likened the broker's head to his reproductive member. He was beginning to get nervous and considered a strategic retreat—why had he made the mistake of taking her to the party anyway?

Dr. Bingham and the farmers accepted Vedeler's ribbing, but Freeman wasn't ready to back down. "Still, Hiram, it all sounds pretty good, but what's all this about buying on margin? I mean, hell, I'm not the smartest fellow in the room, but if one person is buying with money he doesn't have and someone else gets excited and buys that person's stock with money he in turn, doesn't have, well it seems like a house of cards."

"But that's just it, don't you see what you've just described?" Again, Hiram turned to the assembled listeners with a salesman's open-armed gesture, inviting his students to answer the philistine's question. "Leverage, my friends, pure and simple—leverage!"

As the others waited expectantly for Hiram to place his new pearl of wisdom in a setting of purest rhetorical gold, all were momentarily distracted by a loud yawn from Myrna. She shot Hennessy a theatrical expression that could only mean to him, and everybody else in the room, that she was being overcome with terminal ennui.

Vedeler gave an awkward smile but quickly regained his stride. "Ever since the caveman invented the first lever that let him move something he couldn't move without it, he was usin' leverage. That's what lets the workingman pick himself up by his own bootstraps and become great in this country. He can buy stock with money he doesn't have because the market lets him leverage the God-given strength in his arm, his ability to work and earn, against the future. He can obtain what would ordinarily be unobtainable."

Freeman looked over at Hennessy. "What do you think, Dale? You ready to ride the fat-cat train? When are you going to invest?"

Hennessy was caught by surprise. He had been gathering himself with the intention of herding Myrna out of the room when the question broke his concentration.

"Actually, I have. I, uh, just made some significant investments. . . . I know Mom didn't like the market, but even her modest stock holdings ended up serving us very well. I've moved the majority into commodities and radio, and we're doing better than we ever have." Vedeler was nodding in a self-satisfied way, making it clear to everybody whom Hennessy had to thank for advice on his aggressive move into the world of stocks and bonds.

"Well, gentlemen," Myrna said, rising and stretching her arms in a long yawn. "My ass has gone to sleep."

Too late.

Amid nervous laughter, Hiram Vedeler sought to regain his control of the group. "My, my, Miss Logan, all this man talk boring you? Perhaps a round of chat on how to keep house would suit better?"

"Maybe so. At least being around you gallant gentlemen makes a lady feel safe. When the best man talk I can hear is about pork bellies, I figure what's left of my virtue is going to stay pretty much intact."

Some of the men chuckled more raucously, but a few, including Vedeler, raised their eyebrows and went stone silent.

Hennessy shot to his feet, surprised that even his game leg seemed sprightly at the moment. He grabbed Myrna by the elbow and ushered her toward the kitchen, announcing that she "really ought to see the rest of the house."

Then, in a lower tone to his ward, "You know that really wasn't necessary—you aren't getting snockered, are you?"

"Only had a couple. Has Myrna been a bad girl?" Then she pulled her arm away. "For crying out loud, Dale-o, you're getting mighty touchy. If I had to listen to that puffed-up money changer one more minute I'd have—"

"Okay, okay, calm down, let's mix a little." He put his hand in the small of her back in the manner one might have introducing a lady. She complied, but he thought he felt her stiffen when she realized she was being directed toward her gender-mates in the kitchen. He decided to stay with her to soften the sense that she was being relegated to woman talk.

"Hi, ladies. Many of you met Miss Logan earlier."

"Sure did. How you doin', honey? We were just fixin' to talk about Major Hennessy next—but here he is. He wouldn't make for a good subject of hot conversation now."

"Probably wouldn't be good gossip anyway," Myrna responded in an exaggerated faux-confidential manner. Hennessy felt his face redden as the women giggled. "Now if you really want some hot gossip, some of those jokers in there can fill you in on soy futures and pork bellies."

Hennessy started fading back toward an hors d'oeuvres table just in earshot of the women. He was always surprised how groups of women seemed to lose their inhibitions once they thought they were with just their own. One of the ladies said something about being "more interested in what is below their bellies," and the rest of the ladies variably shrieked or tittered in response. Myrna's resonant voice took over in a conspiratorial tone, saying something he couldn't quite catch followed by another outburst of female mirth.

"Oh Lordy, Lordy, hah! You stop that now, Myrna, my sides are hurting, I can't believe you said that. And you, Marilyn, you're just as bad."

Soon all was hushed again as Myrna continued to speak just below his ability to make out what she was saying, then delivered an easily audible punch line: "Give me all you got and I'll let you know when the time's up, mister." The women dissolved into another round of merriment. Apparently the mint juleps were flowing pretty freely among the ladies, and Hennessy realized that relegating Myrna to the kitchen was akin to throwing Br'er Rabbit into the briar patch. If he could gauge by the red faces of some of the women casting guarded glances in his direction, she wasn't regaling the group with her theories of commodities and wheat futures.

As he returned to the men's club, which was just reconstituting itself in the living room, it appeared that Dr. Bingham was interested in directing the conversation to subjects other than the free enterprise system or the outspoken nature of Hennessy's female companion.

He drowned out further prattling by Vedeler with a booming, "Well, Major, how's the fox hunt going? Boyd Calvin and that Negro, you've been keeping up with all that, working with the police, right?"

Hennessy noted that Freeman was out on the porch with a couple of other men, and Bingham had obviously thought the time right to raise an issue that had been on all of their minds.

"No sign of them right now, but won't be long before they surface."

"Speaking of surfacing," said one of the farmers. "That was a couple black guys they found in the quarry, eh?"

"Yeah, I guess it got right confusing. They even told the family of the black fellow, the one who was with Boyd, that he had drowned."

"Damnedest thing," said Hiram. "But hell, can't tell one from the other, can ya?" Most of the men chuckled.

"That the rapist you talking about?" It was Dan Murphy inquiring.

"Yes, that's the one," said Hennessy. "He's accused of raping a white woman who—"

"Can't keep off them white women, can they?" Hiram was looking with a half smile to the others for confirmation as he offered his assessment. His smile faded as he glanced behind Hennessy, who suddenly knew that Myrna must be back from the kitchen.

"Yeah, Hiram, we white women are a real draw, must be 'cause we're so appreciative—"

"Marge—" Hennessy cut Myrna off. He didn't want to hear the rest of her remark, and believed the others could be spared as well. The sudden appearance of their hostess and several other women was the excuse he needed. "This has been a delightful party and I can only say we hope you and the good doctor make a habit of throwing them for the rest of the summer." Many of the other guests had taken the signal and were rising, finishing conversations and beginning the ritual of taking their leave.

Marge elaborately curtsied to Hennessy and said, "We might just do that, honey. And you'll be the first on our list. You come again and bring Miss Logan with you."

Marge walked Hennessy to the door and confided to him in whiskeyed breath, "Honey, Myrna's an absolute hoot, she is just a hoot." Hennessy wondered if her husband, the good doctor, would agree. "The ladies love her, so refreshing, her being from Chi-town and all." Then more conspiratorially, "And she's a fine-looking woman, Dale. Not a bad catch for the most eligible bachelor in town, if you know what I mean."

He murmured an embarrassed "You never know," hugged Marge, and stepped out on the porch. Myrna was already outside with her elbow raised toward him.

"Take me to a place of starry climes and cloudless skies, where I can walk in beauty," she announced dramatically as she slung her derriere from side to side, striding toward the car. He let her lead him quietly to his coupe. They settled in and Hennessy punched the starter.

"Myrna."

"Yes?"

A few seconds passed. "Nothing."

As they began to rumble down their hosts' driveway, Myrna said in a perfectly even and sober tone, almost as if she had just left a boring church picnic, "Dale?"

"Yes?"

"What do you think Boyd Calvin is doing right now?"

The sun was setting as the Blue Island Interurban made its way east toward Calumet City. Boyd and George sat quietly in the back, shoulder to shoulder against the other passengers, bodies crammed tight in the small space of the hot car filled with workers going home, shop girls, laborers, office personnel. Others looked dressed for a night out. Boyd watched the driver with a professional interest.

"We'll get off before Whiting, then hitch a ride or walk. It ain't far." George appeared lost in some inner thought.

Boyd nudged him. "You worried about something?"

George seemed more subdued than usual. He gazed out the dirty window, watching the row houses pass by. After Boyd and Geoge had been riding for the better part of an hour, the tiny lights in the ceiling of the streetcar came on. The dusky glow from the sunset turned the car into a bluish tableau. Boyd thought the lipstick on women seemed darker and richer. Men's eyes became hooded and deeper. The car was silent. A woman about Laurel's age stood next to Boyd. He volunteered his seat to her but she declined. The swaying of the car pushed Boyd's shoulder into the young women's leg and she quickly moved away. Boyd looked up at her as if to apologize but the woman turned her head, probably not wishing to make eye contact.

George made a sound as if to move.

"What'd you say?"

"Let's get off."

The two men made their way to the double doors. George reached high for the bell cord and the car slowed. The doors rattled open and he swung down. Boyd grabbed the pole and, just before alighting, glanced back at the pretty girl. She met his eyes briefly and then once again shied away. It seemed to Boyd there was an accusation in those eyes, and a feeling of pain.

Boyd watched the streetcar move away, the interior lights seeming brighter from the outside. The people swayed, holding their straps. He thought he saw the girl glance his way one last time. But maybe not.

George was halfway across the street. "Let's go."

"Yeah, right."

They walked for about a mile and a half.

"This is Cal City, suppose to meet this guy at Willie's. A dance joint, speakeasy."

After directions from pedestrians and shop owners they finally found Willie's. They were to wait outside to meet George's friend at eight-thirty, but by nine o'clock they still hadn't seen him.

"How you know this guy?"

George looked Boyd's way and shook his head.

Boyd had never seen George like this; usually he was the epitome of cool, but tonight he seemed jumpy, even scared. Boyd strolled the sidewalk, walking several hundred steps north, then back past George and several hundred steps south. George had his hands jammed in his worn blue trousers. On one of Boyd's swings south, he turned to see George talking to a short black man wearing a long coat and a dark snap-brim hat. Something under the coat caused it to swing in a strange way.

"This your whitey friend, George-o? Damn, he don't look like much. You sure he can tote his load?"

George eyed the small man. "He'll do. And who in the hell are you to

question me, Peabody? You show up here an hour late all huffy. We goin'
do this thing or what?"

"Yeah, we be doing it. Don't get your bowels in an uproar. I'm late
'cause I set this thing up and I got a lot to do, Mr. Smart Aleck. Now,
you in or you out?"

"I said we're in, now let's do it."

Boyd watched the two men argue. They both seemed nervous and
speaking out of some pent-up emotion. Boyd wondered if there was
more to this deal than just loading and unloading trucks.

George signaled for Boyd to follow them as the two men walked down
the dark street. After several blocks, they turned into a small alley. Parked
nose to tail were two Ford trucks. The lights blinked on the first truck as
the men approached. Peabody swung up into the passenger seat next to a
black man drumming his fingers on the wheel of the open-cab truck.

"Say hello to my cousin, Boots. He's gonna drive this truck, you guys
follow behind in the other. We're going to Gary. Don't fall too far behind; and George, stop worrying, my man. I done this a number a times.
It's a snap, my brother, a snap." Peabody flashed a big smile as Boots
swung out of the cab to crank the engine.

"I swear, I never thought we was gettin' in this deep," said George as
he and Boyd walked back to the second truck. "Oh yeah, figured we was
gonna move some hooch. But I just thought we would be carrying some
five-gallon cans. You know, laboring and like that."

Boyd didn't answer but stepped up to the passenger side of the truck
and waited for George to swing into the driver's side.

"You gotta drive, my man. I ain't drove no truck." George didn't get in.

"I never drove no truck, either."

"Boy, this is a fucked deal. Never drove a truck? Why in the hell didn't
you say so?"

"You didn't ask. You said it was just loading and unloading, right?"

"Yeah, right." George started walking back toward the first truck that
sat idling.

"George, wait a minute. Let's give it a try. I drove a Dodge truck a
couple times in the army. Just foolin' around. Let's try it."

They did. They set the spark and choke and cranked the heavy truck. It started after a few cranks. Boyd quickly scooted back into the cab and pushed in the clutch. He moved the massive shift lever into what he thought was a low gear but found reverse instead and stalled the engine. Peabody had come out of his seat and was starting back toward them when Boyd recranked the engine. George waved Peabody back, and the two friends fixed their eyes on the red taillights of the first truck.

The trip to Gary was interrupted several times by Boots's confusion about where the hell he was going. Twice they ended up on dead-end streets and were forced to back up while Peabody and George shouted directions.

"This don't seem like it's a well-organized operation," Boyd observed, keeping his eyes on the road. He found it difficult to follow Boots, who rode the brakes, making the rear lights blink continuously. They passed through the outskirts of Gary, the giant steel mills glowing in the night sky. "Did you ever work in the mills?"

George gazed at the heat rising from the open-hearth furnaces. "Nope, never did. Was supposed to, but it never happened. I actually came up from Bama to work the mills. Read it in the *Defender*, how one could get good work. But I got involved in other things."

"What's that, a magazine or something?"

"Nah, just a paper, what a lot of people down south would read. Probably 'cause it was printed up north. You know how people are. Things always seem more interesting if it's from someplace else."

"I used to read a lot. But it seems lately, can't concentrate. Can't seem to get interested in nothing."

"Well, yeah, the *Defender* would be a good thing for you to read, seeing as how you're so interested in the Negro problem and all."

"What is it, one of those throwaway sheets you see laying around?"

"Hell no, it's big. Real big. We're coming, coming round the mountain. I saw an article 'bout how there was good, fair jobs in the Illinois, Indiana region, and me and a couple relatives came up. Well, yes, you met Frederick and Juanita and, course, Jolene. Well, hell man, you're practically part of the family. Yeah, you could pass, let me look at you." George turned in his seat. "Oh hell yeah. I'll get you a copy of the *Chicago Defender* and you can speak out for all of us lonely downtrodden turds."

Boyd could tell that George was under some kind of pressure. He didn't understand what it was exactly, but this testiness was unlike his friend. "What's gotten into you?"

"Nothin', sorry. I guess this clown Peabody's got me in a stitch. Forget it."

Once through the town, they stopped at a crossroads. Peabody ran back to their truck, his long coat flapping in the wind. Boyd could see what looked like a shotgun hidden lengthwise against the small man's side.

"We gonna turn here and head north a mile or so, then parallel the beach 'bout quarter mile. Stay close, you hear?"

They sat watching the man trot back to the truck. "That convict gonna get our butts shot. Sure'n hell," mumbled George.

Boyd didn't answer but engaged the shift lever and eased up close to Boots's truck. "How long you know this guy Peabody?"

"I'm thinking not long enough. Why?"

Boyd fidgeted in his seat. "Just seems a funny name for a black man—no offense meant—but is that his real name?"

"You doing a fair-to-middlin' job hauling this truck around, why you asking questions 'bout that nigga?"

"Oh, don't know, like I said, just seems a strange name for him is all." Boyd felt he had asked an awkward question of George, but as usual, George was forthcoming.

"His real name's Philip Du'taire from New Orleans or someplace south," said George. "Don't know really, but everybody calls him Peabody. I hear tell it was a name they gave him in prison and it stuck. Guess 'cause he's got a small body. You know, like a pea, get it? Peabody. Anyhow, that's what I hear. How'd you pick up that wasn't his name?"

"I guess the way he kind of winced when you called him Peabody." Boyd shrugged.

"You see too much, cracker boy," George said easily.

After five minutes or so the pavement ended and a rutted dirt road wound its way through some scrub oaks. The land became more spread out—after the trees there was what looked like pastureland. Then more trees, until they finally came into an area of marshland loaded with cattails and brush.

The road had changed to hard-packed sand as they turned at a place where a number of cars had come and gone. Boyd could hear the Lake Michigan surf on the other side of the dunes. Boots stopped once again. Peabody got out of the truck and waved to them. Boyd left the truck running. They gathered in front of the headlights of Boots's Ford. Peabody spoke hesitantly, as if scared.

"There's a path that we can get the trucks down that goes next to these big sand dunes. We got to go another quarter mile to the spot. Be careful, hear?"

Boyd looked at George, then Peabody. "That path looks pretty soft, mister. We get down in them dunes and sink in, we'll never get out."

"You scared or somethin'?" Peabody moved in front of Boyd and got his face to within a foot of Boyd's.

"No, ain't scared so much as cautious. I don't wanna get stuck."

Peabody turned to George. "Tell your pale friend to shut his mouth and drive, hear?"

Boots and Peabody drove their truck straight into the path, knocking down brush and weeds on both sides. Boyd watched for a minute, then turned to George.

"Jump out and guide me. I ain't driving down there not knowing if'n I can get out. I'm backing in." George started to protest, but seemed to think better of it and got out. He walked backward down the path, shouting to Boyd and waving his arms as Boyd struggled with the big truck. They were both exhausted when they finally caught up with the second truck. Its engine was dead and its lights were out. "Where in the hell are they, George?"

George pointed to the top of the dunes some fifty or sixty feet above them. One of the men on the top of the dune—they couldn't tell who it was—was waving a red lantern. "What in the hell's he doing?" George muttered.

"Probably signaling to a boat, don't you think?"

George nodded. The two men trudged up the long, steep hill, the sand breaking away as they labored to the top. By the time they caught their breath, Peabody and Boots were already at the water's edge, meeting what looked to be a thirty-foot longboat piled high with five-gallon cans. Three men from the boat were rapidly piling the cans on the beach as Peabody and the man who appeared to be in charge of the boat completed their business. Boyd and George jumped into the waist-deep surf and began hauling the heavy cans out of the boat. No one spoke. Boyd figured they all were thinking the same thing: Let's get this thing unloaded and get the hell out of here. Peabody and the captain were having their differences while the crew unloaded.

The captain jumped into the longboat and turned.

"I'll leave these three men with you while I get the next load. They can help you over the dunes."

He shoved off, having started a loud little auxiliary engine. Boyd could see the mother ship standing about a quarter mile off the beach, its running lights out but still shining brightly with reflected moonlight.

The trip across the dunes with the heavy cans was backbreaking, but the seven men kept at it steadily for the better part of an hour.

Just as they made their last trip, the longboat arrived with the second load. The crew quickly unloaded the boat; then the captain and his men scrambled on board and backed out of the light surf.

Peabody, just coming back over the dunes, yelled, "You bastard, you suppose to help us with these cans." The captain had turned the boat and presented his back to the man. Guiding the boat with his left hand, he waved lazily with his right. Peabody paced the beach for a few minutes but in the end he grabbed two cans and began the long hike over the soft sand. The second load took longer. They finally all collapsed at the base of Boyd's truck. Each vehicle had approximately eighty five-gallon cans on board at thirty-five pounds each, almost a ton and a half. A lot of weight in the sand. The moon was starting to drop. Boyd figured it must be two or two-thirty in the morning. He was anxious to get going. Peabody got up.

"You boys go on ahead, we'll meet ya at the parking spot, then you'll follow us back to Cal City." Peabody seemed to have regained his composure, strutting around whispering some kind of crap in Boots's ear, then breaking up with laughter as if they had just won the Kentucky Derby.

Boyd had a fearful moment when the truck didn't start after the third crank. But he yelled to George to advance the spark and finally the engine caught in the damp night air. Boyd ground the shift lever into gear, sounding as though he had sheared all the teeth from the gearbox, and eased the truck carefully through the brush. The fallen branches of the beach sage actually helped the truck regain traction. Boots wasn't doing so well. Boyd and George stopped to watch the impatient man try to back the heavily laden truck through the brush.

"If he gets off the path, he's a goner."

George nodded.

"Let's go, we'll wait at the parking spot." George and Boyd sat idling in their whiskey-laden truck while back along the dunes they could hear Boots's truck screaming as it tried to gain the path. Boyd and George could tell they were in trouble from the shouts of Peabody and Boots as they hurled accusations at each other. The two men were snickering to themselves when Boyd sat up suddenly.

"We got trouble."

"No, they got trouble," replied George. "We're doing just fine." He smiled and turned to look back at Boots's truck on the trampled path.

"No, I mean up ahead, look." Boyd pointed. Coming from the south three sets of headlights cut their way relentlessly through the twisting sandy road. Boyd pounded the horn twice, trying to alert the stalled truck, then accelerated out of the car park.

"What the hell you doing, idiot? You're going right toward them."

"I'm trying to make it to those trees." Several hundred yards later, Boyd slid the truck into a copse of scrub oaks. He kept his motor running and his lights out. "They'll see Boots's lights and run right past us."

"Who says?" George looked at Boyd.

Boyd pulled the truck carefully through the trees as the last of the cars sped by. "Says I." Boyd eased onto the sand road and drove slowly back south, his lights out. He glanced in the rearview mirror, then pointed toward the water. "Look there."

The two men saw a break in the sand where the years of wind had eroded the dunes enough so you could see the water.

"Boyd, my good man, this whole thing seems to be a setup."

A second boat with a powerful spotlight had stopped the mother ship and was circling her.

George whistled through his teeth. "Serves the prick right. He should have helped us with those cans."

"We didn't have time to do more than give them a honk. Did we?"

"Probably not."

Boyd picked up speed when he saw another car coming. "Ah, Jesus, not again."

"What ya gonna do?"

Boyd gave the big truck all the throttle she had.

"Jesus, man, you're gonna kill us both."

He kept the truck in the middle of the road and gritted his teeth. "You see the light switch on the dashboard? When I tell you, throw that switch on. But not till I say so." The two vehicles came hurtling toward each other, each doing thirty-five or forty on the loose dirt road. At the last possible second, Boyd shouted, "Now, damn it, now!"

George threw the switch and looked up just in time to see the police car blinded by the truck's lights. The car spun crazily off the road and then stopped abruptly in the marsh.

"Turn them back off." Boyd kept the big truck moving at speed until they reached the crossroad, the moon guiding his way. He prayed they wouldn't come upon another police car. At the crossroad, Boyd switched the lights back on and slowed down. He turned to the west and took a deep breath. They traveled silently for several minutes.

"After we pulled outta those trees and just before we saw that last police car," Boyd finally said, "I thought I heard gunfire."

"Yeah, you're right. I thought I heard Peabody's shotgun and maybe more. . . . Hope they made it."

George seemed to reflect for a while.

"When we passed that service station just now, I suddenly realized that if I had been driving, I would have turned the other way at the crossroad. I recognized that station 'cause I saw it when we came out. I . . . well, hell, man. I guess I'm just rambling here. But I tell you, I was shit-scared." He looked at Boyd. "You one strange devil. Yeah, you one strange devil indeed."

Boyd had never really had a friend. He supposed it had something to do with trust. George seemed like someone who took people as he found them. He never questioned Boyd about the death of his ex-wife, or the possibility of Boyd's being involved. Boyd sat behind the wheel of the noisy truck, thinking about the last several hours. A peculiar sense of despair crept over him. Here he was, nearly thirty years old, driving a stolen truck down an unfamiliar highway having just left Lord knows what mayhem at the beach, hoping to unload illegal whiskey onto someone who was obviously going to be a gangster. He wanted just to park the truck and walk away from it. It was only a matter of a couple of bucks, and the risk was enormous. But he kept driving. He noticed that George, after having complimented him, had fallen asleep.

Boyd wondered about himself and why, in the face of danger, he always relaxed. He was sure it had something to do with his early life. The long hours of waiting for Unca Donald to come home and administer his inevitable beating. He had always felt better when he could do something—take action instead of just sitting there. Finally, in the last couple of years of his foster care, he would sit in the dark basement and daydream, transporting himself to an outer edge where kids ran laughing and free, kindly older women prepared lavish fried chicken dinners, and doddering ancient men told startling stories of derring-do. The truck lurched in a pothole, and Boyd fought the wheel as George raised his head. "What?"

"Go back to sleep."

George mumbled and lowered his head. A man with a lunch pail stood on a corner with his thumb extended. They were driving through a desperately poor section, the row houses downtrodden in the early-morning gloom. They went the rest of the way into Calumet City without incident and without speaking. Boyd could smell whiskey. At least one of the cans had burst and was spreading its illegal juice across the bed of the truck.

George finally broke the silence. "If we don't get rid of this truck soon, someone's gonna spot us for sure."

"Why don't we park it right where we started from?"

"Then what?"

"We'll go to Willie's and see if that's where the load was supposed to end up."

"Sounds about right. How you get instincts 'bout all this, you being a white boy?" George wiped his fingers along the dashboard. "You was real nervy back there. That took guts. Now you saying, 'Let's go to Willie's and see if this is their hooch.' Shoot, man, what we suppose to do, just wake ol' Willie up, tell him we got his booze?"

"Yeah, why not?" Boyd laughed. "What's he gonna do, arrest us?"

George slumped down in his seat. Boyd found the same alley close to Willie's, parked the truck, switched off the lights, and sat listening to the hot metal creak and crack as it cooled down. Finally, Boyd eased out of the cab.

"Come on, big boy. They'll never let me in that joint by myself."

They found Willie, who was just closing up. He acted suspicious, probably because he had never met either of them. At first he denied any knowledge of booze or boats and said, "Who in the hell is Peabody?" but in the end, he gave them fifty dollars apiece. But not until they had driven the truck into a garage several blocks away.

The sun was just coming up as Boyd and George walked back toward the interurban line. Boyd wondered if by chance the young woman who had reminded him of Laurel might be on the train. It was just that she had looked at him in such a way that—

"I'm going back to Vermilion."

"What ya mean, going back?"

"Just what I said. I can't be running around doing crazy stuff, pretending that this thing back home hasn't happened in my life. 'Cause it has, and I gotta go back and make it right somehow." They walked across the tracks where they had stepped off the car twelve hours earlier. "What you gonna do, George?"

"Don't know, really. Kick around some. Try not to hook up with any rumrunners and—"

They could see the trolley coming.

"Think I'll mosey on down toward that railroad crossing and try to catch something going south."

"Yeah, well, don't do nothing I wouldn't do, Boyd."

"That gives me a hell of a lot of leeway, don't it." Boyd looked over his shoulder and watched as George boarded the trolley car. When it passed by, Boyd saw George had written "Fuck it" in the dirty window. George didn't wave but nodded just slightly.

"Miss Logan, the *Tribune* lady, is here. She says she needs to talk to you, Major." Betty had an inquisitive look on her face. She seemed to think the Major's reaction to this piece of information might carry significant import.

He said as matter-of-factly as he could, "Miss Logan? Okay, let me have a minute or so and show her in."

He removed Boyd's file from his desk and stuck it in a drawer. Then he positioned a sheaf of administrative papers in front of him as if that were what he had been poring over for the last few hours.

When Myrna was ushered in, she flopped into one of his padded guest chairs before Betty could offer it to her; this was clearly a serious breach of protocol in the secretary's world. Hennessy watched Betty's eyes roll and her nose raise as she remarked, "Be sure to make yourself comfortable, ma'am," and exited more officiously than usual.

Myrna winked at him. "Tillie the Toiler seems a little protective of her Major, eh?"

"Look, she's a fine—"

"Yeah, I know, she's as fine a lapdog as a fella can find these days, but that's not what I'm here about, mi amore."

Hennessy realized from the familiar feeling of heat in his face that he had gone from a reflective, relatively tranquil state of mind to full alert in the few seconds it had taken Myrna to walk into his day.

"Pray tell, just why are you here?"

"I need to know what's happening, Dale."

"How so?"

"I mean, where's Boyd? It's been nice visiting the fine town of Vermilion and getting to know ya, big fella, but I need to know what that rascal is up to. My editor was happy with the escape, but he's gettin' a little tired of pieces on local color while we wait for Boyd's next move."

"Well, I'm sure the police will redouble their efforts knowing you need to keep your Chicago readership satisfied."

"Yeah, yeah, the police. Wedge-head and Fatso are driving around looking important and chumming it up with the state and fed boys. But they don't have a clue where our Boyd is."

"Well, maybe *you* should go find him, then. I mean, if we hicks can't do it—"

"Oh, don't get on your high horse, Dale, I'm just saying I can't wait for these numskulls to get some sort of divine inspiration; I need to report on some progress. Hell, in Chicago they don't know poop from poison either, but they're smart enough to at least give me something to write about, even if it's made up."

Hennessy started drumming his fingers on his desk. He wished Betty had closed the door all the way when she left; he'd be mortified if she was hearing any of this. He could feel his pulse racing and his brain fogging— effects Myrna always seemed to have on him. She lit a cigarette and walked to the window. She was close enough that he could smell the perfume or bath oil she always wore, mingling with some other essence. Her perspiration showed through her blouse even this early in the morning. The bouquet of Myrna, mingled with the tobacco smoke and eau-de-whatever, made him dizzy.

"Just what is it you want me to do?" he asked.

"Let's go find him."

"So, you're Miss Sherlock Logan now?"

"I'm serious, Dale. These bozos haven't even asked the ones who would know."

"They talked to Claudia and Freeman and all the people he knew at work and—"

"That's just it. None of those people are going to know, except maybe Claudia, and she wouldn't tell if she did."

"Then who?"

"The black guy. His people."

"Oh, so you want to go to the Bottoms and interrogate that Matthews fellow's kin. Mind if I don't inconvenience you with my company?"

Myrna's answer was to sit down and take a particularly long pull on her Marlboro as she stared full into Hennessy's eyes. She exhaled slowly through her nose and mouth simultaneously, never averting her gaze. He wondered what it would be like looking in the Bottoms for someone who didn't want to be found.

As they bounced around town in his coupe, Hennessy contemplated how different a place Vermilion must be for a black man. He had never before considered the question. He also tried to characterize the attitude of the neighborhood's denizens toward him and Myrna. It certainly wasn't hostility, more a half-suspicious and half-curious distance, a gulf that seemed to exist between him and those he questioned. "No, sorry, can't help ya there, mister," and "Nope, don't know no George Matthews. He live roun' here?" and so on. The one breakthrough was a woman remarking, "If Juanita didn't know, no one else would."

Myrna looked at the list of possible relatives they had picked up at the county clerk's office and said, "There's a Juanita Matthews on Washington Street. Wonder if that's her?"

Myrna's mood seemed to change as they made their way around the Bottoms. Hennessy knew better than to inquire. If Myrna's mood was going to change, he had learned, asking about it didn't help things. At the Matthews residence they were greeted by a heavyset lady named Juanita, who appeared to be the lady of the house. Myrna stood behind Hennesy as he made introductions and explained to the stern-faced Mrs. Matthews why they were inquiring about her cousin—that he and Miss Logan, who was from the *Chicago Tribune,* had important business with Boyd Calvin, who was a friend of George Matthews.

Myrna had become abnormally quiet, almost reflective, letting Hennessy handle the questions. Hennessy couldn't recall how he had suddenly been positioned on the front lines of their inquiry. Not much earlier he had been protesting the search, and here he was taking the brunt of Mrs. Matthews' glare. He pointed out awkwardly, "We're intending to help Boyd, and maybe we can help George. We certainly don't intend to turn him in."

"Well, thass nice, yes, uh-huh, that certainly is nice of you. Expect me to tell you where my cousin is so you can find a Mr. Boyd? And here, you won' even turn him in?" She yelled back in the house to what must have been her husband, "Fred, honey, we lucky today. They's some white folks out here looking for George and they say they won' turn him in or hang him or nothin'. Jus' lookin' for some cracker name Boyd who's with 'im. . . . Ain' that nice?"

Hennessy sighed and turned to leave, but Myrna was standing her ground. Her expression was subdued but stolid. She looked Juanita in the eye, and said in a low voice, "You know where he is, don't you?"

"Honey, I don' know what you be selling, but I'm not buying. I ain't seen George in a coon's age, I say a *coon's age,* and what's more, I haven't missed him. So don't you take it personally, just take it out of here."

"Okay, we'll be going, but, well . . ." Myrna hesitated several seconds as if weighing her words. "I think it's nice that you protect George. Good for you."

Juanita raised her eyebrows. Apparently, it wasn't a comment she'd expected from the Chi-town news lady. "Well, of course I protect him, what you think?" But the sass in her tone wasn't quite as thick as it had been.

"Maybe you're right. You shouldn't tell us anything."

Hennessy couldn't believe his ears. "Uh . . . Myrna."

"No, she's right. We don't give a damn about her. Hell, I don't even know George isn't guilty, but we could hurt his chances."

Hennessy could think of nothing to say. Juanita had calmed down and was clearly now as curious as he about this turn of events. Myrna turned and started back up the walkway. There were tears in her eyes. If this wasn't the most perplexing women he had ever seen, he didn't know who was.

"What in the dickens is your problem, miss?" The hostility in Juanita's voice had now totally evaporated.

"Nothing the matter with me, just good to know some people still stick up for their kin. Some of us don't, that's all. Sorry we bothered you."

Hennessy felt Juanita's stare, and he could only turn to her and shrug his shoulders. "Well, I guess that's all. I, uh, if you should change your mind—"

"Let's go, Dale."

As they made their way back to the car, Hennessy could hear a rooster, whose timing was obviously off, crow from the direction of the Matthews' coop. Then he thought he heard something from the direction of the house. Standing on the porch, Juanita repeated herself: "Hey now, you—newspaper lady."

Myrna turned.

"C'mon back here a minute, honey."

Hennessy watched Myrna walk tentatively back toward the house and he started to accompany her. "Not'choo, mister, I'm talking to this lady here." He hung back and so could hear only bits and snatches of the two women speaking on the porch; something about "George" and "Pat," somebody "on the prairie," then a couple mentions of Boyd.

When they seemed to be finished, Juanita abruptly turned and reentered her house while Myrna scuffed back up the walk, giving Hennessy a brusque "Let's go" as she passed. Somehow he had lost stature as a major and become, instead, a chauffeur.

Hennessy took his seat beside Myrna in the coupe without a word. He would be damned if he would be the one to open the conversation.

"Chicago."

"What?"

"That's where they are. Chicago."

"Interesting—they're both country boys and that'd probably be the last place the cops would guess." After a few more minutes of no response, he said, "Nice act. They teach you tricks like that at the *Tribune*?"

Myrna turned a withering look on him that made Juanita's glare seem warm and inviting in comparison.

When Boyd reached the overhead railroad crossing he turned south and started walking along the right-of-way. It was a Friday and there was a lot of ground to cover. The death of Laurel—it may have been the first time he admitted to himself that she was gone. He suspected his own stubbornness had caused their split. He couldn't remember how their troubles started, as discord had accompanied them almost from the beginning.

She had lived with her parents when they met, but Boyd had insisted they live apart from them even though he was broke. Laurel and Boyd married and soon thereafter he went off to war. She kept working at the five-and-dime, writing to Boyd while he was overseas and then writing and visiting him at the Leavenworth stockade in Kansas. He would ask if she ever met anyone on the train rides to Kansas and on one occasion berated her when she mentioned having spoken to a young man on his way to California. Boyd felt he had complete trust in Laurel and always believed she was faithful, but he had an inexplicable and terrible compulsion to blurt out his insecurities. He always regretted it afterward.

They had been sweethearts for several years before marrying, and Boyd knew it was he who had changed after the marriage. He managed to hide his green demon while they were courting, but the truth is, he had always been jealous. Not only of her relationships with others, but of her close family ties, her education, and her independence. He had asked himself a number of times what she saw in him.

He would sit in his cell in Leavenworth for hours, thinking about how he had humiliated himself and her with his loud recriminations and sobbing apologies. These thoughts continued into the time he spent at the Soldiers' Home—those years could easily have been cut in half if not for Boyd's stubborn insistence on his masculine independence. He had kept his vow not to live off of his in-laws, so although seemingly well enough to leave the home, he hung on, the security of the familiar surroundings too much to give up.

A cool wind from the north pushed him toward Vermilion. The weather was changing, the sun starting its relentless climb into a spotted gray morning. Boyd could see dark clouds in front of him, their towering forms soaring thousands of feet in the southern sky. He wished it would rain.

By noon, he had walked out of the city. The houses thinned and large pastures spread out on either side of the tracks. He vaulted a fence and drank deeply from a watering trough, skimming the debris off the top. He dipped his head and scrubbed his knuckles into his scalp, trying to rid himself of the cheerless images that permeated his thoughts. He saw his reflection in the water and looked up to see a passenger train streak by, its many windows full of faces heading perhaps to Chicago or beyond. He thought of the meager clothes he had left in his room at the Western Hotel. They weren't worth going back for. Luckily, he had brought the small stack of money he had earned at the stockyards, what he had from Vermilion, plus the fifty he had got from the job with George.

Starting out once more, he fell into a long period when his thoughts were focused on only the tracks in front of him, their straight lines converging at the darkening horizon. After an hour or so, Boyd could hear a mechanical, rhythmic sound behind him. It wasn't loud enough for a train, but it was definitely coming toward him. He turned to see a handcar with just one man on board. It slowed, but only a bit, as it approached him. As the car began to pass Boyd, the middle-aged man said, "Howdy." Boyd trotted along next to the car as the man pumped up and down on the two handles.

"Hey, mister, give me a lift?"

"Not supposed to. Where you from?"

Boyd stumbled but regained his footing. "Down Vermilion way on the Illinois side, just 'cross the Wabash."

The man glanced behind him as if his supervisor were on another handcar tracking him down. "Well, hell, climb aboard and give us a pump."

The tiny car slowed as the man stopped pumping. Boyd grabbed a low railing and scrambled on board, scraping an elbow in the process. He asked how he could help.

"Stand facing me, and when the pump comes up, take both hands and push down. Just keep pushin', okay?"

Boyd grabbed the horizontal handles and waited a moment, then pushed down; the handle on the other side came up and the handcar man pushed down, and they picked up speed.

"We can cover lots of ground this way. Just keep up a steady rhythm." Both men exerted the same amount of pressure, and it became easier for Boyd when he started to relax. "We gotta cross the Kankakee River 'fore three o'clock, there's a little spur there that we can pull onto and wait for the southbound freight." He spit some tobacco juice over his shoulder. "No, don't think about catching that freight."

Boyd thought he looked quite serious.

"She'll be hitting forty. You'd never make it. Besides"—he looked back to the north again—"it's 'gainst the law."

Boyd kept his head down and pumped. It felt good. His back bent into the work, and he quickly learned to use his weight on the handles, rather than push them down just with his arms. Boyd went back to his daydreaming. Visions of Laurel's flaxen hair waving across the darkening sky. He glanced over his shoulder to the south. It was getting dark. "How far is the river?"

The man kept pumping with one hand while he fished a turnip-sized pocket watch from his vest. "About ten miles. We'll be there in half an hour. Should be enough time."

"What were you gonna do about making it to the spur if I hadn't come along?"

The man didn't answer the question. "Name's Robert. What's yours?"

Boyd thought perhaps the man hadn't heard him. "Calvin, Calvin Waters." They pumped along steadily, Boyd deep into his own thoughts. In another twenty minutes or so, they crossed a steel trestle that spanned a gentle river flowing southwest.

Robert grinned. "That's the mighty Kankakee. The state hospital's over yonder . . . big fence and everything . . . oh, there's the spur." The man pointed a quarter mile ahead. They stopped the handcar and struggled to lift it one end at a time over the switch onto the spur.

"Don't you have a key for the switch, mister, so's you don't have to lift this thing? I don't know how you would have done that alone."

Again, Robert didn't answer. They settled the car on the spur and pumped till they were back several hundred feet next to an abandoned freight. Robert dug out his watch again and lovingly pried open the covered face. "Got plenty of time. Not due for five or ten minutes." Boyd walked around the abandoned freight car, killing time. They must have come twenty-five miles and he was grateful for the lift, but he sure as hell didn't know where he was and wasn't too sure if Robert knew either. The freight came thundering past, right on time. Robert had been right about that, at least. When Boyd looked around for Robert, he found him peeking around the side of the abandoned freight car. "She's a four-eight-four, big giant firebox belching out that power, and those drive wheels are six feet high. My God, what a train. Wonderful sight and sound, ain't it, Collin?"

"It's Calvin, Robert." Boyd watched the man closely. "And yeah, it's great to feel those monsters slam by. What you do for the railroad?"

They walked the handcar back to the switch, stuck the two carrying poles in the end of the car, and lifted it back onto the single track. "I'll stand backward this time so as you can see where you're going."

Boyd climbed aboard with a "Yeah, sure." For the first time, Boyd noticed that the man wore what looked like bedroom slippers. As time passed, he noted that Robert looked almost constantly at the tracks behind Boyd's shoulder.

"I'll have to leave you off in Kentland, okay? I'll be heading east from there."

"Okay. Anything you say." Boyd hesitated. "How long did you say you been working for the railroad?"

"Didn't say, Collin. Kentland in just a few minutes."

Kentland was tiny, not more than a wide spot in the road. There seemed to be only a diner and a couple of grain elevators. Robert stopped the handcar and waited until Boyd got off.

He stuck out his hand and shook Robert's paw. "Much obliged, appreciate the lift."

"Oh, think nothing of it. If you ever get over to the state capital, look me up. I'm one of the representatives there. Bon voyage."

"Whatever you say."

Robert frowned and shrugged his shoulders, making a loud *toot-toot* train sound as he stepped around to face down the tracks. Boyd gave the car a push and then stopped to catch his breath at the side of the tracks. Watching the tiny handcar vanish into the distance, he saw there wasn't a trestle or track crossing heading east, at least not as far as Boyd could see.

The diner was open, much to Boyd's relief. He ordered a hardy lunch of mashed potatoes and gravy, biscuits, and a Dr Pepper. When he finished consuming his feast, Boyd left the diner walking south. A sign at a crossroad read "Route 41." Another, "Carbondale, 30 miles." He still had a long way to go, but felt he was making decent progress. He stood at the intersection, waiting for a car or a wagon to take him south.

A six-door Dodge bus came from the south, the sign over the windshield reading, "Kankakee." It slowed at the intersection and turned west. Sitting next to the window in the third row was Robert, focused straight ahead with a beatific smile. Boyd thought Robert was pretending he didn't see him. *What in the hell is that all about?*

Boyd walked on for three or four miles. Corn grew on both sides of the road. The even rows of mounded dirt formed a brace for the foot-high stalks. Several crows walked proudly along the seeded earth. Boyd watched as the birds fretted among the immature shafts.

He could see the main road starting to bear southeast. But a country dirt road kept straight. He had a better chance for a ride on the hardtop but he didn't know how far east it might go, so he stayed straight ahead and soon came to a railroad track. He could see a trestle and something peculiar jutting out from the track above the one he was standing on. As he came closer, he could see the handcar. Robert had attempted to pull it off the track and maybe slide it down the embankment to mount it on the eastbound track. But in the meantime, it was half on and half off the track. Boyd climbed the embankment and surveyed the stricken handcar. Its wheels were off the track and sitting at a peculiar angle. Why Robert had left it like this, Boyd couldn't imagine.

Boyd slid one of the long poles into its metal bracket and lifted the front of the car off the railroad ties, then moved to the other end and pried with all his strength until the other set of wheels slid off; but the car was still sitting too close to the tracks. Boyd pried the front of the car around so it faced down the embankment; and then with all the effort he could muster, he shoved the heavy handcar down the steep hill, where it flipped over at the bottom. Boyd was bathed in sweat and sat on the track wondering about Robert. He hadn't appeared to be dangerous, but he had done something really foolish. The handcar on the tracks could have caused a catastrophic accident.

Boyd gazed to the south and felt the first sprinkle of rain. From his vantage point on the trestle, he could see for miles, and there was nothing. The closest building was back in Kentland, and he didn't feel like walking back. He could stay under the trestle or just start trekking; he chose to walk.

The rain was just a sprinkle at first and soothed his hot face. After he had walked a mile down the country road, it started coming down harder. The drops started to feel like marbles and formed tiny clouds when they hit the dirt, but soon the dust vanished and became mud. Boyd ran for a tree line that bordered some farmland. The trees were tall with sparse leaves, their spindly branches reaching skyward. The branches provided Boyd with very little shelter so he continued to walk, his clothes becoming soaked, his heavy shoes clumped with mud.

The water poured down his face. The rain wouldn't stop. Soon the driving wind had him leaning forward to keep his balance. The trees along a creek bed were bent almost in half, their leaves flying and vibrating, creating a high-pitched clicking sound. Dried cornstalks flew through the air, and Boyd dodged them. Wet grasses and stalks mixed into a smell of fresh-cut hay. Boyd tried to shield his eyes, and a tin sign with

"Dekalb" printed on it passed just inches from his head as he ducked. Boyd came upon a rabbit hunched down in the middle of the road. It never moved as he passed by. The skin around its eyes peeled back, its ears stretched across its body, the rabbit looked as if it were moving at sixty miles an hour. He trudged on.

It had grown dark. The wind decreased but the rain continued. He crossed several creeks that had spilled over the road, their brown banks cracking and falling into the swift stream. He could barely see, but there appeared to be a house straight ahead, right in the middle of the road. He thought the road would turn, but it didn't; and there was no house, just a covered bridge.

When Boyd finally walked under its roof and collapsed onto the wooden roadbed, he had been walking for hours. The bridge acted as a tunnel, driving cold night air and rain past him. He sat hunched against wooden supports, his arms wrapped tightly around his knees.

At first light, shivering, Boyd stepped out from under the protection of the bridge. Stiff, he hobbled as if paralyzed. His wet clothes clung to his cold skin. What a night.

He had forced himself to get up every hour, walking the length of the bridge several times to keep the circulation in his limbs. He was exhausted, but started south once more.

By midmorning, his clothes were dry in all except the most important places—the crotch of his pants, his socks, and worst of all, under his arms, which chafed and bled. His back was still wet where the sun hadn't reached him. Boyd's stuffy nose and red eyes matched his heavy cough. Chest pains followed every step. He kept walking. *This is my punishment for Laurel. She didn't deserve to die like that. Could have saved her if I were there earlier. Or maybe I should have gone with her.*

A racking cough and sharp pain across Boyd's chest interrupted his thoughts. His lungs were on fire and his hunger hurt, but still he kept walking. By midafternoon, he was having trouble seeing; wandering across the road trying to keep in the center, he fell several times, not understanding why. Choking.

He had to get his gas mask. Where in the hell was it? Did Robert take it? Why couldn't he breathe? He deserved this. Laurel must have something. What was it? Why was she asking his name, was it the police? He heard more voices, they asked him questions, maybe he was dreaming.

"Whassyournamefella?"

"Huh?"

"Your name . . ."

"George, that you?"

"Okay. George, are you sick?"

"No, no. It's the gas. . . ."

"I don't think so, fella. You want to go to the hospital; you're layin' in the middle of the road and your body is hotter than a firecracker." Boyd raised his head to see a man kneeling down next to him.

"No, I'm fine," Boyd croaked. The man looped his arm under Boyd's and lifted him. Boyd couldn't keep his legs under himself. The man maneuvered him easily into the backseat of a Model T Ford. "Watch it, man, the Germans will hear us."

"You have any kinfolk round these parts?" asked the stranger.

Boyd could see a woman sitting next to the man in the front passenger seat. He couldn't hold his head up and slowly slumped into a fetal position. "Vermilion."

"Where in Vermilion, Mr. George?"

Boyd fought to stay awake. "The hotel . . . Claudia. Claudia." Boyd willed his eyes open. "No, the Grant. Ask for my mother. . . . No, I mean ask for Claudia."

The rhythm of the metal wheels clicking on the tracks and the side-to-side swaying of the coach had almost lulled Hennessy into sleep. Air moving against his face through the open window didn't revive him—it was too hot and dank to be refreshing. The east Illinois countryside was drooping as it flashed by, not only from heat and humidity, but from a steady downpour with no wind. The trees seemed sad and somehow bored to him, as if they were tired of the whole damn summer routine— provide shade, drip water, get half dried out in the steaming heat, provide shade again.

He could tell by the sea of heads stirring before him in the coach that Myrna must be making her way back up the aisle. Almost all of the heads belonged to businessmen, and the rule was simple: If Myrna slinked by sitting men, they casually turned their faces to take her in, paused for a pregnant second, and turned wistfully back to whatever they had been doing. For several minutes after her passing he was sure there was one thing men definitely weren't thinking about—their wives.

Myrna bent at the middle to accommodate her skirt over her ample derriere as she slipped in beside him. She offered him a hit from the Coca-Cola bottle in her hand. He declined with a shake of his head. Glancing behind him he caught the eye of a heavyset gentleman, whose breathing was audible because it was so labored. The man was obviously suffering more than most from the heat, and Myrna had probably raised his blood pressure another twenty points. He didn't know whether to feel pride or sadness in Myrna's effect on men. After all, to some extent he was a fraud, not deserving the envious glances the other men cast his way. Any one of them could probably have serviced the lady better than he had.

Neither of them had ever mentioned their amorous interlude. At times Myrna seemed to treat him as if they had hardly shaken hands, and at others, she nagged him almost like a wife. He found it easiest not to dwell on their relationship. He took Myrna a day at a time, or she would have his sanity. She had refused to explain her behavior in the presence of Juanita, brushing it off with "I don't want to talk about it" or "Some other time." But her mood had swung back to being self-assured, even self-satisfied, now that they were "hot on the trail of Boyd the toid."

"Dale-o, whaddya say? Think you can handle the big city?" Before he could respond she reached back over her shoulder and gave an annoyed tug through her blouse at the strap of her brassiere. "Goddamn things carry a woman around like a sack of meat." Hennessy was concerned that the heavy breather behind him would expire on the spot.

"And speaking of meat, that could be what Boyd's up to, ya know."

"Meaning?"

"The stockyards. That would be a good place to find work and blend in. No one keeps much track of people working there, and in the summer, well, you can imagine, it's the one place that it's possible for unskilled men to find work."

"Juanita said South Side. That's all she said, right?"

"Yeah, but that's a big neighborhood. She also said Pat's Place."

"You know, I'm not entirely sure what we're doing. Even if we were to find George and he knew where Boyd was . . . well, we're not police. He could just tell us to stumble off."

"Sure he could, but do you really think he would? He's got to be pretty scared, and the deal with the *Trib* lawyer still holds for Boyd. Hell, it might even be extended to George."

"So you spoke to your editor again?"

"Yes indeed—and as long as Boyd gives us his story, we'll pay for his lawyer."

"Swell. Will you pay for an extra-comfortable noose if he gets convicted?"

"Come on, Dale, you're always spoiling the sport. Anyway, I wouldn't worry about nooses at Joliet, they're using the chair these days."

"We should have hired a private investigator that knows the neighborhood."

"Nah, private dicks wouldn't have any easier time than we would on the South Side. Besides, they'd really scare away anybody who knew anything."

"Well, I'm not so sure I'm not getting scared away myself."

"How so?"

"Look, Myrna. This isn't the Bottoms of Vermilion we'll be cruising around—it's the South Side of Chicago, and—"

"I know where it is, love, remember, I live in this town." Her tone was dismissive. Clearly, that's all she was going to say about it for a while.

She settled back with her Coke, and Hennessy returned to his own thoughts.

But he had stopped dozing. He watched a small town roll by. Some workman keeping the rain off his head with an upturned jacket was peering down into the water tank for the southbound locomotive. Hennessy wondered what could possibly be so interesting in there. And Boyd, how had he gotten to Chicago, if indeed their lead was correct? Had he hitched rides, or had he hopped a freight? If he had been looking for George, as Juanita said, he'd probably wanted to lose no time getting there. As he thought about Boyd and hopping freights, he could see a fire in what appeared to be a hobo jungle camp. It seemed awfully early to be starting a fire in the damnable heat. Maybe they were cooking.

The thought of food reminded him of the dining car. "How about a little early dinner, Miss Logan?"

She didn't react to the exaggerated formality of the invite. She just rose and started on her way back through the gauntlet of turning heads. When they were seated in the diner, he asked her about all the male attention she received. Was she aware of it?

"Men, particularly businessmen, are like alley cats. They walk around in suits and act polite, but their whole world is really centered in their privates."

"Nice talk."

"You asked, Dale-o."

She picked up a menu and began to look through it—as she perused the selections, she remarked offhandedly, "Guess you're becoming a bit of a businessman yourself, aren't you." Hennessy looked at her quizzically and she continued. "The other evening at the party, you seemed to be moving into the world of investment capital."

He realized he was grateful she had noticed. "Actually, that's right. Mother always had some investment in the farm and some conservative grandma-type investments."

"Grandma-type investments? Sounds like something Vedeler would have said."

"Well, yes. But it's true. He showed me the official figures on what people made in the last five years on some of the old faithfuls and then how much could really be done with a little intelligent maneuvering. It was an eye-opener, I tell you."

"Big difference, eh?"

"My Lord, some of the fortunes just made in the last year are remarkable." He knew his voice was cracking a bit with his excitement, and that's not the picture he intended to project of Dale Hennessy at the moment. He took a breath and asked a passing waiter, in what he felt was a quietly strong and authoritative way, for "drinks for the lady and me."

He then explained to Myrna how the market worked and how he had wisely moved out of "soft gainers" into hard-money stocks. One couldn't be timid about the market; either get in or get out. He had decided to get in.

"What kind of hard-money stocks?"

"For one thing, commodities. And then, the newest in electronic holdings. I've looked over past performance and I've moved a large portion of Mother's old investments into RCA. Myrna, you wouldn't believe the potential for growth that stock has. If Mother had invested in that before now, I wouldn't even have to work at the home by now."

"But isn't the home important to you?"

"That's not the point. Men do what they have to to survive and provide for their families. Some men just do it better than others."

"Do what better than others?" He thought she might be playing him again but he had an answer this time.

"It might just be, lady, that men who do one well do the other even better."

Hennessy was proud of himself for that one, and he hoped his easy smile and command of the market were having a modicum of effect on Miss Chicago Reporter Lady. Then Myrna, head still buried in the menu, said something he couldn't make out.

"Excuse me?"

"Alley cats," she said, apparently repeating what she had mumbled earlier. Before he could respond, the waiter asked for their order.

As Myrna listed her choices for dinner, Hennessy stared out the window. He could see the countryside passing behind his own reflection. The rain had stopped and the late-evening sun was burning through bright red in the west on the left side of the train as it headed north to Chicago.

He saw a couple men in a freight car that passed slowly going the other way. One fellow was raising a half-opened tin can to his lips and the other seemed to be nursing a bottle in a brown paper bag. Hennessy looked down at the cloth napkin in front of him and thought about what Myrna had said: alley cats. He glanced up at a strange motion in the roadbed across the other side of the tracks. It appeared as though a man was coming up the side of the hill walking strangely and wearing what for all the world looked like bedroom slippers. There was a railway handcar on its side, visible several yards behind him. He wondered about all the stories there were in the world. All the alley cats of both sexes. Myrna actually looked sort of feline the way she was curled back in her chair. And himself? Well, there was a certain strange appeal in seeing himself as an alley cat. He made a mental note to think about all that when he had time.

"Wake up, George-Porge." Claudia shook Boyd's shoulders. He knew who it was; he just didn't know how he had gotten into her room.

"Why you calling me George?"

Claudia sat on the side of Boyd's bed. "Night a'fore last, the room clerk comes running upstairs beatin' on my door, saying somebody was out in the street with a guy name of George in his backseat and he wanted to drop him off with a Miss Claudia." She patted his shoulder as he lay facedown. "The onliest George I knew was that rascal that was in jail with you so I went down and took a gander. Lord, you looked a mess. The room clerk and I carried you up here. I rented you a room, although if the police find out you're here, you aren't gonna need it much."

Boyd groaned. He felt as if his head were crammed with a bag of nails. "I was walking along a dirt road. It was raining. It's kinda all I remember. I do recall talking to some guy about George, I think." Boyd rolled onto his back. "Thanks for lookin' after me. I know I didn't leave in the proper way—"

"Oh, you left, all right. It was just that you and I know you got unfinished business round these parts. What's your plan, Speedy?"

"How long did I sleep?"

"Oh, I don't know. Day or so, I guess. . . . So?"

"Yeah, right, so, I'll tell you, Claudie. I coulda stayed in Chicago and gotten lost, I don't think the cops would ever have caught me. But all I could think about was what happened to Laurel." Boyd paused. "Lying there in her kitchen, her face all smeared by blood. Who knows what everyone thinks about me running off?"

Claudia grabbed one of her movie magazines and tossed it at Boyd.

"Would you stop? Always going on about what people are gonna think about you. Numbhead. When you gonna stop worrying 'bout what other people think and start worrying about yourself? Idiot. You skedaddled off to Chicago thinking you could just put all this behind you. Damn it, Boyd, it just riles the hell outta me to see you so darn weak." Claudia was crying but she never raised a hand to her face; she just kept digging into Boyd. "You could have made something of yourself, sweetie. Maybe you still can, but you gotta start being a little bit tougher on you-know-who. Stop all this bull, a-thinkin' that everyone's against you." She paced to the door and back. "I've called the attorney. Freeman. He's on his way over."

Boyd started to speak.

"Nope. Don't say a word. You told those people in that car to take you to Claudia. Well, here you are, and Claudie's gonna give you a little advice. So you just sit back and relax. You're in my palace now and you're just another knave."

"Well, Mr. Calvin, I see you're feeling better. Miss Falk tells me you have been going through a bad patch. Needless to say, I am delighted to see that you have come to your senses regarding your recent unpleasantness, and that you are willing, if I understand Claudia correctly, to turn your-self in to the authorities."

Boyd was sitting up in bed. It had been several days of, as Freeman de-scribed it, a "bad patch," and he was finally feeling better. Boyd groggily took a sip of water from a glass on a small nightstand.

The water refreshed his parched throat. "Yeah, I suppose I have to do that."

Mr. Freeman sat in the one chair in the tiny room. "I'm of two minds about what to do in the immediate future. One: Turn yourself in today to avoid being discovered; or two, wait until you're feeling better and then tell the authorities. What do you think, Mr. Calvin?"

Boyd looked at the attorney, and then at Claudia, who was leaning against the door. "The problem, as I see it, sir, is I don't think I can get a fair trial. I was at the scene, people heard gunshots. I was seen running away. I . . ." Boyd stopped again.

Freeman seemed to be wrestling with some weighty problem. "If you believe in yourself and that you are not guilty of this crime, then, young man, you have no choice but to allow me to defend you. Look, Mr. Calvin—"

"Call me Boyd, please."

"All right, Boyd, this backwater town has its faults, Lord knows, but believe me, son, people here are decent. I'll see to it you get a fair shake. I promise you that."

Still pressed against the wood door, staring at the ceiling, Claudia of-fered, "You have to make some kind of decision, shug."

"I really feel kinda lousy. But I don't know. I guess if I get caught be-fore I have a chance to turn myself in, it wouldn't look so hot, right?"

"Yes, correct, it's late in the day, so let's think a bit here. As I understand it, just the three of us know you're here, and the room clerk."

Freeman looked to Claudia, who moved from the door and rested her hand on the attorney's shoulder.

"He won't say anythin', he's good people. We registered Boyd under a different name, so yeah, I think if we could wait until tomorrow, Mr. Pale Lips here might be feeling a little more chipper."

"Why don't I check back with you folks tomorrow, say around noon-time?" The old man gathered his tattered briefcase and shook hands with Boyd and Claudia. "Mr. Calvin, you are a fugitive. I am an officer of the court. My knowledge of your whereabouts could be most detrimental to not only my license as an attorney but my reputation in the community. Please don't do anything, shall we say, stupid. Good day."

Freeman left the room.

Boyd tossed his pillow at the door as it closed.

Claudia picked up the pillow from the base of the doorway. She smoothed it carefully with her hands and laid it gently on the bed. She sat quietly in the straight-back chair. Looped over her shoulder was a large cloth bag. She pulled a mound of knitting wool from it and quietly sorted it into some semblance of a sweater. She had finished the bodice of the piece and one sleeve. The way she touched the material made Boyd think she admired the garment's dark reds, rust-hued stripes, muted gold. Claudia hummed softly as she held the finished sleeve up to the larger piece.

"Toss me the pillow, will you?" Boyd said as he leaned against the bedstead.

Claudia ignored him and kept at her work.

"Aren't you supposed to be at the Lucky cleaning up scraps or some-thing?"

When Claudia still didn't answer, he scooted down to the end of the bed and retrieved his pillow, punching it into the headboard and flopping back into his seated position. "I guess you're steamed up at me." A street-car rattled down below, and Boyd turned toward the window. He felt a wave of nostalgia and all he could do was gaze at his hands; his nose dripped but he didn't bother to wipe it. A clock on the bed table crowded the room with its incessant ticking. Boyd finally spoke. "Whatcha makin', a scarecrow?"

Claudia glanced up at Boyd. He thought she had some secret thought, and she went back to her knit-one-purl-two-ing.

"Looks like it, Claudia. Yeah. Who you gonna get to wear that thing?"

They sat quietly for several minutes, then Boyd moved down in the

bed and curled away from Claudia, his arm wrapped around his head, trying to keep out the light. Boyd could hear the clock fighting with the
knitting needles and Claudia's half-song. "All right, damn it. Claudia, I
am sorry. What else do you want?" Claudia stopped her knitting and
folded her wool back into her bag, driving the needles deliberately into a
ball of yarn. She draped the bag over her chair back and looked at her
long, tapered fingers, the clear polish neat and clean on her nails.

"I don't know why you think the world owes you a living, Mr.
Smarty." She crossed her legs and settled in. "When I talked with Mr.
Freeman earlier this morning, he was very forgiving and positive when I
told him that you were back and wanted to give yourself up. I also found
out that he had spoken to both the chief of police and a judge about
dropping the charges against you regarding the so-called escape and the
injury of that policeman at the riot. But, of course, him being a gentleman, he didn't mention that to you today. Probably because he didn't
want to get your hopes up, with you being sick."

Claudia started getting a bit more riled. She uncrossed her leg, slamming it down against the thin rug. Boyd straightened up as she rose from
the chair and started pacing the tiny room, not speaking until she had
crossed it a dozen times.

"Some people have it all. Looks, brains, personality, style. You know,
the works. Others like me have maybe one or two of those things. Maybe
with me it was brains, but regardless, what I'm trying to say is, you gotta
be able to figure out what it is that's important about yourself and make
the most of it. Have fun with it. Live by it." Claudia stopped by the bed.
"You don't have to listen to this malarkey if you don't want to, you can
just pack up and—oh, you don't have anything to pack, do you? Oh, pity
you, poor little ruffian, no clothes, just laying there all toughlike, sportin'
that stupid tiger running up your arm. What were you thinking when
you had that done? I heard you braggin' in the lobby one day about how
you'd been drunk with your army buddies in New Jersey and you'd all
gotten a tattoo one night. Did you think it would stretch your manhood?
Did you? Did it change your life?"

Boyd tried to cover a smile.

"Don't you laugh at me, you snipe, you. You been stuck at sixteen for a hell of a long time. Don't you think it's time to grow up? Well, don't you?" Claudia grabbed her bag and started for the door.

"Claudia."

"What?"

"Stay, please."

"You came little-boying it back here, tail between your legs, all snifflin' and contrite. Then when someone goes to help you, you act the fool, spouting your manhood and generally being an ass. Oh, I don't mean just now, but ever since I laid eyes on you. Since I found you here, I see this little scared kid trying to be a big man. Trying his best to insult people and be a real smart aleck. Well, you listen to me, mister. Old Claudia won't be around if you keep acting like you been." She leaned against the door. "I've known you longer than anyone. There isn't a day goes by I don't regret not being able to take care of you when you were a tyke. But there were things out of my control—my sister, I loved her dearly, passing the way she did." Boyd could see she was fighting for control. "Then your mother while she was giving birth." Boyd knew there was something he had to ask Claudia, but only at the right time.

"I'm a person who cares about those around me, Boyd. It's the way I've always been. I been hurt also, trusting folks, falling in love. . . . Oh, you smile, yeah, go ahead. People have loved me. I know a callow twerp like you might find that hard to believe, but it's true. I didn't always appear all dried-up-lookin' like a bulldog. I used to have beautiful skin and pretty good boobs. The rest of me was all right, too. My legs were strong from the dancing, and, well, I was a little bit of all right, if you know what am I talking about. I want what's best for you, sunshine, and if you don't believe an old tramp like me, well I guess there isn't a whole hell of a lot I can do about that. You'll drift off on your own and old Claudia will keep up her cleaning of scraps and her other unmentionable nocturnal habits."

She stood weeping at the door. "Darn you. Promised myself I wasn't gonna cry about my feelings over people, let alone some ignoramus like you . . . oh, fiddle." She went out, but before the door had closed, she was

back inside. "And I'll tell you one other thing, Mr. Know-It-All. It will
be a hot day in the Arctic 'fore you run your tattooed arms through *this*
sweater." The nails in Boyd's head had gotten more plentiful. Rather
than fight the feeling, he slipped back down into the bed and wrapped a
pillow around his head. His ear was folded backward and he could hear a
muffled thumping. He thought how strange it was that both Claudia and
George had come into his life. He had known Claudia for several years,
but had really just found out who she was. A woman who loved him like
a son.

He didn't know if he would ever see George again. Boyd had wanted
to tell Claudia something about his mother, but she was so angry at him
it didn't seem the right time. He had always known that his mother had
died giving birth to him. How he knew was a mystery to him. He just
knew. Did he kill her, too? Like Claudie said, some people have it all. He
wondered if death was what he had.

Seeing Myrna in her home environment was a revelation to Hennessy.
She was not only at home at the *Trib*, she dropped the rebellious manner-
isms she used as a face to the world. Her fellow reporters, all men except
for one other woman who wasn't present during his visit, seemed to treat
Myrna with respect. They used joking sarcasm when they were with her,
but he sensed they didn't particularly resent her. Her demeanor was almost shy and retiring in the presence of her editor, a gruff, sleeves-rolled-
up fellow, chief of the state news desk according to a stenciled sign on a
door that looked like it had never closed properly.

When introduced, Mr. Henry Coble gave him a quick handshake and
asked Hennessy to take a seat. He listened carefully to Myrna's explanation of what she had been up to and Hennessy's role in the whole drama.
After the report, the man politely showed him to a desk outside and sent
a copyboy out to fetch him some coffee. Then Coble handed him the
morning edition and apologized that he needed a few minutes alone with
Myrna. The door remained open, but Hennessy couldn't make out much

of what they were saying. After about twenty minutes, Myrna reappeared and waved him in.

"Major." Myrna was definitely on her best behavior. It had been a while since she had called him that. "Mr. Coble is going to give us *Trib* backing to get downtown and look for George. But he said we can't extend the offer of help to George regarding his own defense—we can't put the paper in the role of doing that unless there's clear reason to expect he isn't guilty. We also want exclusivity with you and access to you for background material on Boyd. Mr. Coble wants me to emphasize the story that one soldier, you—a war hero—is looking for a comrade that might have gone astray. It's a great story."

"What? I'm not, well, I would like to see Boyd given a fair shake but—"

"That's just it. Here you are, at your own time and expense, on a soldier's mission to make sure a fellow veteran is dealt with fairly—I mean that's not that far off, is it?"

Far off? He didn't know—certainly no farther off than his being in Chicago with a journalistic bearcat looking for a black rapist and an escaped felon who used to reside at the home over which he presided. He had to admit, it was exciting to think he might finally be getting public attention for something—it didn't get much bigger than the *Chicago Trib*. He looked at his feet and mumbled a response to Myrna, who had assumed the role of negotiator for her editor. The latter seemed to be silently appraising both of them during the exchange.

"Guess not," Hennessy said.

"Pardon?"

"Guess not, I mean I guess it's not far off." When he really thought about it, heck, her appraisal of his motives was accurate enough.

The paper hired a car and driver to assist them in their quest. Myrna seemed to shed her *Trib* persona before leaving the building. Hennessy had been to Chicago several times before, but he still felt a bit the bumpkin in her presence. The paper had arranged a hotel for Hennessy, but they decided to head right down to the South Side rather than stop and get him settled in a room. Instead of exiting on Michigan Avenue, she took him out through the Circulation Department to a back entrance to meet the car. Here she was already more the Myrna he was coming to know. A couple of whistles followed her passing, and she answered the catcalls with a nonchalantly raised middle finger. "Any time, doll" came back in response from one of the men, but it seemed more a ritual exchange than anything.

On the loading platform she spoke with a couple of dock supervisors about something and then rejoined him. She led him to a Model A with no *Trib* markings of any type and a driver who seemed as though he could be an off-duty grocer. It took almost an hour to make their way to the South Side and find the establishment Juanita had indicated George might frequent.

Hennessy's earlier observation had been correct: The South Side of Chicago looked and felt a lot different than the Bottoms of Vermilion. The stares from the denizens of Pat's speakeasy were piercing—no sign of curiosity or accommodation, only a quick assessment that it wasn't the law or anyone to be concerned about. When they turned away it was because they had lost interest.

Hennessy and Myrna walked toward a vacant gap in the bar and stood. There were no stools at this point, just a brass rail on which to rest their feet. The barkeep, who may also have been the owner, wiped the same glass again and again with a white towel, seemingly oblivious of their presence and expectant looks. People were calling him Pat.

"I can't believe we're doing this," Hennessy mumbled under his breath to Myrna. "This is not what I would call a friendly reception."

"Just be thankful you're not a colored guy walking into a white bar in an Irish or Italian part of town—now that would be unfriendly. Compared to that, this is a welcome party."

Hennessy inspected the bar more closely while waiting for the reluctant barkeep to acknowledge their presence. He was surprised to note in the roiling sea of black faces that there were three white faces in one booth who looked very comfortable. They were engaged in animated conversation among themselves and with several black people who shared the wooden alcove.

"Ah hep you?" The huge bartender had finally edged within speaking distance. He was still studying the glass he was polishing but had at least conceded their existence.

Assuming he was expected to take charge, Hennessy decided that regardless of how uncomfortable it felt, he was going to assert himself. Damn it, he wasn't in the mood for guff from Myrna or surly bartenders or anybody else. He heard what he realized must have been his own disembodied voice say, "Yeah, you can help, I'd like a drink and so would the lady—that's why we're standing here."

"What sorta drink?" If Pat noticed the sharp edge to Hennessy's remark, he didn't show it.

"Beer for me and Canadian whiskey for the lady."

"We got near beer and dark whiskey and light whiskey, don' know nothin' about Canadian—you think this is uptown?"

"Any whiskey is fine . . . and the near beer is fine, too."

The man reached under the counter and pulled out a bottle of dark whiskey. He poured it into a glass and laid it down in front of Myrna. Then he brusquely slapped a beer down in front of Hennessy, making him jump slightly.

"Dollatwenny."

Silently furious that his nervousness had been exposed by the man's maneuver, Hennessy wondered if Myrna had noticed. While counting out his change he felt Myrna brush by him and place an elbow on the bar. He watched her in the mirror as she smiled at the big man and said, "Look, we're not the police—we'd just like to ask you a couple questions."

The man ignored Myrna and looked into Hennessy's eyes. "Ah know you not the police, you look too sorry-ass to be the police. Maybe you and Legs here should tell me what you want. Miss Ofay might get more'n she can handle and not want to leave, she hang around too long."

Hennessy tried hard to maintain his composure—he would *not* be intimidated. "We're looking for somebody, and if we find him maybe we can help him out."

"That so? Hmm, don' tell me now, let me guess. You here looking for George Matthews."

There went the composure. "Well, yes . . . but . . . how did you know that?"

"Easy. 'Cept for that table of jass players over there, they's been three white people in this bar in the last two weeks. You are two of 'em and the other one asked for George, too. Figured he must be collecting crackers for something, maybe to build a white rice museum."

"Look, bartender." Myrna couldn't stay out of it. "We're not looking for trouble, we're just asking if you could help—"

The big man interrupted here, again addressing Hennessy, not Myrna. "Help? Shiiit, mister, you crazy taking this white woman down here, you know that? And tell this cooze with the big white legs I ain't the bartender. My name's Pat and I own this place."

Hennessy had no time to reply. Myrna took over the conversation in her own way. Pat suddenly had a full glass of whiskey rolling down his cheek. Myrna, with her finger in his face, leaned across the bar. "Look, pal, you have something to say *about* me you can damn well say it *to* me, get my meaning?"

Their whole end of the speakeasy had turned to take in the scene, and many patrons now mirrored the jaw-hanging, stunned look on Pat's face.

"Myrna, for God's sake." Hennessy had his hand on her shoulder but she shrugged him off.

"Talking to me like I'm not here, making veiled threats . . . big man, eh?" Myrna dropped her purse and stepped back, glancing about wide-eyed, as if looking for something more potent than whiskey to hurl in Pat's direction. The whole end of the bar was quiet enough that everyone could hear her running commentary to Pat, who stood catatonic watching her performance.

"He didn't bring me anywhere, buster. I don't need anybody bringing me anywhere." She kicked a stool over. "Big black bully—uptown you'd be playing step-and-fetch-it, here you're a big man."

"Damn, Pat, I b'lieve she kick yo' ass, son." The remark came from a tall man with a glint in his eye and an amused look on his face. He was perched at the portion of the bar that had stools instead of a brass step—he'd had to jump out of the way when Myrna kicked the empty stool over. Several others responded with a "Wooeee" and "That mama a handful, she a pistol, man."

To Hennessy, it was one of his bad dreams run amok. Myrna seemed beside herself, shaking with anger and frustration and provoked out of proportion to the insult. Even waving her arms about it was still apparent that she was trembling. Pat had really set her off.

"Cooze? I can't believe you called me that." Suddenly Myrna had her shoe off, and she looked as if she was ready to fling it at Pat when a strong black hand arrested her arm.

"Whoa, mama, whoa." It was the man who had first remarked that now stepped in to subdue the crazy white woman. He lifted Myrna firmly off the ground from behind in a powerful bear hug. With her arms pinned but her feet kicking the air wildly, he brought her over to Hennessy.

"Hey, guvner, you lose this wildcat?" The whole place dissolved in laughter. Even Pat, glancing around at his customers clapping one another on the back and stamping their feet, seemed to go along with the good-natured turn of events. He broke into a smile and shook his head, as if this was just one more trial in the day of a professional speakeasy boss.

"Now I gonna put ya down, lady, if you promise not to go throwing drinks or whacking anybody, you hear?"

"Just put me down, Sambo!" The remark brought the house down again.

"He ain' Sambo, he the Kingfish, mama." Hennessy heard a couple more Amos 'n Andy remarks and wondered if there was any way he could possibly shrink into the woodwork and not ever be noticed again.

"I got all day, sweetness; ah put you down when you stop kickin'."

Myrna, rendered helpless and probably aware of how ridiculous she must look, seemed to calm down—Hennessy had the feeling she was also mollified somehow by the man's tone, which managed to carry an element of gentleness along with its authority.

Hennessy grabbed Myrna by the elbow when the man set her down. Somehow he wasn't surprised at the tears starting to stream down her face. This seemed to happen when she was extremely angry or sad or embarrassed. Her hard, smart-talking shell dissolved into salt water when any strong feelings surfaced. She had once referred to this tendency as the "Irish curse," but he suspected it was a specifically Myrna factor.

Hennessy was not taking chances. He hustled her toward the door, although she was now compliant, like a reprimanded child. The men in the bar let loose with a hail of salutations as she was escorted out. "Later, mama . . . and bring that fine ofay behine when you come back!" Hennessy pulled her hand down as he ushered her through the door into what was becoming night. She had extended it over her head in a final obscene gesture, which was all she could muster in response to the verbal barbs.

Hennessy saw that the *Trib* car had moved about a half block up. He wasted no time talking as he steered her, hand firmly on her elbow, toward the mobile sanctuary. She was blessedly silent. When they were almost there, he felt a strong grip on his own elbow. He swallowed hard when he turned to see the man his ward had just insulted looking intently at him. This is what it must feel like to be on the cusp of hand-to-hand fighting, something he had never experienced in the war.

"Hold on a minute there, folks."

"You?" from Myrna.

"Yeah, it's me, Sambo." The man said it without rancor.

"Look, we're sorry," Hennessy started, "that just all got out of hand, crazy in there."

"Yeah, I'd say." The three of them stood mute. The black man studied Myrna carefully, but she refused to say anything. She only returned the man's look with a now-sniffling defiance.

Then the man broke into a smile, backed up half a step, and extended his hand. Hennessy accepted the offer and shook hands, hoping the extent of the relief he felt wasn't apparent.

The man then turned to Myrna, did a slight but gracious bow, and extended his hand to her. "Ma'am, they was no reason for folks to pick on you in there like that. Pat shouldn't have been disrespectful and called you that name. Everyone deserves respect until they prove otherwise."

"And he shouldn't have spoke to Dale like I wasn't there."

"Thass right, and spoke like you wasn't there." Hennessy felt for all the world that he was watching a schoolteacher talk to a tomboy who'd just been disciplined after a playground fight. How could the woman be so tough and so fragile at the same time?

"If my brothers were around, nobody would have been speaking to me like that," she added, still sniffling.

"Ah, you got some tough Mick brothers, do ya?"

"How do you know I'm Irish?"

"Shit, how you know I'm black?"

That seemed to do it. Myrna laughed despite herself. After she wiped the remnant of her tears away with her sleeve, she commented softly, "Yeah, well, I'm sorry I said some things, too."

"Yeah, you did! Why I figures I jus' shuffle on up the street heah and get me a lantern so's I can light your way."

Myrna now had a broad grin. "Like I said, I apologize. . . . You know, you're pretty strong."

"Oh heckens, Miss, eh, Miss . . ."

"Logan."

"Miss Logan, you light as a feather." He winked at Hennessy. "Mean as a snake but light as a feather."

"Yeah, well, anyway, thanks for helping, but we gotta go." Myrna's whole presence had lightened but her businesslike tone had returned.

"Sho-nuff, ah be goin', too, but I couldn't help hear you say you was looking for that Matthews fella—Joe, George, something like that?"

"You know him?" Hennessy and Myrna chorused.

"Yeah, ah met 'im. Don't know'm well but he seemed a real nice fella, salt-of-the-earth kinda guy. I was wondering why you were looking for him."

The three of them got into the back of the news car and watched the sun go down. The driver had disappeared and returned with a bottle of light whiskey and three glasses. He looked less the grocer and more the citywise chauffeur when he wasn't crouched behind the wheel. He had pulled down a collapsible seat in the back of the Ford so their guest could sit facing Hennessy and Myrna.

"So, you're saying you met the white fella George was with, too?" Hennessy was amazed at their luck.

"Yeah, he was a funny cat but ol' George seemed to like him and was taking care of him. That George, he knows a lot of people. Good-lookin' guy, you know, snappy dresser, smooth with the ladies—he a devil, that boy is."

Myrna had pulled out a notepad but wasn't writing. She quietly studied the man and let Hennessy do the talking. It occurred to Hennessy that he still didn't know the man's name.

"Sorry, you said your name was . . . ?"

"Didn't say. See, Miss Logan? Us black folk sometimes go through life having people talk like we wasn't there, too. So I know why ol' Pat talking like that kind of got to ya. My name's Roland, and thanks for asking, Major."

Hennessy noted a curious thing about Roland's speech. He sometimes sounded like an Amos 'n Andy caricature, but moments later he could be mistaken for an educated white man. He would mention that to Myrna later—right now she had slipped into a quiet I'm-just-here-taking-notes-and-enjoying-the-company demeanor as he asked the questions.

"Now, you know that George is wanted for raping that white woman in Vermilion?"

"Mister, that's a pile. Ol' George, he ain't the type needs to rape any woman, black or white." Roland seemed particularly intent on making this point.

"Why are you so sure?"

"The George I know ain't no saint, mind you, but he don't treat women that way—he just simply don't."

"So you know him pretty well, do you?"

"Excuse me." Myrna suddenly broke in as if something about the line of questioning was making her uncomfortable. "I'd like to get back to Boyd, if you don't mind." But then she looked to Hennessy to continue rather than pursue the questions herself.

"That the white man George was with?" Roland asked.

"Yes, it is."

Hennessy hesitated a moment, then added, "Well, Roland, I know this has been a strange way to get introduced, but we're really not here to hurt either George or Boyd. In fact, it might be that we can actually help Boyd out in his defense."

"Why you wanna help?"

"The best reason, self-interest." Myrna was suddenly taking over. "I'm a reporter doing a story, and he's good grist for the tale. Also, the Major here used to know him and doesn't think he's the sort that would have murdered those people." Hennessy nodded his agreement with her assessment, then sat back and took the role he was more used to with Myrna— observer. Observer and something else. What? Lover? Friend? Partner? Just what was he to Myrna? He found he had been asking himself that question more and more.

He took a sip of the white whiskey as Myrna continued. He noticed Roland at one point appraising him out of the corner of his eye while Myrna asked questions and started making notations in her pad.

"So, do you think if we find George he can help us get to Boyd?"

"Nah, I don't think he knows where Boyd is."

"Why do you say that?"

"Well, I seen George just a couple days ago and he tol' me Boyd went home."

"Went home?" Hennessy saw Myrna's head pop up in sync with his own. "Why would he do that?"

"Because the damn fool says he's innocent and thinks he has to go back to face the music, you know, set things right."

Hennessy couldn't contain himself. "Are you telling me that Boyd's back in Vermilion?"

"Don't know, but George said he's heading that way."

"Well . . . I mean, when?"

"Probably left yesterday."

"Yesterday! But, I thought—" Myrna stopped Hennessy with a hand on his arm.

"Look, Roland. Thanks for telling us all this. I do have one question for you."

"Yes'm."

"Do you think . . . does George think that Boyd committed those murders?"

The black man pulled at his chin reflectively and replied, "Doubt it, ma'am. I surely think George is of the opinion that white boy is a caution in all kinds of ways, but he is not a murderer." There was not the twinkle-in-the-eye humor evident in most of his responses. He looked straight at Myrna and then turned to Hennessy. He didn't blink at all.

Myrna flapped her pad shut. "Well, I guess we're wasting our time here then, aren't we?" But she made no move to leave. She sat sipping her drink in silence for a moment as they soaked in the sounds of street bustle and the odor of chicken frying in a nearby eatery. They were all sweating again, as even the slight breeze they had encountered on leaving Pat's seemed to have abated. Hennessy had the feeling something that he wasn't keyed in to was happening in the car. He started feeling restless as neither Myrna nor their new acquaintance made a move to end the stalemate.

"Okay, then." Myrna seemed to come to some conclusion. "Guess it's time to go. I don't think you'll be needing that hotel room after all, Dale."

Hennessy muttered an affirmative response. Myrna fixed the ebony-skinned man in her gaze again, but he couldn't tell in the darkening car what her expression was saying. Finally, she asked him, "What're you thinking? You seem to be looking inside of me."

Roland chuckled and glanced away for a second. He cut his eyes at Hennessy as if he were eavesdropping on a private conversation. Then he looked back at Myrna and said, "You don't have no big tough Mick brothers, do you?"

After a pause Myrna responded, "No, guess not, at least none that would come stand up for me."

"Okay, then. I guess I be goin'. You take care of yourself, tiger lady. And you too, mister. Good luck in finding yo' man." Roland leaned into the door and started to step out as it swung open into the street.

Myrna stopped him with a hand on his arm. Hennessy couldn't see her face but could tell from the way the man was looking back at her that he was getting the full Myrna see-through stare.

"You really didn't, did you."

"Didn't what?"

"You really didn't rape that woman, did you, George?"

"No I didn't, tiger. I really didn't." He lifted her hand from his arm gently, patted it with his other hand, and repeated, "I surely didn't." Then Hennessy watched George Matthews slip into the night. And something else—he watched Myrna Logan watch George Matthews slip away.

TUESDAY, OCTOBER 22

*H*ear ye, hear ye, all rise, the Fifth Circuit Court for the great state of Illinois is now in session this twenty-second day of October, nineteen hundred and twenty-nine. The Right Honorable Judge Malcolm Everett presiding; please remain standing." The bailiff called the court into session, and the packed courtroom waited.

The judge looking out over the assembly seemed to be surveying his flock, and was obviously savoring this moment. He said softly, "Ladies and gentlemen, welcome to my courtroom. Before we begin today, I will remind you of the grave responsibility we face in this trial and how its outcome will affect our society. Furthermore . . . I expect absolute decorum in my court, meaning there are to be no outbursts or demonstrations of any kind, is that clear?"

Boyd thought that the judge had forgotten what else he was going to say. After a few moments, he abruptly sat down and began riffling through some papers on his desk. The bailiff finally walked up the several steps to the judge's bench and whispered into his ear. The judge looked embarrassed and waved one hand at the courtroom. "Ah, yes, please be seated."

Boyd and Freeman exchanged looks. Boyd had been willing himself for several hours to be calm, to stay focused and accept that things would progress in a reasonable fashion and that there was nothing much he could do about the results. He had managed to calm himself, but this beginning unnerved him again.

The judge nodded to the clerk of the court. "Vincent, would you read the charges, please."

The clerk stood. "The people of the state of Illinois versus Mr. Boyd Calvin, who is charged with two counts of murder in the death of one

Laurel Wheaton Calvin and Ralph Sheridan on or about June sixth, 1929." Boyd caught his breath when he heard Laurel's name; it was hard for him to believe he was sitting in a courtroom being tried for the murder of someone he had loved so deeply.

The judge looked out at the courtroom. "Mr. State's Attorney Wolski, proceed with your opening statement, please."

Boyd had watched the dapper Phillip Wolski in the previous week as the court selected a jury, a process the attorneys referred to as "voir dire." He seemed careful and polite to Boyd, never saying anything until he had thought about it, and always addressing the potential juror in a considerate manner. There was something dangerous about him. The man had quick eyes and impatient hands. His permanent smile made Boyd uncomfortable, as if he had already been found guilty and the trial was a mere formality.

"Good morning, gentlemen." Twelve men of various ages and occupations had been selected for the jury, along with two alternates. Wolski had used all of his preemptory strikes to attain the jury he wanted, and now he was addressing them as a group for the first time. "I'm sorry about this Indian-summer heat. I hope you will all be comfortable." He glanced at Boyd. "It's a shame that because of certain circumstances we have to endure this. If there is anything we can get for you, please do not hesitate to ask."

He spoke to them as if they were guests in his home. *The bastard.*

Freeman scribbled a quick note to Boyd: "Full of bull, don't worry."

Wolski rested his hands on the railing separating him from the jury.

"This is a fairly straightforward case, gentlemen. The evidence will show how Mr. Boyd Calvin, with malice aforethought, deliberately and intentionally took the life of his ex-wife and her innocent companion, Mr. Ralph Sheridan; how Mr. Calvin lay in wait to avenge his honor; how Mr. Calvin deliberately, and with an abandoned and malignant heart, shot and killed his wife and then turned the pistol on his rival, Mr. Sheridan. Evidence will show that in grim anticipation of his demise at the hands of a vengeful murderer, Mr. Calvin's victim underlined the very passage in the Bible that presaged his own death. Testimony will show that Mr. Calvin was seen leaving his ex-wife's premises, and that Mr. Calvin brazenly brandished his pistol at several innocent people who approached the back porch of Mrs. Calvin's home as he attempted to flee. That Mr. Calvin left those premises and was not seen again for a number of days, finally being captured by the Bureau of Investigation for flight into the state of Indiana, and that, to compound his guilt, several days later, during arraignment, he and another prisoner were responsible for a disturbance that turned into a riot while being transferred from the courthouse to the county jail. During this riot, gentlemen, an officer of the law, Officer Tom Blake, while in the performance of his duty, was felled with a crippling injury; and subsequently, as the evidence will show, Mr. Calvin became, once again, a fugitive from the law. Gentlemen, this man"—the state's attorney pointed at Boyd—"Mr. Calvin, is indeed a menace to society. A man who kills without conscience and a man who, and I think you will agree, should be taken off the streets."

Boyd watched as the state's attorney adopted a long-suffering look. Boyd then glanced toward the jury; to a man, they were staring at him. He had never seen such anger, and he felt himself inching lower into his hard-bottomed chair.

"Thank you, citizens, for your attention on this sweltering day." Wolski smiled his best smile at the jury and, with a slight swagger, slowly walked back to his chair.

Freeman shuffled some papers in front of him and rose from his seat. Without actually addressing the jury, he spoke. "Well, I think that now, in my seventieth year, I have finally heard it all."

Boyd could see the tension in Freeman's body.

"This state's attorney, Mr. Wolski, has the audacity to blame my client for the weather."

"Objection, Your Honor. I did no such a thing." Wolski was on his feet.

Boyd watched as the judge looked to Freeman. "Your Honor, his implication was quite clear. Mr. Wolski has an obligation to stay with the issue brought forth by this court and not try to implicate my client in matters over which he has no control. Also, the event of the street riot is not relevant to this case and should not have been mentioned in Mr. Wolski's opening statement. I move for a mistrial, Your Honor."

Judge Everett snapped, "Denied." The judge pulled out a folded white handkerchief. "You'll have to admit, Counsel, it is hot, and I would appreciate it if you would move along."

"Thank you, Your Honor," Freeman politely addressed the judge. "It is hot, and a man's life is at stake." It seemed Freeman had made his point and he turned to the jury. Boyd couldn't help but feel he was going to be part of a nasty scrap if they were even arguing about the weather.

"We are all interested in stories, gentlemen. The state's attorney has woven a tale of intrigue and deception, a fascinating yarn of murder, riots, escape, and capture. 'Abandoned and malignant heart,' Mr. Wolski called it. 'Malice aforethought.' All very curious fictional reading as such, but malice aforethought? I think not. I, on the other hand, would like to give you a short *non*fictional account of my client, Mr. Boyd Calvin." Boyd felt self-conscious as Freeman gestured toward him, referring to him as if he were a lump of salt.

"Boyd is—and I hesitate here to use the term, but must—a bastard. He was born on the wrong side of the blanket. There seems to be no other word for it, my friends. A bastard. An illegitimate baby."

Boyd watched Freeman as he paced in front of the jury. He had no idea what the lawyer hoped to gain by calling him a bastard.

"I say this because I would like you to know who this man is, this citizen of Vermilion, who is fighting for his life today. This man who distinguished himself and fought bravely for his country in the Great War. A young man who spent years recuperating from the stress of battle, recuperating, I must say, in the local Soldiers' Home. A young man who, along with his wife, attempted to build a life here in Vermilion, in this community. A local boy." He made a point of glancing at Wolski. "Gentlemen, this is not a criminal. We, the defense, will be most pleased to prove to you beyond a shadow of a doubt that Boyd Calvin did not, I repeat, did not, commit this atrocious crime. Thank you."

The judge looked at the prosecutor. "Call your first witness, Mr. Wolski."

"Yes, Your Honor, the state calls Mr. Charles Decker."

The bailiff swore him in.

Boyd had never seen his boss with a tie on; his dark suit looked wrinkled and tight. He looked very much as if he would rather be someplace else. Boyd wondered why they would call him.

Wolski stepped to the witness stand. "Mr. Decker, you are employed by the Vermilion Light Rail Company."

"Yes, sir."

"In what capacity, sir?"

"I'm superintendent of the shops, sir."

"And as superintendent, did you yourself have occasion to hire Mr. Boyd Calvin?"

"Yes, sir, I mean no, sir, I didn't really hire him. I had nothing to do with hiring him. I was given him by my superiors. But he was not my choice. I mean, I used him but I didn't hire him, sir."

Boyd glanced at Freeman. It looked as if Freeman felt as disgusted with Decker as Boyd did.

"Mr. Decker, what kind of employee was Mr. Calvin?"

Decker looked around the courtroom, and when he caught Boyd's eye, he quickly looked down. "Oh, he was just average, I'd say."

"Were there ever any disciplinary problems with Mr. Calvin?"

Decker fidgeted in his chair. "Yes, quite a few, actually."

"Describe a few of these problems, please."

Decker chewed on his bottom lip, looked at the jury, and spoke. "He was trouble, right from the beginning. Always mouthing off, telling jokes. Just a day before he killed those people—"

"Objection, Your Honor." Freeman had not stood up.

The judge looked to the witness. "Sustained. Mr. Decker, restrict your testimony to the facts of the case."

Decker dropped his head. It looked to Boyd as if he was angry. "Yes, Your Honor."

Wolski cleared his throat, a half smile on his face. He seemed pleased that Decker had stated his case for him. "Mr. Decker, you were saying, 'Just a day before.' What exactly were you about to say?"

"Well, just the day before the . . . incident, I had to have Boyd into my office, something about a letter someone wrote about him, pushing people around violently or such on his trolley. That's what he does, drive the trolley."

Boyd quickly wrote a note to Freeman saying that the letter had been about his missing some people at night because he hadn't seen them; Decker's version was a lie. Freeman asked Boyd if the letter would still be in the files. Boyd nodded.

Wolski seemed to be enjoying himself. "So, Mr. Decker, would it be fair to say that Mr. Calvin was a problem employee? That he had become violent at times, and had been a disruptive force at the trolley barn?"

"Yes, I would say that would be fair."

Wolski walked back to his table and picked up a half-page document. "Do you own a bicycle, Mr. Decker?"

"Yes, I do, Mr. Wolski."

"And could you tell us what happened to said bicycle on the date in question?"

"Yes, well, I leave my bicycle at work sometimes, so that at lunch hour I can ride around a bit. And on the morning of the sixth, I noticed it was missing, and I immediately thought of Boyd as having taken it."

Freeman got on his feet. "Your Honor, could you restrict Mr. Decker to the facts in the case and leave the suppositions to others."

The judge turned again to Decker. "Mr. Decker, please, I will not admonish you again, sir, I will hold you in contempt. Stick to the facts."

"Yes, sir. Where was I . . ."

Wolski leaned against the jury box, seemingly amused. "The bicycle. You were going to tell us about it."

"Yes, well, it was missing when I came to work and I was just about to call the police and report him—I am sorry, report it—when an officer came to my shop with the bicycle, asking if it was mine."

"Thank you, Mr. Decker. You have been most helpful."

The large man attempted to lever his girth from the witness stand, but

Freeman was already on his feet. "Just one moment, Mr. Decker. I know you're anxious to get to lunch, but I would like for you to straighten out a few points."

Tittering in the courtroom as the man plopped down. Decker looked to the judge for help.

The judge leaned toward him. "It is customary for the defense to be able to cross-examine after the state."

The superintendent settled back into his chair.

"Mr. Decker, what is the average length of time your employees stay at your place of business?"

Decker thought for a bit. "Oh, I couldn't rightly say. Maybe two, three years. We don't have a pension plan, so most of the fellows tend to move on. There's a couple old-timers, but yeah, I'd say three years."

"Do you know how long Mr. Calvin was employed by the Vermilion Light Rail Company?"

It looked as if Decker had built a trap for himself. "I can't remember."

"Really? It wouldn't be hard for us to find out, would it, Mr. Decker?"

Decker pretended to search his memory. "I'd guess five years or so."

"Thank you. Five years? And yet by your admission, he was only an 'average employee,' is that correct?"

Decker didn't answer. Freeman looked to the judge. The judge spoke. "The question requires an answer, Mr. Decker."

"Well, like I said, he was trouble." Decker flashed a look at Freeman.

"Trouble, truly? Why didn't you get rid of him?" Freeman again waited for an answer, then shrugged and went on. "Or why didn't you take your case to your superiors?" He raised his voice. "Mr. Decker, he had been there longer than your 'average' employee. But according to you, he was trouble. Was he always 'trouble,' or did he become 'trouble' when you found out he was a fugitive?"

Wolski rose from his seat. "Objection, Your Honor. I believe the question has been asked and answered."

"Sustained."

Decker sat mute.

Boyd could see that Freeman was unfazed. The lawyer kept after his former boss.

"Mr. Decker, I want you to clear your mind for a moment and think about this so-called letter stating that Mr. Calvin was violent with some of the passengers. Is this an article you can produce, Mr. Decker? If I was to subpoena that letter from your company's archives, is that letter going to reproduce the statements made here by you?"

Decker started breathing hard. Freeman waited. Finally, he asked, "Was there a letter, Mr. Decker? And if so, did it so state that Mr. Calvin had become violent with some passengers? Answer, sir."

Decker fished for a handkerchief and began shaking his head.

"You're nodding your head, but the stenographer cannot note that. A 'yes' or 'no' is required."

"No."

"No what?"

"I might have been wrong. Yeah, there was a letter, but I might have been wrong about him being violent. . . . It might have been someone else."

"Thank you, Mr. Decker. No further questions." Freeman glanced toward the state table with its three high-powered lawyers.

The judge declared a one-hour recess.

The afternoon became even hotter. The old stone courthouse soaked up the sun's rays, and the courtroom, on the southwest side of the building, was stifling. A forensics expert was in the process of telling the prosecutor about fingerprints.

"The three main types of prints, sir, are arches, loops, and whorls. Loops are the most prevalent in the print itself, followed by whorls and arches."

Boyd wondered why Freeman didn't just acknowledge that his client had been at the scene.

The state's attorney paused. "Thank you, sir, for your expertise. Could you now describe, please, how you were able to match the latent print found at the scene to the defendant, Mr. Calvin."

"Yes, of course. The defendant's prints are consistent with the print found at the scene on the edge of an enamel kitchen table. The right slope loop of the right-hand index finger is identical to the defendant's."

"Any other matches?"

"There was a partial print taken from the screen door that is consistent with the defendant's right thumbprint. In other words, there is what we call an 'accidental' whorl on the right thumb of both the defendant and on the screen door handle. . . . There are at least nine other points of identity that are consistent with the defendant's."

"Is there any doubt in your mind, sir, based on your extensive expertise, that this is one and the same person?"

"None."

"Thank you. No further questions."

Freeman never got up from his chair. He spoke respectfully but in a curt manner. "Sir, could you tell the jury how you happened to be here today?"

"I was asked by the state's attorney's office to provide my expert advice on these latent prints, sir."

"And how did they contact you?"

"They called my office in Chicago."

"And are you being paid here today?"

"Yes, sir."

"So the state called you in the big city and paid for, I assume, your transportation, room, board, and salary, is that correct?"

"Yes."

"Why didn't they use someone from Vermilion, sir?"

"I guess it's just too small of a town to have—"

"Thank you. Sir, you stated for the jury before your testimony regarding the fingerprints that you are a forensics expert, is that correct, and that you have fingerprint-analysis expertise?"

"Yes, sir."

"And sir, if you will, explain for the jury just exactly what that means."

"Why, yes. I believe I have gained expertise through my years of experience and the number of cases I have been involved with."

"What fingerprint system do you use, sir?"

"The Henry system, of course."

"Sir, are you not aware of the Vucetich system?"

"I am sorry, I didn't catch the name."

"Vucetich."

"No, sir."

"Well, sir, for your edification, the Vucetich system is used in more than half of the world's police stations. Matter of fact, it is a system that is used almost exclusively in all of the Spanish-speaking countries of the world."

"I didn't know that. We use the Henry system."

"I see. I have no further questions for the expert witness at this time." From Freeman's expression and manner, one would have thought he had just finished questioning an idiot. Freeman leaned in toward Boyd. "Doesn't mean much, but anytime we can show a little doubt to the jury regarding a so-called expert witness, it's one for our side."

During the short recess, Boyd sat toying with a glass of water. He felt someone's eyes burrowing into the back of his neck. When he turned, he saw Claudia three rows back on the aisle. She blew him a kiss. It was very brief and no one saw it except Boyd. Boyd felt good about seeing Claudia; she was always on top of everything. He nodded to her and was startled to hear the voice of the clerk telling everyone to rise.

The judge slid into his seat and pointed to the state's attorney. "You may proceed."

"The state calls Officer Steven Billings."

The police officer hurried to the witness stand and was duly sworn in, and Wolski began.

"Officer Billings, would you tell us the circumstances of your having been called to the deceased's address the morning of June sixth, 1929?"

"Well, I arrived at the scene and there were quite a number of people in the street and some peering into a back window, which I subsequently found out was a kitchen. I tried to clear the people from the immediate vicinity and looked through the window. I could see a man seated at the kitchen table. He was slumped over with his head resting on some books and papers." The officer glanced nervously at his notes. "There was blood visible. He seemed to be deceased. I asked to use a neighbor's phone. I called my sergeant and told him of the circumstances, and he said 'hold tight' until help arrived in the form of a detective."

"Officer Billings, what did you do next?"

"There were some people in the orchard wheeling a bicycle toward me." The officer once again looked at his notes. "The people said it didn't belong there. 'It's not hers.' Meaning, I guess, the deceased woman's, and maybe I should take a look at it. Well, sir, it was Charles Decker's bicycle. Which I found out later. And so I secured it next to my patrol car."

"What did you do next, Officer?"

"Well, I waited for the detectives to arrive, and oh yeah, I talked to some of the people about what they had seen and heard."

Wolski looked a little disappointed. "Which was . . ."

"Well, it seemed the defendant came out on—"

"Objection, Your Honor, calls for hearsay."

"Sustained." The judge admonished the officer. "Keep your remarks to the facts of the case, as you have personal knowledge, please."

The officer seemed confused. "Well, they said it was him."

"Anything else?"

"No, sir. Well, yes, I walked up on the porch and looked through the kitchen screen door. I started to go in but I could see a pair of women's legs sticking out from under the table. There was a lot of blood."

The courtroom grew quiet.

"I sat on the end of the porch and waited for the detective."

After Wolski had thanked the officer and moved away, Freeman strolled to the witness stand as if he had all the time in the world.

"How long have you been a policeman, Officer Billings?"

"Come December it'll be fourteen years, sir."

"In those fourteen years, you've seen a fair number of dead bodies, I shouldn't wonder."

"Yes, sir."

"And of that *fair* number, have you always been able to tell if someone was dead just by looking at them from a distance?"

The officer once again glanced at his notes as if the answer might be there. "Well, sir, if you're referring to my looking into—"

"Just answer the question, please. Are you able to determine if someone is dead by just looking? Seems a simple enough question."

"No, sir. I cannot, always."

"So your looking through the window and ascertaining that Ralph Sheridan was dead might possibly have been a mistaken judgment. Is it at all possible that he might still have been alive?"

"He seemed dead . . . but yes, sir."

"So, Officer Billings, Ralph Sheridan might still have been breathing?"

The officer now seemed resigned. "Yes, it's possible."

"Is it true, Officer, that you were raised not far from the deceased's home and that you were well acquainted with many of the onlookers at this crime scene?"

"Yes, sir, I went to school close by and knew a lot of the folks."

"It became kind of a party scene?"

"Well, sir, insofar as I was the only officer there and, well, some of the folks were doing some gawking—"

"You allowed the scene to spin out of control, then, sir?"

"I tried—"

"You tried what? Isn't it true, sir, that you marched several of your friends up onto the porch to get a better look at these poor victims inside?"

"Yes."

"Yes what?"

"A couple of the ol' boys wanted to see inside, but they didn't touch nothing. I kept them at a respectful distance on the porch."

"Did they lean against the screen door, Billings?"

"I don't know."

"You don't know. You don't know. You truly don't seem to recall or know much about the facts of that night, do you, Officer?" Freeman sat down abruptly in his chair. He was shaking his head.

The judge looked to Freeman. "William, are you finished?"

Freeman looked up at the witness. "I am quite finished with this so-called witness, Your Honor."

"Ask the court to excuse your tone." The judge pointed his finger at Freeman. "Apologize."

"Pardon?"

"Apologize for your last remark or I'll hold you in contempt."

Freeman rose slowly. "Mr. Billings, I apologize to you for my behavior after listening to your testimony. It is inexcusable on my part, for after all these years, I should be used to the carelessness of the police. I apologize, sir, for not being able to bite my tongue when I hear about such unprofessional and inexcusable behavior. I apologize to you, sir, for not cutting off your testimony when I realized what a poor excuse for a policeman you really are—"

As he headed home in his coupe, Hennessy reviewed the day's activity in court. With the trial under way, he told Betty, he would be at the courthouse most of the week and so she should contact him only in an emergency. He was surprised that Myrna hadn't been in the courtroom. She had called less than a week earlier about getting together when she got to town, but that was the last he'd heard from her. She had returned to Vermilion with him the night they talked to George but had stayed only two days before heading back to Chicago to cover another story. She had run into a brick wall regarding interviews with Boyd—Freeman simply wouldn't hear of it. Apparently, the editor thought her time would be better spent elsewhere until she could do some firsthand reporting or the trial commenced.

Since his return from Chicago, time had crept by. Hennessy found he was isolated from preparations for the trial as well as from Myrna. Freeman spent about half an hour questioning Hennessy, and one of Wolski's assistants came by to say they would like to take his deposition during what they called the "discovery process." But the trial started and that deposition still hadn't happened. It appeared that once Boyd was in the bag and the press was gone, the need for Hennessy's input had waned.

He spoke to Myrna a couple of times, but it had been all business regarding Boyd and the upcoming trial. As time passed, Hennessy realized he had no inclination to make it more than that. He and Myrna were becoming increasingly distant. He was weary of feeling not quite up to his own expectations in their relationship, to say nothing of hers. His separation from Myrna was a relief in many ways, as it allowed him time to become more thoughtful about his investments, which were doing wonderfully. He seemed to have a golden touch in the world of finance—he wished his mother were still alive to see how their modest fortune had been steadily growing under his well-informed care.

Hennessy pulled the steering wheel hard left to avoid a dog that darted into the road just ahead of him—it occurred to him that he was driving faster these days and maybe also living faster. In some strange way it made him feel fulfilled to see his wealth grow. It seemed that the worth of a person increased along with his stock portfolio and commodity investments. He spoke often with Vedeler the broker, a man Hennessy believed to be extremely wise beneath all his pomp. Finances had begun to preoccupy Hennessy, as success made him feel like a winner. He read the market reports each day and ruminated about the ways in which serious money might brighten a person's future.

Still, Hennessy had moments of the old gut-wrenching emptiness. Though he had resolved not to let it bother him, he experienced a letdown when Myrna didn't show up at the trial. Maybe she was just too all-fired important for a small-town trial. But after all the effort the *Trib* had put into the story, it was hard to understand her absence.

As he pulled into his driveway, his loneliness vanished. Myrna sat in the porch swing. Sprawled in the shade, she was moving herself back and forth by pushing against the floor with one foot.

She smiled as he climbed his front steps trying to mask his limp. Myrna's outfit of the day was a combination of jaunty yellow and cool green. It summed up her personality pretty well—choir girl and tramp rolled into one.

"Hi, Dale-o, how is the big court drama going?"

"Well enough, I suppose. What brings you back to our humble community?"

"Well, we need to cover Boyd's trial and tribulations, don't we?"

"Thought you'd have been here for today's happenings—where were you?"

"Had some problem getting here, but I dropped by for a while and sat in the back—and I'm getting the transcript."

It didn't sound right. "You could have had the transcript mailed to you. . . . Some reporter."

"Aren't we testy? Say, aren't you going to ask a lady in?"

Hennessy opened his unlocked front door with an "after you" gesture. As Myrna walked through the portal she winked and bathed him again in the glow of her smile. He cursed to himself.

Myrna began asking him questions about Boyd. What did he know of his past? How about Sheridan? It became apparent she now knew considerably more than he did about both subjects. She tossed her purse on the kitchen table and paced around with an unlit cigarette between her index and middle finger.

"You know something, my distinguished friend? I need a drink."

Hennessy complied by pulling a bottle of whiskey from a cupboard and chipping some ice off a block in the icebox. He poured double shots for both of them. She downed hers in about ten seconds and held her glass out for another.

As he refilled it, she remarked, "By the way, sweetie, sometimes the story isn't in the most obvious place. Don't underestimate ol' Myrna."

He didn't know what that meant, but he had reached his limit with the constant turmoil she evoked in him.

"That so? And does ol' Myrna' have a handle on everything else in life, too?" He knew his tone was edgy. "Does she like to play tease with all the men and keep them wrapped around her finger?"

After a moment of considering his question, she leaned forward, half smiled, and kissed him lightly on the forehead. He was suddenly engulfed in her bouquet of perfume and light perspiration—the effect was paralyzing. While his suddenly sluggish brain tried to consider an appropriate response, she stood upright and riveted him to his chair with her eyes. Then deliberately and slowly, she began to undress. She started down the buttons on her blouse and, without glancing away, kicked off her shoes. Hennessy became aware that the noise he heard over the blood pounding in his head was his own heavy breathing. *Jesus Christ.*

When she had her top off, she started fumbling behind her back at her bra strap—and his paralysis became complete.

It was broad daylight in the kitchen of his mother's house. He glanced nervously out the window and back to the vision now almost stark naked in front of him. Thoughts flashed through his mind like images on a movie screen with the projector running slowly.

"Dale, are you saying you didn't miss ol' Myrna?" She straddled him on the chair, her breasts in his face. He started to protest weakly but she cut him off. "I don't want to hear how we can't have fun in Mama's house. She ain't here, honey, and she's never going to be."

Hennessy kissed her breasts and rose to take her to bed. She would have none of it. When he stood, she held her ground. She pulled his suspenders off his shoulders, then put her drink down and with one hand yanked his loose-fitting pants down. Seeing his state of arousal, in a laughing voice she muttered, "Yeah, you're glad to see me." Suddenly, she pushed him back down on the chair, and Myrna was on him for real.

But this time he held his own. He had relived a hundred times in his imagination their tryst some months past. Time and time again he had recalled his own misgivings about his performance. Myrna must have been almost at a full head of steam when he arrived home—he realized with a growing sense of surprise and pride that she was quickly reaching her peak. He was unusually comfortable in this position. With her doing all the moving, he felt as if she was using him, and it was wonderful. His bad leg was irrelevant in a seated position, and in her wild abandon she raced ahead of him until she arched her back and groaned. He followed seconds later, but it didn't matter; he had satisfied her.

She collapsed over him, arms around his neck. When he tried to move, she wouldn't let him. He felt himself slip out of her but she still refused to let him up, muttering, "No, no, just stay here awhile." A moment later she made some semi-lewd comment he didn't entirely catch about his investing, that it must be going well and that she was "glad to see soft gainers turn into hard money."

With Myrna's weight constant on him, Hennessy soon felt his good leg go to sleep; it was as stiff and numb as the other, but still he sat there. It wasn't a moment to ruin. He wasn't sure what he felt for her—love? Maybe some, but mostly he felt proud, happy with his own virility. Eventually she eased off him, and they laughed at how difficult it was for him to walk into the living room with both his legs numb. But Myrna was a creature of habit if nothing else—she always knew what she wanted, and after sex she wanted to be held. She dropped, wet all over from their lovemaking, on his mother's couch; it was *his* damn couch, to hell with the damn stains. She wrapped him between her legs, his back to her, and snuggled without talking as the sun went down.

He must have dozed for a while, because he arose from a slumber to a question.

"The fire, Dale, what happened in that fire?"

His first impulse was to be angry, but he found himself too mellow to care.

"I told you, we had to get the inmates out and some of them were tough to deal with. So I opened the door and directed them toward me but the fire came with them . . . and Boyd had been helpful and . . . I don't know, I fell down and I suppose he pulled me a ways. . . . Why?"

"Because you have more reason than what you have told me to think he couldn't have committed murder."

"It's no secret what happened."

"I know, lover, it's no secret, but that's not the way it's come down since then, and it might help for people to know what Boyd did."

"You sound like you're on the defense team."

"Maybe I don't like seeing a guy not get a fair shake—seems like the public needs to hear about Boyd from others because he's not very damn good himself at getting folks to appreciate him. He's kind of clumsy with people."

In a low voice, Hennessy asked, "Was it me who first made you think Boyd might be innocent or was it . . . was it the interview with that darky—George?" He knew the "darky" language was beneath him, but he couldn't help it.

"I don't know. But hey, Major, the way you're hopping around there, it looks like you're gettin' ready to salute ol' Myrna again."

So he was. She ignored his question, but he didn't really care.

*B*oyd *started* thinking that Freeman was a really interesting old guy—full of surprises. It was as if he were waking up from a long sleep and getting stronger as the hours went by. He observed him questioning one of the men who had been at the murder scene. He rarely looked at notes and seemed effortlessly in charge.

"Sir, you said earlier to Mr. Wolski that the defendant Mr. Calvin 'brandished' his pistol at you, is that correct?"

Boyd watched Freeman walk around the courtroom from the witness stand to the jury box, then back, fiddling with a pencil. "Sir, did the defendant give you any reason to believe he had killed the two people inside?"

"Well, yes he did. When he came out onto the back porch, he said, 'They're all dead. I killed them, they're all dead.'"

"Did anyone else hear the defendant say those words?"

"I don't know, but that's what I thought I heard."

"Well now, Jeff, did you hear him say 'I killed them' or not?"

Jeff thought for a moment. "I honestly think that's what I heard . . . or something very close to that."

"Something very close?"

Boyd watched as Freeman made sure the jury was aware of the slight doubt in Jeff's statement.

"Well, when the defendant came out onto the porch, did he seem agitated?"

"Yes, he seemed—"

"Just a 'yes' or 'no,' please."

"Yes."

"Did he seem shocked?"

214

"Yes."

"Did he ask for help in any way?"

"No, he just jumped off the porch, fell down, and then ran down the alley."

"And what did you do?"

"I yelled to him to come back and wait for the police but he just kept running."

Freeman pounced on him angrily. "Were you invited to view the deceased by your friend Officer Billings?"

Boyd thought he saw Jeff hesitate, as if he were going to tell a lie, but then he spoke.

"Yeah."

"'Yeah' what, Mr. Graham?"

"Well, yes, Stevie said he thought it would be all right."

"Well, did 'Stevie' say anything about not touching anything?"

Graham shrugged.

"I need an answer."

"I don't remember."

"You don't remember. You didn't seem to have any trouble with the rest of your story, but this part you 'don't remember.'"

"We were all just foolin' around. You know how it is. There had been shots, a guy comes out on the porch spouting off. It was real dark and you couldn't see much unless you were up close, so I don't know, it was kinda exciting, I guess."

"Earlier, when the prosecutor asked you to identify the defendant, you pointed to him without hesitation. Is that correct?"

"Yes."

"So it was 'real dark' most of the time. The kitchen lights were on bright, but the defendant was on the porch in the dark. Him—you could see quite clearly, correct?"

"Well, you don't understand, you see—"

"Yes, indeed, I don't understand. That will be all, Mr. Graham."

Boyd sat wondering where all of this would end. Even though Freeman was able to discredit most of the witnesses in some fashion, that still didn't negate the fact that he, Boyd Calvin, had been there when the gun went off. Freeman had told him that he wasn't sure if he would put him on the witness stand.

There was a lull in the proceedings while the clerk seemed to be catching up with paperwork. Boyd glanced quickly at the box to see whether the jury was watching him. They all seemed preoccupied. Boyd was sure one of the men sitting in the back was a passenger he had carried on his trolley. A bitter-looking fellow in his forties, kind of farmerlike, always seemed alone.

"The state calls Detective Sergeant Terrence Petrel."

Boyd leaned into Freeman. "Who's that?"

"He's the detective that worked the crime scene. We'll just have to wait and see."

Wolski stood next to his table piled high with law books and stacks of paper. "Detective Sergeant Petrel, you were the man in charge on the night in question. Would you tell us, please, exactly what you found."

"In the early-morning hours of June sixth, I was called to the scene. I found two bodies, one later identified as Ralph Sheridan, the other as Mrs. Laurel Wheaton Calvin. Both had been shot once in the head. They had been dead approximately two hours."

"Detective, how were the bodies positioned?"

"The female was lying partially under the kitchen table and the male was seated at the table, slumped over. His head resting on a book and things."

"What was your immediate reaction to this scene?"

"Do you mean what did I think had happened?"

"Yes."

"It seemed likely this was a double murder. The position of the bodies, the absence of a note indicating suicide. And the lack of a weapon, which there surely would have been if it had been a murder-suicide. . . . Then, of course, the underlined passage in the Bible sitting right there, well that clinched it."

Wolski picked up the Bible from where it was lying on the evidence table still open to the page in question. After first looking to the judge for approval and receiving a cursory nod, he carefully held it up within reading distance of the policeman's face.

"And what exactly does the underlined passage say, Detective Sergeant Petrel?"

"Well, it says . . . I mean, it's in Leviticus, chapter twenty, verse ten, and the underlined part says 'And the man that commiteth adultery with another man's wife, even he that committed adultery with his neighbor's wife, the adulterer and the adulteress shall surely be put to death.'"

Wolski let the words sink in, then gave a meaningful glance toward the jury box before solemnly returning the Good Book to the evidence table. He checked his notes briefly, then addressed Petrel.

"Thank you, sir, no further questions."

Freeman was slow to rise. He greeted the detective and then asked him a few questions about his experience and length of time on the force. "Is it your experience, Detective, that there is always a suicide note?"

"No, sir, not always."

"Thank you, sir, that will be all at this time."

It surprised Boyd that Freeman had asked so few questions. "What's up, can't you get anything out of him?"

"Maybe later. I can recall him later. Something just occurred to me."

He was a strange duck, this Freeman. Boyd could never tell what he was thinking.

Several additional witnesses from the neighborhood were called, except they all remembered slightly different versions of Boyd's statement on the porch. Wolski then called for Mrs. Bernice Wheaton.

Boyd sat up. He turned to see his mother-in-law make her way through the courtroom. She gave Boyd a withering look as she passed the defense table. She had never liked him. Now was her chance.

". . . and they had been separated about a year."

Wolski was Mr. Polite to Laurel's mother. "Mrs. Wheaton, at any time after the separation, did Mr. Calvin attempt to see your daughter?"

"Yes."

"Would you tell us, please, those circumstances?"

The prim woman paused. Boyd remembered quite well how, when she was annoyed, she would stop and take stock, gathering her forces. "He came to the house several times, uninvited, I might add. Well, he would sit on the front porch, waiting for Laurel. . . ."

She hesitated, trying to hold back the tears.

"Do you need a moment, Mrs. Wheaton?"

"No. As I said, he would sit there, even after I told him to scoot. He'd just sit there rocking on the swing. When Laurel would get home from the five-and-dime, sometimes she would sit and talk to him. Other times, she would come in the house crying."

"Mrs. Wheaton, were there any other communications between them?"

Boyd could see the old gal was bursting to say more.

"Yes, Boyd sent Laurel a number of letters. Some of them she didn't even read, others she burned."

"Mrs. Wheaton, did you have occasion to show me any of those letters?"

"Yes, I did."

"If the court pleases, I would like to offer into evidence this letter addressed to 'Laurel Calvin, 18 Maple Street,' with a return address of 'Boyd Calvin in care of the Grant Hotel, Vermilion, Illinois.'" The court clerk took the letter from the evidence table and handed it to Wolski. "Would you read parts of the letter please, Mrs. Wheaton?"

The woman seemed to take pleasure in opening the letter, as she did so with a flourish. "It's dated May twentieth. Just a couple of weeks before . . . 'My dearest Laurel. Please, sweetheart, read this in full, try not to be angry with'—well, anyway, it goes on for some time about a lot of stuff Boyd was trying to get across but the most important thing is here on the third page.

"'There are a number of things I can do, I hate to make threats and all but . . .'"

Boyd said to Freeman, "Make her read the first two pages."

"Your Honor, could we have a short recess," said Freeman. "I apologize to Mrs. Wheaton for this distraction."

The judge seemed slightly irritated but granted a recess.

"All right, Boyd, what's with this letter?" Freeman asked.

"I wrote it in desperation. It may sound a little different from the way I intended unless it's read in full."

"You think it's damaging?"

"Depends how it's taken."

When the court reconvened, Freeman stood up. "Your Honor, if it pleases, we would like the letter read in full and not have parts of it taken out of context."

"I think that's fair, Counsel. Mrs. Wheaton, start again, please, and read the letter in its entirety."

The woman made several annoying attempts to smooth her lap and then once again started reading. " 'My dearest Laurel, please, sweetheart, read this in full, try not to be angry with me. I realize that we are divorced and as painful as that is to me, I am trying hard to accept that. I still love you very much, as you well know, and miss you each day. Here's what I would like you to consider. Would you allow me to take you out once in a while? Yeah, I know it seems nuts but . . . ' " She stopped reading. "Your Honor, I can't. I am sorry. I just can't read this drivel."

The judge seemed sympathetic.

The judge looked at Wolski. "Mr. Wolski, would you proceed reading the letter, please."

"Objection, Your Honor." Freeman was on his feet.

"So noted. Please proceed, Mr. Wolski."

Boyd could see that Wolski wasn't pleased about reading the letter, but he began.

" 'Yeah, I know it seems nuts, but you know me, I am kind of a nutty guy. I just thought maybe we could go to a movie once in a while or get something to eat. I'd like to be able to show you I'm okay. You know, I'm not a crazy, like some people think. Did I tell you I love you? Well, if I didn't, I love you. I know, Laurel, that I can change if given the chance.' "

Wolski looked up to the judge. "Your Honor, is this really necessary? The part that is relevant is at the back end—"

"Read the damn letter in its entirety, Mr. Wolski. You obviously have read the letter before, that's why you had Mrs. Wheaton bring it in. If you think you can slip a fast one by me, sir, you can think again. Now proceed."

Wolski started again. " 'I can change if given the chance. I know what you're thinking, sweetheart, I've been given lots of chances. You're right. But please, please sweetie, think about this, will you? Do you remember coming home from Kansas? How we made love on the train that night; we both giggled so loud and you were terrified someone would see or hear us. That was so sweet. I'll remember that always, I love you, please think about some of these good times, darling. I can't sleep at night thinking about all the mistakes I've made with you. I don't really know why I'm so jealous. I'll try to not be in the future.' " Wolski stopped, and when he began reading again, it was with a much louder, clearer voice. " 'I've been so worried about you, sweetheart. I know you're seeing *some-one*, and it drives me crazy. I don't know what I'll do. I feel really desper-ate at times. There are a number of things I can do, I hate to make threats and all but the idea of you with someone else is just too much. Please give me another chance, darling. I love you, your always to be husband, Boyd. P.S. I'm really afraid of what I might do. If you can't love me, *I've had some awful thoughts.*' " Wolski emphasized the last clause.

Freeman turned to Boyd as recess was called and the courtroom cleared. Amid the low rumble of people discussing the case, Boyd found it hard to drag his eyes away from the tabletop. He knew he looked guilty. He also felt guilty.

"I don't know. I guess I was just kind of desperate. She wouldn't see me; and even when she would, I always seemed to annoy her. I always said the wrong thing. Or maybe it was the right thing. But I said it in the wrong way. . . . You don't want to hear this crap, do you?" Boyd still hadn't looked at Freeman.

"Look, sonny, I want to hear everything that's relevant to this case. Stop worrying about what I want. Go on and explain to me what you meant in that letter."

Boyd looked at his hands on the table. He pulled them from the table and buried them in his lap. "When I say 'I'm really afraid of what I might do,' I was talkin' about myself. . . ." Boyd looked at the old man's tired eyes. "Ah, well, the hell with it, I don't know."

Freeman reached over to Boyd and laid his hand on the younger man's arm.

A deputy jailer made a sound as he waited close to the defense table.

"Give us a few minutes, will you, Deputy?"

The man nodded and stepped back.

Boyd fought back the tightness in his throat. "I really didn't mean any harm, Mr. Freeman. I know it sounds—but—"

"What you're saying is that you thought about taking your own life. Is that right?"

Boyd nodded.

"Did you seriously consider this?"

"I went out to the railroad bridge in the East end a couple of times. Just stood there, staring down. But I guess I didn't really have the guts or maybe I'm just not tough enough to do what's right. But anyway, I couldn't do it."

Freeman slid his arm around Boyd's shoulders. "Thank God you didn't." The old man's eyes were wet. "Get some rest, Boyd. Tomorrow is another day."

THURSDAY, OCTOBER 24

*B*oyd scanned the gray painted walls of the holding cell. Someone had scratched a calendar in the paint, then crossed out the days, seven. A heart-shaped design with a "For a good time, meet here Friday nights, Paula," message in the middle. Another said, "A life of crime ain't no shame, it's all a part of the devil's game, signed John Dillinger. Ha ha." In a very precise and neat hand, the words "Fuck all the niggas," and then in a different hand, "No thanks." Boyd twisted his head around to try to read what someone had written upside down. It looked like "I hate grils." The reply, also in a different hand, said, "What's the matter with us grils?" He had only scanned about half of the graffiti when the bailiff came in to take him back to court.

The coroner was on the stand, explaining how Laurel and Ralph died.

"There was one gunshot wound to the head of each of them, almost identical. The temple area being the softest part of the skull in an adult. It would appear that whoever did this seemed to know something of anatomy or was expert at killing. Or both."

Wolski wrote a note to himself and then spoke to the coroner again. "Were there any other distinguishing features to the assault, sir?"

"Yes, there was tattooing of the male victim."

"When you say 'tattooing,' sir, would you explain that, please?"

"When a pistol, in this case a thirty-two caliber, is fired at close range, the excess powder in the cartridge makes small burnlike marks on the victim's skin, hence tattooing."

"Thank you, sir. No further questions."

Boyd watched as Freeman gathered some notes and walked toward the coroner.

"Sir, when you speak of tattooing, why weren't there marks on the body of Mrs. Calvin?"

"Probably because she was shot from farther away. You see, the residue dissipates at about two feet or so."

"In your opinion, did these people suffer at all?"

"No, sir, I would think they would have been rendered unconscious immediately, and died within seconds."

"Sir, you voiced an opinion to the prosecutor that you thought this act was committed by an 'expert.' Could it possibly have been a murder-suicide?"

"In my opinion, no. There didn't seem to be enough tattooing on the male victim to indicate a self-inflicted gunshot wound. In other words, his arms would have had to be very long in order to hold the pistol far enough away from his head for the burn marks not to be more prevalent on the left temple."

"But there was some tattooing on the victim, indicating the weapon was closer than it was to Mrs. Calvin."

"Yes, that is correct."

"But wouldn't you agree, sir, that each pistol, weapon, would have different characteristics—wouldn't the load, the ammunition, vary from box to box?"

"Yes, that's possible."

"So that, although from your experience there should be more marks for a self-inflicted wound, wouldn't you agree, sir, given the various elements going into the actual firing of a weapon—ammunition, variance in pistols—that it might just be possible for this to be a suicide? Would you agree to that, sir?"

"Yes, I suppose it's possible."

"Thank you, sir. Nothing further."

"The court calls Mrs. Ralph Sheridan."

Boyd watched as a plump young woman in a floral print dress took the stand. She had on too much makeup.

Wolski approached her carefully. "Mrs. Sheridan, would you please tell us the circumstances in which you found yourself during the spring of this past year."

The woman wrapped her handkerchief tightly around her fingers. "I was married to Ralph for more than ten years and he never done nothing the likes of this thing."

"And exactly what was this 'thing,' Mrs. Sheridan?"

"Well, the going out with someone, a course."

"The 'going out,' do you mean he was stepping out on you, Mrs. Sheridan?"

"Yeah, well, that's what I said. I've got children, you know. Three of them. And that sum-a-bitch should hafta pay." She pointed her finger at Boyd.

"Mrs. Sheridan, how did this affair with the deceased start?"

"Deceased?"

"How did your husband become involved with Mrs. Calvin?"

"S'pose down to the five-and-dime, they both worked there. He tol' me he wanted to leave 'cause he was crazy in love with this bitch down to the store. I said to him, 'Ralph, you leave, you're gonna be plenty sorry, that girl don't care a hill of beans 'bout you.' He knew I was probably right 'bout that. But he was gonna try her anyway. Well, he came home later with his tail 'tween his legs like some whipped hound dog and I tol' him to keep right on travelin'. I wouldn't have him back. He was damn sorry then, let me tell ya. He loved his oldest son, Kenny, a whole hell of a lot, but I wouldn't let him see the boy. Some people call me hard, but no. I'm just a practical kinda woman."

"Mrs. Sheridan. Did Ralph have a gun? Did he own one?"

"No, I don't think so, couldn't afford one. No, pretty sure he didn't have one."

"Your witness, Mr. Freeman."

Boyd could see Wolski had gained respect for Freeman over the past several days.

"Mrs. Sheridan, you said to Prosecutor Wolski that Ralph, your husband, didn't own a gun. Is that correct?"

"Yes."

"Well, let me ask you, if I may, to take a look at this weapon we have here in exhibit." Freeman walked to the evidence table and picked up the .32 caliber handgun with the bone handle partially broken off. "Do you recognize this, Mrs. Sheridan?"

"Nope. Sure don't."

Freeman handed the unloaded pistol to her. The witness took it rather reluctantly in her hands.

"Would you please examine the weapon and see if it is at all familiar to you?"

The woman turned the gun to all sides as if inspecting it.

"Mrs. Sheridan, may I ask you what your maiden name was, please?"

"Objection, Your Honor. Relevance?" Wolski asked.

"Yes, Mr. Freeman. What road are we going down, sir? This lady is not on trial here."

"Yes, Your Honor, I realize that. If you would just indulge me here a few more moments."

"All right, Counsel. Just show some relevance. Tie this up, please."

"Thank you. Mrs. Sheridan, I'll repeat my question."

"Young."

"Your maiden name was Young?"

"Correct."

"And what may I ask was your father's name?"

"His name was Young also."

"Yes, of course, excuse me. I meant, his first name?"

"Alfred Young."

"His initials would have been A.Y., is that correct?"

"Yes."

"Did he have a middle name?"

"Orville."

"So it would have been A.O.Y., am I right?"

"Yes."

"Would you look, please, on the bottom of the trigger guard and read for me what it says there."

"There's some letters, I guess."

"What exactly are they, Mrs. Sheridan?"

"Can't read them."

"Turn the pistol the other way."

"'A.O.Y.,' I guess."

"A.O.Y. That would be your father's initials, am I right, Mrs. Sheridan?"

"S'pose so."

"Did you give this gun to your husband, missus? Mrs. Sheridan, I might remind you that you are still under oath."

"I didn't give it to him. He probably just took it. I had it hidden under my socks in a dresser drawer. He probably just took it. Don't know why."

"So you did see the gun before."

"Well, it was just a little old peashooter."

"Thank you, missus. No further questions." Freeman took the gun from Mrs. Sheridan and laid it neatly back on the evidence table next to the blood-spattered Bible.

Wolski stood. "Your Honor, with your permission, may I step out of sequence here, please? I would like to call Detective Manion."

"Proceed, Mr. Wolski." The detective had been waiting in the hall with several other witnesses. He took the witness stand.

"Detective Manion. Am I right in my information that yesterday you were asked by Mr. Freeman if he could reexamine the evidence in this case?"

"Yes, that's right."

"Where did this happen, sir?"

"The evidence locker at the police station."

"Were you in the room with Mr. Freeman the whole time?"

"Yes, he examined the papers and the books that were on the kitchen table. He looked through the Bible and then examined the gun."

"And you were with him the whole time?"

"Yeah, well except for when I answered the phone for a couple minutes."

"Was your back to Mr. Freeman, sir?"

"Part of the time, yes."

"What was he doing while you were on the phone?"

"He was looking at the gun."

"Thank you."

Freeman got up from his desk tiredly. "Your honor, is the state's attorney implying that I scratched those initials on that gun?"

Wolski didn't bother to rise. "No, I am not implying anything. I'm just pointing out that you had opportunity."

"The state calls Peggy Trotter."

"She's Laurel's friend from work," Freeman said to Boyd. "Nothing to worry about."

Wolski was solicitous with an extremely nervous Miss Trotter.

"Did you ever have an occasion to meet the defendant, Boyd Calvin?"

"No, I never met him, but I saw him a couple times in the alley behind the store. He would be waiting for Laurel."

"What, if anything, would happen at these times?"

"He would approach Laurel and ask if he could talk with her."

"And did she stop and talk with him?"

"Not the couple times when I was with her, she didn't."

"Miss Trotter, if you would, could you describe the defendant's attitude, his demeanor during these times?"

"Objection, Your Honor." Freeman had gotten to his feet. "It's impossible for this witness to know the state of mind of my client during those so-called meetings."

"Sustained, Mr. Wolski. Rephrase your question, please."

"I'm sorry, Your Honor. Miss Trotter, did you have occasion to see Mr. Calvin act upon his anger in any way?"

"Yes, this one particular time, after Laurel said she wouldn't speak with him, we were walking away toward the corner when we heard this loud crash. We didn't look back but just kept hightailing it toward the street."

"And what was the crash, Mrs. Trotter?"

"We heard later it was a garbage can having been thrown through the back window of the five-and-dime."

It was a lie. He'd only kicked the can.

"What, if you remember, please, was Mrs. Calvin's reaction to that incident?"

"Well, Laurel was real frightened, she started crying, said that Boyd scared her some. She still cared for him but was afraid. Because, and if I remember correctly, she used the word 'passionate' to describe his behavior."

"Did Laurel ever say whether Boyd had been physical with her, you know, in a violent way?"

Peggy looked quickly at Boyd. She started to answer but dropped her head and shook no.

"Are you indicating 'no,' Miss Trotter?"

"Yes, I am. She never told me about any beatings or anything, although some mornings her eyes were swollen and red. Didn't look so good."

"So to summarize." Wolski walked over closer to the jury. "Your friend Laurel was not only afraid of Mr. Calvin, but had experienced a passionate episode with him, and from your own experience at the back door of the five-and-dime, you had been witness to some sort of violent event. Would that be a fair summary, Miss Trotter?"

"Yes, I think so."

"Thank you. No further questions at this time."

Freeman had been scribbling notes, but when he rose he left them on the table. "Miss Trotter, you say you never met my client, Mr. Calvin, correct?"

"Yes, sir."

"Miss Trotter, you say that Mrs. Calvin used the word 'passionate.' "
"Yes."

"You are aware that the word has a number of meanings, relating to amorousness, desire, love. You are aware of that, are you not?"

"Yes."

It looked as though Peggy was losing some of her resolve. Freeman walked quickly back to his desk, glanced at his notes, and spoke to the witness as he returned to the stand.

"Miss Trotter, when was the last time you noticed Mrs. Calvin's eyes swollen and red?"

"I don't think I can remember."

"Some people are sensitive to pollen. Aren't they, Miss Trotter?"

"Yes."

"Thank you, Miss Trotter, no further questions."

The judge called a brief recess. Hennessy met Myrna outside the court-room, where she lit her inevitable cigarette and paced in the shadow of the building, apparently seeking shade.

"Quite a show in there, don't ya think, Dale-o? They ought to put tri-als on the radio for people's entertainment."

"I suppose."

Hennessy would have been more bothered by her offhandedness if he hadn't had something else bothering him. Myrna acted as though they had shaken hands the night before instead of engaging in the most torrid lovemaking of his life, but that was to be expected of the fickle woman. What really had him riled was something he had spotted in the newspa-per he clutched in his hand. Even the Vermilion paper had given the quirky day in the market almost equal play to the trial of Boyd.

"Yeah, Mrs. Sheridan, Fatso, and Peggy hot-to-Trotter; I could use those characters in a pulp story but no one would believe they're real."

"What?"

"What do you mean, 'what'? Something on your mind—Major?" A passing couple were the reason for Myrna's sudden switch to formal ad-dress. As they passed out of earshot, she continued. "What gives, lover boy?"

"Nothing. I mean—well, the market's unpredictably strange lately, and today a lot of stocks really dropped."

"Yeah, I saw that in the Vermilion privy-liner." She jutted her chin to-ward the rolled-up paper in Hennessy's hand. "The *Trib*'s got it above the fold, too."

Sometimes her contempt for the *Vermilion Herald* irked him—his fam-ily had once been involved in that paper—but today he couldn't rise to it. He had hardly followed the trial that morning, and he'd noticed that

Vedeler wasn't in the courtroom today. A few of the more well-to-do Vermilion society folk were conspicuously absent, come to think of it.

"So, the alley cats tripped over an empty trash can this week, huh?"

"Whatever the hell's that supposed to mean?"

"Lighten up, lov—Major."

Manion came brushing by them on his way back to the court, Petrel a few feet behind. They nodded greetings back and forth. Then Myrna turned to Hennessy.

"Really, Dale, there are more important things going on today than the problems the fat cats are having in moneyland, aren't there? I mean, so you gain a few bucks, you lose a few, what's the big deal?"

"Easy for you to say."

"Yeah, maybe." She stubbed out her butt on the sidewalk. "How much you have wrapped up in that game of craps anyway?"

"Game of craps? The stock market is hardly that. It's the lifeblood of this nation—how do you think you're able to wear those fancy clothes and travel about safe in one of the richest nations on earth? It's because men of substance are willing to gamble on the might and moxie of America."

"Criminy, Dale. You've been listening to that snake-oil peddler Vermin Vedeler too much. You're getting yourself in an uproar over some numbers in the paper while we've got Boyd on trial for his life here."

"Don't preach to me about Boyd!"

Myrna stared at him as though he were an escaped inmate from his own facility.

Where was Vedeler anyway? Hennessy had a few questions for him and needed the reassurance of his calm demeanor—he really should have been available today, as some of his clients might be upset. When he turned to speak to Myrna, he realized she had gone back inside.

Boyd watched a black ant crawl across his polished shoe. He had buffed his work boots to a glisten. Freeman insisted that Boyd wear a coat and tie, but the candy-striped shirt didn't feel right with the dark coat he had been given, and it was hot. But as Freeman said, "You've got to look like a million." His jailhouse haircut felt strange, the clippers having been freely used on the sides, the top sticking up in several unruly cowlicks.

He was surprised to hear Claudia's name called. She marched down the aisle with a determined look.

After she had been sworn in, the prosecutor made a strange pronouncement. "Be it noted that Mrs. Claudia Falk is a hostile witness for the state."

Boyd was wondering what that meant when Freeman scribbled a note: "She's been subpoenaed by the prosecutor against her will. Keep your fingers crossed."

Wolski held a document in his hands. "Miss Falk, may I call you Claudia?"

"You may not."

Wolski paused for a moment to gather himself. "Miss Falk, I have here an incident report signed by Officer Tom Blake. This report describes in detail the early morning hours of June sixth, 1929. Officer Blake had been searching for Mr. Boyd Calvin at his place of residence, the Grant Hotel. Could you tell the court, please, where you presently make your domicile?"

Claudia gave Boyd a furtive glance. "Do you mean, what place do I call my abode?"

"Yes, please."

"I'm currently in residence at the Grant Hotel." She tightened her back and sat up. "Of course, that's just temporary."

"Of course. Now, Mrs. Falk, according to Officer Blake's report, he met you in the lobby of the Grant several minutes after a loud disturbance on the roof of the hotel, is that correct?"

"I think I remember seeing an officer of the law that night, yes."

"Mrs. Falk, what, may I ask, were you doing in the lobby of the hotel at 3:30 A.M., please?"

"There were a number of people in the lobby. I was just one of many lonely souls wandering those marble halls."

"Mrs. Falk, please. Did you have occasion to see or visit with the defendant in this case on the night in question?"

"I'm sorry. I was under the impression that you had said it was 3:30 A.M. in the morning."

"Yes, Mrs. Falk, let me rephrase—"

"No need, the answer is no, and why would I? What's your implication, that I meet strange young men in the wee hours, please?"

Wolski appeared perplexed. Boyd wondered how long he would put up with Claudia. "Officer Blake's remarks indicate that you were observed coming from the street into the lobby of the hotel. Is that correct?"

"I don't recall."

"I'll read the officer's notes to you. 'I saw this older woman wearing a nightgown and thin robe come into the lobby from the street. Her hair was disheveled and she looked as if she had been crying. I took her name. She seemed nervous and high-strung. I asked if she'd seen Boyd Calvin and she said, 'No, not lately, sugar.' I attempted to question her further but to no avail. Do you recall that incident, Mrs. Falk?"

"That couldn't have been me. Older woman, indeed."

"Mrs. Falk, are you in the habit of parading around in the middle of the night—I am sorry, in the early-morning hours—out on the street in your nightgown?"

Claudia took a moment, and her face magically changed from the lovable gamine's to the tortured heroine's.

"I had been aroused, excuse me, awakened from a deep session of being in the arms of Morpheus. There had been a thunderous crash, almost that of titans struggling on Mount Olympus. There were screams of fright echoing in the darkened passageways. I was certain that the building was about to alight onto my crown, pardon, my head. I fled to the grand staircase and slipped into the darkness. There were a number of similar souls praying outside of the inn. We hovered like street urchins until we were able to observe the constable in the lobby. As for my appearance, I think it was probably appropriate for the occasion."

Wolski looked to the judge. "Your Honor?"

Muffled laughter could be heard. The judge rapped his gavel lightly.

"Order. Mrs. Falk, please keep your remarks directed to the questions, please. We don't take murder lightly here. We are trying to prove who committed a terrible deed, Mrs. Falk."

"And well you should, Your Honor."

Exasperated, the judge looked away.

Wolski laced his fingers across his expensive suit. "Did you know Boyd Calvin?"

"Yes."

"For how long, Mrs. Falk?"

"Oh, about twenty-nine years or so."

"The defendant is twenty-nine. Are you saying you knew him from birth?"

"Yes, that's what I'm saying."

Wolski paused. "You were seen outside the entrance to the Grant Hotel helping the defendant down a ladder. Isn't that the truth, Mrs. Falk?"

"Objection, not in evidence."

"Sustained, unless you have a witness. Mr. Prosecutor, stick with what is known."

"Your Honor, as you well know, Officer Blake was incapacitated in the riot a few days after this incident. In his notes, he says he spoke to a man across the street from the hotel who observed the witness and the defendant conversing before the defendant ran from the scene. I was hoping, sir, that you would provide me a little leeway here, in honor of this fallen hero, Officer Blake."

"Did the officer note the man's name and address?"

"Yes, sir, but we have been unable to ascertain his whereabouts."

"Where in this line of questioning, Mr. Wolski, might I ask, are you proceeding?"

"Your Honor, I'm trying to establish that the defendant did, through trickery and deceit, escape from the crime scene and make his way back to the hotel in preparation for his continued fugitive status, contributing to his guilt in relationship to these heinous crimes." Wolski once again turned to Claudia.

"Would it be fair to say that you and the defendant, Mr. Calvin, are extremely good friends and that you would say and do almost anything for each other?"

"Well, yes, we are good friends, but if you are implying that I would lie in a court of law for him, no, of course not. I am a good citizen, Mr. Wolski."

"Wouldn't you characterize your friendship as one of complete trust in each other? And in order to preserve that relationship, would you not go to great lengths to keep your friend out of way of any harm?"

Boyd could see the prosecutor's eyebrows arch as he posed the question.

"I think what he's asking, Your Honor"—Claudia had turned to the judge—"is the same thing he asked just a moment ago. And with all due respect, I will have to say what I said previously." Claudia turned back to Wolski. "No, damn it."

Wolski rigidly set his jaw. Boyd could see him working to keep his composure.

"Wouldn't it be fair, Mrs. Falk, to say that in fact Boyd Calvin confessed to you in the early-morning hours of June sixth, and that in that confession he recited chapter and verse about what had taken place just a few hours before? Wouldn't that be fair to say, Mrs. Falk?"

"It wouldn't be fair, as you say, because it wouldn't be the truth, Mr. Wol-skee."

Wolski looked as though he was stumped by Claudia. Boyd could see the prosecutor was itching to try again, but finally he thought better of it and sat down.

The judge waited a moment. "Do you have any further questions for this witness?"

"No, Your Honor." Wolski stared at Claudia. "Not at this time. But I would like her kept available." Claudia made a slight face at Wolski as he turned away.

Freeman stood ten feet from Claudia. "What kind of man is Boyd Calvin?"

Claudia became her old self again. Relaxed and confident. "Boyd is, I think, a warm and lovable human being. I've known him a number of years. I've never heard him raise his voice at anyone or harm them in any way." Claudia dug a small handkerchief from her purse. "Boyd just couldn't have done this thing. He—"

"He's never been violent?"

"No, never."

"Ever see him fight or be disrespectful to anyone?"

"No, never." Boyd wondered if the jury noticed her pause slightly before she answered.

"Did you see him on the morning in question, Mrs. Falk?"

"No, I most certainly did not. If I would have seen him, I would have said so."

"Anything you would like to add, Mrs. Falk?"

Claudia looked to Boyd. "He's the sweetest person I've ever met. For anyone to think that he could kill those people, well, to me, that's ludicrous." She turned to the jury, her eyes wide and teary, head slightly cocked to one side.

"Thank you, Mrs. Falk."

Boyd watched as she made her way slowly through the courtroom. Just before she reached the large double doors, she let out a mournful sob. Then she was gone. All in all, Boyd thought, it had been a masterly performance.

*F*reeman turned to Boyd with a list of names that had been given to him by the prosecutor. "Do you know this person?"

Boyd scanned the list briefly and settled where Freeman was pointing: Felix O. Roush. "Nope, doesn't sound familiar."

"Well, his address is the Grant Hotel, so he must know you."

One of the officers of the court could be heard calling for Felix O. Roush in the hallway. When he finally came in, Boyd was surprised to see Odem. He had never known his real name; everyone just called him Odem. *With a name like Felix, why not?*

"Mr. Roush, where do you currently reside, please?"

"At the Grant."

"The Grant being the hotel here in Vermilion, correct?"

"Yeah, right."

"Mr. Roush, do you know the defendant, Mr. Boyd Calvin?"

"Know him? I don't think anyone really knows him, but yeah, I see him round the lobby from time to time."

Wolski glanced down at his notes. "What line of work are you in, Mr. Roush?"

"I'm a bricklayer, but I'm currently between jobs."

"I see. Mr. Roush, on the night of June fifth, 1929, would you tell this court where you were?"

Odem resettled himself in the hard-backed chair. "It was hot, I couldn't sleep, the hotel was like a steam bath. I laid there on the wet sheets till I couldn't take it any longer. Then I got my Luckies and went up on the roof, trying to catch a breeze."

"Approximately how long did you stay on the roof, Mr. Roush?"

"I don't really know, it must've been a couple hours or so."

"And what, if anything, happened on the roof that night, Mr. Roush?"

"Well, as I said, I'd been up there awhile when I hear someone in the alley down below making some kinda shushing sound, you know, like trying to shoo away a cat or a dog. . . ."

"Yes, go on."

"Well, as I had nothing better to do, I sat on the parapet of the roof and watched as this guy starts climbing up—first to Miller's, the building next door, then he swings up on the fire escape of the hotel, and finally up on the roof."

"What happened then, Mr. Roush?"

"Well, I started to ask him what'n the hell he was doing there—you know, thinking maybe he was a thief or something—when I see it's Boyd."

"And by Boyd, do you mean Mr. Calvin?"

"Yeah."

"Do you see the person that was on the roof in the courtroom, Mr. Roush?"

"Yeah, sure, he's sittin' over there, next to the old fellow in the blue suit." Odem pointed to Boyd with not a little bit of glee.

"Have it so noted that the witness has identified the defendant. All right, Mr. Roush, what happened next?"

"Well, when I saw it was old Mr. Jesus H. Christ hisself—"

The judge cleared his throat. "Language, Mr. Roush, language."

"Oh, right, sorry. I dropped down in the shadow of the parapet and just watched. He came up to the roof and peered over like he was look-ing for someone. Several times I started to speak to him, but he was really acting strange, like he had killed someone or something—"

"Objection."

"Sustained. Mr. Wolski, instruct your witness, please."

"Mr. Roush, keep your testimony to the facts, please."

"All right, but he was acting real peculiar, I'll tell you. Anyway, he picked up an armful of tiles that had been left on the roof and just tossed them for no good reason. Just tossed them down on the fire escape on the third floor. Boy, it made a helluva"—he glanced at the judge, and the older man nodded back—"made an awful racket. Must've woke every-one in the old joint. Well, ol' Boyd slipped down the stairs about then and I followed. There were people scurrying about, it was a treat to see. I drifted down to the lobby, then out on the street to watch. I guess people thought the old building was gonna come down."

"Then what happened, Mr. Roush?"

"I see Boyd slip outta his window, and lo and behold, he's climbing down the face of the building. He stopped at the second floor and spoke to someone, then slid on down. Busted himself in the nuts pretty good at the bottom."

A slight rustling in the audience made the judge tap quietly. Wolski again asked Roush to proceed.

"Well, the old biddy Falk comes flouncing out of the lobby, nightgown and robe flapping around. Tell you, it was a sight. Well, she goes out to the street to get a bag that Boyd must've throwed down, then they talk awhile, and Boyd ran away."

"Could you hear what they were talking about, Mr. Roush?"

"Yeah, well, Boyd was bragging about havin' killed this fella and his ex-wife. Old Claudia was wailing away, feeling sorry for everybody, screaming about his havin' kilt a paramour and illicit love. I don't know, it seemed they were in an awful mess."

"Approximately how long did they speak?"

"Oh, five minutes or so, I'd guess."

"Thank you, Mr. Roush. No further questions."

Freeman seemed anxious to get to Odem. Boyd could tell by his pace and manner that this would be quick.

"Did you have a watch on, Mr. Roush? At the time in question, were you wearing your watch? You had just gotten up, right?"

"No, I don't own a watch."

"But you could tell that it was two hours on the roof? And also I think you said five minutes in front of the hotel, correct?"

"Well, yeah, about, I'd say."

"About?"

"Well, you know, roughly."

"You say there were a lot of people scurrying about in the halls. Did you see the policeman, Mr. Roush?"

"Not then. That wasn't until later."

"How much later?"

"Oh, I'd say ten minutes. When things settled down, I spoke to him in the lobby."

"Do you know Officer Blake, sir?"

"Yeah, I'd seen him around some."

"In your earlier testimony, you described your work as 'bricklayer' and that you were between jobs, correct?"

"Yes."

"Where did you learn your profession, Mr. Roush?"

"Objection, Your Honor, relevance please?"

"Yes, Mr. Freeman. Where are you going here, sir?"

"I'm trying to determine this witness's credibility, sir. He says he heard my client confess to murder. I'd like to see if he's a reliable witness. It's that simple."

"All right, Counselor. But quickly, please."

Freeman looked at Roush. "Your job? You were going to tell us how you acquired your expertise?"

Roush sat for a moment trying to decide how to begin. "I laid brick over by Williamstown for a couple years."

"And by whom were you employed, sir?"

"The state."

"Is that the state pen, by chance?"

Roush nodded.

"You're nodding, sir."

"Yeah, well, I did some time. Currently on parole."

"Since you brought it up, what did you do time for, sir?"

"Robbery."

"So when you saw someone coming up the side of the building at three-thirty in the morning, it wasn't such an unusual sight, was it?"

"I suppose."

"Mr. Roush, are you friendly with Claudia Falk?"

"No, not really."

"How would you describe your relationship with her?"

"We didn't have no relationship, really. I'd see her in the lobby or in the hall at night. You know, the community toilet."

"Did you like her, sir?"

"Not particularly."

"Mr. Roush, are the words 'paramour' and 'illicit' normally in your lexicon, sir?"

"In my what?"

"Vocabulary. You used those words earlier, sir."

"Well, I was just repeatin' what I heard."

"Did you hear those words, sir, or did you read them in the newspaper? They are not words we use in everyday conversation, are they, Mr. Roush?"

"No, I guess not. I mighta read it. But I'm tellin' you what I heard."

"Thank you, Mr. Roush. Nothing further."

Wolski rose majestically. Boyd thought he looked like a cat. A very slick one. "The state calls Mr. Vernon Hill."

Wolski questioned the federal agent for quite some time.

"And sir, when the defendant whom you have identified finally gave himself up, what, may I ask, did he have in his possession?"

"A Remington thirty-two-caliber pistol, sir."

"Is this the said pistol, sir?"

The agent took the gun in his hands. "Yes."

"And how do you recognize this weapon with just a cursory glance, Mr. Hill?"

"The bone handle on the weapon has been broken off. I recognize the gun from that break, sir."

"You spent twenty years in law enforcement. Were you asked by the state to do a forensics exam of this weapon?"

"Yes, sir."

"And what was your determination, sir?"

"The bullets fired into the skulls of the decedents were without a doubt fired from this weapon."

"And how did you determine that, sir?"

"The lanes and grooves from the barrel of the thirty-two are identical to the striations found on the spent rounds in the victims."

"Thank you, sir."

Freeman rose wearily. Boyd could see the old man was worn out.

"I have only one question, Your Honor. Mr. Hill, did my client resist in any way? Did he show aggression or threaten anyone at the capture?"

"No."

"Thank you, sir."

Wolski walked to the witness stand and accompanied the bureau agent to the gate leading out of the courtroom, looking as if he were leading an honored guest out of his home.

"Your Honor, if it pleases the court, I would like to set my case aside at this point. I have several witnesses who are currently not available. With Mr. Freeman's indulgence and the court's forbearance, would it be possible for Mr. Freeman to present his case?"

The judge nodded assent toward the defense table. "Mr. Freeman, what do you say? It is unusual. Not unprecedented, but unusual."

Freeman stood. "I would like some reassurances of the leeway that would be granted me in this instance."

"I can assure you, Mr. Freeman, that you will be treated fairly."

Walking out of the courtroom at recess, Hennessy almost bumped into Juanita. "Oh, excuse me."

"You." She turned, gave him a strange look, and stopped in her tracks. Some other black men, maybe relatives, almost walked into her, apparently not understanding any better than Hennessy her reaction.

He wasn't in the mood to tolerate any sass at the moment, and this was not the Bottoms; it was downtown Vermilion. Mustering his most dignified carriage, he looked her straight in the eye. "Yes? Is there some problem?"

Juanita shocked him by taking his hand and squeezing it. "I don't know your name, sir, I can't remember, but I thank you."

Her hand was trembling as it held his tightly, and there was moisture in

her eyes. With everything going on, Hennessy would have thought nothing else could grab his attention today, but the hard-faced black woman,
her features and demeanor softened like this, stopped him cold.

"You and that reporter lady, you done us right." She let his hand go,
nodded her departure, and made her way to the balcony of the courtroom. "I'll never forget that, either, mister, never. You done right by us."

What in blazes has gotten into her?

He continued into the courtroom, and with several minutes to spare before being called to order, he unfolded the *Herald* on his knee. He forced his
eyes from the market coverage and skimmed over the local reporter's take
on the trial. It seemed verbose, but he knew that most people were waiting
for the evening train to bring the *Trib* from Chicago. Myrna was spending
an hour a night on the phone, sending copy up on the noon and late trains,
and twice he had seen special couriers arrive for her typed text and photos.

No question about it, she was good. Her coverage was not only balanced and accurate but human. She got across a sense of the people beyond the facts of the case. She made the trial more compelling even for
someone like himself who sat in the same room all day. Her description
of Boyd, her assessment of his manner and the way he answered questions, was empathetic and sometimes eye-opening.

Without directly criticizing any testimony, she could present it with a
sense of irony, making the reader raise a skeptical eyebrow at some of the
comments made by Boyd's accusers. Hennessy had to admit it might be
more than her legs and her "fine ofay behine" that had got her where she
was. Myrna was a hell of a reporter. In some ways that pleased him, in
others it did not—but it added to his unsettling feeling that she might be
slumming when she was with him.

Oh well, he'd just have to make do this morning with the Vermilion
rag of which Myrna was so scornful. He flipped the page to check the local news—Myrna's byline popped into view. What the hell. In the Vermilion paper? It was a special to the *Herald* and people of Vermilion from
Myrna Logan, *Chicago Tribune*. The text was accompanied by a photo of
George Matthews, probably taken at least five years earlier, and a sketch of
Millie Mae Moss.

Hearing a flurry of activity in the direction of the judge's chambers, Hennessy read intently and quickly, not wanting to be interrupted.

TRIB REPORTER WARNS CITIZENRY ABOUT PREJUDGING.

Special to the *Vermilion Herald* by Myrna Logan

Reporter at Large *Chicago Tribune*

While conducting background investigations on the trial of Mr. Boyd Calvin, I had the opportunity to scrutinize the case of Mr. George Matthews, a black man accused of raping a white woman, Millie Mae Moss. The unwanted attentions Miss Moss received from Mr. Matthews are particularly troubling since she is unfortunate enough to have been subjected to abuse from scurrilous males in this manner more than once. I note that in the arrest reports for August 12 of this year, several months after suffering the attack by the accused George Matthews, Miss Moss was once again taken against her will by a black man, this time unidentified except as "a large muscular Negro known as Toby." He apparently dragged her into an alley and poured liquor down her throat before committing nameless acts of lust. She was found the following morning by the Vermilion police, who mistook her at first for a drunk. On learning the true nature of her plight they quickly adjusted their reports and put out an all points bulletin for Toby.

A record check in the clippings morgue of the *Tribune* revealed that the unfortunate trend that ended in Vermilion actually had roots in Chicago, where the poor woman had almost the identical problem with another black man, this one at her place of work. Before the wheels of justice could turn too far, the man left, taking his family of four and guilty conscience with him to points unknown.

I attempted to conduct a follow-up interview with Miss Moss on the matter, but she informed me that she had nothing further to say and was considering returning to Benton, Georgia, "where women are still treated with respect." I checked with the *Benton Daily News* and it appeared that even in Georgia, the heartland of southern chivalry, she had been harassed by black men.

On the off chance that Mr. Matthews ran because he was afraid of backwater justice and not because he knew he was guilty—I recommend caution in prejudgment. If Mr. Matthews is caught and returned to Vermilion for justice, let us remember the curious complexities of his case and accord him the respect of a fellow citizen who just might be the victim of his color and not of his own unbridled passions.

So this is why Juanita acted the way she did.

As the bailiff started bringing the court back to order, Hennessy felt Myrna slip into the seat beside him.

"Well, it appears you're quite the heroine of the oppressed."

Her blank look prompted him further.

"You know, poor old George . . . old 'fellow citizen' George."

Seeing the open paper, she nodded her understanding. "Yeah, I decided somebody should say something about that business—that Millie Mae Moss seems to have been a serial victim."

"I'd say."

They turned back to the proceedings, but the deepening hush settling over the room suddenly lifted and people started drifting back into open conversation. Apparently, there was some problem with the court reporter, and the bailiff announced an additional ten minutes of break. A few people sitting next to them got up to walk about and stretch, leaving them again in comparative privacy.

"So, did you see a lot of George when you were up there?"

"No, just a few times."

"A few times? You needed to see him more than once for the story?"

He knew his jealousy had to be showing. Myrna's expression was getting a bit taut and distant.

"Look, Dale, I like the man. We had several meetings where I got background on Boyd and we talked about all kinds of things. George made me . . . he made me feel good."

"I'll bet he did."

"Not that way. You can think what you want, but that's not what I meant."

"What *did* you mean?"

"He made me feel safe and he made me laugh."

Hennessy was amazed how angry this all made him feel.

"It was more than just an interview, though, wasn't it?"

"I told you, we talked. He has a great sense of humor but he's also sensitive. . . . He asked about my family, my brothers."

"Your brothers. What about your brothers?" He couldn't believe that this man knew things about her that he didn't.

She looked around to see if anyone was listening and said, "I don't really know if I want to talk about it now, Dale."

"Great, nice. You won't tell me things you told him."

"It's kind of embarrassing."

Hennessy hoped his folded arms and stiff demeanor implied all he meant them to.

"It's just, my dad . . . he used to rough me up when I was young—even when not so young." Her voice trailed off and she looked away. "He'd whip me on my legs and backside with a strap; called me a tramp. And no, goddamn it, I didn't deserve it. I was a virgin until after I went to work for the *Trib*—I was terrified of boys."

"You?" They had gotten loud enough that a couple of ladies a few benches away glanced in their direction.

"Think what you want." She looked as if she was starting to clam up. He knew he had to ease up on her if he expected her to keep talking.

In a gentler voice he said, "Well, what does all this have to do with your brothers?"

"I'm sorry now I brought it up."

"C'mon, you don't have to turn to ice on me."

"I don't know why it bothers me so much, but they were both older and they never helped. Oh sure, they'd act all tough around everybody else, and I wanted to look up to them, but they never helped." A tear appeared at the corner of her eye but she brushed it away angrily. "Yeah, they acted tough, palling around with him and drinking beer, but they were afraid of Dad." Her eyes suddenly bore into him. "Can you imagine strapping your fourteen-year-old girl in her panties in front of your drunken, leering friends? And your brothers, they act kind of nervous and laugh along with the rest?"

"But what does that have to do with George?"

She forced herself to calm down, and muttered as if in closing, "Heck, I don't know, Dale. I told him about that and he just said something thoughtful and kind."

"What'd he say?"

"That I was a 'real fine lady.' He got real serious for a minute and said that. And then he said he reckoned nobody would be hitting me with any strap if he was my brother—not twice, anyway." Just then, the bailiff marched out imperiously and quickly started hustling everyone for the trial to commence.

A minute later Hennessy sat there in knots—Myrna had regained her composure and was taking notes as if nothing had passed between them.

Boyd had been taken into a holding cell to have his lunch. He balanced the cold tin plate on his knees. As he played with the remains of the corn and beans and made small designs in the congealed gravy, the phrase "eat your veggies" pushed against his conscience.

The morning had been endless; the four-day-old trial seemed punishment enough. Boyd wondered, Why bother with prison? Just sentence people to a thirty-day trial. No one would ever commit another crime. Certainly not him.

As he was led into the courtroom, Boyd experienced the same embarrassment he had felt since the first day. The shackles were released from his hands and he was seated. Freeman busily pored over his notes for the afternoon. He looked at Boyd.

"This is it, kiddo. Our defense is you. You're all we got. So when I ask you a question, be forthright and honest. Try not to drop your head or be shifty-eyed. Don't gaze around the courtroom like you're looking for a way out. And tell the truth. You got it all?"

Boyd nodded. He looked over his shoulder to where Claudia usually sat. She wasn't there.

"Mr. Freeman, are you ready to present your case, sir?" The judge had leaned over his tall bench and was peering down at the defendant and his attorney.

"Yes, Your Honor. The defense calls Boyd Calvin."

The gallery stirred immediately. It was not unheard of, but it was unusual, for the defendant to take the stand. When Freeman had talked to Boyd about this move, he had explained that it might be dangerous, but because of the many circumstantial pieces of evidence—the eyewitness that saw him on the porch, the broken gun discovered on him in the silo in Indiana, and maybe worst of all, the motive, one of jealousy and rage— they had to take the chance if they expected to win. Boyd walked to the stand and thought he could feel a hundred sets of eyes drilling into the back of his neck.

"State your name, please."

"Boyd Calvin." As he spoke his name, he heard a distant laugh through the open window. Someone in the street going about his business, not aware of the serious proceedings in the second-story room. He couldn't help thinking it would be nice to trade places. Boyd looked up to see Claudia tiptoeing down the aisle and sliding into her seat. She had her finger to her lips, as if that would keep her from making noises.

"Mr. Calvin, would you describe yourself as of sound mind and body?"

"Yes, sir." Freeman had adopted a studious pose, as if he were about to prove some scholarly thesis.

"Are you currently under a doctor's care?"

"No, sir."

"Have you, in the past five years, been admitted to a hospital or a nursing home?"

"I was at the Soldiers' Home briefly a couple years ago."

"And what were you being treated for, please."

"I had been feeling bad, probably from the war. Kinda blue all the time. Got over it, though."

"We'll come back to your war record directly. Boyd, tell us, if you please, what your daily routine would be?"

"Well, I work late at night at the Light Rail, so I try to sleep in the morning till about ten or so, have lunch, then go back to work. That's about it."

"So your life is fairly routine, would you say that?"

"Yes, sir."

"You live a fairly everyday sort of existence, correct?"

"Yes, sir."

"How did you meet your wife, Boyd?"

"Well, sir . . . we met at the skating rink."

"Is that the rink on River Road?"

"Yes, sir. We started to skate together and that was that. We were married just before I went overseas."

"How long were you separated, Boyd?"

"Oh, I'd say maybe three years."

"Boyd, would you tell us, please, in your own words, what transpired on the evening of June fifth, 1929?"

Boyd looked around the courtroom. Claudia wiggled her fingers at him. His eyes settled briefly on Wolski. The lawyer's eyes cut deep into him.

"I drive a trolley. . . ."

The sound of his own voice startled Boyd. He wondered if his face was red; his collar felt tight around his neck. He had started out wrong. It seemed a dumb thing to say.

"I mean, my job is a motorman, and on that night I was on a familiar run, which I would get about two out of every ten times. This particular run happens to go past my wife's house. On this night, after my third run, I thought I saw someone, or something, in the orchard behind her house."

"Were you at all worried about what you had seen?"

"Well, no, I didn't think anything of it for a few minutes. Then about halfway to the car barn—it was my last run—I got to thinking maybe I should check in on Laurel. I thought I would take a ride out there to see if everything was all right."

"And how did you get out there?"

Boyd shook his head as if he had done something foolish. "Well, I borrowed Chuck Decker's bicycle. I knew it weren't right without asking permission and all, but I sure couldn't call him at midnight. So anyway I rode out to the east end of town."

"Did you think that your concern for Laurel, your ex-wife, was justifiable enough to 'borrow' Mr. Decker's bicycle, Boyd?"

"Objection, Your Honor. Leading the witness."

Boyd could see that Wolski had said this without a lot of enthusiasm. "Overruled. Continue, Mr. Calvin."

"Well, yeah, I didn't think he would mind once I explained it to him. Well heck, he probably wouldn't never even have known if—"

Boyd stopped. The image of Laurel's legs, all white and bare, flashed across his eyes.

"Boyd, do you need a moment?"

Boyd took a deep breath. "No, I'm okay."

"You were telling us about riding to the east end."

"When I got out there, I was kinda pooped, so I came down the alley thinking I would catch my breath for a bit before I went in. I could see there was a light on in the kitchen, so I knew she was up."

"You knew your wife was still awake, correct?"

"Yeah. I stood in the orchard and leaned the bike against a fence. Then I heard some people talking. At first I thought it was coming from the house. But then I saw a couple people in the front, on the sidewalk, and a couple more across the street."

"Had you heard anything at all as you were riding up to the orchard, Boyd?"

"No, I don't think I could have heard anything over the sound of my breathing. Anyway, I kinda crept through the trees so as not to be seen by the folks in the street."

"Boyd, why didn't you just walk up to the house boldly? After all, she was your wife. You had a right to be there, correct?"

"Well, yeah, but I don't know. It was kinda spooky. The people in the street, the kitchen lights casting this funny glow across the yard, and there didn't seem to be any movement in the house."

Boyd looked to Freeman for help. He didn't want to tell the next part. Freeman had sat down and given Boyd the whole courtroom to himself. But now he rose for support.

"Tell us what you did then, Boyd."

"I walked in the shadow of the trees. When I reached the porch, I stood there for a minute or so. I could see someone at the kitchen table. He was hunched over like he was studying or something."

"What then, Boyd?"

"I called out Laurel's name. There was no answer, so I opened the door."

Boyd braced his hands against his knees.

"The fellow inside said something about 'being finished' and I stopped halfway. He looked at me with this strange grin. I asked where Laurel was and he gestured with a pencil toward his left. I thought maybe she was in the bedroom, and I felt kinda stupid just standing there. After a couple seconds, I could sense he was pointing with the pencil toward the floor, and there she was."

Tears welled up in his eyes; the muscles in his neck fought with his breathing. He struggled as if he couldn't get enough air. Boyd could hear his gasps as if they were coming from a far-off place. He held his hand up to ask for a moment, the courtroom very still. A car a block away honked an angry *ah-ooh-ah*. The judge asked Boyd if he needed a recess.

"No, sir, I'll be okay."

Freeman waited another moment, then spoke. "Would you like to tell us what happened next, Boyd?"

"I don't know. I almost fell over. I could see Laurel's legs sticking out from under the kitchen table. She was bloody . . . an awful lot of blood." Boyd bit down on his lip. "I felt like my head was gonna come off. . . . I loved her very much. I looked at this fellow at the table. He had the gun in his hand, pointing at me. Then all of a sudden he turned it toward himself and there was a loud explosion. I don't know if I ducked so hard that I fell, but I found myself on the floor, trying to figure out what had happened."

"What then, Boyd?"

"My ears were ringing and I couldn't take my eyes off Laurel. I tried shaking my head to clear it and that's when I saw the gun. It had fallen off of the table after the guy did what he did, and it landed hard on the linoleum, breaking the bone part of the pistol grip. I swear to God, I don't know why, but I picked it up and just stared at it. . . . I heard some people outside shouting, and I knew I better go for help."

"Continue, Boyd."

"Well, I went out to the back porch and some people started shouting at me. I don't know, I guess I just panicked."

"Did you run for your life, Boyd?"

"Yeah, I guess I just couldn't think straight. . . . She was gone. Just gone, and I ran."

"Boyd, did you kill Ralph Sheridan?"

"No, sir, I did not."

"Did you kill your wife that night, Boyd?"

Boyd buried his head in his hands, shaking his head no. The courtroom could hear his muffled denials.

Back in the holding cell, Boyd felt drained. He sat on a hard wooden chair and thought about his testimony. He wished he could do it over, as difficult as it had been. He felt he hadn't sufficiently explained himself. But it was now too late.

Boyd scanned the dingy room. A heavy wire screen with a padlock had been fitted over the filthy glass window. Someone must have lost the key. He could see the top of the Grant Hotel and next to it, Miller's Notions. The climb up to the roof seemed ages ago. In the other direction, the car barn seemed dilapidated, the brick facade crumbled and sad. As he watched, a trolley turned the corner and coasted toward the barn, swaying drunkenly on the old tracks, looking for all the world like an elderly man stumbling home from work.

"Court's back in session in ten minutes, Calvin." The bailiff had stuck his head through the anteroom door.

Ten minutes.

Boyd's legs felt wobbly as he walked back to the stand. He glanced at the judge, who looked away quickly. Boyd didn't think that was a good sign.

"Are you feeling better?" asked Freeman.

"Yes, sir."

"You have stated that you did not commit these crimes of which you are accused. Did you feel as if you were an integral part of this community, Boyd?"

"Yes, sir."

"You wanted to raise a family, is that fair to say, Boyd?"

"Yes, sir."

"Did you feel as though your wife had given you a fair shake regarding any kind of reconciliation?"

"Yes, sir. She tried real hard to understand me. I guess I didn't do my share in trying to make things work. . . . But yes, sir. She sure did her bit."

"And your attempts at trying to get back together with her were, shall we say, done in a civilized way?"

"Yes, sir. After the separation I attempted to see her a few times but it was always, as you say, civilized. I guess you could say that we had been apart a lot, with me being in the service and all, and I felt we hadn't given the marriage a chance."

"Let's talk about your service, Boyd. You enlisted quite young, am I right?"

"Yes, sir, just turned seventeen."

"And where did you serve?"

"After basic training, I was sent right off to France and Belgium."

"Did you see action, Boyd?"

"Yes, sir, quite a lot—more than I wanted, if the truth be told."

"Were you decorated, Boyd?"

"Well, yes, sir."

"Tell us about those decorations, would you please."

"Well, I was wounded once and my unit got a citation also."

"How long did you serve, Boyd?"

He started to answer, then stopped as if trying to remember the exact time length. "I think all and all 'bout fourteen months, something like that." His eye was pulled toward the prosecutor's table; a junior lawyer wrote furiously on his notepad.

"So you served your country honorably and then tried to establish yourself back in this community, correct?"

"Yes, sir."

"I'm going to ask you one more time, Boyd, did you commit these crimes?"

"No, sir, I did not."

"No more questions, Your Honor."

The judge had been writing some notes without looking up. He called to Wolski. "Sir, are you ready to proceed with this witness?"

"Your Honor, may we have a side conference, please."

The judge motioned for both Wolski and Freeman to come to the side of his raised pedestal away from the jury.

"All right, Mr. Wolski, what's up?"

"Your Honor, I have a witness that I've been trying desperately to contact, but without any luck. Since it's late Friday—"

Freeman interrupted the prosecutor. "There aren't any more witnesses on your list. What are you trying to pull here, Wolski?"

The prosecutor didn't look at Freeman but pleaded to the judge. "Your Honor, could we possibly have a continuance until Monday, sir? I realize this is unusual, but I'm asking in the name of justice, sir."

Freeman shook his head violently. "Your Honor, my learned counterpart should have prepared his case better. The defense has done its fair part in these proceedings, and I expect the prestigious prosecutor to do the same."

"Please, Your Honor."

The judge seemed to be thinking; he shuffled his notes. "I realize this is an unusual request and normally I wouldn't grant it, but with this stifling heat and the amount of testimony we all must absorb, I'm going to allow it. We'll take the rest of the afternoon off and reconvene Monday morning. Mr. Wolski, don't disappoint me, sir. I will go hard on you if you're not being forthright here."

"Yes, sir. Thank you, sir."

Freeman walked back to his desk as the judge dismissed the court, explaining to all his reasons.

Boyd could see that Freeman was troubled. "What's the matter, Mr. Freeman?"

The old lawyer started packing his briefcase. "Toward the end of my questioning of you, there was a bit of commotion at the prosecution's table. It seemed strange. . . . I just don't know. It was as if they had heard something in your testimony that rang a bell."

The attorney finished up his housekeeping and rose from the table.

"You're not holding back on me, are you, son?"

Boyd tried to think what he had said that might have caused a fuss. "No, sir. I've told the truth right on through. Beginning to end. I swear."

Freeman's shoulders were sagging. His blue suit seemed to hang from his bony shoulders like limp laundry.

"Well, it's gonna be a long weekend, sonny. Get some rest."

Boyd watched as the old man trudged past the beehivelike table of the prosecution. Wolski had rallied his troops, and their heads were just inches apart, whispering. It looked to Boyd as if the enemy camp was preparing an all-out assault.

Hennessy stood in Freeman's office, trying, with limited success, to carry on a conversation with the older man.

"I don't get it. What's happening? You seem bothered. Seems to me like things are going okay."

"Something's wrong, damn it. Wolski's up to something. Everett shouldn't have granted that continuance, but there is not much I can do about it."

"Yes, but even if they do have a witness who speaks ill of Boyd, I don't see why that should be all that important—people obviously see Boyd in a different light. I think I can bring out some of his more positive aspects when I'm on the stand."

"You'll bring out pretty much what Wolski pulls out of you." Freeman sighed and smiled half apologetically. "Sorry, don't mean to sound curt, but this pattern of last-minute key witnesses and the like has me concerned. I don't think Wolski's just grandstanding, because he knows the judge will have him for breakfast Monday morning if he doesn't have enough to justify holding us over. I hope that knucklehead Boyd hasn't held back on something; that's what would hurt us the most."

Hennessy and Freeman were both startled when the phone rang loudly in the quiet room. The old lawyer had the new rotary dial type, rare in Vermilion, that had the mouth and earpiece all in one—he could snatch it up and use it with just one hand.

He handed the receiver to Hennessy. "It's a call for you from the home."

"Mr. H, it's Betty."

"Betty, what's up?"

"I don't know, this fellow showed up, some officer of the court, and handed me a subpoena." From the agitated tone of her voice it was obvious to Hennessy that Betty didn't care for receiving official-looking court documents late on a Friday afternoon. He knew she was looking forward to a long weekend with her cats. With her husband deceased and her sons having flown the coop, her feline charges occupied most of her time.

"They couldn't find you and they told me that because they were delivering it to your place of work it was my duty to ensure that you were informed of the contents of this document by whatever means at my disposal."

"Can you tell me what's in it? Do you know what they're asking me to do?"

"I read it. It tells you to produce all relevant records and information on Boyd, or some such, when you testify on Monday."

"I'll be there within the hour."

By the time he put the phone down, Freeman, whose frown had deepened as he listened to Hennessy's part of the phone conversation, was rising to greet Myrna, who had just arrived with her usual purposeful air. It was obvious the old man had begun to take a shine to her—no different from most males that Hennessy had seen spend any time around her. He had a brief taste of that familiar queasy feeling he got when he suspected that most men would gladly give up a limb to spend time between the sheets with Miss Logan. He had the opportunity, and still couldn't figure out if he was better or worse for it.

Hennessy continued as if there had been no interruption, directing his comments to Freeman. "Well, whatever Wolski has up his sleeve, it apparently involves something in my files."

The attorney absently waved Myrna toward a chair as he responded to Hennessy. "Do you know what this is about, Dale?"

"I really don't." This was mainly true, but not entirely. Racing his mind back over the testimony he had heard in the courtroom, a vague uneasiness started to take hold. It occurred to him that there might have been some parts of Boyd's war record that he hadn't recounted in court. Preoccupied, he bid Freeman good evening, nodded a good-bye to Myrna, and left.

Myrna caught up with him as he was heading for his car.

"Hey, what gives? What's Freeman nervous about, and where in the heck are you rushing off to? What'd I miss?"

Hennessy explained to her a little of Freeman's distress but said nothing about the growing suspicion in his own mind. He opened the passenger-side door of his car, knowing that Myrna had no intention of letting him depart alone now that she knew he might have some newsworthy information for her.

As they sped along Main Street, Myrna watched him drive for a moment, then said, "Well, you're a bit more together today—things better at the races?"

"If you mean the market, I wouldn't worry, things will even out."

"I'm not worried. My money is under my mattress in a sock."

He refused to be goaded by her. "Yeah, well, we'll see if that's wise in a few weeks or so. Anyway, I don't want to talk about it—radio said the trading dropped way off today. Vedeler said the experts spoke on the radio and agreed there are no real worries for the economy—bunch of people who turned tail yesterday will be crying in their beer soon. We're holding pat."

Myrna seemed to find something real interesting to study out the window and had nothing more to say.

Hennessy was pleased to note that Betty, ever the competent secretary, had pulled everything on Boyd without his asking. Myrna pulled a folder out and was already perusing it.

"Make yourself at home with our confidential files."

"Thanks, I will. I expect they aren't going to be so confidential come Monday, when you're sitting there in court answering questions from them."

Hennessy grunted and grabbed a couple of thick files for himself. He realized most of what he had was bureaucratic folderol: medical records, semiannual reviews of patient progress, and a host of half-page confirmations of the most routine functions.

"Dale, what's this?"

"I don't know—some letters and odds and ends from the earliest of Boyd's transfer documents. Hard for me to tell exactly, because you snatched it from me before I could see it, don't you think?" After no response for a moment, he looked back at Myrna to see she was still glued to one piece of correspondence. "Why, what do you have there?"

By way of answer, she just asked another question. "What's the court asking for, anyway?"

He pointed at the packet back on Betty's desk. "It says on the subpoena, 'Service record and other pertinent material relating to Boyd's time in the United States Army.' Why?"

"Have you read this letter? The one from Colonel Wells."

"How could I have? You snatched it up." Then, with no repartee returned by Myrna, and seeing the serious look on her face, he added, "Not in several years."

"You better take a look." She handed a two-page letter to him.

Hennessy sat back in his rocker and examined the piece of correspondence. It was from a Col. Matthew Wells, Leavenworth Stockade, Leavenworth, Kansas. Hennessy felt suddenly queasy; yes, he remembered this letter. He imagined reading it out loud in court on Monday.

                                        Colonel Matthew Wells, M.D.
                                        Fort Leavenworth Stockade
                                        Leavenworth, Kansas

        Major Dale Hennessey
        Soldiers' Home
        Vermilion, Illinois

        MAY 10, 1920

        Sir:

    The following will serve as cover letter for a detailed report and transfer of records on inmate Mr. Boyd Calvin, 060719.

    Mr. Calvin has been a prisoner of this facility for the past eighteen months, having been transferred to this stockade after his sentencing at a general court-martial that took place in Neufchâteau, France, on or about November 30, 1918.

    It was in my power as medical director to recommend that Warden Burns commute Mr. Calvin's sentence from five years to the above-mentioned eighteen months. The circumstances of Mr. Calvin's offenses were vague at best and, coming so close to the armistice, were rife with innuendo and thus possible inaccuracies.

    Mr. Calvin has been an exemplary inmate at this facility and shows signs of possibly being rehabilitated and joining a successful and fruitful civilian life.

    The following tendencies have been exhibited by Mr. Calvin:

1. A decidedly antisocial demeanor in the general prison population.
2. A marked inability to concentrate on military protocol.
3. Extreme agitation and fright when subjected to loud noises.
4. Generalized manifestations of confusion and guilt over the
   traumatic circumstances surrounding the death of Lieutenant
   Charles Eddie in the final days of the war.

The above-mentioned traits collectively seem abhorrent and possibly
diametrically opposed to what one might think of as a candidate for
release from prison, but it is my belief that Mr. Calvin can be a useful
citizen.

This inmate has shown tendencies to try to better himself, and although not highly educated, he is, I believe, in possession of a higher-
than-average intelligence quotient.

I have determined that it is in this inmate's best interests to have access to both medical and, possibly, psychiatric doctors, who will be better equipped to deal with Mr. Calvin's problems. Also, the fact that Mr.
Calvin would be exposed to his hometown and a supportive family
structure will, I believe, help improve his disposition.

Striking an officer, as we all know, is a serious offense, especially in
times of war. But as previously stated, the war was over, for all intents
and purposes, and the offense, as I understand it, came at the end of a
long and arduous campaign.

In 1919, during the much-publicized riot we had at Leavenworth,
Mr. Calvin showed both courage and compassion tending to prisoners
and prison personnel in the facility's hospital as a volunteer.

Yours in truth and valor,
Col. Matthew Wells, M.D.

He wasn't sure which bothered him more—the content, or Myrna's penetrating gaze when he finally looked up. "Nothing here all that surprising, just the colonel agreeing that Boyd isn't a bad sort."

Myrna gave him a funny look, and quickly added, "Sure, and it catches Boyd in a barefaced lie about his military record."

"How do you mean? Just because—"

"Stop it, Dale."

"What do you mean, 'stop it'?"

She stubbed out her second cigarette in yet another of Betty's clean ashtrays—Hennessy noted that she was already absently reaching for a third one; apparently not one of Betty's collection of Murano glass ashtrays would be clean by the end of the evening. She seemed distant and wouldn't answer until she finally muttered, "You know what I mean."

"Now look, what are you asking me? You know darned well that I'm legally obliged to turn this all over to the court."

"You don't have to turn anything over that you don't find." She said it softly, but her intent was anything but soft. It was somehow almost accusatory. "Dale, there are times when a man needs to decide what's right rather than what's proper."

He found he was really angry. The "man" reference held special import to him, and he resented it.

"Look, damn it, I'll decide what's right *and* what's proper. It seems not very long ago you were ready to cinch the noose on Boyd's neck yourself. Now, all of a sudden you're the Goddess of Compassion and Fair Play. Hell, you're ready to see me perjure myself to keep poor buddy Boyd from justice."

"Justice? You really think that's what this court is fixing to give Boyd? Justice?"

"I don't get it. Who are you to decide? Just because you were enamored of Mr. Black Stud, now you're the angel of mercy?"

Hennessy was sorry he said it the moment it came out of his mouth. Myrna gathered herself and made for the door. No question of a ride to the inn, nothing about getting her a cab. She just headed out into the sultry evening air and disappeared. He would be damned if he would play

her games. Hennessy looked down at the letter in his hand and cursed
when he saw how much his hand was shaking.

With court adjourned for the weekend, Boyd spent Friday afternoon read-
ing. He had borrowed a couple of dog-eared pulp magazines from Morris.
The cover of one said, *Amazing Stories, Scientifiction, a Compilation of Startling
Tales.* A rocket ship zoomed toward the stars, fire shooting out of its tail.

Boyd read the daring deeds of someone by the name of Buck Rogers.
He had completely lost himself in the exploits of the handsome rocke-
teer. His friends were all beautiful, too. Boyd felt it was a world he
wanted to live in; Buck was fighting evil, and he stood for what was right
and proper. Unlike some people he knew.

By Saturday afternoon, Boyd was ensconced comfortably in an outer-
space dreamworld to which he would gladly have succumbed for the rest
of his life. It would be just him and his beautiful friends, twirling end-
lessly in the azure sky.

"*Should we go to full power, Commander Boyd?*"

"*Yes, full power, let's try to overtake Killer Kane before he reaches the planet
Nebus.*"

"*Right, sir.*"

Boyd ran his fingers along the lines of the illustrated rocket ship. He lay
on the hard cot of his subterranean cell; Morris had given him his old spot
back. He could shimmy up the wall and grasp the barred window and, for
as long as his arms held out, watch the rest of the world walk by freely.

"Boyd, you got a visitor."

He was startled to hear his name called out. "Don't call me Boyd,
Morris. My name is Buck now."

"Well, Mr. Buck, Mrs. Falk is here."

Claudia came lightly down the corridor. She was humming softly.
"Hi, sugar."

"Hi, Claudie."

"How you keeping?"

"Oh, I'm keeping."

Claudia dragged up a hard-backed wooden chair outside of Boyd's cell. "Do you feel like having some company, shug?"

"Well, I don't feel like I'm fit for human exposure."

"Oh, that's a bunch of hooey, you know better than that."

"I've been reading, taking my mind off of things."

"Well, it'll be over soon, one way or the other."

Boyd thought his friend seemed to have gotten older in the months since the murders. He had never noticed the lines around her eyes and the sag under her chin. But her voice was still strong, if a shade softer. She had visited him almost every day since he had been put in jail awaiting trial, but the weeks had crept by. Some days she would just sit and knit or read. Other days she couldn't stay long and she would just "Ta-ta" and be off. Boyd didn't know how to react to her most of the time. With the exception of Laurel, she was the only woman he had ever really known.

"Whatcha' thinkin', baby?"

"Oh, don't know, really, just about women in general, I guess."

"Well, they are a necessary evil, my friend. So get used to it."

"I maybe won't have to get used to it. If you know what I mean."

Claudia clasped her hands on her hips in mock anger. "You just listen to me, Mr. Boyd Calvin. You gotta keep a good thought about this thing. I been at the trial almost every day, and I'm here to tell you that it don't look all that bad. Every time one of those witnesses makes a point for ol' Wolski, our guy Freeman manages to cut 'im down, or at least soften the blow some."

Boyd stretched his arms and folded them behind his neck. He eased his head back against the flaking wall. "Whenever I'm on the stand and start thinking about Laurel, I just kinda lose my way."

"Sure do. Funny, you know, how you ended up with someone who worked at the five-and-dime. You remember I told you that your mom and I worked at the Kresge's five-and-dime in Chicago."

"Oh, right, almost forgot. She was a good gal, my Laurel. Miss her. Wish—oh, the hell with it."

"You wish what, hon?"

"Oh, I don't know, wish I could have told her how sweet she was to me. I mean, I told her that plenty, but I wish I could have been more convincing."

Boyd remained quiet for several moments.

"About the closest we ever were was on a hot July night. We couldn't sleep. It was at least a hundred at midnight. We decided to dress and go outside. We took an old flannel blanket and a milk bottle full of water with a couple pieces of chipped ice in it. We walked a heck of a way, finally ended up in a grassy area up to Wilson Heights. A slight breeze came across the lake and we were on this bluff. It actually felt cooler, probably around ninety-five."

Claudia laughed.

"Well, we laid there and I could feel the heat rising off me like a loco-motive. I pulled my shirt off and stuffed it behind my head. Laurel hiked her skirt up to her hips and we just laid there, looking up at the stars through an old oak tree. Think I fell asleep for a while with Laurel's hand in mine. I could feel her rings. They were so tiny, those stones, but she loved them. Her breathing was deep and regular. I thought she was asleep. 'I want a baby, Boyd. I really do.' It had been six months since her mis-carriage and I was scared for her. I took a drink of the cool water and caught a piece of ice in my mouth, kissing her neck and shoulder with my cold tongue. She looked at me. 'I'll always love you, Boyd. Whatever happens.' That kinda startled me, but she went on to tell me she had this, I think she called it a—"

"Premonition?"

"Yeah, said she was sure she would go before me. I tried to kid her out of it, but she just smiled and took me in her arms. I remember the moon played funny tricks across her face as we made love. An old hoot owl seemed disturbed that we were ruffling the grass. He laughed at us and then flew away. We fell asleep and woke with the mosquitoes trying to carry us over the bluff. We'd been there almost all night, so we finished the water, which had gotten warm, and walked home. I had a terrible crick in my neck and she tried to rub it out while we were walking. 'If we have a boy, I want him to be just like you, sweetheart.' But I guess it was just not to be."

Claudia looked down at her feet. "You've been through a lot. I was so upset when you were on the stand, talking about your time in the service. It must have been awful for you."

Boyd got up from the cot, his eyes swollen and red. Stretching his neck, he paced to the wall and pushed hard against the crumbling plaster. He didn't want to delve into the past, but it was coming anyway.

"The worst thing that happened is we got lost."

"Lost?"

"Yeah, we had been out on patrol, the whole platoon, and Lieutenant—well, it wasn't really his fault. You see, after this one heavy bombardment, I guess we got disoriented. Lieutenant got us moving the wrong way and we got way deep inside the German lines. I'll tell you, I was shit-scared."

"I can't imagine what men have to do in war. It must be horrible."

"I saw lots of people get killed, Claudie."

"Did you ever have to shoot your gun?"

"Couple times I did, yeah." Boyd took a quick look at Claudia. He thought she was so wonderful, just sitting there not prying or digging into his thoughts, waiting for him to take the lead.

The sally-port door banged shut and Morris called out, "You got another visitor, killer—not s'pose to, but seeing as how the place is empty—should I send him to you?"

Boyd could see it was Hennessy in uniform and looking spiffy. The Major brought a small wooden stool and his obligatory cane down the hallway with him. Boyd wondered what he wanted; he had seen him a few times in court with the woman from Chicago and felt he had to be polite. "Hi ya, Major. You know Miss Falk, don't you? Claudia, 'member Major Dale?"

"Oh yes, nice to see you again." Claudia was sort of overly gracious.

"Don't let me interrupt." Hennessy sat primly on the small stool. "I just wanted to say hello and . . . wish you well. I can speak to you later if it would be more comfortable for you."

Boyd didn't know what this was about. "No, stick around. What's on your mind?"

"Oh, nothing really. It can wait." Hennessy tapped the floor with his cane.

"I can go," piped Claudia. "I just popped in to rattle Boyd's cage."

Boyd knew this was getting uncomfortable, but they still exchanged pleasantries for what seemed too long a while. Finally, Hennessy blurted, "Boyd, you look as if you're going through something. Is it the nightmares you were having or . . ."

Boyd felt a warmth in his cheeks. He knew his eyes were swollen and he felt embarrassed in front of the Major. "I was telling Claudia about . . . about a patrol where we got lost and . . ." They sat in silence once again.

Hennessy spoke to Boyd in a soft yet authoritative voice. "I'd like to hear about it, Boyd. Why don't you tell us?"

"You don't want to hear about that stuff, do you?"

"If you feel like talking, do so. Maybe it will make you feel better."

"Well, like I told Claudia, the lieutenant was dead and there wasn't anybody in charge." Boyd ran his hands over his face. "I tried to get some of the guys organized but I was just a kid. I had just turned eighteen and of course nobody wanted to listen—not that I had the answers. I had been up moving around doing this and that. . . . The rest of them were just dug into the sides of this ravine." Boyd paused. He didn't know if he would be able to finish this. "I remembered which direction we had come from, and tried to get the people moving back that way. The German guns were real close and they knew we were there, so I started crawling back toward our lines. The rest of them just bolted toward the Germans, not fighting, just running hell-bent for leather—I can still remember their screams."

Hennessy edged closer to the bars. "What had happened to your superior officer, Boyd. Your lieutenant?"

"Well, like I said, he had been hit. . . . He screamed bloody murder and . . ." Boyd stared at the small window in his cell for a few moments, aware of Hennessy's total concentration on him. Why had he used the

words "bloody murder"? Did he feel as if the Major was here to interview him? Boyd sensed Claudia's frown was out of concern for him.
Boyd had to get this story out, regardless.

"Later, the Krauts came back toward us. That's when I got hit. Finally
got away and, after a long stretch in and out of German lines, hooked up
with the three other guys, white as rabbits, from the platoon. All of them
huddled up under a footbridge in the middle of this damn forest. I probably didn't look much better. The Germans had just given me a gunning
and I had been scampering around for a spell. I remember one of the
guys, a religious-type fellow from Ohio, saying, 'Calvin, we thought you
were a goner.' Where did everybody get to? Damn, I didn't know a
whole heck of a lot more than they did, except I knew the whole platoon
was dead. I told them and they just collapsed. I think,'cause I had been
running and dodging around, and they'd just been huddled and just kinda
hip-deep in fear. They just couldn't get themselves together." Boyd stumbled for a moment.

"Don't put yourself through this, Boyd," said Claudia.

But Boyd continued.

"Well, anyway, about that time, a German light machine gun opened
up and we all hit the mud."

"Probably a captured English Lewis gun," Hennessy said quickly.
"They had thousands of them that they modified and—" He caught
himself. "Excuse me, go on."

Boyd took a deep breath. "I could tell it was coming from where I had
run into a whole bunch of Krauts. They didn't have us zeroed in, but
were spraying the area, trying to get us to run. I was sure glad the trees
were so thick in those woods. I told them to keep their heads down and I
would be right back. The ravine we were in was about thirty feet wide at
this point. I sprinted across and eased up on the other side, keeping my
head under a couple large ferns.

"I could just barely see the Germans—three of them had set up at a
spot to cover the ravine where it kinda opened up. If we'd kept walking
down that stream bed, they would have cut us to pieces. We had these
British-made Enfield rifles but they were pretty good anyway. I knew I

couldn't get all three of them with my rifle, so I decided to try and take out the machine gun. Then all they could do was chase us with their rifles. I didn't think they would do that, as they didn't know how well armed we were."

Boyd wished he could forget the image.

"If they'd known I was the only one with a weapon, we would have been goners. The other guys from the platoon had dropped their rifles back at the original bivouac area when Lieutenant—well—" Boyd looked at Claudia. She had her eyes closed and was kind of rocking back and forth. "I took a chance and plinked that ol' German machine gun real good; I could hear the heavy metal ricochet as the bullet went careening off into the woods. Must have done considerable damage, because the Germans were hell-mad. I ripped off a couple more rounds to keep their heads down and fell back down the ravine. I hissed at the three guys under the bridge and was angry when they wouldn't budge, but I finally got them to running and we made it across the open space okay. I'll tell you, that was plenty close."

"That's enough," said Claudia.

"Yes, Boyd, take a break." Hennessy had eased even closer to the bars. "Give yourself some time."

"I'm okay." Boyd's hands were shaking. "These guys were petrified and I had to prod them to keep moving—they wanted to stop and huddle under every big rock they saw. A mortar round suddenly exploded close by. We had heard its whistle as it arched through the sky, so we were all down. I kept the guys on their bellies for about a fifty-yard stretch. We came across what must have been a German latrine. We were gonna try and skirt it but I heard voices so we had to plow through. I took my Enfield and tried to push the awful stuff to the side as we crawled on but it was bad, real bad. I could hear the guys retching and gasping. One of them got to his knees, saying he'd rather die. I swatted him with my gasmask bag and told him to shut up. It seemed like we crawled a mile through that stuff, but it probably was only ten yards."

Claudia gasped and dug a handkerchief from her bag. "My God, oh my God."

"We finally made it through and I listened for a minute and then we trotted what felt like about four or five hundred yards."

"Were they following you, Boyd? Did you cover your rear quarter?"

Boyd wondered if Hennessy was grading him on his infantry tactics. He ignored him and went on. "That ravine kept turning and winding back on itself. It felt good to get a breeze. I was worried the ravine was gonna take us back toward the enemy lines. About then we hear a 'Halt' and some yea-hoo fires off a round at us. I yelled that we were the Second Platoon of the First Battalion. Some officer finally came up to the line and shouted that we were to identify ourselves. Couple of the boys wanted to walk right on in, but I convinced them it was worth waiting a couple minutes. I talked to some lieutenant, we shouted back and forth about this and that. It seems our whole platoon had been listed as casualties—we'd been gone about four days and they had given up on us. I shouted to him that our lieutenant was dead and we were all that was left. In the end, he told me to walk on out with my rifle up over my head. Someone said something in German and I can tell you, my heart sank, but they were just trying to see who we were."

Claudia got up from her chair. "Now it's really enough. Boyd, I'll stop in tomorrow or at court. Or—well anyway, I love you, sweetie."

Boyd could hear her weeping as she left. She called out a strangled "Good-bye" to Hennessy and slipped out.

"She's a very nice friend, Boyd. I like her."

"Yep, she's all right. Where was I?"

"You had just gotten back to the U.S. lines." Hennessy massaged his bum leg.

"Right, well, we were filthy and smelled to heaven. They gave us water and took us to a captain's tent about half a mile past the lines. This guy kept shouting at me about desertion and dereliction of duty. He said, 'Sergeant, I'll have your stripes.' Course, I weren't no sergeant so there wasn't much to have. When I tried to explain that I was just a corporal, he wouldn't believe me. Said he'd see I was court-martialed. To this day, I don't know what the hell had gotten into this guy. He singled me out. When the lieutenant who had brought us in tried to intervene, he told him to shut up and ordered him out of the tent. He had a long leather thing with a loop on the end that he kept wiggling in my face—"

"A riding crop?"

"Yeah, I guess. Well, all of a sudden, he bashes me in the nose with this damn thing. When he drew back to hit me again, I tried to grab it away from him—"

"Were there any other witnesses in the tent with you?" Hennessy interrupted.

"Yeah, sure, the other guys from my platoon, but . . . about then, the lieutenant, hearing the commotion, comes running back into the tent. The captain screams out that I had struck him. I remember turning to the lieutenant and trying to explain to him what happened. But the captain had the bit in his teeth then and he called for the officer of the day. They arrested me and I eventually got a court-martial."

Boyd realized he was still upset. His hands and face were soaked in sweat, his short hair plastered to his skull.

"If the end of the war hadn't come just that week, I think I could have been shot. You know, striking an officer in time of war. I was lucky to get off with the time I did in Leavenworth. It bothered me that those guys didn't stand up for me. Maybe they were too embarrassed. I did some awful things during the war. If this trial doesn't turn out well, I guess it's just my payback for past deeds." Boyd ducked his head down to his shirtsleeve and tried to get some sweat off himself.

"You know, I've never told anyone about this stuff, been holding it in for quite a spell. It hurts, damn it." Boyd mopped his head and hands with a face towel. "I'm sorry, didn't really intend to get into all this but . . ."

Hennessy tapped his cane slowly against the cell's bars. "I've been asked to bring in some of your papers, Boyd."

"Bring them in?"

"To the trial . . . I've been subpoenaed. I'm required by law to turn over what I have." Hennessy continued with the tapping. "Why didn't you . . . did you have a lawyer at your court-martial or—"

"No, just the shit-scared guys from the platoon, and all they could think about was getting home."

"I wanted to ask you about your lieutenant and how he died. Was it instantaneous?" The tapping stopped.

Boyd felt Hennessy's stare. "He got killed. A mortar round or something. Damn, I don't get it, whatcha need to know for?"

"I told you, Boyd, I have to bring in your papers and I wanted to hear your side first. I have a letter from Dr. Matthew Wells talking about a number of things; your court-martial, your deportment while at Leavenworth, and your lieutenant. I would like to help you, Boyd, but if I bring these things in, it opens up your past record, and of course that can work against you. I would like very much—"

Boyd interrupted. "Why don't you just do whatever you're big enough to do, Major?"

"What do you mean, Boyd? I'm trying to understand you, if you'll just help me a little."

"Help you . . . I don't think so. I think you're going to do whatever it takes to get Major Dale Hennessy through this looking as clean as possible, so if you've come down here for some kind of forgiveness before committing the offense, forget it. Do whatever you see fit—officers usually do, don't they?"

Hennessy pulled his cane into his lap. "I like you, Boyd. I think you got a raw deal in this murder rap."

Boyd watched as Hennessy ran his fingers along the polished hickory surface. It seemed he was always searching for the right word. "And I thought I could explain to you why I have to—"

"Do you really need that?"

"Pardon?"

"Do you really have to walk with a cane?"

"No wonder you're always in trouble, Calvin. You're insubordinate."

Boyd had his hands wrapped tightly around the bars. He looked at Hennessy defiantly. "If you have something you feel compelled to tell the court, tell them, damn it."

"You're a difficult man, Calvin. I really don't think you recognize when someone is trying to do you a service."

Hennessy rose awkwardly. Shoulders ramrod stiff, he walked purpose-fully down the hall. Boyd had effectively released him from any friendly obligation, and felt a wave of depression descending upon him. He could tell Hennessy was now on a mission. Boyd didn't dislike Hennessy, but he knew he didn't like him, either.

*M*onday *morning* was bright and brisk. Fall leaves were starting to turn, and the heat had subsided. If he hadn't been in a crowded courtroom, fighting for his life, Boyd would have felt fine.

Wolski was explaining to the judge something about his witness not yet arriving, so he would like to cross-examine Boyd in the afternoon. "If it so pleases Your Honor."

"You are trying my patience, young man." The judge shook a finger at the prosecutor.

"The state would like to call at this time Major Dale Hennessy."

Boyd watched as the officer, with a leather briefcase tucked under his arm, limped into the courtroom with a decidedly military bearing. He had a certain air of resignation about him. Boyd could see the female reporter from Chicago. She was busy taking notes and didn't look up as the man walked by. While the Major was being sworn in, Boyd observed the courtroom. There seemed to be a new atmosphere. People were in an expectant mood. There was a sense that the end might be near and no one wanted to miss the excitement.

"Major, would you tell us, please, what your current job is, sir?"

Hennessy cleared his throat. "I am currently superintendent of the Soldiers' Home here in Vermilion."

"You were subpoenaed this morning, sir, along with certain records. Would you tell us, please, what those records contain?"

"Yes, sir, the subpoena read that I was to bring Boyd Calvin's military record and any other pertinent documents."

"Thank you. Would you show us those records, please?"

Boyd could tell from Hennessy's attitude that he was reluctant to delve into his briefcase. He finally dug out a large envelope, which he handed to Wolski. The lawyer took the papers and spoke to the judge.

"Your Honor"—Freeman was on his feet—"the defense, sir, has not had an opportunity to review this evidence."

"That was my next question, Your Honor." Wolski had walked up to the judge's bench. "Should we take a recess, sir, to let Mr. Freeman read the material, or would he like to read it while I question the witness?"

"Mr. Freeman."

"I'll just take a minute here, Your Honor." Freeman examined the documents, including the letter from the Leavenworth stockade.

"When possible, sir, I would like a copy of this evidence." Freeman sat down heavily next to Boyd. "Prison?"

Boyd's face went red. "I didn't think—"

"Exactly. You didn't think. You may have bought yourself a length of rope, Mr. Calvin."

Wolski lifted the papers from the evidence table. "Major Hennessy, would you read please this letter I have in my hand."

Hennessy took the letter and quickly glanced around the courtroom. "It's addressed to me, from a Dr. Matthew Wells at the stockade in Leavenworth, Kansas."

"Rather than read the whole letter, with Mr. Freeman's permission, would you give us the gist of the paper, sir?"

"Your Honor, in the interest of time, the defense will stipulate to the contents of the letter," said Freeman.

Boyd sensed an attitude of defeat from the older man. Hennessy looked to the judge. The judge nodded to the Major.

"It's a letter stating that Boyd Calvin was being transferred from the prison in Leavenworth to the hospital facility in Vermilion. The doctor, a Colonel Wells, had been instrumental in having Mr. Calvin's sentence commuted. That's about it."

"That's about it, Major? Would you read, please, in the fifth paragraph, the sentence under the fourth heading?"

Hennessy scanned down the paper with his finger. " 'The following tendencies have been exhibited by Mr. Calvin' . . . and then under number four, it reads "Generalized manifestations of confusion and guilt over the traumatic circumstances surrounding the death of Lieutenant Charles Eddie in the final days of the war.' "

"Would you now read the postscript, please."

Hennessy turned to the second page. With a deep breath, he read, "Striking an officer, as we all know, is a serious offense, especially in times of war—"

"Were you personally acquainted with the defendant?" interjected Wolski.

"I knew him, yes. We were not close friends, as you can imagine—given the difference in age and all."

"What do you recall of Mr. Calvin's behavior at the Soldiers' Home?"

"He seemed an average patient. Kept to himself, and was not disruptive. Except for a few . . . episodes."

"Episodes?"

"Yes, he seemed to have nightmares. Or to put it a better way, at certain times he would lose himself in these episodes . . . sudden memories of disquieting events in his past."

"I think that should be enough. The other documents that you have brought me—do they include an honorable discharge?"

"No, they do not."

"No further questions, Your Honor."

Boyd could hear Freeman take a deep breath. "Your Honor, we were not notified of the appearance of this witness. I would like to have him available to question at a later time."

"That will be your prerogative, Mr. Freeman."

Wolski was still on his feet. "Your Honor, at this time the state would like to recall the defendant, Mr. Boyd Calvin."

Boyd was aware of the scraping of his chair as he pushed it back, the sound reverberating through the old courtroom.

"I'll remind you, sir, that you are still under oath. When being questioned by Mr. Freeman on Friday, you were asked how long you served, correct?"

"Yes."

"And your answer?"

"About fourteen months."

"And when asked if you served honorably your answer?"

"I think I said, 'Yes, sir.'"

"Well, that wasn't the truth, was it, Boyd?" He paused. "Who was Lieutenant Charles Eddie, Mr. Calvin?"

"He was the commanding officer of the platoon I was in."

And what happened to Lieutenant Eddie?"

"He was killed in action."

"Were you present when Lieutenant Eddie was killed?"

"Yes."

Freeman rose unsteadily to his feet. The old man was visibly shaken. "Your Honor, I would like to object, sir. The prosecutor has gone far afield with his line of questions. My client is not on trial here for his deeds in the war. On the contrary, he served in an exemplary fashion, nor should any record of his past life relating to prison have been brought into these proceedings."

"Your Honor, my learned colleague brought up Mr. Calvin's record himself." A half smile appeared on Wolski's face. "And as for Mr. Calvin's time spent in prison, that was discovered, Your Honor, when we were checking on Mr. Calvin's military records. We believe that it is part and parcel of the same thing. Mr. Calvin lied about serving honorably, and we think that goes to his lying about his actions on the morning of June sixth. Also, my next witness, we think, will clear up much of this in his testimony."

The judge played with a pencil. "Mr. Freeman, I'm going to have to allow this line of questioning. You did, sir, bring up your client's war record."

"Yes, sir." The old man eased his thin frame back into his hard chair.

"Mr. Calvin, we were speaking of Lieutenant Eddie. Exactly how was he killed?"

Boyd blinked several times, reliving the explosion that shattered Lieutenant Eddie. "He was hit by enemy mortar fire."

"Did he die right away, Mr. Calvin?"

"I don't know. I don't believe so."

"Did you have anything to do with his death, Boyd?"

"No."

"Thank you, Mr. Calvin. Step down, please—unless Mr. Freeman would like to redirect?"

Freeman said nothing.

"Your Honor, the state would like to call at this time Mr. Arthur Campbell."

Boyd looked at the judge. He rolled his head to relieve a tightness in his neck and bumped into the defense table. When he got to his chair, Freeman would not meet his eye.

Boyd moved in his seat to see a heavyset man in an elegant suit come striding down the aisle. There was a resemblance to the Art Campbell he had known, but he would never have recognized him on the street. As he walked past Boyd, he gave him a thumbs-up and a wink. Maybe it would be all right.

"Mr. Campbell, where do you make your home, sir?"

Campbell pulled his suit coat down in front to straighten his collar.

"St. Louis, sir, and proud to say it. I drove up last night, and a lovely drive it was. I am a distributor for the Hupp Motor Car Corporation and just in passing I tooled up here in a new eight-cylinder Century model."

The judge advised Mr. Campbell to answer only what was asked, and Wolski proceeded. "Mr. Campbell, did you have occasion to serve in the AEF with the defendant, Mr. Calvin?"

"Yes."

"Do you see Mr. Calvin in the courtroom, sir?"

"That's him sitting there with the older fellow." He pointed toward Boyd.

"Mr. Campbell, sometime in October of 1918, were you, in fact, on a patrol with the defendant?"

"Yessiree. We was shot all to hell and Boyd here saved our bacon."

"Would you like to tell us the circumstances of that patrol, sir?"

Boyd could see Campbell was trying hard to be earnest.

"We got ourselves good and proper lost, I'll tell you. We had been out for maybe three or four days. We were leaderless and the patrol had been shot to heck and back. Well, we got separated. . . . There were only four of us left and we just ran like the dickens. Boyd tried to stop us but we got—like I said, separated."

"There were four of you that survived?"

"Well, yes, but we ran down this ravine, the three of us, that is, and Boyd was, I guess, back with the rest of the platoon. I heard later that they were all killed by the Germans 'cept for Boyd. I guess he managed to get under a body when the Germans overran the bivouac area."

"What, do you recall, happened then?"

"We finally holed up under a bridge till Boyd found us and led us outta there. I'll tell you, we woulda been goners if he hadn't kicked our butts along that stream bed."

"And why was Mr. Calvin leading you out of danger? Shouldn't that have been the duty of your commanding officer?"

"Well, yeah, it shoulda, but Lieutenant Eddie was dead and there really wasn't anyone who kinda had it together 'cept for Boyd."

"You say that Lieutenant Eddie was dead. Would you tell the court, please, how that happened."

"He was hit real bad by, I think, it might have been a German eighty-eight."

"And explain, please, what that is?"

"It's a large-caliber artillery weapon that the Germans were damn adept at using."

"Now, then, Mr. Campbell. We have heard in previous testimony that Lieutenant Eddie was hit by a mortar."

"Well, could have been. I don't remember exactly, there was a heck of a lot going on, I just know he was blown all to hell."

"Did the lieutenant die immediately?"

Campbell let his eyes wander. "I don't remember. . . . He was a goner. There was no doubt 'bout that part. And old Boyd saved our bacon, as I said before."

"Yes, that's fine, Mr. Campbell. But answer the question, please. Did Lieutenant Charles Eddie die immediately, sir?"

Boyd caught Campbell looking at him. It seemed he was trying not to tell the rest of his story. Boyd nodded, taking the man off the hook.

"Well, no he didn't."

"What transpired then, sir?"

"I really hate talking about the war . . . so many things—"

"Sir, do you recall a conversation that you and I had on the telephone Friday afternoon of this past week?"

"Yes, sir."

"Would you now, under oath, repeat the gist of that phone call?"

It was apparent to Boyd that the man was trying his damnedest to keep from telling the prosecutor what he wanted to hear.

"I would remind you, once again, that you are under oath, and are subject to penalties for perjury."

Campbell once again looked to Boyd.

"Go ahead and tell them, Soup. It don't make no nevermind, anyhow."

The judge rapped his gavel as the courtroom buzzed with Boyd's outburst. Freeman leaned into Boyd. "You're tying that knot tighter and tighter, sonny."

Wolski proceeded. "We're waiting, sir."

"Well, hell . . ." He put his hands to his face. "We were all bunched up in this ravine and the lieutenant was saying something about backtracking outta there when this German round came in. We all grabbed the earth except maybe the lieutenant. He didn't go down or it was too close, anyway—he was hit real bad. Boyd came running over to the lieutenant and I couldn't hear everything that was said, 'cept something about flanking the enemy. It was pretty clear to everyone that Eddie was delirious. In a couple minutes, the lieutenant started screaming. We all wanted to help in some way but Boyd told everyone to stay put. I tell you, he was right there in the open and I know the Germans could see him, 'cause you could hear the small-arms rounds striking the rocks close to Boyd and the lieutenant."

"All right, Mr. Campbell, get on with it, please," Wolski said impatiently.

"I'll tell the damn thing in my own time or not at all, Mr. Wolski."

"Sir, that will be the last of that kind of thing." The judge pulled off his glasses.

"Your Honor, when Mr. Wolski talked to me Friday, he assured me I would be able to tell the whole thing and I intend, sir, to hold him to that."

"Mr. Wolski?"

The prosecutor pushed his hands in his pockets and shrugged. The judge waited. "All right, Mr. Campbell, tell your story."

"Thank you, sir. Well, the lieutenant's screams were, I got to tell you, hair-raising. He was begging for some relief. His legs were all twisted and grotesque. I could see a gaping hole in his stomach where the blood was just gushing. Boyd had taken the lieutenant's pistol from him and we all just sat there kinda transfixed. I could see Boyd trying to soothe him, talk to him, but the lieutenant was grasping at him, begging. Well, we all was thinking the same thing, and finally, Boyd did it."

A deep silence grew in the courtroom. Boyd could hear a woman somewhere weeping softly. It was strange for Boyd hearing someone tell that story. He had repeated it so many times in his head, he'd wondered if it had really happened.

Wolski looked disgusted. "Did what, Mr. Campbell, did what?"

"Well, he shot him."

"Who shot him?"

"You're a real bastard, Wolski—Boyd shot the lieutenant."

"You're saying that Boyd Calvin murdered this poor wounded soldier?"

"He didn't murder him, damn it to hell. It was a merciful thing."

"Have you practiced medicine long, Mr. Campbell?"

"What?"

"Are you a medical doctor, sir? Could you tell without a doubt that Lieutenant Eddie was a 'goner?' I'm waiting."

"No, I'm not a doctor, but that was one of the bravest things I've ever witnessed." Campbell was angry and bewildered. "And for you to force me to tell that story on a man who saved my life, I don't understand."

"I have no further questions for this witness, Your Honor."

Wolski went to his table head held high. Boyd looked at Art Campbell as he came down from the stand. "Sorry, Boyd."

"Mr. Campbell, nothing further from you, sir." The judge brought his gavel down again.

Boyd made an "okay" sign with his fingers and smiled as Campbell walked by. "Don't worry about it, Soup."

"Mr. Freeman, instruct your client not to speak aloud in the court-room."

The old attorney said nothing, just turned to Boyd and shook his head slightly.

The impact of Art Campbell's testimony left the courtroom in sham-bles. The gallery could not be quieted by the judge's incessant rapping of his gavel, so he finally had the bailiff declare a ten-minute recess.

Wolski's table was alive with lawyers shuffling papers and reading briefs; a certain air of self-congratulation seemed to float from the prose-cution team. Boyd watched as two young legal assistants in their smart suits and ties went about their tasks. Boyd wondered what that would be like, sending folks to jail, playing God. Had he done that with Lieutenant Eddie?

As Boyd watched the lawyers, he was also aware that Freeman had im-mediately gotten up when recess was called. Boyd figured the old man just didn't want to be close to him after the debacle of the last hour. Free-man was wandering around the evidence table, touching nothing, but peering intently. First at the gun, then at the various documents, then at the Bible and books that had been on the kitchen table where Sheridan had died. Boyd liked the old man. He was dead honest and a real scrap-per. He felt bad that he had not told him about prison and Lieutenant Eddie. He just didn't think it was important. Hell, it was years ago.

Boyd arched his head back and watched the wood fan turn slowly. The late-afternoon light made streaking shadows across the ceiling. The or-nate carvings lit up as if being photographed by a reporter's flashbulb. He wondered if his picture would be in the papers when they convicted him.

Later, when the bailiff suddenly pulled a shade down, the light show was gone, and Boyd pondered whether his death at Joliet would happen just as quickly.

Freeman finally drifted back to the table. "Boyd, something has been bothering me for some time. You told the court that Sheridan was doing something in the Bible."

"Yeah, he was writing in it."

"That's right, those are the words you used when you first told me. But later you agreed under oath that he was marking in it."

"What's the difference, writing, marking? Hell, everyone saw what he did in it, he underlined that junk about adultery and all." Boyd couldn't understand why at a time like this Freeman would fixate on such a minor point. But then, he had thought his problems after the war were unimportant, too.

"Son, look at me, think carefully, and tell me exactly what you saw."

"Well, he was writing when I first came up, I mean you can tell the difference, the pencil was going up and down, and at, uh, the end, he was marking when I asked for Laurel." The old man was staring through him; then he turned his gaze toward the Bible on the evidence table.

When court was called back into session, Freeman asked if the court would see fit to reexamine the physical evidence that had been entered by Wolski.

"Do you wish to redirect with Mr. Calvin, sir?"

"Yes, Your Honor, and I would like to examine, with Mr. Wolski, the evidence currently on this table, especially the Bible."

Wolski didn't bother to get up. "Your Honor, I'm ready to give my closing statement. If Mr. Freeman chooses to fish around in some desperate attempt to find some magic potion that will shed light on his case, let him proceed."

"That's most kind of you, sir. Thank you."

The sarcasm was not lost on Wolski. Boyd retook his seat on the witness stand.

"Mr. Calvin, there have always been troubling things about this case, not the least of which is the physical evidence." Freeman walked to the evidence table, stumbling slightly on the way. He spoke quietly. "Your Honor, as previously discussed, I had an opportunity to examine these various objects under the watchful eye of Detective Manion. What I was not able to do, and what I would like the defendant to do at this time, is to lift open the blood–stuck pages of the Bible, which he had given to his wife as a gift."

Wolski, set to give his closing arguments, was upset at this diversion. "Your Honor, at this late stage of the proceedings, doesn't it appear just a little too desperate, this dramatic probing of this hallowed book? What, indeed, does Mr. Freeman expect to find in this Bible, sir?"

"Your Honor, please, Mr. Wolski has enjoyed considerable leeway in the closing stages of this trial. If the court so pleases, would you indulge an old man, sir?"

"Proceed, Mr. Freeman."

Boyd didn't understand what was happening. He watched as Freeman came back to the defense table.

"Your Honor, could we have the court clerk read back Mr. Calvin's testimony regarding Mr. Ralph Sheridan's behavior as Boyd came into the kitchen on the night in question?"

"Very well." It took quite a while for the clerk to find the passage. He read, " 'I walked in the shadow of the trees. . . . ' "

"A little later, sir."

" 'He was hunched over like he was studying.' " The clerk looked up quizzically.

"Keep reading, please."

The clerk ran a finger down his notes. " 'The fellow inside said something about "being finished" and I stopped halfways. He looked at me with this strange grin. I asked where Laurel was and he gestured with a pencil toward his left.' "

"Thank you, sir." The clerk gathered his notes and sat back at his table. Freeman had been writing quickly while the clerk was reading his transcription. "Mr. Calvin clearly stated, 'He was hunched over like he was studying'. . . . Then he said something about 'being finished' and finally he 'gestured with a pencil.' This clearly sounds to me as though Mr. Sheridan was writing in the Bible. Is that correct, Boyd?"

"That's what I saw, except I was pretty upset about then."

"Your Honor, this is all supposition, sir; can we please get on with closing arguments?" Wolski protested.

Freeman looked Boyd square in the eye. "Boyd, do you know what happened to the Bible after the police arrived?"

"Nope, I sure don't. I heard the shot, then I dropped down real quick; as I said before, then there was a lot of blood and stuff, and then I just took off."

Freeman walked to the evidence table and grasped the Bible firmly in his hand. "I believe in the interests of justice that the court should examine this Bible. There may be information here that might be beneficial to my client. With the court's permission, may I have Mr. Calvin open this book, sir?"

"Proceed, Mr. Freeman."

Boyd leafed through the Bible, stopping toward the end. "There are several pages stuck together here from Sheridan's blood."

"With your permission, may I have Mr. Calvin pull them apart, Your Honor? It appears some pages must be peeled back."

"Mr. Freeman, do you have information that you're holding back?"

"No, Your Honor. Just a very strong hunch."

Wolski's curiosity had gotten the better of him, and he shouldered his way past the old lawyer to take the Bible from his hands. "This is state's evidence, and should be handled by the state."

The judge rapped quietly with his gavel. "Sit down, Mr. Wolski. Your time will come."

The judge looked over to Boyd. "Go ahead, Mr. Calvin. Pry open your Bible."

While he was working, Freeman turned to the judge. "I believe that when Mr. Sheridan's body was moved, someone, possibly a policeman, closed the Bible to preserve it as evidence. The wet blood stuck the pages in question together."

The courtroom fell silent and the only sound heard was that of the pages finally being peeled open.

"There's some writing here, sir. But, it's all smudged, can't make out a word of it." Boyd showed the Bible first to the judge, then to Freeman.

Freeman's face fell. He took the old book from Boyd's hands and fanned the pages in frustration. Boyd hadn't seen him look so close to losing his composure before. He placed the book down and started to walk away. The court was eerily silent; it seemed that even the judge was giving the old attorney some slack.

Finally Wolski commented, not unkindly, "Sorry, Counselor, I don't think we're going to find any full-blown confessions that exonerate your client penciled in the midst of the Holy Scriptures."

The gavel sounded, but before His Honor could speak, Freeman looked at Wolski as if the man had just offered a great suggestion, turned sharply, and grabbed the Bible back up off the table. This time he seemed to know what he was looking for; he placed the Good Book on its front cover and opened the last page in the binding. Almost immediately the old man went white, glanced toward Wolski, then Boyd, and then the judge.

"What is it, Counselor?" The judge's voice reflected the solemnity in Freeman's face.

Freeman gathered himself and spoke in a low, intense voice. "Your Honor, Mr. Wolski is correct—there is nothing to exonerate my client penciled into the Scriptures. But I ask your forbearance to have him read something in the family ledger wherein is inscribed the records of births, marriages, and deaths of his extended family. It is the only thing, I might add, that is written in pencil."

As the judge nodded his approval, Boyd could feel the suddenly anxious Wolski step up to look over his shoulder as he began to read. Boyd's head began to swim as realization dawned with his reading of the neat notations—the last one he recognized as being one he wrote in blue pen when he and Laurel were married. Then there was another he had never seen before, inscribed below it in neat pencil.

"It says, the last one says,

" 'Laurel Wheaton Calvin, born January tenth, 1901. Died June fifth, 1929. Smitten down for her iniquities at the hands of a soldier of the Lord whose life she ruined and who shall soon join her in a more perfect world.' "

Pandemonium seemed to break loose in the courtroom. Wolski had taken the book and was staring quietly at the offending words. Freeman sat heavily, like someone had just removed a heavy weight from his shoulders, and put his face in his hands.

The judge seemed as puzzled as everyone else in the courtroom, and could not maintain order. He called a recess until the next day at 10:00 A.M., when he wanted to hear arguments from both sides on dismissal.

I maintain, Your Honor, that this so-called 'confession' has absolutely no bearing on this case." Wolski had started off bright and chipper, but Boyd felt he was starting to wind down, becoming desperate. "The fact that the evidence was exposed to who knows how many souls in this backwater police station . . ."

Boyd could see the judge diligently making notes, looking up only occasionally when Wolski made disparaging remarks about either the level of jurisprudence in Vermilion or the personalities involved in this case.

". . . as far as I can see, this message, this obviously faked treatise, this, this bogus piece of irrelevant flimflam, has no place in these proceedings. Your Honor, the police in this case were obviously derelict in keeping the chain of evidence secure. Even Mr. Freeman could have written this. As I have stated before, he had opportunity."

A loud *pop* could be heard as old man Freeman clapped his bare hand down on the defense table. He said nothing, just looked at his reddening hand.

"Mr. Wolski, sir, you have tried very hard to get on my wrong side, and I think you have finally succeeded," said the judge. "We are a small community here, sir. We don't enjoy the privileges and pleasures of the big cities. Nevertheless, Mr. Wolski, we are not so deep in the backwoods that we don't recognize a rude remark when we hear one. Your father, sir, would have been ashamed to hear that unworthy attack."

Wolski dutifully took his berating. Until the mention of his father.

"Ah, yes, Mr. Wolski. That got your attention, did it not? I went to school with Joseph Wolski at Northwestern, sir, and he became a fine jurist, one that you could well emulate. Have you quite finished?"

"Yes, sir, I have, and my apologies, sir." Boyd watched as the young lawyers at the prosecution table busied themselves with papers, apparently trying not to make eye contact with their boss.

"Mr. Freeman, your argument, sir."

Old man Freeman looked to Boyd for all the world like a punch-drunk fighter.

"The innocence of my client is so painfully clear, Your Honor, as to be almost laughable. Mr. Wolski argues that anyone could have written this 'so-called confession.' Your Honor, let's bring Mrs. Sheridan back on the stand, let's have her bring copies of Mr. Sheridan's handwriting. Let's compare them, sir. The defense is in no hurry. We'll wait until doomsday to get this right. I think at the bottom, in Mr. Wolski's bed, when he stares at the ceiling in the middle of the night and his eyes refuse to close, even he will say, Your Honor, that Boyd Calvin is innocent. Throughout this trial Mr. Wolski has tried to make us believe that the sun rises in the west, that a pound of beans weighs more than a pound of feathers. Boyd Calvin may have committed what society deems a crime during the war some ten years ago. But Boyd Calvin, my client, did not commit these crimes. It is evident in the circumstantial evidence brought forth, and more than evident in this written confession that Mr. Wolski read to us so eloquently. Your Honor, the defense is ready to proceed with this trial to its inevitable conclusion. If Your Honor concludes that dismissal is not prudent, I feel confident that this jury, if it comes to that, will find my client innocent of all charges. Thank you, sir."

The judge continued to make notes, then glanced at his pocket watch. "This court will stand in recess until 1:00 P.M., at which time I will render a judgment."

Boyd was afraid to look at Freeman. He was afraid he might see defeat in his eyes. He was fearful that his soaring hopes would crash like so many dominoes. As the bailiff escorted Boyd out, Claudia came up to the partition separating the gallery from the judge and lawyers. "I am buying you pork chops and collard greens at the Lucky tonight, shug."

The hours passed slowly for Boyd until 2:00 P.M. The judge and the attorneys had apparently been busy in the interim. At one-thirty, Freeman
had been ushered into his holding cell to give him the news. The judge
would reconvene the court, but it would probably be just a formality, as
Wolski was going to "throw in the towel."

Throw in the towel? Boyd almost cried, feeling a combination of great
relief and anger. He was relieved that he was going to go free, and angry
that the prosecutor acted as if he had just lost a great prizefight, instead of
being part of a system that tried to get at the truth for justice's sake. Did
that mean that if Wolski had done better and the defense had had to
"throw in the towel," an innocent man could go to death row and that
was okay with the prosecutor? Maybe George was right about not trusting the whole damn bunch of them.

Boyd felt as if he were in a dreamworld during the actual formal dismissal of charges in the courtroom. The judge seemed to be talking to
everyone but him—he heard the words "I hereby dismiss" and "free,"
and didn't much pay attention to the rest. Everyone started hollering and
some people he didn't even know clapped him on the back. Wolski
seemed to take it pretty well in the courtroom—he even came over and
congratulated Boyd and extended his hand. Boyd just nodded to the
man—as if he wanted to shake the hand of somebody who was making a
game out of trying to execute him. He'd never felt so many strong feelings at once. Freeman laughed when Boyd asked if they could get him
again on the same charge. "No, son, it's called 'double jeopardy.' Can't
try you again."

Something made him look over toward where Miss Logan had been
sitting, and unlike everybody else, who was milling around, she was still
sitting right there, just watching him as if she were looking down on the
world of people from a cloud. He looked at her and shrugged—she finally let her face crack into a smile and gave him the thumbs-up signal
before turning back to her notepad.

Morris looked around for directions from the bailiff, who seemed just
as unsure as he was. Then some people came up toward Boyd; Morris
started acting as if he was in charge and wanted to show he knew his

stuff. Although his eyes were flitting around, he walked Boyd with a great show of authority to a desk at the entrance to the jail. He had Boyd sign for his meager possessions and sent him off. The jailer stood at the door. "Have a feeling you'll be back, killer." Boyd felt too good to allow Morris to get to him. He took in the sights from the top step of the old building. It was late in the afternoon and he looked forward to the walk up Main Street to the Lucky.

Hennessy's head was still spinning from everything that had happened at the trial when Freeman broke away from a crowd of well-wishers and approached him. "Major, I wonder if you would accompany me to the judge's chambers? I know this is short notice, but who'd have thought we'd be where we are with this case at this moment?"

"You're telling me. That was about as dramatic a moment as I've witnessed—how could you have known, and if not . . ."

"I *didn't* know. But I had played Boyd's account of that murder over and over in my mind like a moving-picture show, and that writing business always had me curious. Frankly, I wouldn't have tried it except in desperation—you can imagine, I'd certainly have looked the fool if there was nothing there but some doodling."

"All I can say is I'm impressed." Then, remembering that Freeman had sought him out for a purpose, he added, "But what can I do for you with the judge? I mean it's over, isn't it?"

"Not exactly. Everybody's in a dither and I don't even know where Boyd's run off to, but there's another issue that didn't have much importance until now."

"That being?"

"That being the fact that Boyd has also been charged with respect to the injury of Officer Blake and others in the crowd—those charges are still pending."

"But that has turned out not to be his fault, right? He only ran because of the mob."

"Even if not purposeful, if it's determined that those events occurred

during commission of the crime of felony escape and interstate flight,
well . . ."

"Still doesn't sound right . . . but how can I help?"

Freeman explained how as he led him toward the judge's chamber.
Hennessy felt his limp worsen and his stride slow. He couldn't believe that
someone was trying to cross his and Boyd's stars again—why the hell
couldn't he just be free of the man? True, he was happy for the way things
had turned out for Boyd, but Lord, he was a difficult person.

Hennessy saw Myrna give him a questioning glance from across the
courtroom, and he just shrugged in response before losing sight of her as
Freeman ushered him along by the elbow into a narrow hallway to the
inner sanctum of Illinois justice. The judge waved them both in and toward a couple leather chairs of the officious maroon color that Hennessy
associated with funeral parlors and law firms.

"Major, I take it that Mr. Freeman has briefed you on the content of
our last side conference?"

"Well, he started to, Your Honor—sounds like Boyd is still in some
trouble."

"Actually, if we were being totally proper, he would still be in the
lockup. But, this being Vermilion and Morris being a numskull and the
bailiff not much better, Mr. Calvin's walking around free as a lark until
we pick him up again." Aside from rolling his eyes and shaking his head,
the judge didn't seem inclined to take steps to remedy the temporary
lapse of protocol. He pulled his black robe off and tossed it aside, then
poured a glass of water for each of them from a pitcher that someone
must have left for him, judging from the fresh ice. His Honor seemed to
be considering his next words carefully. "None of that really matters—
the point is that Boyd is freed on the major charges but he still has a court
appearance pending on the whole escape issue."

"Yes, that's what I understand."

"Now, Major, even though we've learned of extenuating circumstances, escape is still escape, and frankly, I wouldn't be surprised if Boyd
still got a bit of hard time . . . although considering what's transpired, and
the fact that he turned himself in, it might boil down to time served."

Hennessy just nodded in response and waited for the judge to gulp a drink of water before continuing.

"So this is what I'm driving at. Boyd will be arraigned on the other charges, and it will move along in the courts for at least a couple months before being adjudicated." Hennessy was interested where this was going, but damn it, he had his own problems—he wondered what the ticker tapes had been doing to his future all day. Only the drama of the court finale could have been enough to divert him from his anxiety over his own fortunes. Things seemed to be straightening out in the market. Yesterday the cooler heads had prevailed, as Vedeler had said they would. But there had been a couple of real scares last week, and he wouldn't feel reassured until he could get around the radio and confirm that things were getting back to normal. He really was glad that Boyd wasn't going to get the chair, but he had to force himself to pay attention to the judge.

"So, Major, it boils down to this—with Boyd's background and the fact that he is a demonstrated flight risk"—here the judge raised his hands in an "I know" gesture—"even *if* it was under extraordinary circumstances, and even *though* he turned himself in, well, I simply can't release him under his own recognizance."

Hennessy sat mute. Freeman had said he needed his help, but this was going a different direction than he had assumed. He was ready to put in a good word for Boyd, but he was beginning to suspect more was being asked for.

"Mr. Freeman has suggested that you might consider having Boyd remanded to your custody at the home for temporary safekeeping? Now, I know that you've been a great mentor for the veterans in this region, but are you really ready to take on a responsibility like this?"

Hennessy couldn't believe his ears. He looked briefly at Freeman, who was busy staring at his feet. The old son of a bitch had put him on the hot seat—all he had asked on the walk to Judge Everett's chambers was if he would vouch for Boyd's character if released. Now what would Hennessy do? Defend the offer he had never made? Argue for taking Boyd under his wing? Goddamn that old bastard, he takes his advocate role too seriously . . . acts the friend and confidant and . . . His head was swimming. He took a deep breath.

"Well, Judge, you know the world has come down pretty hard on Boyd in the past few months"—he couldn't believe he was saying this— "and, well, although the home isn't a place truly for incarceration, it has really served in that role for certain classes of involuntary residents." Myrna's mocking assessment of that term popped briefly into his head. "So we're actually in a reasonably good position to keep inmates in fairly, eh, secure environments."

"Yes, but this is a man that escaped while under felony arrest. So, again, are you prepared to take on that kind of responsibility? I mean, it's admirable that you would stand by your fellow comrades-in-arms, but this would be exceptional." Now Hennessy wondered if the judge hadn't been in on the thing with Freeman from the start. He knew the judge was buttering him but he had to admit he wasn't unfazed by the kind words. After all, in some ways he really did provide an anchor to the established mainstream of the community for some war-damaged men.

"Well, Your Honor . . ."

Freeman then came to his aid. "Your Honor, I think the people of Vermilion and the county, and the whole state for that matter, would see the merit of such a creative solution. Your Honor is known for your deep convictions about punishment fitting the crime, and what with this case being so well covered by the press . . . it would seem that a just, but humane, determination on your part—could be an object lesson in itself."

Yeah, and what with it being election year and all—Hennessy filled in the unspoken part of Freeman's monologue in his own head. He worried for a second that he might have mumbled his thoughts out loud. He gave them both a weak smile, sighed, and nodded. "It's true, Judge, I think we all need to remember that this is a case that has caught the imagination of the citizens of the whole state. How we deal with its disposition and treatment of a falsely accused war veteran could have long-term repercussions."

"Major"—the judge did him the honor of rising first in his own chambers—"I'd like to shake your hand. Mr. Freeman and all of us have had a long day, but I believe justice has truly been served. With your gracious gesture, so has mercy and kindness." The judge was suddenly more animated, and changing his tone to a conspiratorial one, looked at Freeman and said, "Now how about shuttin' that damn door so some men of serious responsibility can have a moment of serious relaxation." As the lawyer closed the door, the judge produced a key and unlocked the "Bible cabinet," as it was labeled, in his credenza. He produced a bottle that definitely wasn't full of holy water and added a large dollop to each of their water glasses.

Hennessy had to admit that in the light the judge had just painted it, his own role in this mess could be seen as a noble one. Perhaps he should just accept the fact that a man of consequence was called upon more often than others to make sacrifices. He decided to put aside his uneasiness with Boyd and ignore the outrageous fortune that would throw him and the troublemaker together again. At heart, Boyd was a decent man, even brave in some crude way, and certainly not deserving of more incarceration.

Hennessy accepted Freeman's heartfelt thanks outside the chambers and left a message for Myrna with him detailing where he could be found. He relished the thought that Myrna would bear witness to his taking the prodigal under his wing. Then he made his way toward the diner where he figured he could find Boyd. Maybe for once in his life the lout would be properly grateful and render a modicum of respect where it was due.

On his way out Hennessy noticed that the *Tribune* had finally arrived and was being handed out by a newsboy in front of the boarded-up facade of Lou's Better Lounge. If things had finally calmed down with the market, he would feel a lot better. Then he realized with surprise that it wasn't the *Chicago Tribune* at all, it was the *Vermilion Herald*, which was usually only a morning paper. Then he heard the newsboy—so that was it—it was an "extra." You didn't see many of those in Vermilion, maybe three in his memory.

The newsboy seemed excited to be playing a role usually confined to his big-city cousins—he was reeling off in true Chicago-style voice inflection, learned probably from radio, the "Extree, extree, read all about it." That seemed an awfully fast turnaround for the Boyd drama to have already made it to the presses. He waved the boy over, gave him a nickel, and told him to keep the change. After reading the headline, Hennessy decided he needed to sit down. Perhaps his car. Yes, that would be a good place to sit and gather his thoughts.

Boyd's stroll from the jail to the Lucky had been a treat. The fall air was full of rich smells. People on the street were walking a little faster, as though scrambling out of their summer doldrums, and the light from the setting sun turned the buildings a pink hue. The long shadows cut sharply across the concrete streets as if painted. Boyd swung his arms; he had wanted to run and shout, it felt so good to be free. When he turned the corner at Pine, the Lucky sign had just been switched on and the blue light against the soft red sun looked spectacular. Claudia and Laverne were standing on the sidewalk smoking, and gave Boyd a big greeting.

After he was settled in his seat he began to realize just how hungry he was. He caught a glimpse of Stavro, the owner of the Lucky, and Laverne in a discussion. Boyd was convinced they were talking about him.

"Baby, please, you know that people are gonna talk. It's just human," said Claudia.

"I know, I gotta drop all that and just be happy I made it out. Damn, that was a stroke of what you might call good fortune, weren't it?"

"I don't know if it was good fortune or an observant lawyer."

"I had a talk with Freeman during the recess. I asked him about having Mrs. Sheridan bring in those handwriting samples and . . . and he said he didn't think for a minute that the judge was gonna do that. He was confident all along that once he found that confession, it was all over but the shouting. Someday I'd like to do something nice for that old guy."

"You better hurry, sweetie, he isn't getting any younger. Why'd it take so long for you to get out?"

"Oh, I don't know, they just liked my company. They had lots of paperwork; processing, I think they called it. Sure feels good to be out. Can't describe it, sounds seem deeper and clearer, colors richer. . . ."

Boyd piled into his pork chops as if he had never eaten, remarking that he didn't know if he could finish everything.

"It's okay, sweetie. Also, the guy at the counter wants to buy you a root beer."

Boyd glanced at the back of a fellow he didn't recognize. The man turned and Boyd realized he had seen him in the Lucky a few times. He nodded to the guy. "Think he's a guy I almost had trouble with once. Anyway, nice of him to offer the pop."

" 'Almost had trouble with once' could take in pretty much the whole town with you, baby." Claudia watched as Boyd poked at his potatoes. "Whatcha plans, shug? I know it's only been a couple hours, but are you gonna stick around or what?"

"I don't know, Claudie. I don't think I'd get a real fair shake here in Vermilion. Decker probably wouldn't hire me back, and I don't know if I'd want to work for the guy anyway. He tried to bury me at the trial. Maybe I'll just bum around for a while, don't know."

They sat for a few minutes in silence. "The food was great, Claudie, thank you."

"Well, you need to thank Laverne, too. She wanted to split it with me."

"I'll do that."

Stavro came up to the booth and spoke to Claudia. "When ya done with your jailbird friend, bus the front counter, Miss C. That's if you can spare da time." Boyd met Claudia's eye. She eased out of the leatherette booth. "Hold your temper, sweetie. He's an ass. Claudie's got some interes'in' gossip about that old boy. . . . Don't you just never mind that Greek prick." She walked away, then immediately turned back; from her apron pocket she pulled out a folded envelope. "Almost forgot, this was in my mailbox at the hotel. Was sent to you, don't know why someone would put it in my box." The envelope was addressed to "Calvin Boyd c/o Claudia Falk, Grant Hotel." No stamp. Inside, a single sheet of paper read, "Congrats. Sparks would like to see you and talk about Calif." Who in the hell was Sparks?

The restaurant started filling up and Boyd could see Stavro eyeing his booth. As Boyd walked across the tiled floor, he stopped in the middle of the room and shouted, "The dog!" George must be back, how'n the heck did he know about his release? Stavro had moved up to the counter where Claudia was working. "I am real sorry, Mr. Niccos. I been cooped up so long, I just don't have any control. . . . Real sorry, sir."

Stavro didn't say anything but pointed to the door. Boyd squatted on the street curb, hoping that Claudia would have a chance to come out. Making progress. Didn't smart off to Stavro. Held his temper.

It was dark. A few streetlamps were lit and the moths and fireflies were out. He had almost nothing in the world except the musty clothes he had on, wrinkled from the months of being stored. Sadness started to overcome him as he realized he was out but had nowhere to go. He had been on the curb for a half hour when Claudia emerged.

"You're still here. I was afraid you'd just slip away, like always. I'm proud of you, that you didn't pop old man Niccos. He's such a mean-tempered coot. Laverne and me gonna fix that cowboy real good. We laughed like fools when we decided about what we were gonna do. She's gonna help by bringing her Kodak Brownie. He's gonna be one old surprised Greek, let me tell you. Listen, shug, I gotta get back inside. I know you don't like long good-byes. I'll just say remember old Claudie loves you and I'll always be thinking of you. If you want to sleep on the floor in my room a couple nights, it's okay. If I don't see you in a while . . . take care and . . ." She couldn't finish.

Boyd could feel her heart pounding as she held him tightly. She clasped his hand, pushing an envelope into his palm. They looked at each other, all eyes wet, and Claudia spun around and hurried into the Lucky. Boyd peeled open the crumpled package to find fifty dollars and a note written on the back of a restaurant tab: "Never had no kids of my own, may I call you one of mine? Don't know why I'm asking, going to do it anyway. Love ya shug. Claudia the Flying Falk." Boyd thought it funny to look at someone and realize he might never see her again. He stood in the vestibule of Thomas Shoes while he waited for his eyes to stop watering.

As Boyd started walking away from Thomas Shoes, his mood quickly lightened. He spotted Major Hennessy, rather uncomfortable it appeared, in the driver's seat of his car, and Myrna hurrying into a drugstore. Well, what the heck, he'd just have to say hello. Boyd was even feeling mellow enough at this point to muster some courtesy and good feelings toward an officer.

"Where'd you steal the car, Major? Dang, I didn't know the government paid that well."

At the moment, Hennessy looked as though he was having his own problems—he returned a weak smile. Then the Major took a deep breath and started to speak, but Boyd thought he was acting kind of strange. "It's good to see you walking around a free man, Boyd." He glanced toward the drugstore and then back to Boyd, his hands playing with the top of the steering wheel. "I suspected you never could have done something like that, and I'm glad it worked out. Matter of fact, I've been looking for you—there's something I need to tell you about."

They were interrupted when two young men pedaling by on bicycles squeezed off a couple honks on the black rubber bulbs of their air horns. Boyd nodded back in their direction—obviously he had attained some brief celebrity status in town.

Hennessy tossed another glance in the direction of the drugstore. It looked to Boyd as if he had resolved to say something that was private, man to man, before she got back.

"You know, I've been thinking, Boyd. I've never properly thanked you for helping me in that fire. Aside from helping out the patients, you probably saved my life—that was a pretty brave thing you did."

"Ah, well, that was a long time ago. I'd forgotten about it."

He saw Hennessy make another weak attempt at a smile. "Well, it's something I won't soon forget." Boyd couldn't imagine what was eating at the man. He seemed to be popping in and out of the conversation like a loose wire on the streetcar dynamo, connected one minute and loose the next. But that was like an officer, too distracted to talk to a regular soldier and always talking down. Look, now he's putting aside the damn paper in his lap and gonna be a regular fella.

Then the Major seemed to gather himself fully. Looking Boyd in the eye, he announced, "And not only won't I forget it, I plan to do something about it. A while ago I talked with the judge and discussed the terms of your release."

That did it! Boyd felt the heat rise in his neck. "Whaddya mean? What damn business is that of yours? I ain't in the army anymore."

Hennessy was now looking up at him with a real odd expression, as if he had something on his mind but now was gonna blow his gasket instead. "Now look, Boyd, you damn better well listen to what I have to say this time."

"Is that so, General? How about not doing me any favors." Well, who in the hell did he think he was anyway? Here he was actually thinking he'd have a nice talk with the fella and he acts like he can't be bothered and then gets superior on him telling him he's discussing terms of his release. He'd been bossed around by enough officers in his day.

Boyd tipped his hat in mock salute and was going to walk off when he spotted the newspaper lying where the now red-faced Major had dropped it. It was an extra from the *Vermilion Herald*. Boyd tilted his head so he could read the headline. Then with the beginning of a realization dawning on him, he started to read out loud, slowly and deliberately.

" 'Market Crashes—Banks Next?' "

Even the big news of his trial dismissal had taken a backseat to this. So that's what the brass collar had on his mind.

"Boy, oh howdy. Bet some of those rich muckety-mucks are sweating it out. Well, hell with them, I say, let 'em go out and get a job like the rest of us. See what it's like to put in a ten-hour day."

Hennessy turned crimson—his face looked like a cross between a man and a tomato.

"You . . . you." He was actually spluttering. "You've a lot of nerve to say something like that." Hennessy the volcano was about to erupt. "How would you know about the strains on men who have the means and the will to keep this nation's lifeblood flowing?"

"Is that what they were doing? Hell, I thought they was playing the market trying to get rich." Boyd saw the man's knuckles go white on the steering wheel. He wasn't sure what he had said to get him so riled—he must have money in the market, but the heck with him anyway.

"I'd have thought you'd have learned more from your time in the military—it didn't seem to give you the discipline to keep in step with America's march to the future."

Boyd thought Hennessy's response seemed excessive.

"I'll tell you, Major, what my time in the service did. It taught me that you look out for your buddies in time of need." He fought to keep from losing his temper.

"Yes, you seem to have taken care of your buddy, all right. You took good care of Lieutenant Eddie, didn't you?"

"I did what I had to do. What would you have done, Major? Would you have picked up a phone and called for the medics? We were three days lost, we had no leader, we had no one to tell us what was right, we . . . Ah, the hell with it. You wouldn't understand anything about being loyal or you wouldn'a mouthed off in court."

"If you're referring to the letter from Colonel Wells, I did what I had to."

"Yeah, well, officers stink in my opinion. They don't have any guts when it comes down to it."

"Hey, guys." It was Myrna. "Looks like you're holding a veterans' reunion. That was great news, Boyd. It must be wonderful after such a long haul to be totally exonerated."

He wasn't sure what she'd heard of their talk, but Hennessy also looked bothered that she was there. Boyd took a deep breath and answered her. "Thank you, miss. I tell you, I thought they were goin' to put me away forever." He glanced at Hennessy and then back to Myrna. "I want to thank you for the articles you wrote about me and the trial—they sure were fair. You know, sometimes you can't get an even-steven deal in a little burg like this . . . so I appreciate it. Thanks."

"Just wrote the truth as I saw it—no thanks needed. . . . Say, look, Boyd, I don't know where you're heading, but can we give you a lift anyplace?"

Boyd saw Hennessy cut his eyes toward him for a second and he almost laughed out loud. The Major was biting his lip. Yeah, Boyd was sure he'd love to have him squished in the front seat with his filly.

"Well, no thanks, miss. I appreciate it but I'm just wanderin' downtown to see my old buddy Sparks. Thanks for the offer, though." Hennessy snapped the car in gear, but not in time to avoid a parting shot from Boyd. "See you, Miss Myrna, you too, Major." Boyd started to walk away, then turned. "Hey, Major, if things get tight out at the Soldiers' Home, there's always a place for folks like you running things right in town here. You know, gettin' your hands dirty, showin' us common folk how it's done. Of course, that'd be earning a living instead of sucking on the military tit. . . . 'Cuse me, miss, I forgot my manners." Boyd gave Hennessy a ragtag mock salute and smiled.

"Yeah? Well, I'd rather be running a home than living on the dole in one. You . . . the only wars you're fighting these days are the nightmares in your own twisted brain." Gravel spat from underneath the coupe as Hennessy let the clutch out so fast the wheels spun.

"Well, Dale. It must have been nice to finally get to talk some things out with Boyd."

He wasn't going to bite—he was in no mood for Myrna's irony. He was still calming down from the exchange with Boyd, but even his momentary anger couldn't sustain him—he was falling into a pit inside himself. Boyd had put his finger right in the wound, but even with Boyd gone, the wound was still there.

"You know, big guy, this market thing, it sounds bad, but, I mean isn't that the way it crumbles? People put their extra money in, it fuels the economy, and a lot of folks get rich when it goes up." She shrugged. "Then they, you know, tighten their belts when it goes down . . . right?"

It occurred to him that one of the coupe's cylinders sounded like it was misfiring—he wondered how much it would cost to get it fixed. Funny something like that should suddenly be a real concern.

"How far in are you, Dale?"

How far indeed. He drove mute and stiff-armed like a Buck Rogers robot.

"Everything?"

He felt like he was going to be ill.

"Come on, talk to me."

He turned the wheel as though he were in a trance. Silence was the best answer he could come up with. It was funny how he could feel her stare. It had been that way since they met; he could actually feel Myrna looking at him.

"Uh-oh, it's more than everything. You're way out on the margin, aren't you? Bought with money you didn't have?"

It wasn't that he was choosing not to talk to her—there simply wasn't anything to say. The awkwardness of the silence was broken by the sound and feel of the tires beneath them hitting gravel and crunching up his driveway. He pulled in next to her car, sitting where she had left it. It was just off the drive in the bushes where it wouldn't be so obvious to everyone going by that she might be staying chez Dale.

Hennessy sat glued to his seat. Myrna opened her own door and walked into his house without looking back at him. She emerged a few minutes later with her bag and purse, still not glancing in his direction. She placed them solemnly in the backseat of the *Trib* Ford and took a long look around her. Myrna seemed like a traveler who had broken camp, ready to depart—absorbing her surroundings for memory's sake. Hennessy's property in the Heights actually did have a bit of vertical advantage over much of the town. It was the closest something came to being a hill in this part of Illinois. He watched her walk back to his side of the car and smelled her fragrance as she stood by the window.

"Getting out? I don't think you need to put up a For Sale sign and take up residence in your car yet." She frowned when she saw her attempt at humor fall flat. "Dale, I'm sorry, big guy, I really am." After another moment, she leaned in through the window and kissed him on the cheek. "I've got a little time before I have to head to Chicago. Anything I can do to make you feel better before I go, lover boy?" There was a wink in her voice and her meaning was plain.

Hennessy felt a momentary tug at his vitals, a spark of life that went out as soon as it was lit. He just shook his head.

A few minutes after he heard her Ford's tires stop crunching as they hit the hardtop, he opened his door and walked up onto his porch. He sat in the swing and pushed with his good leg and breathed deeply the evening air. It was cool. Fall had finally come to Vermilion.

Boyd asked himself twice why he felt he had to hide. They said he was free. But something was compelling about watching from the night shadows in the dirt alley behind Juanita and Frederick's house. Boyd could see people moving in the light from the kitchen. It was not unlike standing in the orchard outside of Laurel's house some five months before. To Boyd it felt like five years.

He stepped on a can, and a dog started barking. "Sparks, be quiet. Come here, boy." The dark shape of the dog came sniffing and wagging his tail. If he didn't remember Boyd, he sure pretended he did. A man called out from the back porch. A bearded fellow with glasses stood in the dim light.

"Don't be too friendly with no white folks, Sparks." His voice was soft. "You can't tell what kinda desperate criminals might be poking round in the garbage."

Boyd let himself in through the picket gate.

"Mind the vegetables long the path there, cracker. Us coloreds gotta eat, you know."

Boyd stood below George on the bottom stoop. "That beard put about ten years on you, Mr. Matthews."

"Well, better off looking ten years older than giving the state ten in Joliet. . . . Come on in."

Juanita and Frederick were having coffee in the front room. George sat Boyd at the kitchen table as he cleared the last of some dirty dishes from the white enamel surface.

"Glad to hear you beat those crackers down to the courthouse, Boyd," Juanita called out. "Help yourself to the coffee."

"Thanks, Juanita."

"An' Boyd, that white woman Miss Logan, you tell her when you see her that she's welcome here anytime—now that white woman is a lady. And I don't say that 'bout many women, black or white."

"Yes'm, I'll tell her if I see her." He couldn't hear what she mumbled in response. With Juanita banging around in her pantry, he said in a low voice, "George, you ever get next to that there 'lady'? Seems you two got kinda friendly."

George gave him a solemn look in answer and said, "I always answer questions like that about a woman's virtue the same way: no!"

"Yeah, but did ya?"

"No!"

Frederick mumbled something about "white man's justice" and then the radio came on playing someone's theme song as an announcer extolled the virtues of Wonder Bread.

When the coffee had been poured and the two men sat sipping quietly, George asked, "Was it worth it? Returning to Vermilion, I mean"

Boyd took a drink of the strong brew. "At times I didn't know. I think I came real close to being sent off for quite a spell, or worse. But in the end, yeah, I got off and I think I feel better about the whole thing. Real strange, though, I gotta tell you . . . how'd you know 'bout my getting off?"

"I was there."

"You was where?"

"In the courtroom."

"You weren't."

"I was. Sat in the back row. The old bearded guy with the spectacles and engineer's hat. You know, the one with the shuffle and the bib overalls."

"You're one crazy bastard. You mean you was there today in court?"

"Today and three or four other days. Heard you sniffling and carrying on up there. Shoot, man, you oughta be shamed."

"You took a big chance, Dark Cloud. You coulda been spotted."

"Nah. They was too busy trying to nail your white butt. Learned a lot about you, Boyd, my man. You was a real hero 'over there,' weren't you. Damn kilt that Eddie guy. Sorry. Guess I shouldn't a brought it up—you must've felt bad all these years, right?"

"No, that's all—well, I did feel bad. When I got out of Leavenworth, after about a year, Laurel and I was split up for a short while and I went up to Minnesota trying to find Eddie's family, thinking I could talk to them and I wouldn't feel so awful. I remembered what town he was from. Finally found the house; they were these rich people. I mean, they had this monster-sized mansion and I just stood way back there on the street gawking at this place. I was so scared of going up to that huge place that I froze there staring at their mailbox printed in gold with 'Mr. and Mrs. Charles Eddie.' Guess I stood so long the gardener cutting the grass came over and asked if he could help me. Told him no and started walking away, but right out of the blue he offered me a job. I'd spent all my money trying to find the damn place, so I said, 'Sure. What I have to do?' "

"That was dumb, Boyd. Real dumb."

"Yeah, right. Realized that pretty quick. What the hell was I gonna do? Stop Mr. and Mrs. Eddie as they strolled through the garden and explain to them that I was the new yard assistant and I knew their son and oh yes, by the way, I happened to have killed him. . . . Yeah it was dumb. I eased on out of there after a couple days. Hope they don't hear about this trial. Hell, that would be awful for them finding out in the papers, such a thing."

George finished his coffee and took his cup to the sink. "Want to high-ball it out toward California, see what's shakin'?"

"Yeah, why not."

"Ready to go?"

"Right now?"

"Sure thing." George walked into the sitting room and spoke with Juanita and Frederick. He returned with a gunnysack. "Meetcha in the alley." Boyd petted Sparks, then walked outside. When George came out, he was holding a second bag, which he handed to Boyd. "Your wardrobe."

They had hours to kill so they walked leisurely toward the railroad junction. Close to the tracks they found an abandoned building that had once been used as a Nazarene church. The roof was full of holes and the windows were all broken. George suggested they build a fire, and as Boyd gathered dry sticks and leaves outside, he wondered what was on George's mind; his friend had not said or done anything out of the ordinary. But there was something, some niggling thing, that kept itching at him.

There had been a fireplace in the old church, so the blaze that the two men started roared steadily. They sat transfixed by the orange flames. "What's on your mind, George?"

"Me? Oh nothing, really."

"Come on, you been dying to tell me something for hours. Spit it out."

"Ah, well. Hell with it. There's couple things I'm meaning to talk about. Guess hearing you have to tell 'bout your war experiences just got me thinking about some things is all. It's nothing, really."

Just silence between them. Boyd felt either George would eventually tell him what was on his mind or he wouldn't. There was no hurrying him.

"Do you remember the story I told you 'bout my uncle gettin' himself lynched?"

Boyd adjusted his legs uneasily. "Yeah, sure I remember. Felt real bad hearing what you had to go through."

"Well, Boyd-o, I didn't quite tell you the whole thing. You see, sometimes stories have a way of winding in and out, you know? They sometimes have more to them than what appears." George looked at Boyd for a moment and then in a strong, soft voice, said, "After Uncle died, my dad would just sit for hours, not speaking, just sittin' there, his mouth moving but nothing coming out. I had to grow up fast, but I was a strong young guy, so I guess it must have been several years later and old Bobby Tom Dillard and I had a long talk one evening.

"With the help of some friends, I found the farm he worked on. Spent many days and nights watching him work around the old place. He seemed to be a hard worker and quite a likable sort. Or so he would have people believe. I watched him for the better part of a year, hunched down in my little hole, scared of being caught, shivering, crying. It was like my secret. Anytime I was feeling sad or out a sorts or Daddy wouldn't talk to me, I'd go out to the woods and hope I could get a glimpse of Bobby Tom.

"I waited and waited in the woods and then one night I got my courage a-goin' and walked right up and caught him outside the wood-shed havin' a smoke. I rapped him once with an ax handle and frog-marched him through tall corn back to the woods. As I said, Bobby Tom and I discussed the finer points of lynching and such and he finally agreed with me that it probably wasn't right and if I remember correctly he was actually down on his knees at one point trying to tell me that the Lord would bless us all if we were to just see our way clear to forgiveness and so on. Of course, Bobby Tom didn't stick around long enough to hear everything I had in mind, as he was bleeding real heavy by then. As I re-member, the last thing he said was, 'Don't know who jumped that nigga's back, no sir, don't.'

"I don't tell these things to frighten, Mr. Boyd. Just in passin', just in passin'."

George poked the fire with a long stick, the sparks showering their legs. Boyd watched as an ember ate into his heavy shoe, the tiny flame slowly dissolving to ash. He began to think George had never told anyone that story.

The men lay by the fire, George with his head propped up by his gun-nysack, Boyd finally curling up across from him.

When they awoke from the cold, the fire was out and the light from the early sun crept through the broken-glass windows. Stiff and hungry, Boyd shook George, and they stumbled out to the tracks. The fall chill had them beating their hands against their sides.

Boyd and George sat facing each other across the wooden expanse of the boxcar. The empty car reverberated like a drum, its creaking walls fight-ing to stay together, picking up every imperfection in the worn steel tracks. They watched Vermilion's highest buildings disappear in the valley as the locomotive struggled, heading north.

Boyd could feel George's stare. "What?"

"Did you kill him?"

Boyd's arms pulled tighter against his legs, his knees almost hiding his face. He rubbed his two-day-old beard against the rough material of his worn trousers. "Yeah, I killed him. I mean I guess he was gonna do himself, anyway, but yeah, I done him."

George nodded in recognition. "And the girl?"

Boyd's eyes flicked to his friend sitting casually across from him. "No, she was dead when I came into the kitchen. Her legs were sticking out from under the table. Her skirt was hiked up to her waist 'cause she had slid down from the chair. Lot of blood on the floor. When I saw her lying there, it was as if my world tilted. I had to hold myself by the table to keep from falling. Smug bastard Sheridan sat there writing, as if nothing much happened. Guess I went nuts. I grabbed his gun. It was next to the Bible. He turned away from me at the last second. The bastard was smiling. I shot him in the temple pretty close up from just across the table."

Boyd paused. He thought he felt better, having told someone of what he had done. He wished he could have said something to Claudia. He wanted to be honest with her. He loved her so much.

George was still nodding. "I figured as much."

Boyd turned to the open door of the boxcar. The small town was rapidly disappearing in the fall haze. Someone was burning leaves; the rich smell of the white smoke drifted briefly into the car and then, like Vermilion, it was gone.

ACKNOWLEDGMENTS

The authors wish to express their gratitude to a few people essential to the successful completion of this novel:

Our agent, Noah Lukeman, for suggesting helpful course changes in the formative stages of the story and for, once again, guiding us through the publishing process. George Witte and his staff at St. Martin's Press: Brad Wood, Daniela Rapp, Bob Berkel, Adam Goldberger, and Henry Yee, for their fine editing and commitment to the best presentation of our novel.

Our wives, Betsy and Barbara, for being both fans and critics, encouraging and brutal as the situation demanded. And Patricia Lenihan for research and literary advice.

Collaboration in fiction is a tricky business; it has both advantages and perils. Of the latter are the twin pitfalls of agreeing too much and agreeing too little. Betsy Hackman plays an especially demanding role in our joint creative process—she keeps production on line, not only by interpreting scrawls, but also by reminding us that we have to do more than congratulate ourselves when we agree. She also keeps us from killing each other when we disagree.